SECRET WARFARE

Secret Warfare

Special Operations Forces from the Great Game to the SAS

Adrian Weale

CORONET BOOKS
Hodder and Stoughton

First published in Great Britain in 1997 by Hodder and Stoughton
First published in paperback in 1998 by Hodder and Stoughton
A division of Hodder Headline PLC
A Coronet paperback

10 9 8 7 6 5 4 3 2 1

ISBN 0 340 65824 X

Printed and bound in Great Britain by
Mackays of Chatham plc, Chatham, Kent

Hodder and Stoughton
A division of Hodder Headline PLC
338 Euston Road
London NW1 3BH

Contents

List of Illustrations

Section Two

Two members of 22 SAS 'Special Projects' team at the window of the
  Iranian Embassy
BBC journalist Sim Harris escapes through the front window of the
  Iranian Embassy
Firemen remove the body of a terrorist from the remains of the
  Embassy
British special forces personnel training in two-man Klepper canoes
Captain Robert Nairac GC
Members of the SAS Special Projects team training in the Garrabach
  Range near Hereford
Remains of an Argentine Pucara aircraft at Pebble Island airbase in the
  Falklands
Commandos of the Royal Marines Mountain and Arctic Warfare Cadre
  practise river crossing
Chinook helicopter of the RAF's Special Forces Flight during the
  Gulf War
SBS men abseil from a Royal Navy Sea King helicopter in Kuwait
  City
British Special Forces members in HALO parachuting kit
An SAS Trooper during a hostage rescue exercise
US Special Forces personnel carrying M16 Armalite rifles
British HALO parachutist dropping in full kit
SAS HALO parachutist coming in to land
US Navy SEALs
Members of a 22 Boat Troop prepare to dive from a Klepper canoe

Introduction

They were a most mad ten days, but Kim enjoyed himself too much to reflect on their craziness. In the morning they played the Jewel Game – sometimes with veritable stones, sometimes with piles of swords and daggers, sometimes with photographs of natives. Through the afternoons he and the Hindu boy would mount guard in the shop, sitting dumb behind a carpet-bale or a screen and watching Mr Lurgan's many and very curious visitors. There were small Rajahs, escorts coughing in the veranda, who came to buy curiosities – such as phonographs and mechanical toys. There were ladies in search of necklaces, and men, it seemed to Kim – but his mind may have been vitiated by early training – in search of ladies; natives from independent and feudatory Courts whose ostensible business was the repair of broken necklaces – rivers of light poured out upon the table – but whose true end seemed to be to raise money for angry Maharanees or young Rajahs. There were Babus to whom Lurgan Sahib talked with austerity and authority, but at the end of each interview he gave them money in coined silver and currency notes. There were occasional gatherings of long-coated theatrical natives who discussed metaphysics in English and Bengali, to Mr Lurgan's great edification. He was always interested in religions. At the end of the day, Kim and the Hindu boy – whose name varied at Lurgan's pleasure – were expected to give a detailed account of all that they had seen and heard – their view of each man's character, as shown in his face, talk, and manner, and their notions of his real errand.

Rudyard Kipling, Kim

Kim's game – the jewel game – was a technique used to train the young Kimball O'Hara to observe and memorise the many things he would see as a player of the 'Great Game' in British India and in central Asia. Kim was a fictional member of the tiny, secretive group of highly trained British and Indian operators who took part in the covert campaign against Imperial Russian subversion and expansion southwards in the nineteenth century, whilst at the same time paving the way for the consolidation of the northern flanks of the British Indian Empire. To my great regret, I did not read Kipling's *Kim* until the summer of 1995 but I had long been familiar with the jewel game: to this day it forms part of the training received by British special forces and military intelligence personnel, preparing for covert operations in Northern Ireland and elsewhere.[1]

Kim was originally published – to considerable acclaim – in 1901 but even before then the world of espionage, military adventure and covert operations, both fictional and actual, exerted a strong fascination on the public mind in Britain, the United States and much of Europe which has continued to this day. Books about the British Army's Special Air Service Regiment have been a recent publishing phenomenon in the United Kingdom,[2] but it is worth remembering that the first best-selling SAS memoir, the late Sir Fitzroy Maclean's *Eastern Approaches*, appeared in September 1949 (and was reprinted twice in that month, twice in October 1949 and at least once in November 1949!).[3] In Hollywood, military special operations have, for many years, proved an effective vehicle for action/adventure/drama movies ranging from *Apocalypse Now* to *The Dirty Dozen*.

In the meantime, special forces themselves, having been *ad hoc*, informal entities prior to the Second World War, have become mainstream elements within most modern armed forces, often claiming an élite status previously reserved for household praetorian troops like Britain's Brigade of Guards. Such is the appeal of glamorous, relatively cheap but undoubtedly effective special forces units to politicians that they have emerged relatively unscathed, and in some cases enhanced, from the financial restrictions which have been increasingly applied to conventional military organisations and services, particularly since the end of the Cold War between NATO and the Warsaw Pact countries. Indeed, during the 1980s both the United States and the United Kingdom established special operations commands incorporating naval, army and air force elements. When the British Ministry of Defence established the Permanent Joint Headquarters for all 'out-of-area' (i.e. non-NATO) deployments in September 1996, the special forces element within any expeditionary joint force was made a 'one star' command equal to the command of the naval, land, air and logistics elements.[4] Nevertheless, despite the thoroughly up-to-date nature of special forces, the strand which links the Great Game of the soldiers/adventurers/spies of the nineteenth century with modern-day military covert operations is not merely an interesting literary curiosity. There is a very real sense in which modern-day military special forces – the British Special Air Service, the United States' Green Berets and Delta Force – are the direct descendants of the Great Gamers, both in the aims they hope to achieve and, indeed, in the way that they seek to achieve them. Special forces have survived and evolved down the years because the relatively small number of soldiers required to mount special operations have apparently achieved results that far outweigh the efforts required to mount them.

Examples of this are legion and the pro-special forces lobby are happy to quote them. In 1941–2, the Special Air Service, which at that time consisted of fewer than two hundred combat soldiers (and had started with less than seventy), was responsible for the destruction, on the ground, of approximately three hundred aircraft of the Italian and German forces based in North Africa. In 1943, ninety German paratroopers under the command of Major Otto Skorzeny of the Waffen-SS were able to rescue Benito Mussolini, the Italian Fascist leader, from his captors without a single shot being fired. Later the same year, a tiny flotilla of two-man submarines attacked and crippled the German heavy-battleship *Tirpitz* in its base in a Norwegian fjord, rendering it permanently unfit for operations. The next year, a team of British-trained Norwegian Commandos of the Special Operations Executive (SOE) attacked and destroyed the heavy water plant at Vermork, northern Norway, thus bringing Hitler's nuclear weapons programme to a standstill.

Since the end of the Second World War, special forces operations have become, if anything, more widespread. In their early days, there was dislike and scepticism towards special forces but this has been replaced by enormous enthusiasm, and special forces have played a central role in a number of major conflicts, ranging from the Malayan Emergency of 1948–60, through the Arab-Israeli conflicts, the Vietnam War, the Falklands Campaign, the Gulf War, and up to the Balkan wars which are still simmering at the time of writing. Simultaneously, the rise of terrorism has prompted further growth in special forces numbers and operational tasks to the extent that several countries have created specialist counter-terrorist organisations, which fall under the general umbrella of special forces, *in addition* to their military special forces units.[5] The extent of special forces involvement in long-term counter-terrorist operations can be judged by the fact that during the period 1976–87, when there were never less than 12,000 British soldiers involved in security operations in Northern Ireland, special forces were responsible for the deaths of thirty of the forty-four Republican terrorists killed by the security forces.[6] For much of that period, there were fewer than a hundred and fifty operational special forces personnel in the province.[7]

There is, of course, an opposite view of the growth of special forces: the desert campaign was won by General Montgomery's relentless use of British superiority in men and *matériel* and by the Allied exploitation of 'ULTRA' to prevent supplies crossing the Mediterranean. The SAS attacks on Axis airfields – the SAS's finest hour – were a sideshow with a marginal impact, at best, on the course of operations. Skorzeny's rescue of Mussolini created, if anything, a drain on German resources: after 1943 Mussolini's Italian Social Republic needed extensive German support to continue to function whilst the rump of the Fascist-supporting Italian military were uncertain and unreliable at best. The threat from the *Tirpitz* had been effectively neutralised both by the Nazis' failure to build aircraft carriers and by dramatic improvements in long-range maritime patrol aircraft and radar during the first half of the war, and building a fleet of special miniature submarines and training the high-ability crews to man them was a waste of scarce resources. Finally, the attack on the Vermork heavy water plant was irrelevant to the German nuclear programme which was fatally stalled by fundamental scientific miscalculations of the critical mass of uranium 238 required to initiate a self-sustaining atomic bomb – in reality, the German nuclear physicist Heisenberg and his team would not have been close to producing a bomb before 1950 at the earliest.

Since the end of the Second World War, despite the hype that has surrounded them, special forces successes have been minimal and unimpressive: in Malaya, 22 SAS was responsible for less than two per cent of terrorist casualties despite being one of the few British units deployed there throughout the campaign; in the Falklands, the presence of the SAS was a hindrance to the conventional forces operating there rather than a 'force multiplier'; in the Gulf, despite the deployment of two and a half full squadrons of 22 SAS, one squadron of Delta Force and many more specialist long-range reconnaissance troops, *not a single* Iraqi Scud missile was destroyed by the coalition forces before launch. In Northern Ireland, the use of highly trained special forces to kill terrorists represents a *de facto* 'shoot to kill' policy which potentially criminalises soldiers but also undermines the government's claim to be the upholder of law and order in the province.

These two contrasting positions are, of course, somewhat extreme, yet it would not be difficult to find partisans of both, and particularly the first. The inference to be drawn from the two together is that the value of special forces and special operations is by no means proven in all cases: there is room for doubt, at least, whether the British tabloid newspaper war-cry 'Send for the SAS!' is always appropriate.

This book is an attempt to put special forces in perspective and to explain why military establishments do not necessarily share the enthusiasm of politicians and journalists for them. Readers should note that I do not claim to have written an exhaustive or comprehensive history: to attempt to do so would take a lifetime; but I have selected and described what I believe to have been the most important and influential campaigns, operations, units and personalities which have exerted the strongest influence on special forces in this century.

Acknowledgements

A number of people who contributed to this book cannot be, or do not wish to be, acknowledged by name because they are serving or recent members of British special forces against whom there is a genuine threat of terrorist attack, and of retribution by their own employers for breaching military *omertà*. I should, nevertheless, like to register my gratitude to them. Additionally I would like to particularly thank the late Sir Fitzroy Maclean for his help and encouragement and for providing me with several useful introductions, and Professor M.R.D. Foot for the same reasons.

I was very much helped by the staff of the Imperial War Museum Library, the Kensington Public Library, the Office of the Defence Attaché at the United States Embassy, London, the Public Records Office at Kew, and the Special Forces Club in London.

Finally, I must express my gratitude to Roland Philipps for commissioning the book, to Andrew Lownie for his usual hard-nosed agenting and to my wife Mary, without whose support I would still be on Chapter 1.

Adrian Weale
London, March 1997

1

Historical Origins

But now change your theme and sing to us of the stratagem of the Wooden Horse, which Epeius built with Athene's help, and which the good Odysseus contrived to get taken one day into the citadel of Troy as an ambush, manned by the warriors who then sacked the town. If you can tell this story as it really happened I shall proclaim to the world how generously the god has endowed you with the generous gift of song.

Odysseus finished speaking, and the bard, beginning with an invocation to the gods, unfolded the tale. He took it up at the point where the Argives after setting fire to their huts had embarked on their ships and were sailing away, while the renowned Odysseus and his party were already sitting in the assembly-place in Troy, concealed within the Horse, which the Trojans had themselves dragged into the citadel. There stood the Horse, with the Trojans sitting around it endlessly arguing. Three policies commended themselves. Some were for piercing the wooden frame with a pitiless bronze spear; others would have dragged it to the edge of the heights and hurled it down to the rocks; others again wished to let it stand as a magnificent offering to appease the gods – and that was what happened in the end. For it was destiny that they should perish when Troy received within its walls that mighty Wooden Horse, laden with the flower of the Argive might bringing doom and slaughter to the Trojans.

Homer, *The Odyssey*

On the night of 27–28 March 1942, Odysseus' clever ploy to breach the defences of Troy was replayed in a modern setting. HMS *Campbeltown*, an elderly US destroyer which had been given to Britain under the Anglo-US lend-lease scheme, had been disguised as a German torpedo boat of the *Möwe* class. Accompanied by two Hunt-class destroyers, a motor gunboat and a number of small launches and flying German ensigns, the *Campbeltown* entered the mouth of the River Loire on the west coast of France and began to carefully negotiate the mud flats of the estuary. As the force made its way upriver – the two modern destroyers guarded the mouth of the river – it was challenged from the shore but a British seaman, in the uniform of a German petty officer, signalled back sufficient real German code to briefly convince the shore batteries not to fire.

The *Campbeltown*'s fake signals bought the British ships at least five minutes' clear steaming time, taking them further upriver and past the heaviest German batteries before the coastal defences' suspicions got the better of them and the Germans opened fire in earnest. At this point the British lowered their German colours, ran up the Royal Navy's white ensign and returned fire.

Seven minutes later HMS *Campbeltown* crashed into the gates of the enormous *Normandie* dry-dock in the port of St Nazaire. Immediately afterwards, British Commandos led by Lieutenant Colonel Charles Newman came ashore, in the face of withering fire from the German defenders, and started to plant charges on important dockside installations:

> My hands had been cut with small pieces of shell which made the handling of the charge somewhat awkward but Sergeant Dockerill stayed with me in case my wounds should prevent me from firing the charges, while I sent the rest of the party upstairs to warn the neighbourhood of the coming explosion.
>
> We raced outside and lay on the ground completely exposed on the concrete paving. Fortunately we shifted a further ten yards away a second later, for when the explosion did come huge concrete blocks hurtled through the air perilously near.
>
> After the explosion we took our remaining explosives in our rucksacks and raced back to the pumping station to complete the work of destruction by blowing up the electric motors and installations.[1]

In fact the Commandos were in a desperate situation because only a minority of them had got ashore in good order from the *Campbeltown* or from the small fleet of motor launches that had accompanied the ship. Despite this, a number of demolition targets were hit and after a short period, Newman was able to give the order to his Commandos to fall back to their pre-arranged pick-up points. Only then was it discovered that most of the motor launches had been either sunk or forced to withdraw. Undaunted, Newman decided to conduct a fighting withdrawal through the town and for his force to split up and attempt to evade south to neutral Spain. Although the majority were killed or captured within a few hours, a corporal, three lance-corporals and a private soldier managed to make their way back to Britain.

As it became light, the German occupiers of St Nazaire were greeted by the bizarre sight of the elderly destroyer stuck fast in the gates of the dry-dock and a small crowd gathered on the dockside whilst parties of German naval officers toured the British ship. At the same time, it was decided that the wardroom of the British vessel would make a suitable venue for the questioning of prisoners, and two young Commando officers were taken there to answer questions about the strange operation. The real answer was provided at noon on 28 March: five tons of explosives hidden in the bows of the *Campbeltown* detonated, bringing 'doom and slaughter' to everyone on board (including the two British officers who had been aware of what was about to happen) and wrecking the caisson of the dry-dock, which promptly flooded.

Like the Wooden Horse stratagem, the St Nazaire raid was a strategic operation. Odysseus' trick had allowed the Greeks to finally penetrate the citadel of Troy and win the war; the St Nazaire raid was launched to prevent the German battleship *Tirpitz*, the most powerful surface ship in the world at that time, from deploying into the Atlantic. The *Normandie* dock was the only dry-dock in Europe outside Germany capable of receiving the enormous battleship, and its destruction meant that the *Tirpitz* would not be able to deploy far from its bolthole in a Norwegian fjord for fear of sustaining irreparable damage. This freed up the resources of the Royal Navy in the North Atlantic to concentrate on the crucial duties of convoy escorting without the necessity of maintaining a standing force to counter the threat of the *Tirpitz*. Special operations evidently have a long pedigree.

In fact it isn't difficult to produce examples of special operations and raids from throughout history; they are many and varied, but it is worth pausing briefly to ensure that we understand what is meant by a 'special operation'. The United States Special Operations Command applies the following definition:

> Special Operations are defined as operations conducted by specially trained, equipped and organised Department of Defence forces against strategic or tactical targets in pursuit of national military, political, economic or psychological objectives. These operations may be conducted during periods of peace or hostilities. They may support conventional operations, or they may be undertaken independently when the use of conventional forces is either inappropriate or infeasible [*sic*].[2]

Which admirably sums up the current picture in the US where special operations forces are maintained on a much greater scale than elsewhere. A less long-winded definition, to which I shall adhere in this book, is as follows:

> In conventional warfare, special operations are *tactical* military operations and campaigns, usually carried out by specially formed units or teams, implemented by high-level commanders with the aim of achieving a disproportionate *strategic* effect on the outcome of a campaign.

And it follows from this that 'special forces' are the units formed primarily to carry out special operations.

From this broad definition, the range of tasks conducted by special forces can be more easily explained by placing them in more specific categories:

1. Information Reporting

The collection of information and intelligence by special forces is probably the oldest and most 'traditional' task that they undertake. Although military commanders have historically – and almost insanely – been suspicious of 'intelligence' (in both senses of the word, more often than not), it is nevertheless a much repeated maxim in the British Army, at least, that 'time spent on reconnaissance is seldom wasted'[3] and the original Great Gamers were primarily tasked with mapping the relatively, and sometimes completely, unknown parts of central Asia into which the Russian Empire was encroaching. In the Second World War one of the most effective uses of special forces was the 'roadwatch' on Axis main supply routes by patrols of the Long Range Desert Group in the Western Desert between 1941 and 1943. Subsequently, similar tasking was undertaken by US Green Beret patrols in Vietnam and by SAS patrols in Borneo. The most recent examples were in the Gulf War: the famous SAS Bravo Two Zero patrol, which went so spectacularly wrong, was primarily tasked as a roadwatch.

2. Offensive Action

The range of offensive action tasks undertaken, or at least envisaged, by special forces is, if anything, wider than the information-reporting role. Apart from classic military and industrial sabotage attacks against strategic targets – attacking airfields, blowing up bridges, destroying industrial plant – special forces capabilities might also include the assassination of political and military leaders, kidnapping of key figures and the rescue of prisoners of war, all of which have been attempted within recent memory. It should be stressed, however, that most small-scale raids are just small-scale raids with limited, tactical justification, whatever their intended outcome.

3. Training and Advice

Probably the least glamorous aspect of special forces activity is the training of allied conventional and unconventional forces. Although 'modern' armies have been providing help and advice to less advanced allies for hundreds of years, the role was brought up to date by the activities of T.E. Lawrence and his colleagues with the Arab Army during the First World War. Thereafter British officers were sent to Russia to help the White Army fight the Bolsheviks and, in the Second World War, paramilitary agents of the British SOE, the American Office of Strategic Services (OSS) and, eventually, the SAS were parachuted into occupied Europe to provide tactical know-how, logistic support and guidance to resistance movements. Probably the best-known of these military missions was that of Fitzroy Maclean to Marshal Tito's Partisans in Yugoslavia but they took place, in one form or another, throughout Europe, the Mediterranean and Japanese-occupied Asia (the communist guerrilla leaders Chin Peng in Malaya, and Ho Chi Minh in Vietnam were both recipients of substantial quantities of arms and support from British and American sources).

4. Psychological Operations

Psyops is an aspect of special forces activity that rarely receives the attention it deserves, not least because it is – like advisory work – relatively unglamorous. It has become a modern-day military commonplace that to win any counter-insurgency campaign, it is necessary to 'win the hearts and minds' of the indigenous population. This notion grew up during the British campaign in Malaya when patrols of the SAS began to visit villages and settlements deep in the jungle and found that by befriending and helping the inhabitants rather than bullying them, they effectively denied large swathes of territory as a safe haven for their terrorist opposition. A result of this is that 'civil action' will now often be a significant feature of special forces operations in both high- and low-intensity warfare.

5. Counter-Terrorism

Counter-terrorism is the newest and most dramatic area of special forces activity; in some respects it is also the most controversial. There are three basic tasks for special forces in counter-terrorism: surveillance of terrorists and terrorist groups; interdiction and arrest of terrorists; and the rescue of terrorist hostages from various environments, including aircraft, buildings, ships, vehicles and so on.

A significant factor in the definition of special forces, other than by the tasks allotted to them, has always been in the level of tactical excellence to which they aspire. In 1759, Major Robert Rogers commanded a small unit of scouts and raiders in what was then Britain's American colonies, fighting against the French and the native American Indians. The standing orders for his unit represent a blueprint for the tactical operations of special forces even now:

Rogers' Rangers Standing Orders

By Major Robert Rogers, 1759

1. Don't forget nothing.
2. Have your musket clean as a whistle, hatchet scoured, sixty rounds powder and ball, and be ready to march at a minute's warning.
3. When you're on the march, act the way you would if you was sneaking up on a deer. See the enemy first.
4. Tell the truth about what you see and do. There is an army depending on us for correct information. You can lie all you please when you tell other folks about the Rangers, but don't never lie to a Ranger or officer.
5. Don't never take a chance you don't have to.
6. When we're on the march we march single file, far enough apart so one shot can't go through two men.
7. If we strike swamps, or soft ground, we spread out abreast, so it's hard to track us.
8. When we march, we keep moving til dark, so as to give the enemy the least possible chance at us.
9. When we camp, half the party stays awake while the other half sleeps.
10. If we take prisoners, we keep 'em separate 'til we have had time to examine them, so they can't cook up a story between 'em.
11. Don't ever march home the same way. Take a different route so you won't be ambushed.
12. No matter whether we travel in big parties or little ones, each party has to keep a scout 20 yards ahead, twenty yards on each flank and twenty yards in the rear, so the main body can't be surprised and wiped out.
13. Every night you'll be told where to meet if surrounded by a superior force.

14. Don't sit down to eat without posting sentries.
15. Don't sleep beyond dawn. Dawn's when the French and Indians attack.
16. Don't cross a river by a regular ford.
17. If somebody's trailing you, make a circle, come back onto your own tracks, and ambush the folks that aim to ambush you.
18. Don't stand up when the enemy's coming against you. Kneel down. Hide behind a tree.
19. Let the enemy come till he's almost close enough to touch. Then let him have it and jump out and finish him up with your hatchet.[4]

But despite these precedents, the real roots of modern Anglo-American-influenced special forces lie on the frontiers of British India. In 1807, the Emperor Napoleon Bonaparte of France suggested to Czar Alexander I of Russia that together they should unite and conquer India. Bonaparte's plan was to march a French army of 50,000 men through Persia and Afghanistan to join forces with Alexander, before sweeping down across the Indus.

The British had not, until this time, taken much interest in the land routes into India, but faced with this dual threat, the East India Company gave immediate orders that they should be surveyed and mapped, and diplomatic missions were sent to Persia and Afghanistan in the hope of dissuading their rulers from co-operation with the Franco-Russian menace.

In fact Bonaparte and Alexander soon fell out and the intended invasion never materialised, as the French armies swept into Russia in 1812 and were then driven out by the implacable opposition of Alexander's Cossacks and Russia's climate. Instead, after they had beaten Bonaparte, it was the Russians themselves who emerged as the main threat to India: 'For four centuries the Russian Empire had been expanding at the rate of some 55 square miles a day, or around 20,000 square miles a year. By the end of it [the gap between the British and Russian Empires] had shrunk to a few hundred miles, and in parts of the Pamir region, less than twenty.'[5]

The Great Game, as it came to be called, was a low-intensity conflict fought out in some of the most hostile territory on earth. The players were usually professional military officers or 'politicals', British and

Russian, who, either with small detachments of troops or on their own, ventured into what was largely unknown territory, surveying the ground, gathering intelligence on the operations of their opponents and seeking to influence the decisions of suspicious, and often capricious, local rulers.

In January 1810, for example, Captain Charles Christie and Lieutenant Henry Pottinger of the 5th Bengal Native Light Infantry set off on a reconnaissance of the wilds of Baluchistan and Afghanistan at the behest of General John Malcolm, the governor-general of India's Emissary to the Shah of Persia. The two men parted in March at the oasis of Nushki in the north of Baluchistan, with Christie going off to the mysterious Afghan city of Herat (which only one other living European had set eyes on) whilst Pottinger, who was just twenty years old, undertook a 900-mile journey through Baluchistan and Persia, surveying the likely routes of an invading army. Both men were escorted, but by hired Baluchis who believed them to be Tartar, and thus Muslim, horse traders.

Four months later they met again, both unharmed, in a caravanserai in Isfahan. Both were still in native dress and they initially failed to recognize each other. 'In all, since first setting foot in Baluchistan, Christie had ridden 2,250 miles through some of the most dangerous country in the world, while Pottinger had exceeded this by a further 162 miles.'[6] Apart from being extraordinary feats of daring and endurance, their exploit was a textbook strategic reconnaissance: the information they supplied was intended to be used at the highest level to plan the defence of British India.

Pottinger and Christie were followed by dozens of Great Gamers on similar missions, dispatched by the East India Company, the Indian government and the Indian army to acquire intelligence and dispense influence, using their military skills and initiative to survive. Notable individuals included: Alexander Burnes, whose career culminated in an appointment as British political resident in Kabul, where he was murdered shortly before the rout of the Army of the Indus in 1842; Arthur Conolly who coined the phrase 'the Great Game' but was executed by the Emir of Bokhara during a mission in 1842; and finally Francis Younghusband, the last of the Great Gamers, who in 1889 jousted with the Russians high up in the Himalayan kingdom of Hunza and in 1904 led the British expedition to Lhasa, capital of Tibet, which was to prove the last substantial episode of the Great Game.

The link between the Great Gamers themselves lay in the nature of the tasks set for them and the way in which they carried them out; what connected the Great Gamers and their successors, the early exponents of special operations, was that many were still alive and their exploits still celebrated even after the First World War. Francis Younghusband, for example, survived until 1942 and was an active writer and lecturer (and advocate of universal religion and free love) until shortly before then. The legacy of the Great Game, and the *Boys' Own* accounts that it inspired, undoubtedly helped to convince later generations that brave and intrepid individuals or small groups could make a difference.

2

Lawrence and the Arab Revolt

Those who dream by night in the dusty recesses of their minds wake in the day to find that it was vanity: but the dreamers of the day are dangerous men, for they may act their dream with open eyes, to make it possible.

T.E. Lawrence, *Seven Pillars of Wisdom*

The First World War, 'the Great War to End Wars' as it came to be described, was a titanic struggle between a set of enemies with little to distinguish between them in terms of military, cultural and scientific achievement. The focus of the war, the Western Front, consumed many of the finest young men of the three most advanced countries on earth, Great Britain, Germany and France, in a maelstrom of death and destruction unrivalled in its single-minded ferocity. The static brutality of trench warfare – which remained the norm through four years of fighting – cried out for creative thinking, an indirect approach that would enable the combatants to escape from their hideous confrontation; and yet none was found. The few opportunities that arose – the British tank attack at Cambrai in 1917; the German use of poison gas at Ypres in 1915 – were, by and large, squandered by commanders who failed to react in time to genuine victories. Nevertheless, the first genuine modern special operations campaign took place during the First World War, albeit on a small scale as the 'sideshow of a sideshow', and it was to have a profound effect on subsequent generations.

Thomas Edward ('Ned') Lawrence was born in the small town of Tremadoc in North Wales on 16 August 1888, the second of five sons born to Thomas and Sarah Lawrence. The Lawrences lived a peripatetic existence – after Wales they lived briefly in Hampshire and France – until 1896 when they settled into a northern suburb of Oxford.

By birth, Lawrence's father – in reality Thomas Chapman – was a member of the Anglo-Irish Protestant squirearchy, the grandson of a baronet and the owner of a small manor house and estate in Westmeath. He had abandoned his shrewish and unpleasant first wife and their four daughters, and changed his name to live as man and wife with Sarah Junner, their nanny, in England and Wales. Thus T.E. Lawrence and all his four brothers were illegitimate – a considerable stigma in late Victorian and Edwardian England, and one which the family were careful to conceal.

T.E. Lawrence was educated at Oxford High School, a fee-paying day school, where he excelled academically but, unusually for a middle-class schoolboy in late Victorian England, he avoided team games whenever possible. But although physically small – his final height was a little under five feet six inches – he was fit and athletic as a result of constant exercise and a somewhat cranky but very rigorous vegetarian diet that he followed for several years as an adolescent.

As a schoolboy Lawrence developed a consuming interest in history and antiquarianism which manifested itself in a passion for collecting 'medieval artefacts, pieces of pottery, fragments of glass, and brass jettons [trading tokens]',[1] as well as stimulating an enthusiasm for making brass-rubbings in Oxfordshire churches. From this grew an interest, in his late teens, in medieval high culture, warfare, the Crusades and, particularly, the design and use of castles.

In 1907, Lawrence won a scholarship to read modern history at Jesus College, Oxford, where he came under the influence of Dr David Hogarth, the Keeper of the Ashmolean Museum and a fellow of Magdalen College. Despite his distinguished academic career, Hogarth was an adventurer and something of a romantic, with a passion for field archaeology in remote parts of the Middle East. Hogarth had first come across Lawrence when he had brought his finds to the Ashmolean as a schoolboy and had helped to nurture the boy's interests and direct them towards field archaeology and his own areas of study. With Hogarth's encouragement, Lawrence began a study of the influence of the design of Crusader castles on those in western Europe.

As Lawrence's academic interests were developing, so his personality was maturing. Throughout his adolescence he had sought to emphasise a certain distance from his parents and particularly his mother who, although by most accounts loving, was domineering and strict. As he grew towards manhood, Lawrence developed an equally forceful personality which manifested in a variety of highly individualistic ways. Aside from his rigorous asceticism – as well as maintaining a careful diet he neither smoked nor drank in an era when both carried little stigma – he shied away from contact with the opposite sex and from the other typical activities of Edwardian undergraduates. The custom at Oxford during Lawrence's time as an undergraduate was that students attended lectures or study during the morning, took exercise after luncheon, worked or chatted between tea and dinner and socialised throughout the evening: 'No gentleman works after dinner.'[2] By contrast, Lawrence would indulge in extended late-night study marathons, or conduct solitary explorations around Oxford, including, it would seem, strange journeys through the sewers in a canoe, armed with a revolver, which he would occasionally discharge to frighten passers-by in the streets above. Around this time his literary attentions became focused, in part at least, on the work of a group who styled themselves the 'Uranians'.

The inspiration of the Uranians was the celebration, essentially homoerotic, of the 'innocence and sensuality'[3] of young boys. As homosexual activity remained a serious crime, the writing of Uranian poetry and fiction provided a relatively respectable outlet for urges that society and the law sought to suppress. There is certainly no reason to suppose that Lawrence was an active homosexual at this stage of his life. In part, Lawrence's association with the Uranians may have been prompted by a desire to be controversial, and he may well have been attracted by the colourful personalities of other members of the society, but it is equally clear that Lawrence was, to all intents and purposes, homosexual.

Another enthusiasm that Lawrence developed at Oxford was with the military. In later life he was to claim that he had run away from home for a brief period to serve as a boy soldier with the Royal Garrison Artillery in Cornwall. This incident supposedly happened in 1905 but there is no evidence to support the claim. Accounts of Lawrence's life are invariably coloured by his inventions and fantasies. However, his first real contact with the army seems to have been when he joined the Cyclist Section of the Oxford University Officer Training Corps in 1908.

University OTCs were (and indeed are) a means of giving university undergraduates sufficient military training to qualify them for service as officers in the reserve forces, and Lawrence seems to have been an eager participant at Oxford, noted as a good rifle shot and an effective scout. Whilst gaining this practical training in soldiering, Lawrence was also delving into the theoretical side, as he later explained: 'In military theory I was tolerably read, my Oxford curiosity having taken me past Napoleon to Clausewitz and his school, to Caemmerer and Moltke, and the recent Frenchmen. They had all seemed to be one-sided; and after looking at Jomini and Willisen, I had found broader principles in Saxe and Guibert and the eighteenth century.'[4] And it would be fair to argue that he had a breadth of military knowledge that would not normally be equalled by professional officers of the time,[5] even if the depth of his knowledge of the basic practicalities of military life was somewhat limited.

After graduating with first-class honours in the summer of 1910 (having submitted a notable thesis entitled 'The Influence of the Crusades on European Military Architecture to the End of the 12th Century'), Lawrence spent much of the following four years, leading up to the outbreak of war, involved in the excavation of Karkemis near Jerablus in Syria. As one of a very small number of Europeans involved in the dig, acting as his mentor Hogarth's assistant, Lawrence spent much time with their Arab and Kurdish labourers, becoming familiar with their language and customs, developing a paternal affection for them and becoming an enthusiastic champion of Arab nationalism. Lawrence's passionate pro-Arab sentiment was inspired, it would seem, at least in part, by the strong but probably innocent affection he conceived for his servant at Karkemis, a teenaged boy nicknamed Dahoum. Evidently intelligent, physically attractive and anxious to improve himself, whilst at the same time having a simple outlook and being at home in the harsh Middle Eastern environment, Dahoum seemed to embody everything that Lawrence found admirable in the Arabs; and which seemed to contrast favourably with their Turkish rulers. At this time Syria remained a part of the Ottoman Empire, an entity which Lawrence despised: 'Turkish rule was gendarme rule, and Turkish political theory as crude as its practice. The Turks taught the Arabs that the interests of the sect were higher than those of patriotism: that the petty concerns of the province were more than nationality.'[6]

He day-dreamed of freeing the Arabs from Ottoman despotism, envisaging them 'maturing' as a nation under the benevolent rule of the British Empire, in the same way, as it was then fashionable to argue, that India was doing: for all his intellectual sophistication and education, he remained intensely patriotic in the schoolboyish way that appears to us now as an odd but endearing hallmark of that time.

Perhaps less endearing, but also of its time, was the contemptuous way that Lawrence and his fellow Englishmen dealt with the Ottoman officials they encountered. In the years leading up to the outbreak of the First World War, the Ottoman Empire was spiralling into decline. The traditional rule of the Sultan, which had lasted for 628 years, had been overthrown in 1909 by the so-called 'Young Turks', a group of relatively cosmopolitan militarists determined to modernise and secularise the country, but they showed little interest in responding to the growing nationalist aspirations of the sixty or so per cent of the subjects of the empire who were not of Turkish origin.

When war broke out in August 1914, with the Central Powers – Germany and Austria-Hungary – ranged against Britain and France in the west and Russia to the east, the Ottoman Empire was faced with a difficult choice. The pro-German group, led by Enver Pasha, argued that if the empire stayed neutral it would inevitably be dismembered by Britain, France and Italy, which all had designs on parts of it, whereas if it joined the war as an equal partner of Germany and Austria-Hungary it would receive a significant boost to prestige amongst its subject peoples and, in the likely event of victory, would acquire both Egypt, which was then under British occupation, and territory in the Caucasus.[7]

The Ottoman Empire did, in fact, join the war in October 1914, sending forces to attack the Russians across the Black Sea in Odessa and, more pertinently, to menace the British garrison along the Suez Canal. This operation was not, of itself, a success, the Turkish forces withdrawing into Palestine in February 1915: 'The Sinai desert was a check on an invasion in strength, and the two small detachments which got across were easily repulsed, at Ismailia and Tussum, although allowed to make good their retreat. But if [this] was a tactical failure, [it was] of great strategic value to Germany by pinning down large . . . British Forces.'[8]

It was into this situation of relative stalemate that Lawrence arrived in December 1914. One activity that he had been involved in since leaving Oxford was a project to survey the Sinai peninsula, which had taken place in early 1914. Lawrence and a fellow Karkemis archaeologist, Leonard Woolley, had joined forces with Captain Stewart Newcombe of the Royal Engineers, who learned that their part in the expedition was to act as a cover for a military survey, by Newcombe and his assistants, of the country beyond the frontier of Egypt. Although there does not seem to have been any greater significance to the survey than this, it nevertheless meant that Lawrence's name was familiar in those circles of military intelligence – at that time, a very tightly knit community – dealing with the Middle East. In consequence, when war did break out between Britain and the Ottoman Empire, Lawrence swiftly found employment (initially as a civilian; he was deemed too short at that time for service in the forces and it was largely because regular officers found it 'difficult' to deal with non-military personnel that Lawrence was commissioned) in the Geographical Section of the General Staff at the War Office in London, preparing 1:250,000 mapping of Sinai. He impressed his employing officer, Colonel Sir Coote Hedley, sufficiently to be recommended as ' "the ideal officer" for Egyptian intelligence work'.[9] He was part of the first draft of five officers, led by Captain Newcombe, to be sent out to reinforce the Intelligence Section of GHQ Cairo (the others being Woolley, the dashing Aubrey Herbert MP and George Lloyd MP) which had been started a few weeks before under the command of Colonel Gilbert Clayton.

Although Lawrence was inclined, in later life, to romanticise (and fantasise to some extent) his work during the next two years as an intelligence officer on the General Staff in Cairo, there is nothing to indicate that he did anything that was particularly unusual for an officer in that role. His day-to-day activities centred around geographical tasks, updating mapping (and, more prosaically, supplying maps to other sections of the staff), and on piecing together the Turkish order of battle (ORBAT) from the various sources of information that were available. Lawrence's linguistic abilities suited him for interrogating prisoners of war and, by his own account, his knowledge of the home areas of many of the prisoners gave him an advantage that he could use to considerable effect.

As an intelligence staff officer, Lawrence would also have been aware of, and would have read the reports of, any agents that the intelligence department was running. In fact, the majority of the spies working for the British in the Middle East seem to have been 'casual contacts' (spies are generally classified as 'agents' who can be tasked to report on specific subjects as opposed to casual contacts ('cascons') who generally can't). These casual contacts were of dubious value, having a strong tendency to report what they thought the British wanted to hear. Nevertheless, it was largely through this medium that Lawrence was able to keep his finger on the pulse of Arab nationalism which had become an abiding interest for him.

Although essentially desk-bound in Cairo, Lawrence did, from time to time, escape to various parts of the Middle East theatre of operations. In April 1915, the Middle East had assumed a new prominence in the war as a result of the landings on the Gallipoli peninsula, close to Constantinople, which had been launched in order to relieve pressure on the Russians' Caucasus front. For several months, British, Australian and New Zealand troops had floundered in the various beach-heads created by the initial landings and subsequent operations, assailed by dreadful living conditions, poor logistics, their own lack of training, and incompetence almost without parallel in British military history, before withdrawing in November of the same year. More or less simultaneously, Indian forces (which were, of course, British-commanded and included some British-manned units), having seized the strategically important oil port of Basra at the top of the Persian Gulf, were advancing into Mesopotamia – modern-day Iraq. They did so along the valleys of the Euphrates and Tigris where, having underestimated Turkish fighting ability, they too were to come unstuck as a result of dismal and unimaginative leadership, lack of supplies and manpower. A division commanded by General Townshend was besieged by a Turkish force in the town of Kut al Amarah in December 1915 and was slowly ground down, despite desperate attempts to rescue it. Although his campaign had been modestly successful up to this point – Liddell Hart claimed that he had written 'a glorious page in military history'[10] – Townshend was apparently unmanned by the experience of being besieged and began to promulgate an increasingly bizarre series of rescue schemes, one of which involved paying the Turks a multi-million-pound ransom for his force. It was around this time, the end of March 1916, that Lawrence was sent from Cairo to Basra to see whether there might be scope for relieving the pressure on Kut by means of subversion.

It would seem that this was the first time that Lawrence's operational skills were subjected to any form of test. Although he liked to paint a picture of himself in subsequent years as one of the pioneering supporters of the Arab revolt against the Ottoman Empire, the idea had been circulating amongst senior British officers in the Middle East and in London for some time. Hogarth, now a commander in the Royal Navy, was put in charge of an organisation called the Arab Bureau, set up in January 1916 to report on and encourage Arab nationalism. Through the Bureau, GHQ in Cairo had access to a number of Arab dissidents, many of whom had considerable military experience, and there had also been contacts with Sharif Hussein of Mecca, the Arabs' figurehead leader.

The plan devised for Lawrence in Mesopotamia was to attempt to bribe a senior Turkish officer into sowing disaffection and discord amongst Arab units of the Turkish Army. Both of these aims relied on the use of local Arab nationalists as agents and, to Lawrence's dismay, there were none deemed sufficiently trustworthy. Instead, as an Arabic speaker, it fell to Lawrence, together with his colleague Aubrey Herbert who spoke Turkish, and Colonel Bill Beach, to negotiate Townshend's surrender, which duly took place on 29 April 1916. Notoriously, Townshend took little further interest in the welfare of his force. He went into a comfortable house-arrest in Constantinople – even requesting, at one point, that his wife be allowed to join him – whilst the men endured several years of dreadful privation in Turkish prisons from which many did not return.

Lawrence's disappointment at the failure of his mission was tempered by his realisation that his superiors had perceived the military advantage to be taken of the Arab nationalists for whom he had become an enthusiastic advocate. At the same time, however, he had also run into the entrenched conservatism of the regular army, and particularly the Indian Army, who had been aghast at his plans to sow mutiny amongst the Arabs, not only because the loyalty of Britain's Indian troops was increasingly uncertain but also because of plans by the Indian government to colonise Iraq. Lawrence reacted to this, and the general air of incompetence that surrounded the Mesopotamian campaign, with 'a passion of contempt for the regular army'.[11] Nevertheless, he was perceived by his superiors to have performed a difficult mission creditably and he returned to Cairo to carry on with his regular duties.

In June 1916 the Arab revolt against Ottoman rule, long hoped for by Lawrence and many of his colleagues at GHQ Intelligence in Cairo, finally broke out. Notwithstanding subsequent propaganda, there was little spontaneity about it. Sharif Hussein of Mecca had negotiated long and hard to obtain favourable terms from the British before launching his uprising. Before he would consider taking on the Turks and their German advisors, he had secured money, arms and the promise of naval and air support together with pledges regarding the distribution of territory in any post-war settlement. The latter was very important to him: although an Arab nationalist who resented the Turks' domination of the Arab world, he was a political reactionary very much interested in extending his own power and influence in the Middle East.

The location for the revolt was the western seaboard of the Arabian peninsula, the Hejaz, bordering onto the Red Sea and thus within relatively easy reach of British-controlled territory in Sudan and Egypt. The Turks had been able to maintain their hold on this region by means of the Hejaz railway, which linked Medina, their main garrison in Hejaz, with Damascus in Syria and ultimately with Constantinople. A division of about sixteen thousand men, armed with relatively modern weaponry including field artillery, was based in and around Mecca, Jeddah and Medina in barracks, forts and other defensible locations. Sharif Hussein, on the other hand, had access to up to fifty thousand tribesmen but their loyalty was somewhat shaky and most had only sketchy training and little experience of combat, particularly against modern weapons. In any case, the Arabs possessed at that time only about ten thousand rifles – many of which were somewhat antiquated – and no significant support weapons of their own. Nevertheless, in the first few days of the revolt, after it was launched on 5 June, they achieved several notable successes including the seizure of the Holy City of Mecca, and the port of Jeddah which was taken with the aid of British naval gunfire and seaplane bombers on 15 June.

Officers of the Arab Bureau were in Hejaz shortly after the revolt broke out to assess the situation and see how the British could help. There had been considerable debate amongst Allied policymakers over how much help and encouragement should be given to the Arabs because, although it was recognised that a revolt would be a substantial drain on Turkish resources, there were strong feelings that encouraging nationalist sentiments in a colonised people could be a very dangerous double-edged sword for imperial powers like Britain and France. There was also the matter of a secret deal: the Sykes–Picot agreement between Britain and France divided the Middle East into 'spheres of influence' which took little account of nationalist sentiment in the region. Nevertheless the decision to encourage and support the revolt had been made.

The first interim measure to be taken was the despatch of artillery to support the rebels. A significant problem facing the Allies was the hostility of the local tribes to the presence of European infidels in close proximity to some of the holiest sites of Islam (an issue which foreshadowed similar worries during the Gulf War of 1990–1) and there was genuine concern that support for Hussein might fall away if too many Christians appeared in the Hejaz. This was overcome in the short term by sending Muslim soldiers of the Egyptian Army with mountain artillery and machine guns but during the next few months, as the revolt wavered in the face of Turkish military superiority, a debate took place within the British hierarchy over whether a British brigade group should be sent to support the Arab Army, whose most effective element was under the command of Hussein's son Feisal.

Lawrence, a respected but still relatively junior intelligence officer, was of the opinion that British troops were not the best way of supporting the revolt, but other more senior personalities disagreed, notably Sir Henry MacMahon, High Commissioner in Egypt, and General Sir Reginald Wingate, the governor-general of Sudan who was of the opinion that 'the Arabs would be swamped by the Turkish offensive [which was widely expected to follow the revolt], a disaster which could be prevented only if a brigade of British infantry were sent to Rabigh'.[12] General Murray, the military Commander-in-Chief at Cairo, and the General Staff in London knew well that in the late summer and autumn of 1916, in the wake of the battle of the Somme, when 50,000 men had been killed, wounded or captured on the first day, even a brigade would be hard won. In October, Clayton, who by now was acting as Murray's chief advisor on Arab affairs as well as 'chief-of-staff' to the small force of advisors and technical specialists attached to the revolt, obtained General Murray's agreement to send Lawrence to Hejaz to make an independent assessment.

Why was it that Lawrence was selected to go to Hejaz? Although he was widely regarded by the GHQ staff in Cairo as a slovenly and unsoldierly individual – his scruffy uniform and relatively long hair were the subject of much comment – he was nevertheless respected for his intellect and for the special knowledge of, and affinity for, the Arabs that he evidently possessed. Lawrence's views on the Arab revolt were well known to his peers: there was no question but that he was not in favour of sending British soldiers to fight alongside the rebellion; even so, he was regarded as sufficiently professional to produce a dispassionate analysis. Although Lawrence subsequently took pains to present himself as a difficult rebel during his time in Cairo, and his behaviour was certainly regarded as eccentric by the regular officers he was serving with (as at Oxford, he continued to shun the majority of the conventional social aspects of life), he was evidently also deemed to be competent: had he not been, it is almost inconceivable that he would have been given the responsibilities that subsequently fell to him.

Lawrence made his first visit to Hejaz in October 1916. His itinerary included discussions with the handful of British officers who were already working with the Arabs but, more importantly, visits to the Arab Army and its leaders. Hussein's chief military advisor at the time was Colonel Cyril Wilson, the British Consul at Jeddah, who was in favour of sending British soldiers but who was suspected by Clayton of doctoring his reports to favour his own opinions; there was also concern that he was close to a breakdown.[13] It is apparent that he and Lawrence did not get on: 'Lawrence wants kicking and kicking hard at that . . . I look on him as a bumptious young ass who spoils his undoubted knowledge of Syrian Arabs &c. by making himself out to be the only authority on war, engineering, HM's ships and everything else. He put every single person's back up I've met from the Admiral down to the most junior fellow on the Red Sea.'[14]

Lawrence's contacts with the Arabs were more successful. The senior field commanders of Hussein's rebellion were his sons; Lawrence met the second son, Abdulla, at a conference in Jeddah before travelling by sea to the port of Rabigh to meet the eldest, Ali, but neither impressed him as having the qualities necessary to steer the revolt on the course that Lawrence wanted it to follow. The third son, Feisal, whom Lawrence met after obtaining permission from Hussein to journey up-country, was a great deal more promising. He was encamped, with 4,000 irregulars and the Egyptian artillery battery, at Al Hamra. Lawrence's description of their first meeting has become almost legendary:

> He led me to an inner court, on whose further side, framed between the uprights of a black doorway, stood a white figure waiting tensely for me. I felt at first glance that this was the man I had come to Arabia to seek – the leader who would bring the Arab revolt to full glory. Feisal looked very tall and pillar-like, very slender, in his long white silk robes and his brown head cloth bound with a brilliant scarlet and gold cord. His eyelids were dropped; and his black beard and colourless face were like a mask against the strange, still watchfulness of his body. His hands were crossed in front of him on his dagger.
>
> I greeted him. He made way for me into the room, and sat down on his carpet near the door. As my eyes grew accustomed to the shade, they saw that the little room held many silent figures, looking at me or at Feisal steadily. He remained staring down at his hands, which were twisting slowly about his dagger. At last he enquired softly how I had found the journey. I spoke of the heat and he asked how long from Rabegh, commenting that I had ridden fast for the season.
>
> 'And do you like our place here in Wadi Safra?'
>
> 'Well; but it is far from Damascus.'
>
> The word had fallen like a sword in their midst. There was a quiver. Then everybody present stiffened where he sat, and held his breath for a silent minute. Some, perhaps, were dreaming of far off success: others may have thought it a reflection on their late defeat. Feisal at length lifted his eyes, smiling at me, and said, 'Praise be to God, there are Turks nearer us than that.' We all smiled with him; and I rose and excused myself for the moment.[15]

Lawrence's romanticisation of Feisal makes it easy to overlook the many qualities that he brought to the task of leading the Arab revolt. Aside from his personal magnetism, intelligence and courage, Feisal was a practised diplomat and politician within the Ottoman Empire and had held high rank in the Turkish Army, giving him a working knowledge, at least, of basic tactics and staff procedures; although he was vacillating and indecisive as a military leader, he was not the ingénu that has occasionally been described. What he lacked, and what he hoped Lawrence might be able to give him, were modern weapons in sufficient quantities, training and assistance, and money. In fact Lawrence knew that all these were on their way and as a consequence he was able to give Feisal assurances that not only had the ring of truth to them but were actually fulfilled shortly after Lawrence's departure, thus enhancing his, and British, prestige.

Lawrence spent a few days in Feisal's camp before returning to Jeddah on 4 November. By this time the British perception was that an acute crisis was facing the Arabs. Lawrence had been able to report on Turkish preparations for an offensive against the Arab-held territory along the coast: Fahreddin Pasha, the Turkish commander, was massing his troops around Medina prior to sweeping down towards Yenbo, Rabegh, Jeddah and Mecca; but he was confident that the Arabs, with the support of British aircraft and naval gunnery, would be able to resist them. At a conference held in Khartoum immediately after he left Hejaz, Lawrence managed to put this viewpoint across, and his subsequent reports on his meetings with Feisal and the other princes, which fitted neatly with his commander-in-chief's view that British troops should not be sent to Hejaz, were given wide circulation (even up to the war cabinet) by a relieved General Murray.

Lawrence left Hejaz thinking that it was unlikely that he would be allowed to return. He knew that, apart from the small numbers of British officers already in Arabia, a team of specialist military advisors had been selected by General Wingate and was being assembled ready to begin operations, and he was not included in it. However, the success of his mission caused his superiors to look upon him in a new light: Lawrence had suggested in his report that a 'reliable intelligence officer'[16] should go to Hejaz and a number of others had picked up on this point. Even better was that Lawrence appeared to have established a relationship with the most active of Hussein's field commanders, Feisal. In consequence, the decision was quickly made to attach him to Feisal's headquarters at Yenbo, as a political and military liaison officer, pending the arrival of the now Colonel Newcombe, who would take over military advisory duties.

It was during this early period with Feisal that Lawrence formulated his ideas on the best way for the revolt to proceed. In the long term it was important that a regular Arab army should be formed, capable of taking on and defeating their enemies on equal terms, but in the short term that would be neither practical nor desirable. With the change of government in Britain in December 1916 came a change in Allied strategy in the Middle East. Senior figures were beginning to doubt whether it would be possible to defeat Germany outright but that advantage could be taken of her allies. As a result Murray was now ordered to push the Turks out of Palestine and launch a full-scale invasion of Syria aimed, ultimately, at the defeat of Turkey. In consequence, the Arabs, who were now perceived as having a key part to play, needed to be put to good use. In fact Lawrence reached the conclusion that David Stirling and his colleagues would arrive at twenty-three years later: that the desert is like a sea, and small, mobile, easily concealed forces can move around it almost at will, virtually immune from detection, but then attack out of nowhere like predatory sharks. The Bedouin Arabs lived in the desert and would not be daunted by it. However, they needed the technical help and guidance of men like Lawrence, who knew how to, for example, dynamite a railway line or interpret an aerial photograph. Provided they received this, they could sustain a lengthy and damaging campaign against the Turkish lines of communication. This would pin the Turks in their garrisons in the Hejaz and dissipate their efforts on futile security duties and reconstruction work whilst the Arabs' conventional strengths were increased. Lawrence subsequently calculated that the campaign against the Hejaz railway, in which he was a prime mover, kept some twenty-seven thousand Turks in the Hejaz, defending Medina and the railway, men who could, and probably should, have been employed fighting the British on the Palestinian/Syrian front.

Despite this appreciation, it took time for Lawrence to fully gain the trust of both Feisal and his superiors. The long-expected Turkish offensive coincided with Lawrence's arrival and he was kept extremely busy during his first few weeks co-ordinating Allied air and naval support, reporting Turkish movements back to Cairo and calming the panicking Arabs. As he had predicted during his first visit, air and sea power proved too much for the Turks who were cautious because of their over-extended lines of communication and lack of air cover, and after initial successes against the Arabs, the cautious Fahreddin withdrew his forces to Medina.

In January 1917 the way was open for the start of the guerrilla campaign against the Hejaz railway which was to continue until the end of the war. British officers, including Lawrence, Newcombe and several others, accompanied by small groups of Arab irregulars, would visit isolated stretches of track, culverts and bridges, and either demolish them there and then or lay mines which would be detonated by passing trains – or indeed both:

> after nightfall we returned to the line, laid thirty charges of gelignite against the most-curved rails and fired them leisurely. The curved rails were chosen since the Turks would have to bring down new ones from Damascus. Actually, this took them three days; and then their construction train stepped on our mine (which we had left as hook behind the demolition's bait) and hurt its locomotive. Traffic ceased for three days while the line was picked over for traps.[17]

But apart from the glamorous but small-scale raids against Turkish lines of communication, Lawrence also engineered several more important *coups de main*. The first major operation that he was involved in, along with Newcombe who had just arrived in Hejaz, was the capture by Feisal's forces of the port of Al Wajh which had been designated as Feisal's base for operations against the Tabuk to El Ela section of the railway. The plan was for Feisal's force of 3,000 tribal irregulars to march 100 miles north of their current base at Umm Lajj on 15 January 1917, and nine days later to assault the small garrison at the port from the south and east whilst a naval vessel shelled the Turkish defences and landed a smaller group of Arab irregulars and a party of British seamen.[18] In fact the operation turned into farce: Feisal's force dawdled and dithered for so long that, on 23 January, the naval commander, with little idea of the Arabs' whereabouts, successfully launched his attack without them. With the town captured by the naval landing party, for the loss of one British seaplane pilot, the Arabs looted it, to the general disgust of the British officers present (though not, of course, Lawrence).

The Al Wajh débâcle caused serious misgivings amongst British commanders over whether the Arabs would ever be sufficiently reliable and disciplined to play a role in the campaign against the Turks: 'In Cairo, Khartoum and Jiddah, this seemed to most people a victory for the professionals and a defeat for the amateurs'[19] but Lawrence was not particularly perturbed: 'The Arab movement had now no opponent in Western Arabia, and had passed beyond danger of collapse . . . and we had learnt the first rules of Beduin warfare.'[20]

Undaunted by failure, Lawrence continued with the railway campaign as he worked out his next strategic move. A central plank of Lawrence's personal Arab strategy was the exclusion of the French from any post-war involvement in Arabia. The Sykes–Picot agreement had promised Syria as a French 'sphere of influence' – as Lawrence knew well – but he was determined to thwart this if possible, convinced that he could manoeuvre Feisal into control there as a *fait accompli*. To achieve this aim, Feisal needed to have both the loyalty of the local inhabitants and physical control of key terrain in Syria. Lawrence set about obtaining both.

Lawrence left Al Wajh on 9 May 1917 with a force of thirty-six men, comprising a handful of senior members of Feisal's entourage and some escorts, on an 800-mile tour of ostensibly Turkish-occupied Syria and Lebanon. His aim was to sound out tribal leaders as to whether they would support Feisal, and to recruit a force to capture the strategically important port of Aqaba at the head of the Red Sea. For both purposes he carried £20,000 in gold sovereigns. Along the way, and partly for propaganda purposes, his group carried out several small-scale ambushes and sabotage attacks against Turkish installations: 'The noise of dynamite explosions we find everywhere to be the most effective propaganda measure possible.'[21]

The first part of Lawrence's mission, the canvassing of tribal leaders, was a mixed success: few were prepared to commit themselves outright to Feisal and the rebellion, adopting a wait-and-see attitude which, if not encouraging, was at least entirely understandable. But the second part was a resounding success: from a 'forward operating base' (for want of a better phrase) at An Kabk, much of the gold was used to recruit a force of Bedouin for the attack on Aqaba. Between 23 June and 4 July, Lawrence led his force of approximately five hundred irregulars on a series of reconnaissances, and through several sharp engagements with Turkish regular troops, before sweeping into Aqaba on 6 July. Almost immediately, he set off across the Sinai desert towards Suez with a small escort in order to get word of his extraordinary achievement to the new British Commander-in-Chief, General Allenby. Lawrence also wanted to obtain help in feeding his own force and evacuating the 600 Turkish prisoners they had taken.

Lawrence's achievement on the Aqaba operation cannot be gainsaid. There is some doubt over whether he actually travelled the entire distance that he claimed; nevertheless he undoubtedly did remain 'at large' far inside enemy-controlled territory for two months, he did raise a force of battalion-strength and he did lead them to capture a key strategic target, although they were probably motivated largely by the money he paid them rather than devotion to the cause of Arab nationalism. Furthermore, he developed a coherent guerrilla strategy during this period which he was able to present to Allenby when they eventually met in Cairo at the end of July: a strategy that Allenby, to Lawrence's surprise, accepted.

Lawrence's plan was to use Aqaba as a base to extend the railway war north into Syria, using his irregulars to harass what was about to become a Turkish flank and pinning down Turkish (and indeed German) troops who would be better employed fighting the regular British forces. From July 1917 until the end of the war, Lawrence acted as liaison officer between Feisal and Allenby, as Feisal's political and strategic advisor and as *de facto* military commander of a series of guerrilla raids against the railway and other Turkish installations.

Throughout this latter post-Aqaba period when Lawrence had, to some extent, acquired a certain amount of freedom of action as a result of his extraordinary success at Aqaba, a conflict of loyalties was developing within him between his romantic attachment to the Bedouin Arabs and the Hashemite dynasty, and his duty of loyalty to Allenby, whom he respected and admired, and the British government, whose post-war plans for Arabia he opposed. One consequence of this is that Lawrence's accounts of events after Aqaba are at increasing variance with what other participants believe to have happened and this has, to some extent, masked what he did actually achieve.

Despite the presence of the large Turkish garrison, loosely besieged by the 'Southern' Arab army at Medina, led by Abdulla (Feisal's elder brother), and outposts along the railway, the Hejaz coastline was now effectively under Arab control, moving the focus of the fighting into Syria. Shorter lines of communication for the Turks and the larger indigenous population in Syria made the battlefield considerably denser as it got further north which, in turn, restricted the operational options open to Lawrence's irregulars and exposed their considerable shortcomings. In reality, even the best of Lawrence's force were unwilling to take on the Turks on anything remotely approaching equal terms; their motivation was poor and largely mercenary; they were prone to lapse into banditry whenever an opportunity presented itself (even robbing their supposed British and French allies) and they committed regular gruesome atrocities against Turkish prisoners. They also required the support of European or Egyptian regulars with support weapons for almost all their operations. But this is not a criticism of Lawrence: history shows us that raising and leading irregular forces, however warlike the traditions of the population from which they are recruited, rarely supplies soldiers of high quality, and by and large local irregulars have little, if any, impact on large-scale conflicts. The fact is that, despite the generally poor quality of the forces available to him, Lawrence's operations did significantly affect the course of the conflict in the Middle East; this was an enormous achievement in itself.

From the special operations point of view one key lesson that can be learned from Lawrence's operations after the capture of Aqaba can be drawn from his scheme to destroy the railway bridge over the River Yarmuk at Tell el Shehab in November 1917. The purpose of the attack was to halt traffic on the Dera–Haifa railway at a crucial phase in General Allenby's offensive against the Gaza–Beersheba line. This railway was a Turkish main supply route and the bridges in the Yarmuk valley were complicated feats of civil engineering, not easily repaired: 'To cut . . . these bridges would isolate the Turkish Army, for one fortnight, from its base in Damascus, and destroy its power of escaping from Allenby's advance'[22] in Lawrence's view and 'Allenby was emphatic that it should be destroyed immediately after the offensive had opened'.[23]

In fact, despite the careful construction of tailor-made charges to destroy the girders of the bridge, a covert approach of more than four hundred miles through Turkish territory, and the presence of a demolition specialist and a party of Indian machine-gun troops, nevertheless the actual 'target attack' came to nothing because one of Lawrence's party dropped his rifle, alerting the Turkish sentry on the bridge who called out the guard and started a firefight. As the bullets began to fly, the Arabs carrying the gelignite sensibly decided to ditch it before it could be accidentally detonated. This left Lawrence, who had reached the span itself unobserved, unable to do more than make his getaway in exasperated annoyance. Instead, Lawrence and his party used their remaining explosives to hit the main Hejaz line, where they derailed a train carrying the Governor of Syria: a moderately satisfactory outcome but lacking the strategic possibilities of the original plan.

This incident illustrates an important truth about special operations in general war: their success *can* conceivably have a major effect on the course of larger operations but success cannot, and should not, be relied upon by high-level commanders. The 'crucial special operation' is a favourite device of thriller-writers and film-makers – *The Guns of Navarone* is a classic example of this genre – but a strategic commander who relies upon the successful outcome of a special operation should be hurriedly sent off to prune his roses. The reasons for this are self-evident: however good the preparation and planning inherent in any particular operation, a successful outcome depends on factors that ultimately cannot be controlled. There is an old military adage that 'No plan survives its first contact with the enemy' but the truth is that the longer and more intricate an operation is (and this is true of any military operation), the more outside factors impinge upon it, and the less likely it is to proceed according to plan. By their nature, most individual special operations take place on a knife-edge between success or failure even before there is any contact with enemy forces, and cannot sustain too much variation from the original concept, for whatever reason, before they are irretrievably derailed.

In fact Allenby was far too sensible to rely overmuch on the possibility that Lawrence might cut off Turkish supplies for a crucial fortnight. Instead he used his superiority in numbers and equipment to grind down his enemy in Palestine and, by the second week of December 1917, Jerusalem was in Christian hands for the first time in 730 years.

The Arabian campaign effectively ended when Allenby's forces took Damascus in October 1918. Lawrence had striven to get Feisal and his Arabs into the city first in order to set up an administration that was to his own liking but, in fact, Australian units were the first to arrive, and Lawrence was only able to install Feisal as figurehead ruler with Allenby's agreement and British support. The reality of the logistic situation was that Feisal's irregulars couldn't hope to administer the city themselves, even though they had, in the short term, successfully suppressed opposition to Hashemite rule. In the disputes that followed, Lawrence asked to be allowed to return home, Allenby agreed, and he never again commanded soldiers, British or Arab, in the field.

Although analysis of Lawrence's achievement and his military legacy is impeded by the growth of the post-war legend of 'Lawrence of Arabia' (and not least by David Lean's feature film of that name) it is clear that he did illustrate one point to the military establishment. Namely that, in the context of modern warfare, very small, highly mobile units can conduct a campaign of simple, tactical target attacks which can nevertheless achieve a significant impact; that these can be conducted at minimal cost in men and *matériel* (no British soldiers were killed in the course of Lawrence's operations); and that small teams of advisors and leaders, provided with money and basic weapons, can weld untrained, undisciplined, indigenous volunteers into an effective military force that exploits the local knowledge and way of life of its members.

Lawrence achieved this in a fairly mechanical manner. He was able to provide Feisal with what he needed: weapons to arm his tribesmen; gold to pay them; artillery, machine-gun, mortar, air, naval and logistic support when the going got tough; an instinctive grasp of guerrilla warfare; and an educated understanding of broad strategy. Why he did it is a much more complex question.

Lawrence's strong attachment to the Arabs and their cause is difficult to explain adequately. As a young man his personality contained some elements of his mother's Christian evangelism, her desire to teach and to lead, and he was certainly inspired to some extent by prevailing ideas of British imperialism. His close contact with the Arab workers at Karkemis, actually in the setting of the Crusades, was also a very significant factor, helping to give life and substance to what was previously merely an academic enthusiasm for the area; there may also have been some element of homoeroticism involved as well. In fact his sexuality is worth some consideration. There is no convincing or compelling evidence that Lawrence was ever an active or predatory homosexual, although some rumours have surfaced, but it is almost beyond doubt that he was homosexual by inclination, and that, in the years after the First World War, he derived sexual satisfaction from being brutally flogged. As we shall see, several successful twentieth-century unconventional warfare commanders were homosexual and, while homosexuality is clearly neither a necessary nor a sufficient condition for success in special operations, it is curious that the military profession, which, in Britain at least, still abominates homosexuality, should produce such individuals.

However it came about, his pro-Arab sentiment dovetailed neatly with the knowledge he gained of the Hashemite Arab nationalists from his desk in Cairo and he became, as we have seen, a passionate advocate of their cause. Lawrence did not invent the Arab revolt, he was not the only British officer working with the Arab Army and he was not the only commander dynamiting the Hejaz railway, but he was probably the most enthusiastic advocate of all three and, cranky individualist that he certainly was, he was without doubt the right man in the right place at the right time. By applying his ability to think strategically to a coherent campaign of tactical operations, linked with the wider operational aims of his theatre commander, he effectively invented the modern special operation and did so with a degree of success which compares well with a virtually simultaneous parallel campaign that was waged, at a very low intensity, by British forces in Russia.

The prevailing image of the First World War is, for most Britons, Americans and Frenchmen at least, of a struggle that took place over the familiar landscape of Flanders and northern France; but as the great clash between the Entente powers and Germany was taking place in the west, the third member of the alliance, Imperial Russia, was confronting Germany on an even greater scale: 'in spite of disasters and slaughters on an unimaginable scale Russia had remained a faithful and mighty ally. For nearly three years she had held on her front considerably more than half the total number of enemy divisions, and she had lost in this struggle nearly as many men killed as all the other allies put together.'[24] What this meant was that should Russia be eliminated from the war for whatever reason, a huge number of German and Austro-Hungarian troops would be released to serve on other fronts. As the strain of the war in the east increased, this is precisely what happened:

> The conditions of life have become so intolerable, the Russian casualties have been so heavy, the ages and classes subject to military service have been so widely extended, the disorganisation of the administration and the untrustworthiness of the Government have become so notorious that it is not a matter of surprise if the majority of ordinary people reach at any peace straw. Personally, I am convinced that Russia will never fight through another winter.[25]

This was the accurate prediction of Sir Samuel Hoare, Chamberlain's future foreign secretary, in December 1916 as he prepared to finish his tour as the British Secret Service's (then called MI1c) 'resident' in Petrograd. Within three months the Czar had been overthrown and forced to abdicate, and the country was being ruled by the shaky and inexperienced Provisional Government.

There was some speculation in the aftermath of the February Revolution that the new government would be able to 'rejuvenate' the Russian war effort but this failed to understand the depth of misery caused by the war and within a few months Commander Mansfield Cumming, the chief – 'C' – of the British Secret Service, was exploring the possibilities of using covert action to keep Russia in the war.

The attempts at covert action which began after the February Revolution and which were greatly intensified after the Bolshevik *coup d'état* in November 1917 were strange, misconceived, almost pathetic, operations that now seem too bizarre to believe. At the same time, however, more serious military special operations were being organised in an attempt to bolster the substantial number of anti-Bolshevik groups who were still in possession of large sections of the fringes of Imperial Russia. These operations were also intended to organise the defence of large, strategically important areas of the former Russian Empire to defend themselves against Turco-German attack. Just as in the Great Game, the threat to British India seemed palpable, although now there was a choice of potential enemies: Russian Bolsheviks or Germans.

There were many individuals involved in advising the various Russian factions, and no coherent policy seems to have united them, but one particularly striking example was the mission of Captain Reginald Teague-Jones to the strategically vital region of Trans-Caspia in the spring of 1918. Teague-Jones was a military intelligence officer based at GHQ Delhi who, having been brought up in Saint Petersburg, spoke fluent Russian. He had also served for several years in the Indian Police on the frontier, and with the Indian Foreign and Political Department. He was broadly experienced in intelligence work, and was ideally placed to gather intelligence and assert whatever influence he could bring to bear on the political and military leadership he could find in the region, with the particular aim of preventing the Turks and Germans gaining control of the Baku oilfields. What he actually discovered was a situation bordering on chaos:

T. E. Lawrence as a Captain at the beginning of his mission to the Arab Revolt in 1916. *(Imperial War Museum)*

SS-Obergruppenführer Reinhard Heydrich, mastermind of the German special operations that opened the Second World War, and subsequently a victim of assassins sent by SOE. *(Imperial War Museum)*

Members of the Long Range Desert Group on roadwatch in the Western Desert c. 1942. *(Imperial War Museum)*

Major General Robert Laycock inspecting Royal Marine Commandos as Director of Combined Operations in 1942. As commander of No. 8 Commando and Layforce he was a pioneer of special operations. (*Imperial War Museum*)

The darker side of special operations: Lance Corporal William Britten was a member of Layforce left behind on the island of Crete after the German invasion in 1941. Disaffected by his experience, he joined the renegade 'British Free Corps' of the Waffen-SS. (*Public Record Office*)

David Stirling, founder of the SAS, at the wheel of an L Detachment jeep, 1942.

Lieutenant Colonel R. B. 'Paddy' Mayne, Stirling's successor as Commander of 1st SAS Regiment and one of the most highly decorated soldiers in British history. *(Imperial War Museum)*

SS-Obersturmbannführer Otto Skorzeny (left) pictured on the Eastern Front in the spring of 1945. *(Public Record Office)*

An SAS armoured jeep in north-west Europe 1945. Additions since the Western Desert campaign include bullet-proof perspex windscreens. *(Defence Picture Library)*

'Mad Mike" Calvert (left) seen here at a French awards ceremony as commander of the SAS Brigade in 1945. In 1951, Calvert established the Malayan Scouts, laying the foundations for the creation of 22 SAS. *(Imperial War Museum)*

A patrol of 22 SAS poses for the camera in Malaya c. 1957. They carry a variety of weapons including pump-action shotguns, FN rifles, Owen sub-machine guns and M1 carbines. *(Imperial War Museum)*

Members of 22 SAS awaiting pick-up at the end of a patrol in Malaya. Seated at rear is Captain Peter de la Billière who was later to command 22 SAS and subsequently all British forces during the Gulf War. *(Imperial War Museum)*

22 SAS patrol base in Borneo c. 1964. *(Defence Picture Library)*

NCO of 22 SAS patrolling in Borneo c. 1966. *(Defence Picture Library)*

Hearts and minds: an SAS patrol medic treats a local man during a training exercise in Brunei. *(Defence Picture Library)*

The Regimental Quartermaster Sergeant of 22 SAS, WO2 P. J. Amor (right), buying fresh produce in an Omani market. The SAS's reputation for dealing fairly with indigenous populations has been a factor in their success in several counter-insurgency campaigns. *(Imperial War Museum)*

Members of A Squadron, 21 SAS, prepare to move off for a briefing during an exercise in 1992. *(Author)*

To gain a clear understanding of the political situation in Baku, it is necessary to turn back for a moment to the early part of July. The Bolsheviks were then in power in Baku, but although they were in touch with Moscow through Astrakhan, they were daily losing power, owing mainly to their lack of policy and indecision as regards the Turks. The Social Revolutionary Party was rapidly growing in strength, but was afraid to attempt any overt act, as the forces in Baku were entirely dependent on [Bolshevik-controlled] Astrakhan for both food and ammunition.

As this was taking place, the Turkish Army was steadily closing on Baku whilst General Bicherakov, a Cossack leader, fought a rearguard action in the hope of buying time for the defenders of the town: 'as a matter of fact the military authorities in Baku were far too occupied with politics to think of defending the town, with the result that no defence works worth mentioning were ever constructed'.

What transpired was a *coup d'état* by an anti-Bolshevik group following which the Bolsheviks attempted to flee to Astrakhan taking the town's supplies of weapons and ammunition with them. The anti-Bolsheviks, calling themselves 'Centro-Caspians', managed to rescue the armaments from the fleeing communists and immediately called upon the British, through Teague-Jones, to assist them in resisting the advancing Turks. Present nearby was a small detachment of the Indian Army, Dunsterforce, which immediately came forwards to help, to no avail. In the face of squabbling by the main Russian defenders, the Turkish Army broke through into Baku in mid-September 1918 and began a slaughter of up to twenty thousand Armenian civilians.

That the Dunsterforce venture ended in failure in no way reflects discredit on its leader . . . However feasible the original objective of the operation may have appeared, namely to train and equip the large number of anti-Muslim and anti-Turk racial elements in Trans-Caucasia, in practice the venture was doomed to failure because of two main factors (among others): the force was too small for the task assigned to it, and it arrived much too late.[26]

This continued to be the pattern during the British intervention in central Asia (which was halted, having achieved nothing, in 1920).

Unlike the Hejaz, where there existed a single military aim – a cause capable of, superficially at least, uniting many of the factions involved, and strong committed leaders – in Russia, officers like Teague-Jones were pitched into a power struggle where their aim, prevention of Turkish occupation, was well down the list of priorities for the majority of their potential allies and helpers. As we shall see, this was a situation that almost directly parallels the US intervention in Vietnam.

3

On the Road to War

For the armed forces of Great Britain, France and the United States, the 1930s was a decade of relative stagnation. Victory in the First World War had crippled Britain and France economically, whilst the US had entered a phase of political isolationism in which intervention in foreign wars appeared unthinkable; for these three major military powers, large-scale defence spending was both unwelcome and uneconomic. This was not, however, the case in the Soviet Union or in Germany.

The Bolshevik victory in the Russian civil war had torn the old Imperial Army apart. Some units, including the majority of senior officers, had sided with the 'White' anti-communist faction, others with the revolutionaries. Although the Bolsheviks had constructed an effective military machine for the civil war, the Red Army would have been hard put to fend off serious external aggression in the first years following their consolidation of power. The German Army meanwhile had been restricted by the terms of the Versailles peace settlement to a maximum strength of 100,000 men – an almost unimaginably small number in those days for a nation as large as Germany – and had had severe restrictions placed upon the types of weaponry it was permitted to develop and use. Both nations were, therefore, understandably keen to exploit what potential they had to its fullest extent, and both recognised that as international pariahs, albeit for very different reasons, they had a mutuality of interest which could be used to their advantage. Consequently, Reichswehr officers helped to organise and train the new Red Army, whilst the Soviet Union itself was used as a training area where Germany could exercise forbidden weapons and tactics. One result of this was that both the Soviets and the

Germans were at the forefront of the development of special operations techniques and units in the period leading up to the beginning of the Second World War.

Once it is accepted that special forces have a genuine role to play in modern warfare, one of the most daunting problems is how to deploy them. In a relatively empty environment, such as Lawrence found in the Arabian desert, infiltration by land and sea presents few real problems, but in a dense combat zone that is not the case. One of the principal reasons for the relative stagnation of the Western Front during the First World War was that the trenches of the opposing sides ran from the North Sea to the Swiss frontier with no gaps and were sited in depth; the only way through them was by fighting; and even small groups and individuals would be unlikely to evade observation for long whilst attempting to sneak through. Until the arrival of the tank, the only realistic options available to First World War commanders that could create the conditions necessary to be able to pass useful numbers of men through the enemy front line were bombardments with high explosives and poisonous gas, combined with mass assaults by infantry: hardly the best way of infiltrating small units into the enemy rear area. Even when tanks became available and workable tactics had been formulated for their use, they were evidently much better suited for major breakthrough operations.

The situation changed with the great strides forward in aviation which took place in the first half of the twentieth century. It is worth remembering that the first controlled, powered, manned flight took place in 1903 but less than fifteen years later relatively powerful, manoeuvrable military aircraft were dog-fighting over France and Belgium, cities were being bombed from the air and passengers were being carried at unimaginable speeds, out of reach of ground-based weaponry.

Whilst powered flight was making its great leap forward, the military continued to use their only previous means of taking to the air, balloons, for the task of battlefield observation. The arrival of armed fighter aircraft on the military scene made balloon observation a considerably more hazardous occupation and, with no means of defending themselves from attack, observers were issued with simple parachutes to allow them to jump to safety when the enemy appeared. These parachutes, known as 'Guardian Angels', proved to be very safe and reliable, and before long consideration was being given by a few military thinkers to using them to deliver troops to the battlefield. This radical idea failed to advance for lack of any suitable aircraft type and, as the war came to an end, was simply forgotten. The idea of giving parachutes to aircrew was also considered – and rejected on the grounds that possession of a parachute might tempt pilots into abandoning aircraft that were still flyable.

The idea of military parachuting languished until 1927 when the Italian Army began experimenting with a new type of parachute, the Salvatore, which was mounted in a pack on the user's back and opened by a static line attached to the aircraft (the Guardian Angel canopy was actually mounted in an aluminium sleeve attached to the side of the aircraft or balloon basket: the user just wore a harness). The Italians discovered that the static line parachute was reliable and opened quickly, meaning that troops could be dropped relatively close to the ground and would land in a compact group. But having made this interesting breakthrough, they took no further action; no parachute units were formed and it was left to another country to pick up the baton of military parachuting.

In fact it was the Soviet Army that pioneered the use of parachute troops. In 1930, a group of nine soldiers was dropped by parachute during a small-scale experimental exercise and, this having proved successful, the following year a Test Airborne Landing Detachment was formed in the Leningrad Military District. The Soviet idea was that parachute troops would act as pathfinders, dropping in to seize areas into which larger groups could then be landed. In January 1932, airborne motorised detachments were established in Belorussia, Ukraine, Moscow and Leningrad, and within a year, an airborne brigade (complete with its own aircraft) and twenty-nine independent airborne infantry battalions had been formed throughout the Soviet Union.

The Soviets continued to expand their airborne forces and, in the annual Red Army manoeuvres in the autumn of 1935, demonstrated them for the first time to foreign observers. At a training area outside Kiev, an invited group of Moscow-based military attachés saw 2,500 parachutists land within a ten-minute period; around the same date, elsewhere in the Soviet Union, a force of 5,700 parachutists were landed in the same timespan in what was, at that time, the largest ever mass parachute drop: 'The attaches were much impressed and their reports lost nothing in the telling. Other countries began to take notice.'[1]

One result of the Soviet airborne demonstration was that France, Germany, Poland, Rumania and Hungary immediately set about organising military parachuting schools and units. At this stage, airborne troops were conceived as being specialist assault infantry for use in *coup de main* operations against key tactical targets. Prior to the introduction of radar, the detection of military aircraft relied on patrolling aircraft and observers on the ground with fast, efficient communications that would allow reports to be collated rapidly and effective counter-measures organised: an unlikely scenario which probably led to the prevalent view that 'the bomber will always get through'. Lack of effective early warning also meant that paratroops would, most likely, take their immediate objectives by surprise when they were dropped, allowing them to seize bridges and engage strongpoints, for example, ahead of advancing columns of conventional infantry and tanks, without causing the collateral destruction associated with artillery bombardment or aerial bombing. The German High Command was sufficiently enthusiastic about the prospects for airborne troops, and the way in which their concept of operations meshed with Germany's revolutionary Blitzkrieg tactics, that by the summer of 1938 they had created the 7th Fallschirmjäger Division as a Luftwaffe formation under Major General Kurt Student.

In parallel with the development of airborne forces came another idea for revolutionising warfare, and this was also carried forward by the German Wehrmacht: a purpose-created special operations unit.

In the aftermath of Germany's defeat in the First World War, a series of studies were commissioned by the German High Command to analyse what had gone wrong: why had Germany ultimately lost a war that it had specifically and systematically prepared to fight? One of those who worked on the studies was a Hauptmann von Hippel who had spent the war years fighting in East Africa as a member of General von Lettow-Vorbeck's small colonial force. Von Hippel studied the British campaign in the Middle East and took a particular interest in

the role of Colonel T.E. Lawrence ... and his contribution to the Allied victory. The German officer was fascinated by the exploitation of Arab nationalist feelings and the potential which guerrilla warfare offered; that an elusive band of saboteurs could create chaos in the enemy's rear; could bring confusion to his military plans and win for themselves victories out of all proportion to their numbers, even though they lacked heavy weapons, firm bases or proper supply routes. The successes enjoyed by Lawrence, the ease with which he penetrated the Turkish lines in disguise, coupled with his ability to keep large numbers of enemy soldiers tied down in searching for him and his Arab bands, dominated von Hippel's thoughts.[2]

As a result, he conceived the idea of creating a small force of specialists who would be selected, trained and equipped to take advantage of any opportunities that arose to conduct unconventional guerrilla warfare in future conflicts.

Von Hippel's views on unconventional warfare would probably not have developed had the Nazi Party not achieved power in Germany in January 1933. After Germany's defeat in 1918, the Allied powers had – as we have seen – attempted to impose a form of compulsory pacifism on the post-war German government, largely by tightly restricting the size of Germany's armed forces and by controlling the types and numbers of weapons systems they were permitted to use. At the same time, the Allies, and particularly France, tried to extort enormous sums of money from Germany as war reparations, money that Germany did not, in reality, possess. Not surprisingly this fuelled resentment in broad sections of German society, not least because Germany's military defeat in 1918 had been largely invisible to the public at home: the German army's collapse had taken place on foreign soil. The Nazi Party came to power having surfed the wave of resentment created by Germany's defeat and the Allies' peace terms, with an avowed intention of disowning the Versailles Treaty and rearming Germany at least to the extent that the major European powers would have to take seriously German demands for fair treatment. With the enthusiastic support of much of Germany's civilian population as well as the military establishment, Hitler authorised the creation and arming of the Wehrmacht: at its peak the most effective armed force of the twentieth century.

The organisation within the German Wehrmacht which had acquired responsibility for clandestine operations was military intelligence – the Abwehr – under the control of Admiral Wilhelm Canaris, an anti-Nazi

German nationalist. After taking over the Abwehr in January 1935, Canaris started a programme of expansion in parallel with the huge expansion of German military power that had followed the Nazi accession to power in 1933. Von Hippel discussed his ideas with Canaris, who broadly accepted them and authorised officers of Abwehr II, the section with responsibility for sabotage operations, to begin recruiting. They were looking for 'independently-minded, tough and resilient men, inured to hardship and with knowledge of foreign languages, customs and cultures',[3] and by the summer of 1939, sufficient suitable men had been assembled (and trained in basic military skills, demolition and parachuting) to consider their operational use in Germany's forthcoming campaigns of conquest in Europe.

Details of the operations of the Abwehr commandos during the Nazi invasion of Poland remain obscure: von Hippel's special unit was not, at that time, operational. It is known that the Königsberg Abwehr station successfully sent a detachment to seize important bridges over the River Vistula and to hold them until relieved by German motorcycle units; and it is believed that teams were infiltrated into western Poland with the intention of preventing the demolition of industrial plant and *matériel* by the Polish authorities, although there is no clear evidence available as to how they fared.[4] But, in any case, the first hostile act of the Second World War was a special operation conducted by another part of the German war machine: the Sicherheitsdienst (the SD – literally the 'security service') of Himmler's SS empire.

The Schutzstaffel or SS was one of the most interesting organisations which came into being under Nazism, not only because of the primary responsibility of its members for the horrors of the holocaust, but also because it came to resemble a parallel, politically motivated and controlled armed force, entirely separate from the legally constituted military forces of the German state. It was originally founded in 1925 as an 'élite' and well-disciplined bodyguard unit (Schutzstaffel literally means 'protection squad') to guard important Nazis during meetings and rallies. Under the organisational tutelage of Heinrich Himmler, who became head of the organisation (Reichsführer-SS) in 1929, it grew, after 1933, into a large and powerful instrument of totalitarian repression, gaining control over the German police and inserting itself into a surprisingly wide area of German life.

The SD was the intelligence organisation of the SS, set up in 1931 as a means by which the Nazi Party hierarchy could keep tabs on the many petty chieftains who had risen to prominence alongside the party. It was led by Reinhard Heydrich, an embittered former naval officer 'ideally equipped to be head of a secret service',[5] with a sharp, analytical mind, and a character of almost comic-book ruthlessness. Heydrich had ambitions to extend the reach of the SD outside the confines of the Nazi Party and from fairly soon after the Nazi seizure of power he began to dabble in overseas intelligence and covert operations.

Originally, Heydrich's overseas ploys were crude operations aimed at the elimination of defectors and opponents of the regime like Otto Strasser, an early member of the Nazi Party who had fallen out with Hitler, but with the passage of time they became more ambitious. In 1935, for example, an SD Untersturmführer (Second Lieutenant) named Alfred Naujocks, a former mechanic, was sent to Czechoslovakia to kidnap one of Strasser's assistants who was operating an anti-Nazi radio transmitter from a hotel near Prague. As it turned out, Naujocks bungled the plot so badly that he ended up killing the radio operator and fire-bombing the radio set itself. A little less than two years later, however, Heydrich and his henchmen fed a set of false documents to the Russians which apparently persuaded the paranoid Stalin to launch a massive series of purges that killed off the majority of the Red Army's most effective officers, ranging from junior lieutenants all the way up to Marshal Tukachevsky, Deputy Commissar for War. It has been widely speculated that Heydrich was himself tricked by the Soviets; certainly the 3,000,000 roubles that the Russians paid for the information were forged. However, Stalin's security apparatus undoubtedly eliminated a huge number of officers (90 per cent of Soviet generals and 80 per cent of Soviet colonels were killed or disgraced; in all over thirty-five thousand officers were 'liquidated') and considerably reduced the Russian military capacity for no sensible reason beyond Stalin's paranoia. Even if Heydrich's forgeries provided only part of the justification for the massacres, it was a far more sophisticated operation than previous schemes.

For the historian gifted with 20:20 hindsight, there is no doubt that the drift towards war in Europe began with the Nazi accession to power in 1933. In 1934, following the death of Paul Hindenburg, the German President, Hitler made himself head of state and commander-in-chief of Germany's armed forces. In 1935 he introduced universal military service in defiance of the Versailles Treaty. In 1936 he reoccupied the 'demilitarised' Rhineland, set up as a buffer between Germany and France. In 1938 he forcibly united Germany and Austria, and demanded – and was granted – territory in the German-speaking Sudetenland of Czechoslovakia, ceded at Munich by the craven emissaries of Great Britain and France with virtually no reference to the Czechoslovak government.

The Munich agreement was signed on 1 October 1938. Neville Chamberlain, the British Prime Minister, flew into Croydon Airport waving a piece of paper which he believed would guarantee 'peace in our time', whilst in Germany the realisation had dawned on Hitler and his fellow Nazi leaders that Britain and France would do anything to avoid war. Hitler now knew that if he did have to fight Britain and France, he could do so to a timescale that suited him: in March 1939 he concluded the Pact of Steel (otherwise known as the Rome–Berlin Axis) with Mussolini's Fascist government in Italy; in August, to Europe-wide surprise and dismay, Nazi Germany and Soviet Russia concluded a 'non-aggression' pact which, in effect, secured Germany's eastern flank if and when Hitler decided to take action over Germany's territorial claims in Poland.

Hitler's decision to go to war was announced to his military chiefs at a conference held on 22 August 1939 at the Berghof, his mountain retreat near Salzburg. In a speech lasting several hours he outlined the reasons for going to war against Poland: the weakness of Britain and France; the non-aggression pact with the Soviets. As he outlined his ideas, his voice reached a frenzied pitch: 'Close your hearts to pity! Act brutally! Eighty million people must obtain what is their right.' Calming himself suddenly, he informed his audience: 'I shall give a propagandist reason for starting the war – never mind whether it is plausible or not. The victor will not be asked afterwards whether he told the truth. In starting and waging a war, it is not right that matters but victory.'[6] The 'propagandist reason' was to be the first special operation of the war.

In fact the operation had been set in train some two weeks before this. Alerted to the fact that a German attack on Poland was imminent, Heydrich had proposed engineering a series of bogus frontier incidents which would, on the face of it, give Germany a reason for going to war. Himmler had submitted the idea to Hitler who eagerly accepted it.

The plan, codenamed Operation Hindenburg, was for detachments of SD men, armed, and dressed in Polish uniforms, to attack several German targets close to the Polish border: a customs post, a forestry station and the German radio rebroadcast station at Gleiwitz. In a gruesome twist, the SD men would leave bodies, in reality inmates of Sachsenhausen concentration camp, to be found and photographed by the world's press.

By 25 August the operation was ready and, that afternoon, Hitler gave his generals the order to commence hostilities against Poland. At the same time, Heydrich's various detachments set off to begin their carefully planned operation. It was at this point that things began to go awry.

With the Wehrmacht already moving forwards into 'jumping-off' positions, two key pieces of information reached the German government. The first was that Mussolini's Italian government 'felt unable to participate'[7] in warlike operations against the Poles; the second was that Britain and Poland had concluded a mutual assistance agreement: if the Germans attacked Poland they would most likely find themselves at war with Britain as well. Needing time to consider these developments, Hitler ordered the postponement of the invasion.

Unfortunately for Heydrich's men, by the time this news reached them the team preparing for the attack on Hochlinden customs post were out of communications with base and in position ready to begin the charade. At the appointed hour they duly attacked the customs post and a firefight developed that was only brought to an end by the intervention of a senior SS officer who had hurried to the scene (in fact this was SS-Oberführer Müller, head of the Gestapo, who was in charge of providing the corpses). The two team commanders, SS-Oberführer Mehlhorn and SS-Obersturmbannführer Hellwig, were dismissed but there were no further repercussions: both sides in the firefight were privy to the plan and there were no casualties.

The operation was played out for a second time during the evening of 31 August. By now Hitler had decided to go ahead with the invasion, come what may, and this time the bogus frontier incidents went more or less as planned. At Gleiwitz radio station a team led by Alfred Naujocks burst in waving revolvers at the surprised staff and firing shots into the ceiling 'in order to make a bit of a shindy and frighten people'.[8] Unfortunately they then found that the station was simply relaying a programme from Breslau and they had a frantic search in order to find a microphone which would allow them to break into the broadcast. When they finally managed this, a Polish-speaking member of the unit read a short harangue and they fired a few more shots before making off, leaving the staff handcuffed in the cellars. At the front gate, they came across the body, in Polish Army uniform, of a concentration camp prisoner, executed earlier that day by lethal injection, then shot and mutilated to simulate death in combat and to disguise his identity.

Proceedings ran equally smoothly at the forestry station and at Hochlinden, now subject to its second fake attack in five days, and within a few hours photographic plates were being rushed to Berlin for development and distribution to the world's press, whilst a mock murder investigation was set up, conducted by Arthur Nebe, the head of the Criminal Police (Kripo) and Heinrich Müller, chief of the Gestapo, who had supervised the murders in the first place.

Leaving aside the breathtaking cynicism and fundamental criminality of Operation Hindenburg, it is worth asking, at this point, what it achieved. The aim was simple: to create a plausible excuse for a full-scale German assault on Poland, a political rather than military aim. Hitler had himself told his generals that 'In starting and waging a war, it is not right that matters but victory'[9] and in this case he was quite correct: few historical sources now refer to the border incidents except as another indicator of Nazi evil, and there is little evidence that anyone outside Germany (or inside, for that matter) took them at face value. Although the false claims of the German propagandists caused some confusion during the first few hours of the invasion, this was not significant from a military or a political standpoint: there was no question of any outside agency being prevented from acting by the confusion and there was no disguising the fact that fifty-seven divisions cannot be mobilised in a few hours in response to petty border violations.

With the benefit of hindsight it is obvious that the phoney border violations did more to assuage the guilty conscience of the OKW (Oberkommando der Wehrmacht: Armed Forces High Command) than persuade anyone that Germany was embarking on a just war, and it is difficult to fathom why the Germans bothered with them, particularly if one considers that if they had gone seriously wrong, they would have resulted in a major propaganda catastrophe. On this point it is worth noting how difficult it is to get even the simplest special operations to work according to plan. Even without an enemy to complicate matters, the border incidents did not go smoothly, and one is left to ponder why the relatively hard-headed planners involved didn't simply take the option of telling outright lies about the whole episode rather than acting out a potentially dangerous charade. This is a difficult question to answer and, as we shall see, it is a curious feature of the history of special operations that many of them seem to be entirely unnecessary.

So it was that the first shots fired in the Second World War came from the pistol of an SS thug simulating a Polish attack on a German radio station. As Naujocks and his team acted out their little drama, David Stirling, a Scottish aristocrat aged twenty-four, was climbing in New Mexico;[10] Otto Skorzeny, a thirty-one-year-old Austrian engineer, was staying with the family of Professor Ferdinand Porsche, the inventor of the Volkswagen, on the Wörthersee;[11] and Mike Calvert, a twenty-six-year-old regular army captain, was adjutant of the London District Engineers, working long, long days mobilising his unit from its peacetime establishment to a war footing:[12] they, along with many others, were to play a crucial part in the succeeding four years in the development of special operations.

After two days of confused dithering and contradictory advice from his political colleagues, Neville Chamberlain, the British Prime Minister, made a speech to the nation allowing that, as from that morning, 3 September 1939, a state of war existed between Britain and Germany; shortly afterwards, the French government made a similar declaration.

4

Leopards

The Prime Minister's broadcast informed us that we were already at war, and he had scarcely ceased speaking when a strange, prolonged, wailing noise, afterwards to become familiar, broke upon the ear. My wife came into the room and commented favourably upon the German promptitude and precision, and we went up to the flat top of the house to see what was going on.

Sir Winston Churchill, *The Gathering Storm*

Fighting in Poland came to an end on 28 September, less than a month after it had started, although any hope that the Poles had had of holding their German invaders had been dashed within a week by the ferocity of the German Blitzkrieg attack. This new tactical doctrine had been developed as a result of the British experience with tanks during the First World War. In the British attack at Cambrai in November 1917, a force of 381 tanks, with supporting infantry, had driven a hole ten miles across and up to five miles deep in the supposedly impregnable Hindenburg line, which had surprised* and deeply impressed both sides.

During the 1920s and 1930s, forward-thinking military theorists throughout Europe and North America had pondered the 'problems' of tank warfare and come up with a theoretical tactical doctrine which seemed to make the best use of the mobility, firepower and protection offered by tanks. The consensus was, put simply, that by organising large masses of tanks into mobile formations with integral mechanised infantry and artillery support, and by co-operating

---

* Not least the British commanders, who failed to move quickly enough to exploit this extraordinary and unprecedented success.

closely with tactical air support, it would be possible to concentrate overwhelming force on weak points of an enemy defence and, having broken through, exploit success sufficiently quickly to unhinge any defensive counter-measures.

This revolutionary doctrine was widely discussed by military professionals and theorists during the period between the wars: advocates included such diverse figures as J.F.C. Fuller in Britain, Guderian in Germany, De Gaulle in France, and Patton in the United States; but it was only in Germany that it became the accepted military practice. Britain preferred to concentrate on colonial policing; France was skulking behind the Maginot line, its hugely expensive defensive white elephant; whilst the United States was gripped by isolationism.

Poland had been able to mobilise some thirty divisions to meet the threat posed by Germany's fifty-seven and had not been at all prepared for the Soviet invasion of eastern Poland which had begun on 17 September. The unexpectedly quick German victory meant that the campaign was over before the British Expeditionary Force had even established its headquarters in France. Nevertheless, Germany made no attempt during the autumn and winter of 1939 to open hostilities against Britain and France in western Europe and instead the situation developed into the 'phoney war', as the armies of the major belligerent powers faced off from either side of the French defensive system, and the Benelux countries twittered about their neutrality.

Neither Britain nor France possessed military special forces during this period, and nor did they intend to create them,* but in contrast, von Hippel's scheme for a German special unit was just coming to fruition. In fact in September 1939 the first Abwehr special unit was established, under the cover designation Bau-Lehr Kompanie Nr. 1 (Deutsch Kompanie) (No. 1 Construction Training Company (German Company)), commanded by a Leutnant Grabert. This happened slightly too late for their participation in the invasion of Poland but the Abwehr were sufficiently convinced of the value of special units to add a second company in October and to create a battalion structure, under the command of von Hippel, in January 1940 (as Bau-Lehr Bataillon z. b. V. Nr. 800) with its depot at Brandenburg/Havel.

The training programme followed by the men of this unit is

---

* MI6 had established Section D which is discussed in Chapter 5.

fascinating, not least because of the close resemblance it bears to present-day special forces units (it is much closer to modern-day SAS training, for example, than that of the wartime SAS). Members of the unit were taught fieldcraft and survival; demolitions, including improvised and home-made explosives; advanced signalling; parachuting; the use of canoes and small boats; unarmed combat; marksmanship to a high level; skiing; and a wide range of complementary military skills normally reserved for specialist technical troops.[1] In fact, the most significant difference between this original special forces unit and present-day equivalents were the selection criteria: in 1940, the Abwehr was looking primarily for men with the ability to blend in with their potential enemies but who could be trained to be good soldiers, whereas nowadays the reverse usually applies.

As Germany prepared to launch its assault on the West in the spring of 1940, Bau-Lehr Bataillon 800 was readied for its first combat operation, comprising the seizure of several bridges linking Jutland with the Danish islands. This involved an activity that was to become a 'signature' of German special forces: dressing in enemy uniforms.

Contrary to popular supposition, posing as enemy soldiers for the purpose of tactical deception does not constitute a war crime in itself, but is a legitimate *ruse de guerre*. It is only if soldiers open fire whilst so disguised that they are held to have breached international law. This situation did not actually arise during the German invasion of Denmark, which began at 4.15 a.m. on 9 April 1940 and ended a few hours later. Danish resistance was negligible, limited to a few army units in north Schleswig which engaged the German invaders until the government ordered a cease-fire at 6 a.m. And the Bau-Lehr Bataillon 800 operation passed off entirely successfully: the German special forces simply took over 'guard duties' on the bridges and waited for the main body of the invasion force to arrive.

The simultaneous invasion of Norway was, however, somewhat more fiercely contested. In Denmark, Luftwaffe parachute troops had made unopposed landings at Madnesø fortress and Aalborg Airport – the first ever airborne operations – but in Norway similar assaults at Oslo and Stavanger did meet with resistance although both were rapidly successful. In fact, though novel, these were not special operations in the strategic sense of the term, but a conventional use of airborne infantry, and are thus outside the scope of this work. However, the

Norwegian campaign provoked the first stirrings of special forces on the British side.

Emboldened by his stirring success in occupying eastern Poland in September 1939, Stalin decided in November of the same year to invade Finland, which had been independent of Russia since 1917. The Soviets' motivation was not entirely unreasonable: the geography of Karelia meant that Leningrad, the USSR's second city, was open to attack from the Baltic or through Finland itself; and Stalin had tried to negotiate mutually acceptable frontier adjustments with the Finns, only to be rebuffed by the staunchly anti-Soviet Finnish government. Nevertheless, the Soviet invasion on 30 November provoked widespread international outrage and offers of help from individual volunteers and friendly governments.

One such offer, from the British government, was of a battalion of volunteers specially trained in skiing and winter warfare. This was accepted and, in December 1939, a circular was issued to units in Britain asking for volunteers for '5th Battalion Scots Guards'. Amongst a number of individuals that put themselves forward were David Stirling, who was a Second Lieutenant in the Scots Guards supplementary reserve anyway, and Captain Mike Calvert of the Royal Engineers:*

> After a week or two at Bordon we went out to Chamonix, near the Swiss-French border, for ski training with the crack French ski troops, the *Chasseurs Alpins*. We spent a hectic time climbing mountains and rushing down them again on skis, and it wasn't until some time afterwards that I discovered the land we were supposed to fight over in Finland was dead flat. Presumably the need to get us ready and away was so urgent that no one had enquired what sort of country we would find out there: they knew we had to ski and obviously that meant training on ski slopes. I suppose it was a fair enough assumption and in any case it got us used to wearing the things, although personally I never got on well with them.
>
> About six weeks after we had first gathered at Bordon we were told that our rough and ready training was finished and we were on our way to Finland. We travelled back to England from Chamonix

---

* All volunteers for 5 Scots Guards were reverted to private. Calvert then became a platoon sergeant, David Stirling a sergeant and skiing instructor.

and on up to Gareloch, on the Clyde, where we embarked on the
Polish liner *Batory*. It was March 1940, and I was glad to think
that before long I would be in action again . . .

Then, just before we sailed, news came through that the Finns
had been beaten and their three month struggle was over.[2]

The 5th Scots Guards was promptly disbanded and its personnel
dispersed back to their original units but, after the German invasion
of Norway, the idea of specialist winter warfare troops was revived and
many of the original volunteers for 5th Scots Guards were incorporated
into several 'independent companies' (in fact, ten were formed but only
five were committed to action). Although the independent companies
were essentially conventional troops – they had had no real opportunity
for specialist training – they did, nevertheless, have a strategic role:
denying Norwegian fjords to the Germans as U-boat bases and attacking
German lines of communication. The circumstances of the campaign
in Norway actually meant that their only job was fighting desperate
rearguard actions, safeguarding the retreat and evacuation of other
troops, and they had no opportunity for raiding. Even so, their
existence is a simple indication that special forces were, at least,
under consideration prior to the fall of France.

Fighting continued in Norway until early June, by which time the
German invasion of western Europe had relegated it to a sideshow,
notwithstanding the loss of nearly four and a half thousand British
lives, five and a half thousand Germans and some eighteen hundred
Norwegians. It had proved a depressing and dispiriting campaign for
the British soldiers involved, demonstrating the ineffectiveness of the
piecemeal and amateurish British approach to war-fighting in contrast
with the well-drilled, well-prepared Wehrmacht. It was, however, only
a prelude to the disaster which would befall the British and French
armies in France and Belgium in May and June of the same year.

The German invasion of France and the Low Countries began on
10 May and was, once again, preceded by special operations by the
Wehrmacht. France at this time possessed by far the largest army in
western Europe, consisting of over five million men after mobilisation,
with more tanks and more artillery than the Germans. This, combined
with the heavily fortified Maginot line which ran from Switzerland to
the French borders with Belgium and Luxembourg, led most French

and British military planners to conclude that any German attack would be held, much as Germany had been stopped in the First World War. In fact the German strategy, devised by General Erich von Manstein, was to launch an initial attack into the Netherlands and northern Belgium, drawing the British Expeditionary Force and the powerful French forces north-east into Belgium, before launching the German main effort through the heavily wooded and mountainous Ardennes region of southern Belgium, an area deemed by French strategists to be impassable to large armoured formations. For this reason, it had relatively light protection.

Not surprisingly in a campaign in which nearly two hundred divisions (in total) were committed, the impact of the Wehrmacht's single special forces battalion was somewhat limited. The task set for the unit involved the seizure of several key road and rail bridges which would facilitate the passage of larger bodies of troops through enemy defensive positions with only the minimum of fighting. The most important operation undertaken by the Bau-Lehr Bataillon 800 involved capturing the railway bridge over the River Maas at Gennep in the Netherlands.

The 400-metre-long Gennep bridge was built to carry the railway from Goch in Germany into western Holland. It stands nearly three kilometres inside Dutch territory but the German plan was to take control of it before the main body of German troops had crossed the border at the opening of the offensive. This would, of course, require penetration of neutral Holland before any declaration of hostilities, so would represent an undoubtedly warlike attack on Holland in its own right.

Shortly before midnight on 9 May, the small detachment of Germans, disguised in the uniform of Dutch military police, crossed the border under command of a Dutch-speaking corporal, and quietly moved themselves into position near the eastern end of the bridge. As dawn approached on 10 May and the German Army prepared to cross the borders of France, Belgium, Luxembourg and the Netherlands, the special forces team left their hiding place and boldly marched up to the sentry position on the eastern end of the bridge. The Dutch Armed Forces had been on alert for a German invasion since 10 p.m. the previous evening and demolition charges had been placed on strategic bridges, but the sentries did not, at first, suspect that the group of six men that were approaching them in Dutch uniform could be enemy forces. Meanwhile, just before the six newcomers arrived, a telephone message was received at the guard position from the military police in the town of Gennep to the effect that the railway station was under attack. In reality they were reporting the arrival of two German troop-carrying trains from across the border, the follow-up to the Bau-Lehr Bataillon 800 operation.

As the six-man group of Germans reached the guard post the three sentries realised that only two of the new arrivals were properly dressed in Dutch uniform, whilst the others were wearing military-style raincoats, but by then it was too late. When they got close to the guards the Germans put their unarmed combat skills to good use and overpowered the sentries without a shot being fired: they were now in control of the eastern end of the bridge.

A quick examination by the German commander ascertained that the demolition charges on the bridge could not be fired from the eastern end and, consequently, further subterfuge was required. He therefore put through a call on the Dutch guards' field telephone to the western guard post asking them to send an escort to the centre of the bridge to pick up four German prisoners, and the six Germans set off again, leaving the Dutch guards secured in the eastern guardroom. In the middle of the bridge, the four German 'prisoners' were handed over and their new captors began to escort them to the western guardroom.

By now, the two German troop trains were approaching the bridge and a panicky phone call reached the western guardroom, probably from Gennep itself, demanding that the guard commander set off the demolition charges. Unfortunately, the guard commander was escorting the Germans and the only man in the western guardroom, a fifty-one-year-old sergeant, dithered over passing on the order. Before he had reached a decision, the German trains, carrying the 481st Infantry Regiment, had arrived: the bridge was captured intact.

The success of the Gennep bridge operation, and of other attacks by Bau-Lehr Bataillon 800 on bridges over the River Maas and the Juliana Canal, must have been encouraging for the Abwehr. Even though they cannot be described as vital or strategic operations – if they hadn't worked, their failure would have imposed an insignificant delay on

German operations against the Dutch Army – the technical achievement was an important indicator that more ambitious plans could be worth considering.

At the same time it was emerging that there was a psychological value to special operations: German radio stations, particularly the so-called 'secret stations' run by Goebbels' Propaganda Ministry's Büro Concordia, specifically sought to give the impression that there was an active fifth column of subversives and saboteurs operating behind Allied lines. Stations like La Voix de la Paix aimed at France and Belgium, and the New British Broadcasting Station, put out bogus instructions to sabotage groups and, in the case of the former, false reports of the military situation designed to throw the civilian population, and the military, into panic. Garbled rumours of German soldiers and Nazi fifth columnists operating in disguise undoubtedly added to the fear and uncertainty that gripped France and Belgium as the Germans relentlessly advanced, and echoes of this can even be heard today, in reruns of the popular British television comedy *Dad's Army* which features a running joke about the danger of German parachutists dressed as nuns.

Within forty-eight hours of the start of the invasion, the Netherlands had virtually collapsed and Belgian defences were weakening, hastened by the brilliant assault by a German airborne engineer detachment which had landed by glider in and around the fortress of Eben Emael, destroying many of the guns and occupying the defenders' attention, whilst paratroopers seized bridges over the nearby Albert Canal. Despite this, the main effort remained the panzer assault through the Ardennes, and by 13 May, German forces under General Guderian had already crossed the Meuse at Sedan and were heading west towards the English Channel.

Within the next two days, the battle of France was effectively lost. The Allies possessed no strategic reserve with which to counter the bridgehead over the Meuse and by 19 May, Guderian's 19th Panzer Corps had reached the English Channel at Abbeville, effectively cutting off the best of the French Army, together with the British Expeditionary Force, in a large pocket of Belgium and north-eastern France. By this time, defeatism was rife in the French High Command and government and there was little will to continue the struggle. Although plans were made for the armies in the north to break through the German flank and link up with the mass of the French Army to the south, little attempt was made to execute them and the British commander, Lord Gort (who had won the VC, three DSOs and the MC during the First World War), unilaterally began to withdraw his forces to the Channel on 25 May, in the hope that they could be evacuated. Operation Dynamo, the Dunkirk evacuation, began during the evening of 26 May 1940.

Dunkirk has been variously portrayed as a glorious victory and a catastrophic defeat: in truth, there were elements of both about it. Between 26 May and 3 June, approximately three hundred and thirty-eight thousand British, French and Belgian troops were rescued, most of whom were fit to fight again later in the war. But whilst most managed to take their personal weapons with them, virtually all of the BEF's heavy equipment, tanks, transport, artillery, mortars, machine guns, ammunition, rations and stores, was abandoned to the Germans. Although the Netherlands, Belgium and France had been thoroughly defeated in the north, there were still strong French forces available on the Somme and further south who maintained resistance for ten days before the final collapse took place, and the French government, now under Marshal Pétain, sought armistice terms from the Germans.

The fall of France in May and June 1940 was the major catalyst which led to Great Britain embracing the concept of military special operations forces and ultimately (and wrongly) coming to regard them as a strategic weapon in total war. On 10 May, as Germany's armoured spearheads rolled into France, Winston Churchill succeeded the appeaser, Neville Chamberlain, as British Prime Minister. Although he was regarded, in Conservative political circles at least, as an unbalanced adventurer, Churchill was remarkably well qualified to lead Britain in wartime, having had tenure of most of the high political offices of state, as well as serving as a soldier in Cuba, with the Malakand Field Force, and at the battle of Omdurman. He had also acted as a war correspondent in the Boer War and returned to the army to command a battalion of the Royal Scots in 1915–16. Throughout the 1930s he had urged rearmament as a deterrent against the expansionist plans of Hitler and the lesser European dictators; and he had been surreptitiously fed a diet of up-to-the minute military and intelligence information by sympathisers within Whitehall who shared his anxieties. In consequence, his military views were soundly rooted in a thorough knowledge of the subject, which combined well with his practical experience of high policy and military strategy.

Two significant strategic problems faced Britain in June 1940. The first, short-term issue was the immediate threat of German invasion. The Wehrmacht was, in some respects, as surprised as the Allies had been by the extraordinarily rapid success of their invasion of western Europe and they had not made any significant preparations to invade the British mainland, expecting instead that Britain would seek peace terms. When, in July 1940, it became clear that this was not going to happen, planning was put into effect for Operation Sealion which would launch the 9th and 16th Armies across the Channel between Folkestone and Newhaven, once the RAF had been effectively eliminated by Goering's Luftwaffe.

For the British defenders the situation was grave. As the struggle for air supremacy took place – the Battle of Britain – an invasion was anticipated at any time and, although a great many troops had been evacuated from Dunkirk (to the extent that the army was now stronger on the British mainland than it had ever been), very few heavy weapons had come with them, making it most unlikely that the army could have successfully resisted a full-scale invasion.

Aside from the immediate defensive problem, however, came the second important strategic issue. Churchill's intention, even in the dark days of near defeat in 1940, was to win the war, which ultimately meant that Britain, and the British Empire, would have to go onto the offensive at some point. In the immediate aftermath of Dunkirk, there was clearly no prospect of major offensive action in Europe for some time, probably years. But in the shorter term, there was a need to strike back at the Germans for reasons of public and military morale, and, to some extent, for training. The difficulty would be to find a way of doing this without diverting resources from the more important tasks of defence and recovery.

One answer was suggested by Lieutenant Colonel Dudley Clarke, military assistant to the Chief of the Imperial General Staff, General Sir John Dill. On the last day of the Dunkirk evacuation he wrote a short paper outlining his ideas on launching some form of guerrilla warfare against Germany: 'To anyone accustomed to the normal workings of government, the next stage of the story is little short of fantastic: 5 June: Clarke tells Dill his idea. 6 June: Dill tells Winston Churchill, the Prime Minister. 8 June: Dill tells Clarke the scheme is approved and that afternoon, Section MO9 of the War Office is brought into being.'[3] Clarke was instructed to mount a cross-Channel raid at the earliest opportunity, provided that he did not divert any unit from essential defensive tasks and could do so with the minimum of heavy weapons.

The idea of a specialist, small-scale offensive guerrilla unit clearly appealed to Churchill, who had witnessed the activities of Boer Kommandos during the South African War. On 6 June he directed General Ismay that 'Enterprises must be prepared, with specially-trained troops of the hunter class, who can develop a reign of terror down these coasts, first of all on the "butcher and bolt" policy.'[4] Whilst casting around for ideas that might help the defensive situation, Churchill minuted his chief-of-staff on 18 June 1940:

> What are the ideas of C.-in-C., H. F., about Storm Troops . . .
> There ought to be at least twenty thousand Storm Troops or
> 'Leopards' drawn from existing units, ready to spring at the
> throat of any small landings or descents. These officers and
> men should be armed with the latest equipment, tommy guns,
> grenades, etc., and should be given great facilities in motor cycles
> and armoured cars.[5]

Prime Ministerial enthusiasm gave Clarke's concept the impetus it needed. Within a month Lieutenant General Alan Bourne, the Adjutant General of the Royal Marines, had been appointed Commander of Raiding Operations on coasts in enemy occupation, and the first raid was mounted as early as 23 June 1940.

The first commando raids are worth examining, not least because of their almost total futility. Major Ronnie Tod, who had previously commanded one of the independent companies in Norway, put together a small force of 120 men under the designation 11 Independent Company. Using a number of air-sea rescue boats borrowed from the RAF, Tod and his men crossed the Channel and landed parties at Boulogne and Le Touquet. In actuality there was no real target for the raid, so the group at Boulogne sought out and attacked a German beach patrol, whilst the second found a guarded building at Le Touquet and attacked that. The Boulogne group's brush with the Germans proved to be indecisive and the only casualty on either side was Colonel Clarke, who had accompanied the raid as an observer,

whose ear was nearly shot off. The Le Touquet squad believed that
they had killed two German sentries at the building they attacked,
after which they had thrown grenades through the windows before
withdrawing. A similar raid, mounted on the night of 14–15 July against
the newly installed German garrison on the island of Guernsey, achieved
equally unimpressive results, leading Churchill to remark that 'It would
be most unwise to disturb the coasts of [the occupied] countries by the
kind of silly fiascos perpetrated at Boulogne and Guernsey. The idea of
working all these coasts up against us by pin-prick raids and fulsome
communiqués is one to be strictly avoided.'[6] The only real justification
that can be made for either operation is that they raised civilian morale
at a difficult time and confirmed that it was technically feasible to land
Commando groups across the Channel.

The more important task now was to establish the Commando
units* properly and find suitable men to lead and man them. After
considering the requirements of flexibility and relative self-sufficiency
that were evidently needed, each Commando was established to consist
of a headquarters and ten Troops of three officers and forty-seven other
ranks. Commando units were formed numbered from 1 to 9, 11 and
12 (10 Commando was formed later as a composite 'inter-Allied' unit
consisting of various different nationalities) and volunteers were urgently
sought from units of the home forces. The criteria laid down for selection
for what was described as 'special service' were that volunteers should
be 'young, absolutely fit, able to drive motor vehicles and unable to
be sea- or airsick'.[7] No details of the kind of work expected of the
soldiers was given. Selection for further training was by interview and
recommendation. Provided that the individual soldier met the basic
standard, he was in.

The nucleus for numbers 1 and 2 Commando came from the
independent companies but the remainder were found by appeals for
volunteers. The actor David Niven was serving with the 2nd Battalion,
Rifle Brigade, when he was 'shown an interesting document by [the
Adjutant], calling for volunteers for a new "élite force" of a highly
secret nature . . . the Tidworth boredom prevailed and "anything to
make a change", I put my name down.'[8]

---

* The name Commando was taken into use shortly after the idea was first mooted
and was derived from the Kommandos of the Boer War.

In practice what happened was that commanding officers were selected from the initial officer volunteers and they could then select the officers they wanted for their Commando. After this, the Troop officers were free to travel to units to trawl for other ranks to join them. Guardsman Cooper had just passed out from basic training at Chelsea Barracks:

> Shortly after Dunkirk, news was posted on the Company notice board about the formation of an irregular type of unit to be known as a Commando ... The notice stated that all those who wished to volunteer should hand in their names to the orderly room and be prepared to be interviewed ... When my turn came I was far from confident and became quite terrified when I saw [the recruiting officer]. He was most impressive, squarely built, broad in the shoulders and with a delightfully broken nose, an obvious legacy from his boxing activities.
>
> 'Well, Guardsman Cooper,' he began. 'You are a bit young for this operation, but what can you do?'
>
> 'Sir, I am a fair shot with a rifle, I have obtained the King's Scout Medal in the 9th Leicester troop and finished as a Rover in the 56th.'
>
> 'Oh,' he replied, 'then you're keen on the outdoor life?' assuming this, I imagined, from my scouting record.
>
> 'How fit are you? Do you drink? Do you smoke?'
>
> 'I'm a teetotaller, sir, and I have never smoked,' I said truthfully ...
>
> Fifty volunteers from the Scots Guards were accepted, to form No. 3 troop of 8 (Guards) Commando.[9]

The motivation of the volunteers for the new force varied but the aura of glamour and mystery that surrounded the Commandos (which were also known as Special Service Battalions) made service with them highly attractive to many young officers and men, and there was no shortage of recruits. No. 8 Commando, for example, was recruited mostly from the Household Division and commanded by Lieutenant Colonel Robert Laycock of the Royal Horse Guards. It is fairly clear that quite a number of his officers were recruited for social reasons as much as for any military qualities that they may have possessed. The son of the Prime

Minister, Randolph Churchill, became 8 Commando's quartermaster, for example, whilst the novelist Evelyn Waugh was liaison officer, and various other 'Buck's Club toughs'[10] (including the brothers David and Bill Stirling) commanded Troops and sections. Few of these characters had any operational military experience (Waugh, oddly enough, was an exception, having taken part in an unsuccessful expedition to seize Dakar from the Vichy French), most having joined up at the beginning of the war, and many were distinctly unimpressive as leaders (it should be noted that the Stirlings were a respected exception). Waugh observed the habits of his fellow officers: 'All the officers have very long hair & lap dogs & cigars & they wear whatever uniform they like ... The standard of efficiency and devotion to duty, particularly among the officers is very much lower [than in the Royal Marines, from which Waugh had been recruited] ... Officers have no scruples about seeing to their own comfort or getting all the leave they can.'[11] Although the other Commandos were drawn from a less tightly delineated social circle, nevertheless it should not be assumed that they constituted an élite at this time, by any standard other than their own inclination to be one.

Training for the Commando forces got underway during the summer of 1940. In July, Admiral of the Fleet Sir Geoffrey Keyes, who had led the raid on Zeebrugge during the First World War and had latterly been an MP and parliamentary supporter of Churchill, had become Director of Combined Operations, and he had supervised the formation of the Special Service Brigade. Meanwhile, the Special Training Centre was established at Lochailort Castle in the Western Highlands of Scotland, staffed by various individuals with esoteric skills, including Mike Calvert, who taught demolitions, and Inspectors Fairbairn and Sykes of the Shanghai Police 'who concentrated on teaching ... a dozen different ways of killing people without making any noise'.[12]

In the early months of the Commandos, their operational concepts were – aside from the intention to raid from boats – somewhat hazy and they were very much shaped by the type of training that they did, which tended to emphasise physical fitness and skills at the individual and Troop rather than Commando level:

We were taught by some Shanghai policemen who were bloody smashing blokes and they taught us a few tricks of the trade.

They used to say, 'You don't need a weapon, all you need is your hands and your feet.' Then Lord Lovat took us out into the blue, up to our necks in heather, and taught us the art of stalking. He had half a dozen instructors with him and he'd say, 'See if you can spot them.' After about ten minutes they'd walk straight into your bloody face. We learnt the art of fishing too; we'd lob a hand grenade into a stream, it'd go off and all the fish would float to the surface. We'd spear them out with bayonets and feast on fish for a couple of days.[13]

Churchill's directive of 6 June had also called for the 'Deployment of parachute troops on a scale equal to five thousand'[14] and this was an area where specialised, well-directed training could begin immediately. No. 2 Commando was designated as a paratroop unit at the end of June 1940 and parachuting began at Ringway Airport, Manchester, in July. Although Churchill wanted a corps of airborne infantry on the German model, 2 Commando were formed, initially at least, into a parachute raiding unit:

Training was largely based on night attack exercises, weapon training and unarmed combat – sticking knives into the backs of sentries, that sort of thing. We found it exciting, but it wasn't very realistic; our commanding officer . . . was a Tank Corps man. There were few of us with any experience of commando or special force fighting,* and we really weren't sure what we were supposed to be doing. We enjoyed the training, except that nobody was terribly keen on marching. So the fact that you couldn't march very far in our specially designed 'shock absorbing' rubber-soled boots suited us well. I suppose we imagined that marching wouldn't come into our operations – we'd just drop behind the lines and, duty done, we'd be spirited out by some unknown means. We were disabused of these fantasies later.[15]

Also being formed at this time were highly secretive Auxiliary Units, intended to form the basis of a British resistance movement in the event

---

* Like the rest of the army!

that the Germans did invade. Several of the instructors from Lochailort were detached to assist with this process:

Our job was to make Kent and Sussex as unsafe and unpleasant as possible for the Germans if they ever got that far. Our instructions came as something of a shock to me. I had been caught up, along with everyone else, by the invasion fever, but this official recognition that desperate measures might soon be needed brought home, as nothing else had, the full gravity of our situation in 1940. We had treated the invasion scare half as a joke, as the British are inclined to do; but clearly the dreaded danger of occupation was all too real.

Peter [Fleming] and I started by trying to put ourselves in the place of invaders, seeing the towns and villages of Kent for the first time and not admiring the scenery but deciding which bridges to cross, which houses to occupy and so on. We then set about mining and booby-trapping all the places we thought the Germans would use.

We covered bridges and railway lines first, then sorted out the big houses which would have made good headquarters and billets. Most of them had cellars or basements of some kind and we crammed them full of explosives which would be safe until a secret switch was pressed to start up a time fuse.

The next job was to pick the right people who could be relied upon to find their way to a switch and press it when the Germans had taken over. Mostly we chose farmers or farm workers, solid chaps who were not likely to lose their heads under the sort of pressures that occupation brings. But there were other people as well, quite ordinary types in normal, everyday jobs, who were entrusted with our secrets and would, I am sure, have given the Germans a most uncomfortable time if they had ever landed in England. There were even one or two country parsons among them!

Nearly all these brave and willing people had brothers, sons or nephews in the forces and the knowledge that they, too, had been asked to 'do their bit' seemed to give them a quiet satisfaction. Quiet it had to be, for they could tell no one else about it. These were the people who would have formed the nucleus of a resistance movement in Britain. None of them knew who the others were, but they would have got together somehow. And they would not have stopped at one blow against the hated invader any more than the French or the Dutch or the Norwegians did.[16]

Thus it was that by the autumn of 1940, from a standing start, Britain had created a special operations structure which encompassed ten Commandos of raiding troops; what was, in effect, a parachute battalion; an organisation of saboteurs for home defence in the event of an invasion; together with an operational headquarters to control and direct their activities, as well as launching two, admittedly rather pathetic, attacks on enemy-occupied territory. Much of this effort had arisen on the crest of a wave of enthusiasm amongst British politicians for cheap and violent military organisations that has yet to diminish, nearly sixty years later. Nevertheless, it was to be early 1941 before the Commandos were to be properly used in anger.

As the threat of a German invasion began to minutely recede in the autumn of 1940, Admiral Keyes' Combined Operations Headquarters began to cast around for appropriate tasks for the Commando Brigade. The first-choice option was a full-scale invasion and seizure of the Azores but this was shelved for political reasons, whilst the second envisaged the capture of Pantelleria, an island in between Sicily and Tunisia in the Mediterranean. When this operation too was cancelled, morale amongst the Commandos began to fall; after all, most members of the brigade had joined in the specific belief that they would see more action than their colleagues in more conventional units.

In February 1941, training began for what would be the first major Commando operation of the war: an attack on the Lofoten Islands off the coast of northern Norway. In the meantime, spirits were revived with Britain's first airborne raid. This, by members of X troop, 11th Special Air Service Battalion – the former 2 Commando, now renamed for purposes of deception – was an attack on an aqueduct over the River Tragino in southern Italy, which provided fresh water to the toe of Italy, with the intention of disrupting the ports of Bari, Brindisi and Taranto. Mounted from Malta on the night of 10 February 1941, it was the first meaningful and technically successful British special operation of the war.

The small group of paratroopers dropped – mostly – within a few

hundred metres of the target aqueduct, which was undefended, and
while a sapper corporal placed charges on the small bridge that led
up to it, a junior officer set explosives on the main target. Lieutenant
Deane-Drummond (who later commanded 22 SAS) described what
happened next:

> Corporal Watson RE, in my stick, set the charges on the tiny
> bridge that led up to the aqueduct. The explosion of one box
> of gun cotton was the signal that the aqueduct was about to
> blow. When we heard that we moved to a safe position. George
> Patterson, in the absence of the senior Royal Engineer officer, who
> had been dropped in the wrong valley about five miles away, had
> decided to put all the explosives, about half a ton of gun cotton,
> on one pier of the aqueduct instead of on three.
>
> Watson lit the fuse and we withdrew. With an almighty blast
> the bridge went up, clouds of flying concrete, iron rails – bits of
> masonry showered everywhere. Our bridge had been cut. Thirty
> seconds later, up went the second enormous explosion from the
> aqueduct.
>
> We now waited higher up for 'Tag' Pritchard to tell us the
> results of the explosion. Tag came back with a smile on his face
> and stopped us talking. 'Listen', he said. What we heard was
> the sound of a great waterfall – we'd done it. We cheered and
> cheered. Not the best thing to do in enemy country, because we
> would have been heard a long way away. But after all our weeks
> of preparation and training it was a great relief. Now we had to
> make it to the coastal rendezvous.[17]

Unfortunately, however, this proved somewhat more difficult than had
been envisaged and, although the group split up to evade back to their
rendezvous, all were captured within three days of the attack. An
Anglo-Italian corporal was tortured by the Fascist militia and murdered.
Deane-Drummond's summary of what the operation achieved was that
'it had a profound psychological effect on the Italians. It was a slap in
the face for Italian pride. It meant that troops were brought from the
front to be on guard duty all over Italy protecting bridges and other
vital installations.'[18] Even so, the water supply was only interrupted
for a few weeks and the disruption to the three ports was minimal.

The attack on the Lofoten Islands had a somewhat more profound effect on the course of the war. The ostensible objects of the raid were: 'to destroy fish-oil factories so as to deprive the Germans of glycerine for the manufacture of explosives; to sink enemy shipping; to enlist volunteers for the Norwegian forces in the United Kingdom; and to capture supporters of the traitor, Vidkun Quisling',[19] none of which was of earth-shattering strategic importance; the real reason, however, was.

The raid took place on 4 March 1941 and the landing force consisted of 3 Commando, 4 Commando, a detachment of sappers for demolitions work, some Norwegian soldiers to act as guides and interpreters and a small party of intelligence officers from the War Office, all mounted in two landing ships. These were escorted and protected by a powerful group of naval escorts including the battleships HMS *Nelson* and *King George V*, the cruisers HMS *Nigeria* and *Dido*, and five destroyers.

To the slight chagrin of some of the Commandos, there was no fighting in the islands. A little over two hundred German personnel were taken prisoner but most were meteorologists and Luftwaffe ground personnel who gave up without a struggle, whilst 315 local inhabitants volunteered to return with the raiders to join the Free Norwegian forces in Britain and sixty Quislings were captured. More importantly, eighteen factories were demolished and approximately eight hundred thousand gallons of fuel destroyed, but the key element of the raid took place without the knowledge of the Commandos.

The strategic aspect of the first Lofoten raid had nothing to do with fish oil. The major targets which justified the deployment of two full Commandos with a massive naval escort were the coding equipment in use at the apparently insignificant weather station and on board an armed trawler that was present in the islands. The 'War Office intelligence officers' were able to capture an intact German Enigma machine complete with key settings: a vital tool in the development of ULTRA intelligence, together with coding information for routine weather reporting, which, although mundane sounding, was a crucial tool in deciphering enemy signals traffic. This alone justified the mission.

Similar, though not identical, concerns brought about the famous Bruneval raid in February 1942. Photographic reconnaissance had identified the site of a Würzburg radar installation at Bruneval near

Le Havre on the French coast. This particular type of radar had
been adapted by the Germans for use as part of their night-fighter
system, the Kammhuber line, aimed at defeating the Allied strategic
air offensive, and British technical intelligence were very interested in
obtaining one to see how it worked, assess its capabilities and devise
counter-measures. Further air reconnaissance and information from
local resistance convinced Allied planners that it might be possible
at least to snatch vital components of the set by mounting a small
raid: the task was passed to Combined Operations, by now under
Lord Louis Mountbatten, who duly allocated the job to C Company of
the 2nd Parachute Battalion, commanded by Major John Frost. Frost's
force included a small team of sappers and, most importantly, an RAF
radar mechanic, Flight Sergeant Cox, whose role was to dismantle and
photograph the radar with the assistance of the Engineers. When they
had finished, Cox was under orders to get as much of the radar as possible
aboard navy landing craft which would come in to evacuate the force. In
the meantime, Frost was under instructions to ensure that Cox didn't
fall into enemy hands; had this looked likely, the paratroopers had
been ordered to kill him. Cox remembers:

> The green light went on and out we went from 300 feet. Twenty
> seconds later I was picking myself up out of several inches of soft
> snow. The six sappers who were my guards, and RSM Strachan
> and Major JD Frost, the commander, landed near by. It was a
> perfectly still night and we could see the big metal parabola of
> the radar station and the house, just as the models had shown.
> I opened my container and took out the tools I would need, the
> camera and flash gear to photograph any of the equipment we
> couldn't dismantle, and a collapsible trolley to wheel the booty
> down to the beach.
>
> One of the engineers helped me to saw off the aerial; another
> took photographs. I used a muffled torch but every time I switched
> it on there would be an oath and the Army would tell me to put
> the fucking thing out. Then the Germans began firing at us and
> bullets ricocheted off the metal installation under my hands, but
> I was too busy to bother. The transmitter was still warm – it
> had obviously plotted our arrival – but the power had been
> switched off. The whole equipment was beautifully made and

its dismantling was made all the easier by sectionalization of all
the important components in neat individual boxes. We stripped
these off and loaded them on our trolley.[20]

Despite a German counter-attack and the late arrival of the evacuation
boats, Cox and the radar were safely removed from the French
coast and carried back to England, and within a few days a
reconstructed Würzburg was operating at the Telecommunications
Research Establishment in Dorset. The raid enabled British scientists
to construct jamming transmitters and ultimately forced the Germans to
change the wavelength of every radar installation from Norway to Africa:
a genuinely far-reaching outcome to what the Germans admiringly called
'a violent technical reconnaissance'.[21]

The role of the Commandos subtly changed as the war continued.
They were originally conceived as highly trained, flexible raiders,
proficient in a broad range of skills, but as time passed their role
narrowed until, by the time of Operation Overlord in 1944, they had
effectively become specialist amphibious assault infantry. This came
about because of the limitations of amphibious operations. To land a
moderately sized body of troops – say 300 men – requires specialised
shipping which, to ensure that they reach their target, will need
protection from sea and air attack. Being lightly armed, Commandos
also require support from naval gunfire and, when possible, aircraft if
they are to achieve anything against defended locations.

5

The Baker Street Irregulars

Not entirely surprisingly Britain's Secret Intelligence Service, SIS, better known as MI6, was ill prepared for the outbreak of the Second World War even though it had acquired a special operations capability in the shape of Section D. At this time MI6 was in a somewhat ramshackle state. For collecting intelligence it relied, for the most part, on a network of officers with consular cover as Passport Control Officers (PCOs), stationed in British missions around the world, and on a separate parallel grouping, the Z Organisation which had been established by a senior officer of the service, Colonel Claude Dansey, in 1936 to overcome deficiencies in the existing system. Although many MI6 officers were effective and professional, the PCO system was hopelessly compromised by the late 1930s and it was, for the most part, a futile disguise. The Z Organisation, on the other hand, operated remotely from the PCOs and was, consequently, much more secure.

However, an operational decision was taken in London in September 1939, on the outbreak of hostilities, to the effect that Z Organisation officers should make contact and pool resources with their local PCO counterparts. In November 1939, the German Sicherheitsdienst organised the kidnapping of the Dutch-based PCO, Captain Best, and his Z Organisation colleague, Major Richard Stevens, on the Dutch-German border at Venlo. Their subsequent interrogation inevitably gave the Germans a fairly clear picture of MI6's intelligence collection apparatus throughout Europe, and meant that only the relatively new sabotage section remained largely unscathed.

Section D (for 'destruction') was actually established in March 1938 by SIS to provide a means of 'attacking potential enemies by means other than the operations of military force'.[1] It was under the command of Major Lawrence Grand of the Royal Engineers, a dashing figure, 'tall and lean',[2] who habitually sported a tightly rolled umbrella and a red carnation in his buttonhole. In the early days of the organisation, Grand fought a fierce turf war with other sections of SIS for funding, against Treasury restrictions, and Section D was only able to survive as the result of the generosity of a friend of Grand, the American-born mining tycoon Sir Chester Beatty, who supplied funds and recruits with knowledge of Section D's likely targets in the Balkans. But following the Venlo fiasco, Section D was the only Europe-based element of MI6 to remain largely unscathed and, as a result, Grand was able, to some extent, to pick up the pieces of the shattered Z network for his own purposes and to recruit more widely. (Amongst others, both Guy Burgess and Kim Philby, the Soviet agents, used Section D as their route into the world of secret intelligence.)

The schemes considered by Section D in the early months of the war were highly imaginative to say the least. Grand was a man who allowed his mind to range 'free and handsome over the whole field of his responsibilities, never shrinking from an idea, however big or wild'.[3] The key operational concept of Section D was that there were individual strategic targets which, if destroyed, would cripple or seriously hamper the German war effort at a stroke. One such was the Rumanian oilfields, principal source of German petroleum.

Section D's plan to halt the flow of oil from Rumania to Germany appears, in retrospect, quite ludicrous. The oil was transported to Germany in barges along the Danube and the scheme involved dynamiting a gorge, known as the Iron Gates, using explosives and expertise from Chester Beatty's Trepca mine, supported by a small force of volunteer naval ratings under the command of Merlin Minshall, 'an eccentric naval intelligence officer'[4] (and supposedly one of Ian Fleming's models for James Bond).

The attack on the Iron Gates was actually launched in March 1940 but failed to achieve the results that Section D hoped for. Although, or perhaps because, they were disguised as a party of art students, the naval ratings were detected by the Rumanian authorities and deported, and their clandestine cargo of weapons and explosives was seized. Other would-be saboteurs fled the country in a hurry. Kim Philby subsequently mused that he 'had seen the Iron Gates, and was duly impressed by the nerve of colleagues who spoke of "blowing them up", as if it were a question of destroying the pintle of a lock-gate in the Regent's Canal',[5] nor was he convinced by suggestions that Section D might put 'the Baku oilfields out of action'. Similar operations were launched, and thwarted, that were intended to halt the supply of Swedish iron ore to Germany at much the same time, and as the Blitzkrieg rolled through western Europe in May and June, most of Section D's efforts were diverted to training the stay-behind Auxiliary Units in Britain.

In parallel with Section D, the War Office had also set up a small unit whose brief included examining the potential for launching strategic sabotage attacks. MI(R) was actually a staff branch of the military intelligence directorate (the 'R' of its title standing for 'research'), run by Colonel Joe Holland, who had taken part in the desert campaign during the First World War and had had peripheral dealings with Lawrence. MI(R) was intended to be a focus for training and doctrine for guerrilla warfare, producing and circulating pamphlets and discussion papers to the rest of the army, but, as war approached, it found itself encompassing an operational role and sent military missions abroad to spread the word on guerrilla warfare, as well as helping to set up the independent companies, forerunners of the Commandos.

A second operational aspect of MI(R)'s work was its research station in Hertfordshire which was dedicated to producing specialist weaponry for guerrillas and intelligence operators. Amongst the many items produced was the Sticky Bomb, an effective hand-held anti-tank bomb for use by untrained resistance personnel, and the Blacker Bombard, a 20mm spigot mortar. Encouragement for this aspect of its work came from Winston Churchill, who was fascinated by the gadgetry of unconventional warfare and organised several demonstrations of MI(R)'s inventions at Chequers, with occasional hazardous consequences for his weekend guests.

Despite the effort and imagination that went into organising sabotage during the early months of the war, by both Section D and MI(R), very little of it was remotely successful, for the very obvious reasons that both organisations had an amateurish approach, both employed amateurs, and neither had a realistic appreciation of what sabotage might achieve. This goes back to the example of T.E. Lawrence and the Yarmuk bridge: in the first place, it is inherently difficult to carry a complex and extended operation through to completion, with or without enemy intervention;

and secondly, the strategic impact of destroying particular targets that is imagined by planners is often wildly optimistic.

The failure of the two pre-war sabotage and guerrilla organisations meant that after the successful German invasion, there was no form of stay-behind network on the European continent which could possibly begin sabotage against the Germans and no immediate means of starting one. Just as the Commandos were a hasty military response to the need to strike back at Germany without jeopardising home defence, so now the intelligence community began a reorganisation that would give it an effective offensive capability without compromising its need to collect intelligence. In July 1940 agreement was reached at cabinet level to merge Section D and MI(R) with a propaganda group known as Department Electra House, into the Special Operations Executive (SOE), under the control of Hugh Dalton, the Minister for Economic Warfare.

The purpose of SOE was set out in a charter issued by Neville Chamberlain (who became Lord President of the Council in Churchill's government) on 19 July 1940 as being to 'co-ordinate all action, by way of sabotage and subversion, against the enemy overseas'.[6] In practice this gave the organisation responsibility for co-ordinating and supplying the resistance movements of occupied countries, arranging for them to receive arms and equipment and, above all, training and leadership, teaching them which targets to attack and how.

In part, according to the official historian of SOE's operations in France, the organisation was 'founded on a misapprehension – the belief that the Germans' successes in overrunning Poland, Denmark, Norway, the Netherlands, Belgium, and France in such short order in 1939–40 had been primarily due to the work of fifth columnists lodged behind their victims' lines before ever a shot had been fired'.[7] Nevertheless, it was to evolve, during its six-year lifespan, into an effective and significant component of the Allied war effort.

SOE, based in an office block in Baker Street, central London, was originally divided into three branches: SO1 handled propaganda; SO2 organised active operations; whilst SO3 acquired responsibility for planning. SO1, the propaganda arm, was, however, something of an anomaly within SOE and, following a year of feuding between SOE, the Ministry of Information, the Ministry of Economic Warfare and even the BBC, it was removed from the control of SOE to become the Political Warfare Executive (PWE) in August 1941.

Once SOE was up and running, its operational aspects were organised on regional lines. Broadly speaking, a section was established to co-ordinate activities in each target country, normally in co-operation, to some extent at least, with the government in exile, if one existed. This caused problems when there were competing exiled groups and competing resistance movements in the target country; there were, for example, six separate sections organising activities in France in 1944.

The basic premise of SOE operations was that agents would be infiltrated into target countries where they would join up with local resistance elements, introduce them to techniques of sabotage and destruction, organise reception committees for agents and drops of arms, supplies and money, plan and carry out raids, and build up the strength of resistance groups. This was easier said than done. In the early days of SOE nobody knew where agents would be able to land by parachute and find safe refuge from the Germans, where they could hide their equipment and who might prove reliable. The first SOE agents to be dropped into western Europe – three who were parachuted into France in May 1941 – went in blind, relying on their luck and their training.

In fact selection and training was a crucial element in all SOE operations and was extraordinarily thorough. Recruiting originally followed the common pattern for the secret services at that time: word of mouth and the old boy network. One particularly good example of the latter is illustrated by the recruitment of James Klugmann in Cairo. Brigadier Terence Airey was brought a cup of tea one day by an NCO whom he recognised as having been 'the cleverest boy who had ever been at his school'.[8] The NCO was soon promoted to major and given an influential task organising aid to the Balkan resistance movements. Unfortunately what Airey didn't know was that Klugmann was a former secretary of the Cambridge University Communist Party, was almost certainly connected with the Comintern and that his M15 file listing his affiliations had been destroyed by an incendiary bomb. As a result, it is possible that he had an undue and malign influence on the eventual British decision to support Tito's communist partisans in Yugoslavia and discard Mihailovic's royalist Serb Chetnik movement. But as time passed and the need for large numbers of good-quality personnel increased, recruiting methods became more systematic. Volunteers were interviewed by a senior officer of SOE to determine their degree of fluency in their foreign language and to make an assessment of their character. If the candidate looked promising, they were asked back to a second interview whilst a check was made with MI5 to ensure that nothing serious was recorded against them. At the second interview the candidate was given more information about what he – or she – might expect to be doing if accepted and at which it was suggested that the chances of survival as an agent in the field were 'about evens'. Candidates were then given a few days to consider whether they still wanted to volunteer and if they did so, they were accepted for training. In June 1943, when the early rush of volunteers for secret work had slowed down, this changed to a board system run along similar lines to military officer and civil servant recruitment boards, during which candidates were examined over a period of several days by committees.

The next stage after recruitment was paramilitary training. The first phase of this, run at one of several country houses (one for each major national group) in the south of England, consisted of basic map reading and physical fitness but this was followed by a month at Lochailort, the Special Training Centre where the original Commandos had been taught their trade. Many of the same instructors taught SOE recruits as had trained the Commandos, including Sykes and Fairbairn of the Shanghai Police. These two individuals, more than any others, have had an enormous and enduring influence on certain techniques taught to members of special forces. They pioneered two-handed pistol shooting and the 'double-tap' method of firing two rapid shots into each target; they taught rapid-draw techniques from hip and shoulder holsters and handbags, and they instructed students in a violent form of unarmed combat which, according to one of their trainees:

> gave [them] more and more self-confidence which rapidly grew into a sense of physical power and superiority that few men ever acquire. By the time we finished our training, I would have willingly tackled any man, whatever his size, strength or ability. [Fairbairn] taught us to face the possibility of a fight without the slightest tremor of apprehension, a state of mind which very few professional boxers ever enjoy and which so often means more than half the battle. Strange as this may seem, it is understandable

when a man knows for certain that he can hurt, maul, injure or even kill with the greatest of ease, and that during every split second of a fight he has not one but a dozen different openings, different possibilities, to choose from.[9]

This phase of the course also included demolitions, intensive cross-country endurance exercises (not dissimilar to current SAS selection tests), infantry tactics and other military skills, and if the recruit passed – about three-quarters normally did – they were then passed on to a course in the more esoteric skills required to live successfully in occupied Europe.

'Group B' training was conducted in a number of country houses around Beaulieu in Hampshire. There recruits learned the techniques of the security forces that would be trying to catch them in occupied Europe, and how to avoid falling into their traps. They were taught basic acting techniques that would allow them to deal with spot-checks and controls without arousing suspicion, and they learned to differentiate the uniforms of the various German and collaborationist organisations that they might encounter. It also included a simulated interrogation: students would be woken and frog-marched to a cell by men in German uniforms, before being subjected to harsh cross-questioning.

The training process culminated in a short exercise during which recruits were sent out in small groups to put some of their skills to the test. They might be tasked to 'steal a machine gun from a barracks, or place explosives on the points at a busy railway junction, or steal a chief constable's car'[10] whilst being searched for by the police who had been alerted and given their description.

The final phase of training might include a parachute course or signals instruction, or even burglary or safe-breaking, before an agent was deemed ready to be moved on to their actual operational task.

The key element of SOE's success was not in any particular individual operations that they carried out, although some of them were undoubtedly important, but in the sheer volume of their operations. The SOE training process turned out some eleven and a half thousand graduates for work throughout the world (of whom 7,500 were destined to work in Europe), but, as we have seen, SOE agents were primarily organisers and leaders, and the actual number of saboteurs and resisters that were controlled or helped by SOE was vastly greater. In France for example, by the time of the invasion in 1944, SOE had armed, with the help of the RAF, more than half a million Frenchmen to fight the occupiers, whilst in Burma, Karen tribesmen trained by SOE's Far Eastern organisation – Force 136 – were responsible for killing nearly seventeen thousand Japanese troops in the closing months of the war. Some more detailed statistics are worth examination: in one month alone (25 October – 25 November 1943) 3,000 acts of sabotage were carried out against the French railway system, resulting in derailed trains, serious damage to the permanent way and the deaths of a number of German soldiers. During the same period, sabotage attacks disrupted the operations of the German U-boat broadcast (the continuous transmission of information to U-boats at sea, designed to allow the submarines to operate without recourse to potentially dangerous transmission and reception schedules) into the Atlantic and halted production at the Peugeot works near Belfort where turrets were made for German tanks.

There were, however, significant failures. Several of the most important early networks were compromised and their members arrested and usually executed. The first circuit established in France, Autogiro, was compromised by an agent arrested while carrying a scrap of paper with the address of a safe-house written on it and in October 1941 the Abwehr arrested many of its members. The Prosper *réseau* was infiltrated in 1943 and broken up, whilst in the Netherlands the entire SOE network was controlled by the Germans between March 1942 and November 1943.

This came about because of routine failures of procedure that were ignored at the London end. By March 1942, five of the fourteen MI6 and SOE agents infiltrated into Holland had been captured. One of the two captured SOE agents, a radio operator called Lauwers, was persuaded by the Germans to begin transmitting to London on their behalf. He ultimately agreed to do this because the eventuality had been anticipated and he had been given a procedure – a security check in each of his transmissions – which would inform his controllers that he was under German control. However, when he began transmission, the head of the SOE Dutch section, Major Charles Blizard, accepted his messages as genuine, despite the lack of the security check, and began to send operational instructions to Lauwers to pass on to other members of the SOE network. This, of course, led to the arrests of most of the remaining agents.

During the course of the following eighteen months the Abwehr and the SD, under Hermann Giskes and Josef Schreieder, effectively controlled SOE activities in the Netherlands and persuaded London to drop them large amounts of *matériel* and a number of further agents, the majority of whom were arrested and executed. This took place despite the fact that the captured operators often continued to transmit without their security checks and even after direct warnings were received that agents had been arrested. The *Englandspiel*, as the Abwehr termed it, only began to unravel when two captured agents escaped and made their way to Switzerland in November 1943. Even then they were distrusted and imprisoned on their arrival in Britain. In all, the incompetence of SOE's Dutch Section cost some 132 lives and set back the development of Dutch resistance by two years.

Together with the relatively low-profile sabotage campaigns and the major failures, SOE also conducted several successful high-profile operations which have contributed greatly to the organisation's reputation. One of the most controversial was the assassination, by SOE-trained Czech agents, of Reinhard Heydrich, the SS security chief and mastermind of the bogus Polish border incidents of August 1939.

In September 1941 Reinhard Heydrich was given the job of 'acting Reichsprotektor' of Bohemia and Moravia, the rump of the former Czechoslovakia. It had been expected by the Czech government in exile that Heydrich would prove a harsh ruler but, in fact, after an initial crackdown on the middle classes and the intelligentsia, he made considerable efforts to appease the workers and farmers of the protectorate whose productivity was significant to the German war effort. As a result, industrial production actually began to rise and the Czech government in exile decided to act. With support and training from SOE, two expatriates, Jan Kubiš and Josef Gabcik, were infiltrated into Prague with orders to kill Heydrich in May 1942. On the morning of 27 May, the two Czechs mounted an ambush on Heydrich as he travelled to work at the Hradcany Palace from his country house to the east of the city. Heydrich was sufficiently confident of his safety that he rarely travelled with an escort and on this occasion he was sitting in the front seat of an open-topped car talking to his driver. As the car slowed to negotiate a hairpin bend, Heydrich looked up to see a man step into the road, level a Sten submachine gun at him and pull the trigger. Nothing happened; Gabcik hadn't fitted the magazine correctly.

The driver slewed to a halt and Heydrich pulled out a pistol with which he now fired a few rounds at his attempted assassin. As Gabcik struggled to operate his Sten, Kubiš lobbed a hand-grenade which went off as the athletic Heydrich was attempting to leap from the car. Despite the explosion, Heydrich continued to move towards Gabcik, shouting and firing his pistol, and the SOE agents now decided to make off on bicycles. Even now, Heydrich pursued them for a short distance but, as Gabcik dodged behind a passing tram, Heydrich collapsed clutching at a wound in the small of his back. Shortly afterwards, the Reichsprotektor was loaded onto a bread van and taken to a nearby hospital. There it was discovered that he had been hit by a number of grenade splinters and he was swiftly transferred to a German military hospital.

Although Heydrich's wounds appeared superficial, the grenade fragments had carried a quantity of horsehair stuffing from the seats of the car into his body and severe infection set in. He died on 4 June.

The German reaction to Heydrich's assassination was an appalling orgy of reprisals. Every building in Prague was searched and, by chance, both Gabcik and Kubiš were caught, holed up in a church crypt where, after a prolonged gun battle, they killed themselves rather than submit to the SS. In their belongings the SS found references to the villages of Lidice and Lezaky. Both were razed to the ground and all their inhabitants executed.

Approximately five thousand people were murdered by the Germans in retaliation for the assassination of Heydrich: a heavy price to bear for the life of one man, no matter how important and influential, but it may well be that his death ultimately saved lives. Heydrich's great talent was the organisation of systems of killing and repression: only five months before his death he had convened the Wannsee conference at which the last stages of the implementation of the 'final solution' were decided upon. It may be that his death prevented even greater horrors being perpetrated against the Jews of Europe.

The SOE operation which has been said to alone provide 'justification enough for SOE's existence'[11] took place in Norway in February 1943. Intelligence received in London indicated that the Germans were commandeering supplies of 'heavy water' (deuterium oxide) manufactured in a plant in Vermork in the Rjukan region of northern Norway. Allied scientists knew that heavy water was a key indicator of ongoing research into nuclear fission and there were considerable fears that Germany might be some way towards producing an atomic bomb, an achievement which, as the Allied scientists knew, was at least a year away. In consequence, a force of thirty-four volunteers was flown by glider to Norway on the night of 19 November 1942, but high winds and inexperience led to disaster: both of the gliders crashed and the survivors were executed the same day under the terms of Hitler's Commando Order.

The second attempt, which took place in February, was much more successful. Six Norwegian SOE agents were parachuted onto a frozen lake north-west of Vermork on 16 February 1943. After lying up for several days they rendezvoused with a group of agents sent as an advance party for the glider raid and then spent several more days conducting reconnaissance of the plant. The German nuclear weapons programme had been given such a low priority that they found there were only fifteen guards at the installation.

On the night of 27 February the SOE team moved in, penetrating the defences with marked ease and planting their charges on the eighteen stainless steel electrolysis cells that made up the heavy water production facility. After a short period, the team leader, Knut Haukelid, heard a small explosion which signalled the success of the mission. This was more than the guards did; a German came out of the guard hut and rattled the chain holding the front door shut, but did not bother to investigate; the SOE team got clean away.

Destruction of the Germans' ability to make heavy water set back their nuclear research by at least the year it took to get the plant working again and, it is argued, ensured that the US and Britain won the atomic weapons race. In reality this is quite a difficult argument to sustain: German atomic research who awarded a low priority and, even if Heisenberg's team had reached the conclusion that a bomb was possible and worked out the practicalities by, say, mid-1943, the example of the Anglo-American nuclear project was that an enormous level of effort and organisation was necessary to refine the radioactive isotopes and build the bombs, involving billions of dollars, thousands of scientists and workers and a huge amount of industrial plant. In the continental United States, secure from enemy action, it took until July 1945 for the first two operational bombs to be produced. It is hard to imagine Germany achieving the same timescale.

6

The Laboratory

When war was declared by Britain and France against Germany in 1939, and even at the beginning of the German invasion of western Europe in May 1940, there seemed little danger that fighting would spread towards British possessions in the Middle East. At this time, Gibraltar, Malta and Cyprus were all still British colonies; Palestine (the modern countries of Israel and Jordan) was mandated to British control by the League of Nations; and Egypt and the Sudan, although nominally independent, were effectively occupied and controlled by British forces 'protecting' the Suez Canal, the key communication link with Britain's imperial possessions in India, Australasia and the Far East. This situation changed with Italy's entry into the war in June 1940.

Although Mussolini's Fascist government in Italy was sympathetic to Hitler's Germany, Mussolini himself was no Hitler: he was a bombast with virtually no knowledge of, or interest in, the realities of military administration and warfare, content to bask in the bogus glory he acquired as national leader ('Il Duce'). At the outbreak of war, Mussolini had prudently declared Italian neutrality, recognising that Italy's Armed Forces were hopelessly unready to fight a major war against modern opponents.* But for the Italian leader, considerations of prestige were vital and he secretly hoped to gain advantage from the war between Germany and the Allies by intervening at a moment when the balance was firmly tipped in Germany's favour. Thus, he reasoned, he would buy Italy a place at the peace negotiations on the winning side.

* Italy had never entirely defeated Abyssinian opposition after the invasion of 1935 – Mussolini could not possibly have hoped to beat Britain or France.

Mussolini declared war on Britain and France on 10 June 1940 and gave immediate orders for an attack on France through the Alps. When Mussolini demanded that the army be ready to move in three days, he was somewhat surprised to discover that it would be likely to take somewhat more than three weeks to make the necessary preparations, and in fact, no move had been made by the time France surrendered. This did not, however, deter the Duce, who ordered an attack against a limited sector near the French frontier: this took place on 21 June but ground to a halt when the Italian forces met resistance from French fortifications.

Mussolini's reward from Hitler for his token intervention against France was Italian supervision of a relatively small area of south-west France following the Franco-Italian armistice on 24 June but by now Mussolini had hit on a strategy that would, he believed, considerably expand Italy's power, influence and territory in the post-war world.

Mussolini's calculation was that Germany would ultimately defeat Britain with or without Italian help. Italy, however, could take advantage of its alliance with Germany by committing a token force (of 200 bombers) for the aerial bombardment of Britain, and at the same time launching a series of military operations which would, when the war came to an end, leave Italy in possession of large territories that could be absorbed into an autonomous Italian Empire alongside the mighty Third Reich. One consequence of this 'parallel war' strategy was a demand by Mussolini that the commander of Italian forces in Libya, Marshal Graziani, should advance into Egypt – before Germany invaded Britain – so that Mussolini could claim the area up to Suez when the UK was defeated.

The Italian invasion of Egypt finally began on 13 September 1940 when the Italian 10th Army, under General Mario Berti, began a slow, cautious advance along the Egyptian coastline. By 16 September the Italians had reached Sidi Barrani, approximately fifty miles inside Egypt, but there they stopped to wait for supplies. The Italians were up against the British Western Desert Force, consisting of two partially equipped but mobile divisions, which withdrew in front of Berti's five Italian divisions whilst the British C-in-C, General Wavell, considered his options for counter-attack.

In the meantime, an interesting military unit had been taking shape amidst the British garrison of Egypt. In the years between 1918 and

1939, a number of British Army expeditions had taken place to survey and map the deserts of north-west Africa. By 1938 these expeditions, led by Major Ralph Bagnold of the Royal Signals, were lasting three weeks and covering over a thousand miles, taking in visits to towns and oases deep in the 'sand seas' that made up much of the desert.

When the war started, Bagnold was on his way to a posting in East Africa, but his ship was damaged in the Mediterranean and put into Alexandria for repairs, and during this enforced stopover, Bagnold went to visit friends in Cairo. News of Bagnold's arrival happened to reach the ears of General Wavell the same day and, when he realised that Bagnold might prove a considerable asset to his force, the African posting was cancelled and the major was added to Wavell's staff as a communications officer.

Prior to 10 June, there was a strict injunction on British forces in the Middle East preventing any action which might offend Mussolini's sense of territorial propriety, but unsurprisingly this came to an end with the Italian declaration of war and on 19 June 1940 Bagnold put forward a plan that would allow him to make full and valuable use of his desert experience. The problem that Bagnold set out was that the Italians controlled the oasis at Kufra, and had a garrison and an airstrip near to the Jabal Al 'Uwaynat on the junction between Libya, Egypt and the Sudan. Theoretically, it was possible that the Italians might exploit either of these factors to launch an attack into the French province of Chad (whose black governor, Félix Eboué, was shortly to declare himself and his province for De Gaulle), or even to strike east towards the Nile and Wadi Halfa, cutting the inland route from Cairo to Khartoum. Bagnold suggested that he lead a vehicle-mounted reconnaissance through the desert to find out what was actually happening. Four days later, Wavell gave his approval.

Bagnold's first priority was manpower and, within a few days of receiving Wavell's agreement, he had recruited as many members of his pre-war survey teams as he could find to act as officers. Thereafter he began to look for other ranks and, on the basis that they would have little time for specialised training, concentrated his search amongst volunteers from the New Zealand Division which had recently arrived in theatre, on the premise that men who had lived outdoor lives in a relatively rugged environment would have less difficulty adapting to the rigours of the desert.

This force of about a hundred officers and men was then equipped with Chevrolet 30-cwt trucks, modified to carry heavy loads, extra fuel and machine guns, and equipped for desert use with sun-compasses and radiator condensers; and training began in the rudiments of desert survival and navigation. During July and August 1940, work also started on establishing dumps deep in the desert, where supplies of food, water, ammunition, spare parts, fuel, medical supplies, clothing and tyres were cached for future operational use. This early logistical/training activity had given the Long Range Desert Group (LRDG), as the new unit was christened, a good opportunity to take a look at the 'Uwaynat garrison and ascertain that nothing untoward was happening. As a result, Bagnold decided that the time was now ripe to cross the sand sea for the first time, and have a look at Kufra, deep inside Italian territory. Captain Bill Kennedy-Shaw described this first operation:

> There is nothing like these sand seas anywhere else in the world. Take an area the size of Ireland and cover it with sand. Go on pouring sand on to it till it is two, three or four hundred feet deep. Then, with a giant's rake score the sand into ridges and valleys running north-north-west and south-south-east, and with the ridges, at their highest, five hundred feet from trough to crest.
>
> Late in the evening when the sands cool quickly and the dunes throw long shadows the Sand Sea is one of the most lovely things in the world; no words can properly describe the beauty of those sweeping curves of sand. At a summer midday when the sun beats down all its shapes to one flat glare of sand and the sand drift blows off the dune crests like the snow-plume off Everest, it is as good an imitation of Hell as one could devise. It was across 150 miles of this dead world that Bagnold was proposing to take for the first time a force of heavily loaded trucks.[1]

Which was precisely what they achieved, crossing the Great Sand Sea in two days and penetrating Italian Libya, unobserved, at Big Cairn. After this, the patrol split into two parts; one section, under Captain Clayton, heading down into Chad to talk with the Free French troops at the outpost of Tekro; whilst the second group reconnoitred Kufra, sabotaging petrol pumps and fuel tanks at unmanned Italian airstrips, and fortuitously capturing two Italian civilian trucks which were carrying supplies and mail to Kufra garrison. By 1 October, the entire party was safely back in Egypt and a significant lesson had been learned.

The lesson that was learned, or rather relearned because it was the same one that Lawrence had exploited twenty-three years before, was that it was impossible for a garrisoning army to maintain surveillance over all parts of a vast empty area like a desert simultaneously, whilst, at the same time, maintaining an effective defence, without gigantically large forces. The desert is thus much like a sea, in which populated and defended areas form islands, but skilful operators, with the right training and equipment, can steer round any islands they wish to avoid with little risk of detection, except through chance encounters with ground or air patrols.

The second LRDG operation, which began in late December, was even more daring than the first. By then, the British Western Desert Force had entirely reversed the situation in Egypt. On 9 December British troops spearheaded by 7th Armoured Division had attacked the Italian invaders at Sidi Barrani, and by 15 December the last Italian troops had been chased out of Egypt, leaving behind more than thirty-eight thousand prisoners (British losses were 133 killed, 387 wounded and 8 missing).[2] Now Bagnold proposed to use the LRDG, with Free French co-operation from Fort Lamy in Chad, to reconnoitre and raid targets in western Libya, and specifically the garrison and airfield at Murzuq.

Leaving Cairo on 26 December, the force of seventy-six British and New Zealand officers and men, in twenty-three vehicles, reached their objective just eighteen days later, via a successful rendezvous with nine Free French soldiers in central Libya, and using the services of a nomad *Bedu* sheikh* as an additional guide. After lunch on 11 January 1941 they casually drove into Murzuq, receiving friendly 'buongiornos' from disinterested locals who assumed they were Italian (for three years it was a feature of the desert war that participants found it difficult to distinguish friend from foe because the colours of both uniforms and vehicles were so similar). At this point the force divided into two groups: one to attack the fort; the other to hit the airfield.

---

* Sheikh 'Abd el Galil Seif en Nasr, who had been fighting the Italians since their original occupation of Libya in the 1920s.

As the airfield group approached their target, they heard the sound of mortar and machine-gun fire from the town, and immediately it became a race between the LRDG trying to reach their objectives and the Italian guards trying to get to their sentry positions: by and large, the LRDG won. Sections led by Captain Kennedy-Shaw and Lieutenant Ballantyne took several machine-gun crews prisoner, but a truck containing Captain Clayton and the French commander, Colonel d'Ornano, received heavy fire which killed the French officer and an Italian NCO who had been taken prisoner and pressed into service as a guide. This last pocket of resistance was put out of action by an LRDG vehicle mounting a heavy machine gun, and the patrol then turned its attention to the aircraft hangar. This was found to contain three Ghibli bombers which Kennedy-Shaw promptly soaked in petrol and ignited, producing a result that was 'dramatic in the extreme. The hangar erupted like a giant torch and, as the LRDG men watched, the hangar roof collapsed on to the aircraft below while bombs and ammunition exploded in a highly satisfactory display of pyrotechnics.'[3]

The LRDG action in Murzuq was almost completely successful and the entire force was clear of the town within two hours of the firefight starting. Casualties were light: apart from d'Ornano, a New Zealand sergeant was killed and five men were wounded, one seriously. By contrast, it is believed that at least twenty Italians were killed, including the garrison commander, and all major installations on the airfield were destroyed. Even better, no attempt was made to pursue the LRDG force nor to attack them from the air, thus allowing the group to take prisoner the garrison of a small outpost at Traghen, thirty miles east of Murzuq, before completing their exfiltration to the safety of French West Africa and then Chad.

These early operations by the LRDG were a clear indicator of what a mobile raiding force might achieve in the desert but a much more important strategy was evolved by the unit during the succeeding months. By the beginning of February Wavell's forces had captured much of the Libyan province of Cyrenaica and the Italian Army in North Africa was in a state of near collapse. Altogether the invasion of Egypt had cost the Italians over one hundred and thirty thousand men captured, together with 850 artillery pieces, 400 tanks and so many vehicles that they could not easily be counted. Unwilling to allow Libya to fall completely into British hands, Hitler now decided that Germany must intervene and, on 11 February, Generalmajor Erwin Rommel was despatched to command a scratch force of German troops being sent to assist the Italians – the Deutsches Afrika Korps.

The appearance of well-organised, superbly commanded German combat troops in the Western Desert caused yet another reversal of fortune. The Italians had failed because of deep-rooted structural faults throughout their command and staff system; because they were poorly led and equipped; and because their officers had little conception of how to fight a modern war against a sophisticated enemy. The myth of widespread Italian cowardice in the Second World War is just that: a myth. The reality is that, in their early campaigns, the Italians were simply not ready to fight. The nucleus of the Afrika Korps consisted of two battle-experienced German panzer divisions, led by the star divisional commander of the French campaign of 1940, and they were clearly a different proposition to the amateurish Italians. Consequently, when large elements of the Western Desert Force were moved to Greece following the British victory in Cyrenaica, those that were left in Libya were actually facing a vastly more formidable foe.

Rommel's orders from the OKW were to maintain a defensive posture; Hitler and his senior generals had no intention of making North Africa a major theatre of war, and Britain became aware of this through intercepted ULTRA intelligence, but when Rommel began to deploy his reconnaissance screen in mid-February, he found that he met little resistance and by April he was pushing his combined German-Italian forces back into Cyrenaica, against Hitler's orders.

This sudden reversal of fortune forced the LRDG into a more defensive posture: pinprick raids on isolated outposts were clearly something of a luxury but Bagnold's original conception of the LRDG was in an information-reporting role and it was here that the unit could make a significant contribution. In practical terms this translated into the roadwatch: LRDG patrols and observation posts which were mounted to observe Axis main supply routes and report by radio back to Cairo on the movements of combat formations and supply convoys.

Strategic information reporting from observation posts (OPs) is perhaps the least glamorous occupation for special forces, but it is certainly one of the most important. Although the vast majority of intelligence at the operational and strategic level is now collected by electronic means, and particularly by the interception of communications, this has only been the case since the Second World War, and the tremendous British success in intercepting and reading German Enigma traffic which became ULTRA intelligence. The success of ULTRA, however, revealed the pitfalls that came from over-reliance on a single intelligence source: as we have seen, ULTRA material indicated that Rommel had been ordered not to take the offensive in North Africa and this suggested to the British government that it might be safe to move troops to Greece where an Axis threat was developing. In fact Rommel chose to disobey orders, catching the British at a significant disadvantage. Human sources – spies, the interrogation of enemy prisoners, reconnaissance patrols and observation posts – are independent ways of confirming or contradicting the main source of intelligence. But whereas one cannot rely on being able to recruit a spy or take a prisoner with access to the kind of information that is necessary to make important operational decisions, a highly skilled force like the LRDG can be directed towards specific targets. In the context of the war in North Africa, which was largely fought out in a relatively narrow coastal strip, it was possible to mount a semi-permanent 'round the clock' watch on the routes that would be used to move supplies and combat troops forward in the event of an Axis offensive; this task represented the major contribution of the LRDG to the war.

However, as Rommel began to roll back the British gains in the desert, a new brigade was arriving in the Middle East to reinforce and expand Wavell's capacity to launch offensive operations.* Layforce, under the command of Colonel Robert Laycock, consisted of Nos. 7, 8 and 11 Commandos, joined by 50 and 52 Commandos which had been raised locally. Although they were attached to 6 Division of 8th Army, the ultimate intention was to use the entire force to seize and hold the island of Rhodes to prevent its future use as an airbase by the Luftwaffe.

The first operational task given to Layforce was a raid against Bardia, a Cyrenaican coastal town captured by the British at the beginning of January 1941, and recaptured by Rommel in March. The orders given to Laycock appear to have been somewhat vague: he was to 'harass the

* For the well-heeled officers of No. 8 Commando, the voyage round the Cape had provided much opportunity for amusement. Randolph Churchill, for example, managed to run up gambling debts of around £2,000 playing *chemin-de-fer*, a sum – which he didn't have – equivalent to about £30,000 today.

enemy's lines of communication, and to inflict damage on his supplies and war material',[4] and it is evident from what later happened that intelligence about enemy activity was based more on guesswork than reliable information. In the event, 7 Commando (under the cover designation A Battalion) were despatched on board the landing ship HMS *Glengyle*, escorted by an anti-aircraft cruiser and three destroyers, to a rendezvous with a British submarine two and a half miles off Bardia, from where the Commando would be put ashore in landing craft.

Unfortunately, the submarine, HMS *Triumph*, was attacked *en route* by British aircraft, which caused delays and, when it did reach the rendezvous, a canoeist from the Folboat Troop (a small group of canoe-trained Commandos who worked with Layforce before expanding to become the Special Boat Section) who was supposed to mark the landing beach was unable to launch his canoe because of heavy seas. Despite these setbacks, the majority of the Commandos arrived on their designated beaches roughly on time and were able to start their operation: only the third major Commando raid of the war. Alas, it was to be somewhat disappointing.

The first problem facing the Commandos was that there were no enemy to be found. Men who had landed at 'A' beach sighted two motorcycle patrols and threw hand-grenades at them, without causing any damage, but that was the only contact of the raid. Otherwise, one group placed explosives on four unmanned naval guns, one group attempted – but failed – to blow up a bridge, whilst a third found, and set light to, a store of vehicle tyres. A pumping station, designated as a primary target, was found too late to be demolished.

More seriously, the raid's casualties were entirely self-inflicted: one officer was shot and killed for failing to give the correct password when challenged in the dark by a sentry, whilst a number of other raiders were left behind and taken prisoner on 'B' beach because they failed to find their landing craft in time for evacuation. Rumours also circulated about the behaviour of Lieutenant Colonel Felix Colvin, 7 Commando's commanding officer, who had led the raid. Evelyn Waugh, who accompanied the raid as a member of Laycock's staff, wrote an 'exaggeratedly heroic' account of the raid for *Life* magazine, in which he accounted for the escape of the German motorcyclists:

It was very lucky really that they did escape for it was through them that the enemy learned, as we particularly wanted them to learn, that a landing was taking place. Had they merely seen the blaze and heard the demolitions charges from a distance they might have taken us for an air-raid. As it was, the impression which these men carried away was of a town strongly in enemy hands, and it was due to their report that our major success was achieved. They did exactly what British higher command wanted and sent a strong detachment of tanks and armoured cars to repel the imagined invasion.[5]

But in private he was characteristically scathing, regretting that he didn't report Colvin's rumoured cowardice to Laycock, and this was very much justified: there can be no doubt that the Bardia raid was a wasteful, pointless fiasco of the highest order.

By the time that 7 Commando returned to Egypt on 30 April, the military situation in the Balkans had deteriorated significantly. Italy had invaded Greece in October 1940 as part of Mussolini's parallel war but the invasion had been driven back by the superior, better-led Greek Army. However, on 6 April 1941, Germany had thrown its weight into the Balkan theatre, simultaneously attacking Greece and Yugoslavia in a move that was essential for Hitler to secure his southern flanks before launching the invasion of Russia later that summer.

Yugoslavia collapsed remarkably quickly: Belgrade fell on 12 April and the government surrendered just five days later. Greece managed to hold on a little longer, but British troops began to evacuate on 21 April and by 1 May the formal evacuation had finished, with most of the British forces taken to Crete which thus became next in line for German attention. The loss of Greece and Yugoslavia sounded the death knell for Layforce: the Rhodes operation was clearly a non-starter and the use of much of Wavell's command to reinforce failure in Greece left the British dangerously stretched in the Western Desert. Layforce consequently came to be seen as a source of highly trained reserves to plug gaps that were beginning to appear throughout the Mediterranean and Middle East theatres. Thus parts of 8 Commando were broken up and sent to Tobruk, which was now besieged by German and Italian forces, whilst 11 Commando went to Cyprus which now appeared directly threatened by German successes.

The loss of Greece was followed, on 20 May, by the dramatic invasion of Crete by paratroopers of General Kurt Student's Fliegerkorps 11. Although there were more than thirty-five thousand British and Commonwealth troops present to resist the ten thousand or so German paratroopers, the majority of the defenders were short of heavy weapons and supplies, demoralised by their recent experiences in Greece, and dislocated from their usual command structure. Despite the fact that much of the plan had been revealed to British intelligence by ULTRA intercepts, Freyberg, the British commander, was in a much weaker position than is suggested by first impressions.

The battle for Crete was effectively decided by German success in seizing the important Maleme airfield on 21 May. This meant that they were able to fly in a mountain regiment to link up with the Parachute Division and thus increase pressure on the British defensive position around Canea to the point where, on 26 May, Freyberg ordered the evacuation of Crete.

That was also the date on which advance elements of Layforce arrived on Crete, having been ordered there to help the garrison regain the initiative. With Laycock in command, A and D Battalions (7, 50 and 52 Commandos) of Layforce were to support the garrison at the Maleme airfield. What they found on their arrival was a situation of complete chaos. Having expected to act in an assault role, Laycock's orders from Freyberg were to form a rearguard to cover the withdrawal of the rest of the garrison, a task that was immediately complicated by Colonel Colvin who had broken down in a state of abject panic.

Layforce did fulfil the role of rearguard until the last hours of the evacuation as the Germans closed in on Sphakia, but with the 2nd and 7th Australian Battalions and a Royal Marine battalion still holding the Germans, Laycock ordered his men to try to get away and several hundred managed to force their way aboard the last evacuation ships. This was a clear breach of orders by Laycock and evidence of his not entirely justified view that his Commandos were worth saving before the exhausted British, Australian and New Zealand soldiers who had borne the brunt of the fighting in mainland Greece and Crete; despite this, it did not redound to his discredit.

The loss of Crete, together with a large portion of A and D Battalions (the Commandos lost 600 men killed, wounded and prisoner of war), hastened the demise of Layforce. No. 11 Commando, which had been

sent to Cyprus, was deployed to Palestine at the beginning of June
in order to take part in the invasion of Syria and Lebanon which,
as French 'mandates' in the possession of the Vichy government, had
been allowing German aircraft landing rights, and were thus thought
to be posing a threat to British interests in Iraq and Egypt. Acting as
assault infantry, 11 Commando, drawn from Scottish and Northern
Irish regiments of the army, took part in heavy fighting around the
mouth of the River Litani in Lebanon, losing 123 men – a quarter of
its fighting strength – killed and wounded, before being withdrawn
back to Cyprus.

Layforce was now in a form of military limbo. Those elements of
8 Commando that hadn't been sent to Tobruk were detailed off to a
series of abortive raids along the occupied coastline which were defeated
by bad weather and their inability to achieve surprise with a seaborne
approach, but the majority of the personnel of Layforce were marking
time with a series of virtually meaningless exercises designed to keep the
troops happy. It was during this period that Lieutenant 'Jock' Lewes, an
Australian-born amateur jockey and Oxford rowing blue serving with
8 Commando, managed to obtain a quantity of static line parachutes
which had accidentally been delivered to the Middle East instead of
India. Lewes obtained permission from Laycock to experiment with
them and sought the participation of his friend David Stirling. An
interesting account of what happened next has recently been found:

> Having been frustrated in his plans for a seaborne operation, Lt
> J S Lewes, Welsh Guards, decided to try it by parachute. He
> and his party first went to an RAF HQ located somewhere near
> FUKA and there he discussed the details with an RAF Officer
> who, although none of the party had ever jumped before, was
> most helpful. He showed us the parachutes we were to use. From
> the log-books we saw that the last periodical examination had
> been omitted but Lt Lewes decided they were OK. Next day,
> along with Lt Stirling and Sgt Stone who were hoping to do
> a job in Syria, we made a trial flight. The plane used was a
> Vickers 'Valencia'. We threw out a dummy made from sandbags
> and tent poles. The parachute opened OK but the tent poles were
> smashed on landing. Afterwards we tried a 10ft jump from the
> top of the plane and then a little parachute control.

We reached the landing field towards dusk, landed, fitted our parachutes and decided to jump in the failing light. We were to jump in pairs, Lt Lewes and his servant Gdsmn Davies first. The RAF officer was to despatch. The instructions were to dive out as though going into water. We hooked ourselves up, circled the field, and on a signal from the RAF officer, Lt Lewes and Davies dived out. Next time round, I dived out, and was surprised to see Lt Stirling pass me in the air. Lt Lewes made a perfect landing, next came Davies a little shaken. Lt Stirling injured his spine and also lost his sight for about an hour, next, myself, a little shaken and a few scratches, and lastly Sgt Stone who seemed OK.[6]

In fact Stirling's canopy had briefly caught on the tail of the aircraft, tearing it badly and causing him to fall much faster than he should have done. The damage to his back was to hospitalise him for weeks, giving him time for serious thought about Layforce's failure in the Middle East.

At the time of his injury, David Stirling was twenty-five years old and a veteran, almost from the beginning, of British special forces. Born in 1915 into a wealthy and aristocratic Scottish Catholic family (his father, Brigadier Archibald Stirling, was a member of parliament), he had been raised in an atmosphere of privilege, accustomed to relatively easy access to money, but also subject to the emotional restraint that characterised the British upper classes of that time. He was sent to boarding school (at Ampleforth) at the age of eight and a half, where he was moderately successful academically but also developed a taste for solitary wandering around the local countryside. This enthusiasm for the outdoor life remained with him throughout his adolescence and adulthood, and, in combination with the inevitable game shooting and deer stalking in which he was an avid participant, gave him a natural grounding in fieldcraft.

In the early 1930s Stirling briefly attended Cambridge University, from which he was sent down, and spent eighteen months living in Paris hoping to become an artist. This was followed by a second spell at Cambridge studying architecture and a period in an architectural practice in Edinburgh, which also came to nothing, before he effectively 'dropped out' in 1937 and decided instead to become the first man to climb Mount Everest. Up until this point it would be fair to describe the young Stirling as something of a waster. He relied, for the most part, on his income from his family and used up a good deal of it on socialising and gambling, but after his Everest decision he became somewhat more focused. Financed by his mother, he spent a year in Switzerland learning techniques of alpine climbing and skiing, and in 1938 travelled to Canada and the USA in order to climb in the Rockies, earning extra money by working as a cowboy.

Before leaving for America, Stirling had signed on as a member of the Supplementary Reserve of the Scots Guards, his father's old regiment, in the hope that training in fieldcraft might help him in some way, but he was disappointed to find that most of his basic training consisted of drill and musketry, with some minor tactics, and he gave up without completing his course of instruction. As a result, when war came in 1939 and he returned home from the United States, he was forced, despite his undoubtedly 'officer-like' status, to complete basic training again as a guardsman before he could eventually receive his commission.

Like many individualists who were anxious to 'get involved' in the war, Stirling appears to have been an inveterate volunteer for special duties of one sort or another; and, paradoxically, like many others he discovered that volunteering for special duties often serves to exclude individuals from combat because they are held back for tasks which may, or may not, take place. Certainly, although Stirling served as a member of 5 Scots Guards during the early winter of 1940, and joined 8 Commando in the summer of 1940 as one of its earliest members, he was not involved in any fighting prior to his parachuting accident and, indeed, a board of officers had been convened during the summer of 1941 to decide whether Stirling might be a malingerer, lacking moral fibre, who was exploiting the system to avoid combat.

Whilst lying in hospital in Cairo, Stirling examined the reasons why, he felt, Layforce had achieved nothing concrete in the Middle East, and eventually wrote down his appreciation in the form of a memo which he hoped to present to the Commander-in-Chief, General Sir Claude Auchinleck (who had replaced Wavell in June). The original memo has not survived but it made the following points:

1. The enemy is vulnerable to attack along his lines of communications and at airfields, transport parks, supplies depots etcetera.

2. The scale of commando raids is such that surprise is unlikely to be achieved and the requirement for naval support and transport puts at risk assets that are of a value out of all proportion to the likely results of the raids.

3. There is an advantage to be gained from establishing a unit to attack l-of-c targets by stealth, taking full advantage of surprise and making minimal demands on manpower and equipment. Thus it might be possible to attack ten targets using the same level of resources used by a commando in attacking one.

4. Training for this unit would have to encompass all likely entry means, including parachuting, boats and foot infiltration, and should be designed to allow the unit to use available means of transport rather than having specially allocated and/or modified resources.

5. The unit must be responsible for its own training and operational planning, and the unit commander must operate direct to the commander in chief.

6. The unit should be ready to participate in the November 1941 offensive.

Also appended to the paper was an outline plan to attack enemy airfields at Tmimi and Gazala, using a force of sixty men who would be parachuted into the desert south of their targets under cover of an air-raid, after which they would lie up for the remainder of that night and the next day before infiltrating on foot, blowing up any aircraft that they could find, and exfiltrating to a rendezvous with the Long Range Desert Group who would then ferry them home.

The originality of this plan has been somewhat overstated. As we have seen, the LRDG had been operating deep behind enemy lines for almost a year by July 1941, when Stirling wrote the memo, and they had also demonstrated the feasibility of raiding airfields and line-of-communication targets, just as Lawrence had done in 1917, but the likelihood is that Stirling, as a lowly Commando subaltern, had little or no knowledge of this. What was new was his plan to infiltrate by parachute, and his suggestion that the raiding unit should be directly subordinate to the Commander-in-Chief as the strategic-level commander.

The story of Stirling's daring raid on Middle East Headquarters, where he succeeded in getting his memo read by General Ritchie, Auchinleck's Deputy Chief-of-Staff, has by now passed into legend, but it will suffice to say that there was much to recommend the idea, which was based on sound military logic, with the added benefit that it did not require much support in manpower or resources. At a meeting in mid-July 1941, Stirling was authorised to recruit and train a unit of six officers and sixty other ranks, under the designation L Detachment, 1st Special Air Service Brigade,* to conduct the operation outlined in his original paper.

The majority of Stirling's original recruits were members of 8 Commando, many of whom either had been, or were about to be, sent to regular battalions of their regiments, and the officers were, at this stage, all members of Layforce. Apart from Lewes, who had to be extricated from Tobruk to join Stirling, he had managed to recruit five other Layforce subalterns: Bonnington, Thomas, Fraser, McGonigal and, controversially, Lieutenant Robert Blair Mayne of the Royal Ulster Rifles. 'Paddy' Mayne was a controversial choice because he was, at the time he met Stirling, under close arrest for striking his commanding officer, twenty-four-year-old Lieutenant Colonel Geoffrey Keyes, son of Admiral Keyes, and recent winner of the Military Cross after taking command of 11 Commando during the fighting at the Litani river.

Mayne, who played second row forward for Ireland and had toured South Africa with the British Lions in 1938, was a somewhat complicated character. He was very big and enormously strong but, when sober, was possessed of a deceptively gentle manner. Although he had trained as a solicitor before the war and was intelligent and well educated, he was inarticulate both verbally and on paper, given to sulking and moods, and capable of acts of horrendous, bullying violence towards lesser characters when he was drinking. Sexually he was enormously repressed and was utterly unable to relate to women other than his mother and sister, and it has been suggested that his terrible aggression may have been a symptom of sexual frustration, either because he could not form relationships with women, or because, as has been strongly suggested, he was homosexual. In the field, however, he is remembered as a perfect soldier with an instinctive grasp of any tactical situation, an

* This title was selected as part of a deception plan aimed at convincing the Germans that a parachute brigade was present in the Middle East.

ability to anticipate danger, lightning-fast reactions and an awesome level of controlled aggression. To a large extent, the rapid growth of the SAS legend in the Second World War was directly attributable to Mayne's exploits.

The first task facing the newly formed unit was to construct a camp and a training facility. The unit was allocated a patch of real estate at Kabrit on the Suez Canal, but with very little to equip or furnish it. Much of the unit's original tentage and bedding was simply stolen from a neighbouring camp belonging to the New Zealand Division that was then fighting in Tobruk. With accommodation in hand, training became the next priority. Obviously, the unit was already Commando-trained but parachuting, desert navigation, weapon handling and demolitions skills all needed to be learned or improved:

> Training had a dual purpose. Obviously it was intended to make us fit and equip us for the operations we were going to do, but there was an idea that it was testing our nerve as well. The parachute training, owing to the difficulty of getting an aircraft to jump out of, consisted of two things. One was jumping off a 14-foot tower on to a bit of rather hard desert, and you were told to go into a roll, which was easier said than done. And the other was jumping out of the back of a truck going at 40 miles per hour across the same patch of desert. I think both of them were partly to check our determination and were also a way of eliminating people who were unfit or unlucky: it was training by ordeal![7]

General Wavell had been replaced as Commander-in-Chief in the Middle East because of his reluctance to take the offensive against Rommel until his forces were ready, a position which, for political reasons, Churchill and the war cabinet were unable to accept. Two offensives, Operations Brevity and Battleaxe, which had been launched in May and June 1941 respectively, had both come to nothing and Auchinleck demanded from Churchill, and received, time to plan and prepare for his first offensive, Operation Crusader, which was to be launched in November. It was to this operation that Stirling hoped to contribute his co-ordinated attack on the airfields at Gazala and Tmimi.

Operation Crusader was timed to begin on 18 November and Stirling's aim, which was to disrupt the immediate Axis air response to this large-scale offensive, meant that insertion of his SAS teams would have to take place some time before that. In fact Stirling's plan called for the parachute insertion of five teams of saboteurs on 16 November, who would lie up near to their targets, march out of the desert, attack the airfields, and return to a rendezvous with the Long Range Desert Group who would ferry them back to safety.

The day of the operation brought bad news for Stirling and his team: weather forecasters predicted high winds and poor visibility at the planned drop zone. Even with military parachuting in its infancy – and Stirling's unit had only minimal expertise at this stage – it was known that winds above 20 m.p.h. were likely to lead to a considerable scattering of each 'stick' and its equipment, and could also enormously increase the risk of physical injury to the parachutists.

Stirling was thus faced with a considerable dilemma: if he cancelled or postponed the operation to wait for more propitious conditions, he would lose the key element of strategic co-ordination with Auchinleck's offensive and, at the same time, undermine the morale of a group of men whose training and preparations had geared them for this one operation for months. If he went ahead, he risked failure even before L Detachment had come to grips with the enemy. After canvassing the views of his officers, he decided to go ahead.

The poor weather conditions were to highlight a fundamental truth about special operations that remains current to this day: a successful entry phase is often considerably harder to achieve than the actual action on the objective. Apart from threatening the descent by the SAS group, the bad weather, with winds gusting at 35 m.p.h., was also causing confusion to the relatively inexperienced aircrew (who had never dropped paratroops operationally); cloud and sandstorms had reduced visibility and they were unable to use their usual navigational landmarks. Eventually one of the aircraft was shot down, a second was tricked into landing at a German airfield by an English-speaking air-traffic controller, and only three of the planes dropped their troops. For the soldiers leaving the aircraft, their problems were only just beginning:

> The pilot straightened up and rose back up to five hundred feet. The green light had come on. As we stood up and got ready, Jock said the pilot was not exactly sure of our position because of the

atrocious weather and the activities of the anti-aircraft gunners. He added that the wind-speed was force nine. The navigator came aft to wish us luck and gave us the wind direction. Then suddenly we were given the signal and the whole stick jumped together. I felt a terrific tug as my parachute opened and then I was swinging in comparative quietness except for the wind howling through my rigging lines.

I could see two other parachutes which both seemed to be drifting away at a vast speed. As it was impossible to see the ground I kept my legs braced, but when I hit the desert I suffered a tremendous jolt right through my body. Before I could gather myself properly I found myself being dragged across the desert floor at more than 30mph by the wind. Vainly I banged at the quick release box into which the straps of my harness were clamped, to jettison my parachute, only to realise that in a moment of panic I had failed to turn it first to unlock it. Finally I managed to get clear of the harness and, luckily for me, the parachute that was dragging me along got tangled in a camel thorn bush. I managed to roll clear just as it flew off into the air, never to be seen again.

Climbing stiffly to my feet, I felt for broken bones and realised that apart from bruises, scratches and slight dizziness I was still intact. Finding my compass I started to walk back along the bearing given by the navigator, and almost immediately bumped into another member of my stick. Miraculously, after about an hour, the entire stick was assembled and without injury. All but two containers, however, were missing, with our food, water, Lewes bombs and Thompson sub-machine guns.[8]

Much the same thing had happened to the other sticks that had jumped and, in any case, they were many miles from their planned DZ. Under the circumstances, there was no question of launching the intended attacks, and the survivors of the infiltration instead converged on the LRDG rendezvous for evacuation.

It is to the great credit of everyone then concerned with the SAS, from the Commander-in-Chief at GHQ down to the individual members of L Detachment themselves, that Stirling's experiment was not abandoned after this fiasco. Of the sixty-two men involved, only twenty-two had returned and a good deal of equipment was lost.

The most important lesson learned by Stirling and his team – apart from the need to avoid glamorous but dangerous parachute insertions – was that the LRDG, who had picked them up and exfiltrated them to the safety of the Siwa oasis, were also confident of their ability to insert SAS teams for attacks. For the few days after their return, Stirling set about organising a second operation involving all the survivors but with a drop-off provided by the LRDG.

The second SAS operation was launched on 8 December when Stirling took Lieutenant 'Paddy' Mayne and ten men to attack airfields at Sirte and Tamet, whilst Lieutenant Jock Lewes and his group headed out to attack Agheila on 9 December, and Lieutenant Bill Fraser with his men made for Agedabia on 18 December. This time, L Detachment was to achieve a stunning success. All of the groups penetrated their target airfields, and Mayne, leading a team at Tamet, destroyed a significant number of aircraft:

> It went without a hitch. We didn't meet anything on the way in and before we knew it we were groping around the airfields. Black as pitch it was, couldn't see a thing. Then Paddy spotted this Nissen hut affair and sneaked up to it. He obviously heard something inside because the next thing we knew he'd dragged the bloody door open and was letting rip with his tommy-gun. Screams from inside and the lights went out.

> The buggers inside soon started firing. Paddy put a couple of guys on the ground to keep the Krauts' heads down and the rest of us went after the planes. We got through our bombs pretty quick – brilliant those Lewes bombs. Quick and easy. Afterwards Reg Seekings said there wasn't a bomb left for the last plane and Paddy got so pissed off that he climbed up to the cockpit and demolished it with his bare hands. What a feller!

> We got moving fast, but even so the first bomb went off before we were clear of the airfield. We had to stop and look didn't we. What a sight, flames and much all over the place. We headed straight out to the LRDG lads. There was a bit of a kerfuffle when the Krauts caught on to us using flashing lights to find the RV [rendezvous] – they started flashing their own but we used our whistles as a back up and we got back OK.[9]

The final 'score' for the operation was sixty-one enemy aircraft claimed destroyed: an unprecedented result which secured the future of L Detachment. Instead of heading back to Cairo, Stirling decided to launch further immediate airfield attacks and again, courtesy of the LRDG's 'desert taxi' service, they were spectacularly successful. But this time, the Axis response was quicker and Jock Lewes's team were strafed from the air as they made their getaway: severely wounded in the legs, Lewes, who had been Stirling's sounding board as he worked out the SAS concept, died shortly afterwards.

On their return, Stirling was given authority to replace his losses from the first operation and to begin the expansion of L Detachment. It was a crucial moment in the development of the SAS: 'After the first operation went wrong, I think there were a lot of people in GHQ Middle East – who didn't like David – who would have liked to have got rid of the whole thing, and thought it was useless. That is when the backing of Auchinleck came in.'[10]

With a sound means of insertion available, the bread and butter of SAS operations became attacks on enemy airfields and main supply routes. The benefit of using SAS troops in this way was that it caused disruption and chaos in the enemy rear area at very low cost in terms of manpower and equipment, and without in any way imperilling operations by the 8th Army (as the Western Desert Force – 13th Corps – had been renamed in August 1941 after being augmented by 30th Corps). The SAS were not then, and have never been, 'suicide' troops: nevertheless part of the value of the operations that they carried out at this time lies in the reality that there is relatively little to lose in attempting them, whereas the gains are potentially enormous.

Meanwhile, L Detachment's raids on Tmimi and Gazala were not the only strategic commando operations timed to coincide with Operation Crusader. Even as the survivors of L Detachment's parachute drop were trudging back to their rendezvous with the LRDG on the evening of 17 November, members of 11 Commando were preparing for the final phase of a daring raid, having landed three days earlier from the submarines HMS *Torbay* and *Talisman* at a beach near the coastal town of Beda Littoria, 200 miles behind Axis lines. Their mission was to kill or capture the enemy commander: Rommel.

As we have seen, Layforce began to be broken up almost as soon as it arrived in the Middle East in the spring of 1941 but it was August before it was formally disbanded as a single entity. Thereafter, all Commando and raiding forces in the Middle East were embodied as the Middle East Commando under the administrative command of Laycock. This comprised the Special Boat Section, L Detachment and 11 Commando as, respectively, 1, 2 and 3 Troops (this was a formal nomenclature only – as far as their members were concerned, each unit retained its own name). As part of the planning for Crusader, HQ 8th Army, under General Cunningham, directed Laycock that Middle East Commando should attempt to 'kill or capture' Rommel 'In order to strike at the brain and nerve-centre of the enemy's army at the critical moment'.[11]

Laycock opted to take overall command of the raid but gave responsibility for the tactical phase – the 'action on the objective' in military terminology – to Geoffrey Keyes, the CO of 11 Commando, and the operation duly went ahead. Unfortunately for Laycock, the same bad weather which wrecked L Detachment's parachute landing caused severe disruption to his raid. As the Commandos were attempting to leave the submarines, the heavy swell swept a number of the heavily laden soldiers into the sea and only about half of the unit managed to get ashore safely. There they were met by Captain Haselden, an intelligence officer who had disguised himself as an Arab and been dropped off in the desert by the LRDG. Haselden led them to a wadi where they were to lie up for the day.

The next evening, Keyes set off with his small assault party towards Beda Littoria where he believed Rommel's headquarters to be. By dawn they had reached a small hill just outside the town where they settled down to wait out the rest of the day. Here they encountered a party of armed Arabs whom they managed to befriend through the good offices of a Palestinian Jewish corporal who spoke Arabic. The Arabs brought them food and cigarettes and led them to a cave where they were able to lie up overnight before moving the next morning to a wood carpeted in cyclamen close to their final objective.

The next day Keyes, with the help of an Arab guide, made a final reconnaissance of the target and, during the evening of 17 November, the small group of Commandos closed in on their objective. At around 23.30, the assault team arrived at a house that was believed to be Rommel's living quarters and as Keyes, Captain Campbell and Sergeant Terry made their way into the rear entrance, a German officer suddenly appeared. Campbell describes what happened:

Geoffrey at once closed with him, covering him with his Tommy gun. The man seized the muzzle of Geoffrey's gun and tried to wrest it from him. Before I or Terry could get round behind him he retreated, still holding on to Geoffrey, to a position with his back to the wall and his either side protected by the first and second doors of the entrance. Geoffrey could not draw a knife and neither I nor Terry could get round Geoffrey as the doors were in the way, so I shot the man with my .38 revolver which I knew would make less noise than Geoffrey's Tommy gun. Geoffrey then gave the order to use Tommy guns and grenades, since we had to presume that my revolver shot had been heard. We found ourselves in a large hall with a stone floor and stone stairway leading to the upper stories, and with a number of doors opening out of the hall which was very dimly lit. We heard a man in heavy boots clattering down the stairs. As he came in sight, Sergeant Terry fired a burst with his Tommy gun. The man turned and fled away upstairs.

Geoffrey threw open a door, but the room was empty. Then, pointing to a light shining under the next door, he flung it open. Inside were something like ten Germans in steel helmets, sitting and standing. Geoffrey fired two or three rounds with his Colt .45 automatic and I said: 'Wait, I'll throw a grenade in.' Geoffrey slammed the door shut and held it while I pulled the pin out. I said 'Right,' and Geoffrey opened the door and I threw in the grenade which I saw roll to the middle of the room. 'Well done,' said Keyes. A German fired and hit Geoffrey just above the heart.[12]

As Keyes fell mortally wounded, Campbell slammed the door and the grenade detonated. The lights went out and there was silence. Campbell and Terry carried Keyes from the building but he had died by the time they laid him on the grass outside.

Campbell ran back through the building to the rear entrance where, unfortunately, another Commando shot him in the leg, having mistaken him for a German. Unable to walk, the soldiers offered to carry him the twenty-five miles back to the beach but he ordered them to leave him and to make their escape, and they did so.

Sergeant Terry managed to get the assault group back to the beach but the weather remained too bad for the submarines to take them off and the survivors were forced to remain in hiding in caves where, on 20 November, they were discovered by an Italian patrol who were quickly reinforced by some Germans. A running battle developed until, eventually, Laycock ordered the men to disperse and evade back to British lines. The only two to succeed were Laycock and Sergeant Terry.

The Rommel raid is without doubt a tale of enormous heroism and Keyes was rightly awarded a posthumous Victoria Cross, but it does beg the question of whether it is worth mounting a raid which ultimately incurs 96 per cent casualties in the hope of killing one man. Rommel was undoubtedly a military commander of enormous talent whose abilities were an important factor in the success of the Africa Korps, but he was by no means the only such factor: the Afrika Korps was a success in North Africa because its men were better trained and better led *across the board*. Churchill's suggestion that Rommel's removal from the equation would have struck at the 'brain and nerve-centre of the enemy's army at the critical moment' is also open to question. Almost all military hierarchies are designed to accommodate and overcome the loss of key individuals, including overall commanders, without suffering unduly: there is always a deputy or a chief-of-staff who will be in a position to take over and 'hold the fort' if the commander is killed.

But the key reason for questioning whether the Rommel raid should have gone ahead is that he wasn't there and never had been. The building attacked was actually the headquarters of the Quartermaster General of the Afrika Korps and the highest-ranking officer who worked there was a major; Rommel had been at his field headquarters close to the Egyptian border since August. Why did the Commandos believe that Rommel was in Beda Littoria? Certainly not via ULTRA intelligence which was not made available at such a low level, would not have been allowed to be used as a basis for such a raid, and which would probably not have suggested such a thing anyway. The inevitable conclusion is that the Rommel raid was, like the Tragino viaduct attack, executed with great courage and aplomb but was fundamentally misconceived and, in truth, a futile waste of lives.

Meanwhile, by adopting a pragmatic approach to raiding, taking time to ensure that the approach to the objective was sufficiently stealthy to ensure maximum time on target and thus maximum destruction, the SAS, on their own and in combination with the LRDG, achieved enormous destruction of enemy aircraft particularly, but also of *matériel*: fuel, rations and ammunition, supplies of which were a perennial problem for Rommel because of Italy's failure to control the central Mediterranean sea routes to Tripoli. The range of targets attacked by the SAS is instructive: in January 1942 a party attacked Bouerat harbour destroying fuel bowsers and ration dumps; in March 1942 groups visited four airfields, destroying more than twenty aircraft as well as ammunition dumps; in April and May 1942, teams visited Benghazi harbour on two separate occasions, destroying *matériel* and reconnoitring for future operations; in June 1942 attacks were mounted on eight separate airfields in Libya and Crete, destroying nearly fifty aircraft despite heavy losses; in July, various attacks on airfields netted well over one hundred enemy aircraft. This continual drain on resources could not be sustained in the long term by the Axis.

Nevertheless, serious operational mistakes were made regarding the use of the SAS, most particularly when David Stirling came under pressure to launch more obviously spectacular attacks to co-ordinate with army-level operations.

One of the fundamental tenets of special forces operations is that they are implemented at the strategic level with the intention of creating strategic impact: they are meant to significantly affect the outcome of campaigning in a particular theatre. But the principal beauty of special operations is that they are themselves conducted on a small scale, are simple in character and tie up very few resources in their execution. The strategic impact of the SAS during their first year of operations came from the sheer numbers of relatively small-scale attacks against enemy airfields that they were able to carry out, and the consequent drain on Axis resources that this caused, and certainly not because any one of their targets was particularly valuable. Nevertheless, there is a strong temptation for military planners, and for special forces themselves, to reach the conclusion that an attack on a particular target can have a disproportionate impact in itself; this is undoubtedly an illusion, albeit a very common one. The first occasion in which the SAS was misused in this way was in the simultaneous raid on Benghazi and Tobruk launched in September 1942.

The Benghazi/Tobruk operation was a brainchild of the planners at Middle Eastern Headquarters rather than being developed, as had previous operations, from within the SAS. It envisaged SAS groups attacking the two locations from the landward side, helped by a deception organised by Captain Buck, an intelligence officer who ran a unit of Palestinian/German Jews (the Special Interrogation Group or SIG) trained to impersonate members of the Afrika Korps, whilst Commandos attacked from the sea, supported by naval gunfire. The aim of the raid was for the attacking forces to destroy as much *matériel* as possible in the towns, hold them for a short period, and then withdraw via the Jalo oasis which was to be captured by the Sudan Defence Force. In the event, both parts of the plan went disastrously wrong as this report from a participant makes clear:

Intention

The intention was to drive into TOBRUK in three of the 3-ton lorries disguised as British Prisoners-of-War, with a guard made up of the SIG party in German uniform (increased in number by Lt. MACDONALD, Lt. HARRISON and myself).

The lorries were to turn along the South side of the harbour and drive to the Wadi near MARSA UMM ES SCLAU. Here troops were to de-bus, and divide into two parties. Lt-Col HASELDEN with the SIG, RA detachments, Lt TAYLOR's section, Lt SILLITO's section and Lt MACDONALD's section were to take the small house and gun positions on the West side of the bay. The remainder of the Squadron, under Major CAMPBELL was to take the positions on the East side. Success signals were to be fired by each party on completion of task, and then Major CAMPBELL's party was to proceed two miles East to find out if there were any guns there and to deal with them. Unless it proved to be extremely simple for Lt-Col HASELDEN's party to push on Eastwards and take the AA positions there, they were to hold until the Coy of A & S Highlanders and 1 Platoon R.N.F. were landed from MTBs in the bay.

I was responsible for 'signalling in' the MTBs and meeting the party when they came ashore. The signalling was to take the form of 3 'Ts' flashed every 2 minutes in Red from a point on the West shore of the bay and also from a point just outside the bay to the East.

On the journey up, Major CAMPBELL developed dysentery badly, and, although he insisted on seeing the job through, Lt-Col HASELDEN told me to accompany him as 2nd-in-Command as far as the first objective. My own plan was to station two of the RE party at the Eastern signalling point, with a torch and instructions as to how to signal in case I couldn't get back to them. I was then going back to the small house on the West side (which was to be Col HASELDEN's HQ) to report and to collect F/O SCOTT and his two Aldis lamps. I would substitute F/O SCOTT for the two REs and return myself to signal from the Western point. Signalling was not due to start until 0130 hours so there should have been plenty of time.

The rest of the Plan does not affect the remainder of the report.

Entrance

Owing to a slight miscalculation the party was late getting on to the EL ADEM road and it was dark soon after we had turned on to the main road towards TOBRUK. However, the entrance went smoothly and no check posts were encountered. Further delay was caused by the fact that, apparently considerable alterations (wire fences etc) had been made where the track along the Southern bank of the harbour joined the main road. We were still some way off our debussing point when the bombing started.

After debussing, sorting stores, hiding German uniforms etc the two parties set out.

Action

Immediately on leaving the trucks Major CAMPBELL's party had to negotiate a small minefield. This was done by an RE party with a detector, and caused considerable delay and necessitated the party walking in a long single file. In the middle of this operation a rifle was fired from the other side of the Wadi. This caused further delay. Eventually one section was sent forward (under Lt. ROBERTS) to investigate and I asked permission to reconnoitre the sandy beach. I walked right across the beach without encountering anything, and directed Lt. ROBERTS to take his party up on the high ground to get round the back of whoever had fired the rifle. I then went back to Major CAMPBELL and guided one section across the beach, the rest following at intervals. Lt. ROBERTS in the meanwhile engaged and put out of action a section of enemy who were manning a spandau.

We had taken almost an hour to get across the Wadi. The same procedure of advance was adopted up the Wadi-side and on. I waited on top to guide Lt. ROBERTS and the REs [Royal Engineers] who were labouring under heavy burdens of explosives etc. and it took some time to catch up with the rest, who I eventually found, had struck Eastwards away from the bay. Soon after that I met Lt. DUFFY who said that all the positions near the Bay were empty and unused.

By this time the success signal from Lt-Col HASELDEN's party had been fired.

We proceeded to catch up Major CAMPBELL and soon afterwards came on a small wireless station which was put out of action with its personnel – mainly by Lt. ROBERTS.

In climbing out of that Wadi I discovered it was already 0130 hrs. I urged Major CAMPBELL to fire the success signal, which was done. I then returned alone and as fast as I could towards the bay. This journey was made more difficult by the fact that I had to skirt a small enemy camp in a Wadi which we had missed on the way out. I found the Eastern Signalling point and was relieved to see that F/O SCOTT was signalling from the West side although he was far too high up. The REs had disappeared by this time, and, I presume that they returned to HQ on finding no guns to destroy. I had no watch and only an inadequate torch. I tried to time my signalling with F/O SCOTT's.

After a short while I saw two MTBs [Motor Torpedo Boats] come in. After that however no more appeared. My problem now was whether to stay signalling or to go to meet the landing troops and conduct them to HQ as I was supposed to be doing. I decided to try a compromise by wedging my torch in a rock and leaving it alight. I did this and started back but, before I had gone 200 yds I saw a light flashing out to sea and it appeared to be on an M.T.B. proceeding *away* again. I rushed back to the torch and started to signal again. But nothing materialised. After another half hour I left signalling and started back towards the landing point. On the way back I found that my haversack and Tommy gun had been taken from the Sangar where I had left them before climbing down to the rocks. I later ran into two enemy one of whom I hit with my revolver.

On reaching the landing point I found the two MTBs unloading. Lt. MACDONALD appeared to be organising the landing, so I took one man with me with a Tommy gun and returned at once to continue signalling. During all this time F/O SCOTT was still signalling from the West side.

By the time we got back to the Eastern signalling point the searchlights were sweeping the entrance to the harbour and our own shore. However I resumed signalling. Heavy fire was coming from the opposite shore of the harbour out to sea. Once the MTBs got caught in the searchlights and I could see their wake, and tracer bouncing off one of them. They were well to the East of us however, and it was obvious that there wasn't much chance of them getting in. One of the two MTBs slipped out past me during a slight lull, and appeared to get away safely. At 'first light' I decided to abandon signalling and I returned to the landing point. By the time I got there dawn was breaking and I saw one M.T.B. apparently aground. Sounds of rifle and L.M.G. [Light Machine Gun] fire was coming from just over the West ridge of the Wadi, near where we had left the trucks. I hailed the M.T.B., but getting no answer, I walked around the bay and up the small Wadi to the house which was Lt-Col HASELDEN's HQ. Rifle fire was coming down the Wadi. I got to the house to find it deserted and I saw the heads of about a platoon of enemy lying covering the house from about 300 yds away. I walked back down the small wadi, and thinking I heard a shout aboard the M.T.B., I boarded her, but found no-one. I filled my water bottle and took what food I could find. Lt. RUSSELL, Lt. SILLITO, Pte HILLMAN and Pte WATLER then came aboard. Lt. RUSSELL opened up with

the twin Lewis guns forward on troops on top of the hill. I went
to the engines to see if there was any hope of getting them started,
but not even Pte. WATLER, – a mechanic – could help there. We
then took all we could in the way of food and water and boarded
one of the assault craft lying alongside. We paddled out into the
bay but were forced to go ashore by being fired on from the rocks
on the West side. We saw some of our own men dodging along
the West side of the bay and there were large explosions coming
from behind them. It was impossible to tell who they were, but
I think they may have been the REs dealing with the guns on
the point. We climbed through a minefield and into a wadi.
Here we were joined by Sgt. EVANS. We made for the hills,
having to hide frequently from low-flying aircraft. I looked back
from the higher ground and saw what I now know to have been
HMS ZULU with HMS SIKH in tow. The latter appeared to
be burning and shells were bursting round. We were fired on
heavily, going over a ridge, from the direction of BRIGHTON,
but got safely into a large wadi where we found about 15–20
others waiting. These included 2/Lt. MACDONALD and Lt.
BARLOW also those of the RNF. who had been landed from
the MTBs. We decided it was now useless to resist. No one knew
what had become of Major CAMPBELL's party. It seemed clear
that Col HASELDEN had been killed. We decided to take to the
hills and make for Wadi SHAGRA North of BARDIA, where
we had been told we would be picked up 5 days later.

Escape

We did not stop long in the big Wadi. Lts SILITO and
MACDONALD took their respective sections. I believe their
intention was to make towards the coast further East and try
to get taken off by the MTBs the same day. I have not heard
of any of them since.

    Lt. BARLOW, Lt. RUSSELL and myself went off up the
wadi with eight men. We found a small wadi and lay up all that
day among the bushes. At dusk we disposed of everything we did
not require, divided what food we had into three and ourselves into

three parties. We split up and made for the perimeter that night. Later in the night – after avoiding two enemy posts I joined up again with Lt. BARLOW's party. Soon after we met, we bumped another enemy post and had to take hurriedly to the nearest Wadi. When we regathered Lt. BARLOW was nowhere to be found, and I have not seen or heard of him since. After 'bumping' several more posts we eventually got through the perimeter wire and lay up next day in a cave in a wadi.

We had two nights of dodging camps etc. during part of which we walked on the road. We hid up every day in caves in the Wadis. On the fifth night, just as we were desperate for food and water we found the first Arab village where we were taken in, fed and given water. Pte HILLMAN acted as interpreter. The Arabs knew all about the TOBRUK raid. They also said they could not understand how the English managed to come all the way from KUFRA.

Going from village to village, we eventually reached the Wadi AM REISA. There was a large Carabinieri post at the shore end of this Wadi, the strength of which had recently been doubled, according to the Arabs. They also told us of boats cruising up and down at night – they said they thought they were British. One had landed a party one night and someone had shouted 'Any British here?'

The Arabs then showed us to the Wadi KATTARA about 5 miles North of BARDIA. Here we found an Indian soldier of the 3/18th Garwhal Rifles who had escaped 3 times from TOBRUK and had been living there for 2 months.

We also found Pte. WATLER. His story is as follows:

On leaving us on the night of the 14th, Lt. RUSSELL, Pte. WATLER and one member of the SIG got through the perimeter and walked 'all out' towards BARDIA along the road. They arrived at MERSA SHAGRA one day late. That night they ran into the enemy post in Wadi Am REISA and were fired on. In making their get-away Pte. WATLER got left behind because of bad boots. Nothing further is known of the other two. The man with Lt. RUSSELL spoke only German.

We lived in the Wadi KATTARA for four weeks being fed by the Arabs as best they could. We tried making fires by night to attract the attention of aircraft, but only got a stick of bombs extremely close. The only news or information we got was obtained from Italian, or German soldiers via the Arabs who sold eggs etc. on the road and engaged the soldiers in conversation. It was apparent that the enemy was very low in morale and very short of food. We had to take great care not to get caught because the Italians would undoubtedly have 'wiped out' the village. As it was we saw no one during our four weeks there.

After three weeks Sgt EVANS unfortunately got dysentery and later we had to help him to the road by night and leave him to be picked up the next morning. The same happened a few days later to one of the Leslie twins and his brother went with him. The rains had come heavily and it was very cold and damp. I decided to move. The Indian stayed behind, and so the party consisted of Cpl. WILSON, Pte WATLER, Pte HILLMAN and myself. I was lucky to have a German compass and a small German map, though the latter was not much use being 1:5,000,000. We had some tins of bully-beef, some goat meat and bread and ten water-bottles. We started on Oct 26th.

Apart from getting fired on on the second night our journey was uneventful. We did not see anyone from the day after we climbed through the frontier wire until we were picked up at HIMEIMAT on Friday Nov 18th with the exception of one convoy which looked very like an S.A.S. patrol, – near the SIWA – MERSA MATRUH track on Nov 5th. We walked south of the QATTARA depression for the last four days and thereby missed the 'retreat'.[13]

The failure of the Tobruk/Benghazi operation removed, for the remainder of the war, any enthusiasm within the SAS for using the regiment to mount spectacular raids and attacks against prestige targets. Instead, in the aftermath of the battle of El Alamein in October 1942, as the 8th Army began to pursue the Afrika Korps and their Italian allies across North Africa, the SAS resumed raids, at an increased tempo, against the Axis lines of communication.

During this period, two significant events occurred for the SAS. The first of these was the formation, under David Stirling's brother William, of the 2nd SAS Regiment, from volunteers drawn from 62 Commando, which was intended to pursue a parallel role in the 1st Army to that of 1 SAS in the 8th Army. The second was the capture of David Stirling himself by Italian troops in January 1943.

The plan for 2 SAS was that they would undergo basic training in Britain before moving to the Middle East for advanced training and 'desert hardening' at the SAS headquarters at Kabrit, and then deploy with the 1st Army in Tunisia.* Stirling had by this stage conceived the notion of an SAS Brigade consisting of his and his brother's regiments which would operate throughout the Middle Eastern, North African, Mediterranean and Adriatic theatres of operations, and he already had under his command the Special Boat Section, together with Free French and Greek SAS squadrons, alongside his original L Detachment members. For the post-Alamein operations, 1 SAS was organised into A Squadron, under the command of Major Paddy Mayne, which consisted of more experienced unit members, and B Squadron, under Stirling, whose soldiers were mostly new to operations but which included a cadre of relatively long-serving SAS veterans.

With each squadron allocated a sector of the German lines of communication, they raided roads, railways, airfields and supply depots almost at will. However, the relative inexperience of B Squadron personnel began to show and by the end of January 1943, more than half of them had been killed or captured by Axis patrols and ambushes:

The patrol lead by Capt Murphy, consisting of six Jeeps, entered the area WEST of MALUT on the night of 16.1.43. At about square reference (z) F 22 a network of military roads was encountered. Attempts were made to locate the road to DEHIBAT until 0300 hrs 17.1.43, but without success. One Jeep bent a spring and a second developed engine trouble. The patrol stopped from 0300 hrs to 0630 hrs and then moved SOUTH. A halt was made in a wadi about reference (z) F 2514 at 0930 hrs. Repairs were carried out while the men slept. A guard was mounted on the side of the wadi during this period. At 1200 hrs the guard was dismounted and the men woken for

* Some 2 SAS patrols did operate in Tunisia in March/April 1943 but conditions prevented full-scale deployment of the regiment.

tea prior to moving off. The attack came at about 1220 hrs. Fierce
fire was opened up on us from the Western side of the wadi by
rifles, machine guns and mortars. Capt. Murphy gave the order
to everyone to try and get the Jeeps out of the wadi if possible.
The previous night he had said that if we met any opposition we
were to scatter and assemble South West.

Capt Murphy ran from Jeep to Jeep endeavouring to get the
crews organized and the Jeeps started. I was able to start my own
Jeep and while it warmed up I was able to get a Vickers K into
action against the enemy on the WEST side. After a few minutes
enemy fire commenced from the EAST side of the wadi also and
I transferred my attention to that side. One other Jeep was firing
by that time and one Jeep was burning.

After firing off three magazines my gun jammed so I decided
to try and run Northwards out of the wadi. Pte Heane W., who
had been slightly wounded in the first stages and Pte. Guard were
near me so I told them to prepare to make for my Jeep. At my
order we ran to the Jeep and succeeded in driving about 500 yds
up the wadi. We were fired on fairly fiercely but the Jeep was not
hit in any vital part. We stuck in a ditch but succeeded in digging
out. While digging we noticed that the firing in the wadi had
ceased but we heard an explosion as if a Jeep had blown up.

We carried on and were fired on each time we came into
view of the enemy. We made NORTH, WEST then SOUTH
until we reached a position about 6 miles SOUTH WEST of
the attack. We waited there from 1530 hrs 17.1.43 until 0830
hrs 18.1.43 but no one else turned up. We then carried on
for the operational area and located the rendezvous party on
10.2.43.

At the moment of leaving the wadi the following were seen.

Capt. Murphy, unhurt trying to start a Jeep.

Pte. Hearn A. beside a Jeep.

Pte. Nixon wounded.

Pte. Robinson in cover.

Pte. Buxton running for cover.

Owing to the shape of the wadi and the dispersal of the Jeeps
the remaining members of the patrol were not visible from our
position.[14]

The experienced and wary Stirling avoided these pitfalls but nevertheless it was a showy and unnecessary attempt to become the first ground troops to link up with the 1st Army that was to lead to his capture. Taking a small party through the Gabes Gap, Stirling had the misfortune, in the last week of January 1943, to make a rest stop in an area being used for working-up exercises by a German security battalion being specially trained for anti-SAS operations. Stirling himself suffered the indignity of being captured by the unit's dentist and, although he briefly escaped, he was soon in permanent captivity.

Stirling was originally held in an Italian POW cage in Tunisia where, in the immediate aftermath of his capture, he was subjected to an interrogation by a British traitor, Theodor Schurch, a private in the Royal Army Service Corps who had been taken prisoner by the Italians near Tobruk. Schurch, a Londoner with a British mother and a Swiss father, was a member of the British Union of Fascists and had actually been supplying tit-bits of information to an Italian intelligence official since 1936 so he did not spend long as a POW; he was highly trusted by his Italian controllers and was a specialist in interrogating SAS prisoners. Bearing in mind the resistance-to-interrogation training that is now given to SAS soldiers, it is interesting to note that Schurch claimed, at least, to have obtained valuable information from Stirling by posing as a recently captured British officer (this was strongly denied by Stirling during Schurch's post-war court-martial at which Schurch was sentenced to death and executed for treachery). Stirling was fairly quickly removed to mainland Italy and subsequently to Germany after the Italian surrender; he ended the war in Colditz.

Although it was not difficult to replace Stirling (with Paddy Mayne) as tactical commander of 1 SAS, his capture created enormous problems for the unit because of his tendency to run it as a one-man band. Although he had discussed many aspects of his future plans with members of the regiment and with Colonel 'Shan' Hackett, the staff officer at MEHQ with special responsibility for supporting the SAS, it seems that no single individual other than Stirling had the full picture. In fact, as the North African campaign reached its climax, with the Axis forces squeezed into an ever smaller section of Tunisia, the opportunity to use the SAS in their classic role was disappearing: arguably for ever.

It wasn't until the Normandy invasion on 6 June 1944 that the SAS returned to a role that resembled Stirling's vision of a strategic special force. Following the invasion of Sicily and during subsequent operations on the Italian mainland, 1 SAS under Mayne (now divided into the Special Raiding Squadron and the Special Boat Squadron) and 2 SAS under Bill Stirling conducted a series of raids against targets that were, in some cases, of purely tactical significance and in others required the SAS to operate, in effect, as Commandos rather than special forces. What became evident was that without the benefit of a huge open flank, and faced with a complex security and logistic infrastructure, small-scale raids were much more difficult and achieved considerably less impact. Some operations were set up on a purely speculative basis, including sending parties into enemy-held territory to find and cut telegraph wires, but others, particularly the SRS operations at Bagnara and Termoli, were launched with the aim of achieving very specific results.

The Bagnara operation, in early September 1943, was a coastal assault in which the SRS, commanded by Mayne and accompanied by other Commando units, were directed to seize the port of Bagnara and hold it, thus disrupting German lines of communication and forcing them to retreat in the face of the 8th Army who were, by now, advancing from the Salerno beach-head against dogged opposition. Although a success – SRS achieved their objectives with relatively light casualties (five dead and six wounded) – it was a pointless misuse of a highly specialised capability. The value of lightly armed, mobile and stealthy special forces does not lie in their ability to seize and hold ground, even though they possess the bravery and tactical skills to do so; in Bagnara they were lucky to get away relatively lightly.

The Termoli raid in October 1943 was to be 1 SAS's last operation before returning to the UK for retraining. In some respects it was a rerun of the Bagnara attack, in so far as the SRS were to land with a force of Commandos (from 3 and 40 Commandos) and then go on to seize and hold two key bridges, and the aim was similar. The attack was launched in order to disrupt German counter-moves against British and US forces in the south of Italy. Nevertheless, it was a misuse of the skills of the SAS and on this occasion they were not so lucky.

With surprise on their side SRS quickly achieved its objective in the coastal town of Vasto to the north of the main Commando bridgehead and secured a defensive position around the area. As expected, the Germans launched a swift counter-attack, bringing members of their elite 1st Parachute Division into action to expel the British raiders from their objectives. Knowing that they couldn't hope to hold their position for any length of time, Mayne and his men began to conduct an orderly withdrawal. As the Germans brought armour, artillery and mortars to bear on the lightly armed British:

> this bloody great shell landed right in the middle of the truck. It blew us to hell. We were carrying detonators for the '78' 2-lb grenade in our packs – you never loaded the grenades till you needed. Mine was the only pack not to explode.
>
> A family who lived opposite the truck – three or four girls who did the washing for us – the women were just blown open. The eldest son was running around screaming, with his guts hanging out like a huge balloon. I caught him and shot him – it was the only thing to do. Wounded all over the place. I was covered in blood and bits of flesh – I stank for days after it. Lance-Corporal Grant picked up his own arm, his own arm, and set it to one side. 'I've had it this time,' he said. He died of wounds that day.[15]

In all, twenty-nine members of SRS were killed – more than ten per cent of their strength – in an operation that could quite easily have been handled by a less specialised, less highly skilled unit.

It was only now, after the tide of the war had begun to turn in both the east and the west, that Germany launched its first major *strategic* special operation, the rescue of Benito Mussolini from his Italian captors in the Gran Sasso hotel in central Italy.

The leader of the rescuers, Captain Otto Skorzeny, was an Austrian engineering graduate and Nazi supporter who had volunteered, at the outbreak of the war, for service in the Waffen-SS. Commissioned as a reserve officer, he had fought in the Das Reich Division before being transferred in 1942 to take command of a Waffen-SS special unit being set up in imitation of the Abwehr's special forces, called the Friedenthaler Jagdverbände.

On 23 July 1943, following the Allied invasions of Sicily and southern Italy as the culmination of a series of military defeats, Mussolini had been rejected by the Fascist Grand Council, dismissed by the King and placed under arrest. He was quickly hustled out of Rome to a series of secret locations to prevent him being snatched by remaining loyalists or the Germans, eventually ending up in a ski resort high on the Gran Sasso in central Italy, where he was guarded by a small force of Carabinieri.

Throughout this period, the new Italian government of Marshal Badoglio was conducting secret armistice negotiations with the Allies, whilst German intelligence was making desperate attempts to locate the Duce. In fact both of these were to come to fruition at approximately the same time. On 8 September the Italian government proclaimed an armistice with the Allies and on the same day Skorzeny discovered that Mussolini was in the Albergo Campo Imperatore on the 2,900-metre-high Gran Sasso. Skorzeny now had to move fast and did so; the armistice terms included delivering Mussolini to the Allies and Hitler was adamant that this should not happen. Instead, the SS officer formulated a plan, in conjunction with Luftwaffe General Student of the German Airborne Corps, to land a small force of gliders on the plateau next to the hotel, sending in an Italian general to divert the attention of the Carabinieri, before storming the building and rescuing the Duce.

Skorzeny's plan required himself and nine other members of his unit to enter the hotel and find Mussolini whilst approximately ninety men from the Luftwaffe airborne training battalion secured the hotel, disarmed the sentries, and took control of a nearby airfield where a bomber would be waiting to fly Mussolini to Germany. On 12 September, at 2 p.m., the operation finally went ahead.

In fact, as events turned out, the most hazardous part of the rescue of Mussolini was the glider landing which took place in a short, steep, boulder-strewn meadow. Skorzeny describes his approach to the hotel:

> there were two machine-guns in front of the main entrance to the hotel. We kicked them aside and forced the Italian guards to back away. Behind me someone shouted 'mani in alto!' I pushed against the carabinieri who were bunched up in front of the entrance and fought my way through in a not too gentle fashion. I had seen the Duce on the second floor to the right. A set of stairs led upward. I raced up them, taking three steps at a stride. On the right there was a hallway and a second door. The Duce was there, and with him two

Italian officers and one person in civilian clothes. Untersturmführer Schwerdt bundled them into the hall. Unterscharführer Holzer and Benzer appeared at the window: they had climbed the facade using the lightning conductor. The Duce was in our hands and under our protection. The entire action had been played out in barely four minutes – without a single shot being fired . . .

'Duce, the Führer has given me orders to free you!'

He shook my hand and hugged me, with the words, 'I knew my friend Adolf Hitler would not leave me in the lurch!'[16]

In November 1943 1 SAS returned to the UK to be brought up to strength and retrained for operations in north-west Europe, and they were joined by 2 SAS in March 1944. The LRDG and SBS, meanwhile, continued to operate in the Mediterranean theatre, committed initially to the Dodecanese campaign in the autumn of 1943, conducting raids on the German garrisons of these small Aegean islands from a flotilla of small boats and fishing caiques. Later, they took part in the Italian campaign and the Adriatic, where the LRDG continued their role as a strategic intelligence-collecting force, mounting observation posts, road and shipping watches and small-scale raids as the Mediterranean fighting reached its closing stages.

The Middle East campaign transformed the British Army from its ineffectual and inefficient pre-war state into a force that could challenge the Wehrmacht, if not quite on equal terms. It also raised the status of unconventional warfare from a desperate expedient conceived as the only way of striking back at a virtually victorious enemy into a prized, accepted and respected adjunct of normal operations. There is no doubt that the LRDG, the SAS and the smaller special forces units did play a part in hastening the defeat of the Axis in the Western Desert and North Africa but we must keep that part in perspective: the campaign was won because the Allied armies inflicted a level of attrition on the Axis that it could not sustain and not because of daring raids behind the lines. The destruction of aircraft and *matériel* by the SAS contributed to that attrition, but not as much as, for example, the destruction of Axis supply convoys at sea did, or bombing by the air force. Even so, the contribution of special forces to this relative sideshow was sufficient to guarantee them a role in the more important campaign to follow for the liberation of north-western Europe.

7

D-Day to the End of the War: the final Allied special operations and the German response

By the end of 1943 there were two British SAS regiments, two French Régiments de Chasseurs Parachutistes (one composed of Free French volunteers, one of Vichy soldiers recruited after the liberation of Algeria – relations between the two units were somewhat fraught) and a Belgian independent squadron. These were grouped together into an SAS Brigade under the command of Brigadier R.W. McLeod, a Royal Artillery officer, and based in Scotland to train for operations in Europe. After a certain amount of indecision it was decided that the SAS would operate in France after the invasion, providing a cadre of disciplined but flexible troops to operate in support of, and in some respects to guide, the French resistance forces who would be harassing the German lines of communication. This was a task that had been carried out, to some extent, by 2 SAS during their operations in Italy, when they had linked up with partisan groups operating in rural areas of the country against the German occupiers.

This was considered an important role for the SAS, and it was hard won. One of the early plans for the brigade had been to provide diversionary raids to cover the real invasion – a role of almost suicidal danger which was resisted by Bill Stirling to the point of resignation. At the same time, it put the SAS into competition with SOE. Apart from active SOE agents and networks who had been in France for some time, the organisation planned to send uniformed Jedburgh teams, consisting of a British, an American and a French member as liaison to resistance groups, in order to co-ordinate resupply from England and to pass on orders and instructions.

There was a difference between the envisaged roles of the SAS and of the 'Jeds', but it was a subtle one. SAS troops would be present in sufficient numbers to conduct their own operations, attacking bridges, railways, supply depots and other traditional lines of communication targets; they would also have their own vehicles, armoured jeeps, dropped with them to add to their mobility and operational flexibility.

One crucial stipulation which affected both the SAS and the Jedburgh teams was that they could not be dropped into France prior to the start of the main invasion (Operation Neptune), for fear that their capture might compromise details of the overall plan. As a result, the forty-three members of the SAS Brigade who dropped into France as reconnaissance and advance parties on the night of 5–6 June 1944 – amongst the first Allied soldiers to arrive on French soil – were the first members of the SAS to serve in north-west Europe. They dropped even as gliders and other aircraft dropped paratroopers and air-landing troops to seize key tactical objectives inland of the landing beaches. The SAS Brigade Headquarters summary, prepared at the end of June 1944, describes their tasks:

Top Secret

Place	FRANCE
Date	6 June 44 to 30 June 44
Operation	OVERLORD
Event	Operation NEPTUNE – Summary of SAS participation for JUNE

Pre-arranged SAS participation in NEPTUNE, the assault phase of OVERLORD, comprised the establishment by 4 FRENCH PARA BN of two base areas in BRITTANY (SAMWEST, SW of GUINGAMP and DINGSON in the LANDES DE LANVAUX NE of VANNES), and by 1 SAS Regt of two bases in central France (BULBASKET in the BRENNE marsh west of CHATEAUROUX and HOUNDSWORTH in the MORVAN Mountains N25).

In addition 1 SAS Regt found a small party for a deception operation (TITANIC 4) in connection with the main airborne assault in NORMANDY. From the bases it was intended that small parties should work outwards against enemy road and rail communications, particularly the latter, and such chance targets as dumps, and telephone cables. In BRITTANY, a direct drop (operation COONEY) onto various railway targets was planned for D + 1/D + 2 for a troop of 4 French Para Bn, who were to work back into base afterwards. It was accepted that the first need was to establish a firm base in each area, before feeding in the further offensive parties.

In the event, reconnaissance parties were safely despatched and reported favourably on all areas. The two BRITTANY bases expanded rapidly – too rapidly for they both drew enemy attention after growing to 115 and 328 men plus over 2000 Maquis respectively, and were dispersed by direct attack, but casualties were not excessive, and the whole remainder of 4 French Para Bn (including those dropped as planned for COONEY) was dispersed in small parties in central BRITTANY and spent the rest of the month organising the local Maquis and arming it with weapons flown from the UK.

1 SAS's bases both developed securely; HOUNDSWORTH was reinforced up to 80 men and able to begin offensive operations. The BULBASKET party moved further SW than had been foreseen, to conform with active Maquis groups in support of which it was operating and was reinforced up to 44 men.

Part of this reinforcement was carried out by dropping parties direct onto rail targets in the area (operation LOT) and a similar operation (GAIN) was mounted later in the month in the PARIS-ORLEANS area, where about 25 men were dropped to form a small base. LOT and GAIN were both mounted at very short notice.

By the end of the month a total of 585 SAS Tps had been dropped almost all by 38 Group RAF (a few by 3 Gp) for the loss of only one aircraft and 15 men.

Resupply sorties, principally to BRITTANY, had dropped nine jeeps and 1892 containers of stores. JUNE, therefore, saw nearly a third of the Brigade's operational strength deployed, and laid the foundations for future offensive operations on a wider scale than had been possible while bases were being established.[1]

The bases established by the SAS parties were, by and large, in remote forested areas away from towns and major centres of population, and normally co-located or, at least, close by camps used by the Maquis – French partisans operating as guerrillas on a more or less permanent and semi-overt basis. For short periods, the lifestyle of the SAS with the Maquis produced an almost idyllic illusion:

> When we finally reached the campsite, out came the wine and a sumptuous meal was prepared. Tucking into vast portions of meat and potatoes we were surrounded by grinning Maquis trying to communicate in French and broken English. We were located in the Morvan just to the north of Chateau Chinon, an area of steep hills which was an ideal hiding place for the Maquis. Having eaten our fill, we settled into our sleeping bags and drifted off to sleep. The following morning the Maquis showed us the location of our own bivouac area and told us where we could get wood for cooking and drinking water.[2]

As the SAS bases increased in size, they were joined by signals specialists from the GHQ Liaison Regiment 'Phantom', whose F Squadron was assigned to work with the SAS supplying long-range communications to the tactical HQ of the SAS Brigade at Moor Park in north-west London. Theoretically trained to the same standards as their SAS colleagues, the signals specialists shared the SAS's precarious existence inside France. An interesting insight into the degree of security that the SAS parties felt whilst working with the Maquis is provided by the following extensive list of military equipment carried by members of a 'Phantom' patrol working with the SAS:

Personal Kit Taken by No. 3 Patrol, SAS PHANTOM

Per Man
  1 .45 Automatic and holster
  1   "   spare mags and pouches

1 tin Dubbin
1 Life belt Mk 2
1 Knife, fighting
1   ″   single blade folding
1 Trousers, paratroops
2 Vests, string (too heavy for hot weather)
1 Flashlight US 122A with 1 spare Bty (excellent)
1 Ruc-sac, Bergen, rubber lined
1 Bedding roll, Icelandic with cover (cover too heavy)
1 Entrenching tool with cover
1 Map case, 'Z' type
1 Oil bottle, gauze, and rod
20 rds Amn .45 spare
1 Mess tin
1 Waterbottle
1 Ground sheet
4 prs socks, spare
1 Shirt, spare
1 Pullover, worn
1 Gym shoes prs
1 Washing kit
3 pencils
3 message pads, small
1 First field dressing
1 First aid pack (add foot powder)
1 Steel helmet with net (never used after jumping)
1 Smock, airborne, camouflaged
1 Jumping jacket (never used after jumping)
1 pr Short puttees (gaiters would be better)
4 boxes matches
1 Escape pack
2 Secret compasses
1 Escape money purse (£12)
1 Language booklet
3 24 hr ration packs
2 face veil camouflaged
4 Handkerchiefs
1 Compass, oil

1 pr Binoculars
1 Watch GS
1 Housewife*
1 Luminous ball (not really of use)
1 Anti-dog smell (never used)
1 Maps sets of the area
1 Gas cape (optional) (most useful for bivouacs)
1 Knife, fork, spoon, mug set
1 Carbine American with 5 mags .30
1 Haversacks American type

Carried in the Patrol

2 Jedburgh sets complete with 6 crystals
2 MCR1 with 2 bts each
2 Protractors
2 Code books and 3 silks
2 India rubbers
4 Sets rubber heels and soles
5 Escape maps (2 were paper, 1 silk) sets
5 Grenades No. 36
2 Sets of colour filters for torches[3]

The SAS Brigade's operations in France undoubtedly achieved many successes at the tactical level. The German garrison troops (often actually Russians, Cossacks and even Indians, bribed and blackmailed out of POW camps) against whom they were normally pitted were ill equipped and ill motivated to deal with the highly trained, enthusiastic SAS. Nevertheless, the question of whether they achieved their aim, the disruption of the German lines of communication to the extent that it hampered the main German military effort, is more debatable.

One of the principal objectives of the SAS and the resistance in the immediate aftermath of the invasion was to delay the arrival of the 2nd SS Panzer Division Das Reich in the operational area. Despite its number, the 2nd SS Division was in fact the oldest combat division of the Waffen-SS, probably the best-equipped and certainly the best-led (1st SS Panzer

* A sewing kit.

Division Leibstandarte Adolf Hitler was also well equipped and well led but contained a higher number of officers who owed their position to political and family influence). As the SS-Verfügungs Division it had spearheaded the German invasion of France in 1940 and of the Soviet Union in 1941, and it had taken part in many of the crucial battles in Russia since then. In early 1944, the division was moved to the Toulouse area of southern France to rest and refit and to upgrade its armoured complement. It was recognised by Allied planners that, should the division arrive at the Normandy beach-head during the first few days of the invasion, it would pose an enormous threat to the success of the entire operation.

Deception operations designed to persuade the German High Command that the main Allied landings would take place in the Pas de Calais area successfully delayed Das Reich's move for several days, whilst Allied air superiority limited the Germans' ability to move at all by day. Resistance units in the path of the SS division had been tasked to launch delaying attacks and did so, but the limited firepower available to the resistance meant that these attacks were little more than pinprick efforts against the powerful German formation. Even so, the casualties caused by these efforts outraged the SS, who regarded the resistance as terrorists outside the scope of the Geneva Conventions, sufficiently for them to mount two horrific and brutal reprisal operations against local French civilians. The first of these was the hanging from lamp-posts in the town of Tulle of 99 civilians; the second, on 10 June 1944, was the massacre of 648 men, women and children of the village of Oradour-sur-Glane.

The lightly armed parties of 1 SAS's Operation Bulbasket, who were in the path of Das Reich, not surprisingly avoided direct contact with it but they did report on the position of elements of the division and on the presence of a number of fuel trains in rail sidings at Châtellerault. This fuel was intended for Das Reich but bombing raids by the Allied tactical air force destroyed much of it, imposing more delays on the division.

In the event, it took Das Reich some seventeen days to reach the combat zone: a journey that shouldn't have lasted more than a week (some writers have suggested that the division could have made the journey in three days but this is highly unlikely). The principal reason for this was the air threat to the division's convoys which inhibited daylight movement but as the SAS were directly involved in reporting information to the Allied tactical air force, it is fair to accord them a measure of credit for their role. Nevertheless, the delaying strategy was put in place on the assumption that the division would be a threat if it was thrown into battle straight from the line of march against newly arrived troops, and this does not appear to be part of the German plan. Instead, even after Das Reich had reached the combat zone, they were held in reserve for operations that didn't commence in earnest until early July.

In the meantime, Operation Bulbasket had been compromised and attacked by German security units. One SAS officer, Lieutenant Tomos Stevens, had been killed (beaten to death with a rifle butt as he lay wounded on the ground); three troopers were seriously wounded and captured together with another twenty-seven members of the Bulbasket party who were only lightly wounded or uninjured: all thirty – more than half the Bulbasket group – were executed by the German Army in accordance with Hitler's *Kommandobefehl* which claimed that Commandos and special forces fell outside the Geneva Conventions.

The activities of the SAS, and their SOE and resistance counterparts, behind the lines in occupied France certainly did cause considerable disruption, but whether it was sufficient to seriously affect the Germans' war-fighting ability – as the SAS had certainly done in North Africa – remains clouded by the fog of war. The toll of spending long periods behind enemy lines was large. Apart from the fact that men were lost through death, injury and capture (which they were unlikely to survive, bearing in mind the criminal ruthlessness of the *Kommandobefehl*), psychological stress was severe. On 10 August 1944, Brigadier McLeod, overall commander of the SAS, visited the 2ème Régiment de Chasseurs Parachutistes (usually known as 4th French Para or 4 SAS) and recorded his impressions in a report:

Discipline is first class and morale is extremely high. The unit regards itself as having been largely responsible for liberating Brittany and are more than anxious to get back to grips with the Germans. The majority will jump again if called upon to do so, but in spite of their apparent high morale I consider that they have undergone a very severe nervous strain and should not again be asked to operate with the Maquis behind enemy lines if it can be avoided. There is no doubt that a proportion of the men could not stand the nervous strain of this sort of life again, but are more than anxious to meet the enemy in overt as opposed to clandestine warfare.[4]

By the end of September 1944 the French campaign was over as far as the SAS were concerned. Now that the Germans were being forced back behind the pre-war borders of the Reich, there seemed to be little prospect of using the brigade for much other than armed reconnaissance and this did, in fact, prove to be the case: from January 1945 onwards SAS parties acted in a reconnaissance and liaison role. Strategic operations by special forces in the dying months of the war would have been a waste of resources and a dilution of the main effort; nevertheless, the SAS did play a role as a reconnaissance force and their flexibility was such as to give a notable 'edge' to formation commanders in areas where they were operating. In the last few weeks of the war, SAS troops were amongst the first to reach the Belsen concentration camp, where they found scenes of almost indescribable horror; and the British component of the SAS Brigade played a vital role in supervising the German surrender in Norway at the war's end.

Although the Allies found little use in the closing months of the war in Europe for special operations forces, the same was not true of the Germans. The original Bau-Lehr Bataillon 800 which had conducted small-scale tactical special operations in 1940 had been deemed a success and expanded, becoming the Lehr-Regiment Brandenburg z. b. V. 800 after the French campaign. During the Balkans campaign the Brandenburg Regiment protected the oil facilities at Ploesti in Rumania and seized and held the bridge across the River Vardar in Yugoslavia. They conducted similar tasks during the invasion of the Soviet Union and, on a very small scale, in North Africa. By the end of 1942, the Brandenburg unit consisted of five regiments and had been reclassified as a division but by now was in a state of decline. It was unpopular with the regular army because of its legally equivocal methods, particularly using enemy uniforms and other disguises in combat, and because its operations were increasingly ending in failure or aborting before launch. Partly this could be explained by its leadership – senior officers of the Abwehr were amongst the leading lights in the German resistance to Hitler – but it was also partly a result of the changing priorities of Germany's war effort: up until 1943, Brandenburg units were at their most successful operating in support of operational-level offensives but the essentially defensive nature of German operations thereafter meant less active tasks and the unit was increasingly used in anti-partisan work.

By contrast, the politically loyal Waffen-SS special forces units commanded by Otto Skorzeny began to expand in 1943 following his successful rescue of Mussolini from the Gran Sasso. Promoted and decorated on his return to Germany, he was also nominated commander of all special operations forces and given authority to recruit volunteers from all branches of the armed forces for his SS special forces unit SS-Jägerbataillon 502.

Two highly unusual recruits for this unit were Fusiliers James Brady and Frank Stringer of the 1st Battalion, the Royal Irish Fusiliers. Both had been in prison in Jersey in June 1940 and had been abandoned by their battalion when it evacuated. Taken prisoner of war by the Germans, both volunteered in the autumn of 1940 to join the Abwehr's proposed 'brigade' of anti-British Irish POWs who were being concentrated at Friesack POW camp. The Irish Brigade came to nothing; the majority of those who put themselves forward did so with the sole intention of sabotaging the idea, but Brady and Stringer were both selected for training as intelligence and sabotage agents by the Abwehr and were prepared for insertion into Britain. Neither was actually sent because of unjustified worries, on the part of their controllers, regarding their trustworthiness. After some time working for the Abwehr, both volunteered for the Waffen-SS and were sent to the European volunteers training centre at Sennheim in Alsace. Brady takes up the story:

I was at Sennheim until about March 1944, when Company Commander Menzel [one of Skorzeny's principal officers] visited the camp and interviewed us all. Some of the men were sent to Divisions at the front, but about thirty of us, including Stringer and myself, were kept back. We thirty had been selected to go into a special unit, and we were moved to Friedenthal. Stringer was sick and could not leave Sennheim; he joined us about six weeks later in May, 1944. I was trained in small arms, map reading, grenades and anti-tank warfare. This training lasted about three months. The name of my battalion was changed from 502 Jägerbataillon to Jagdverbände Mitte.

Stringer and myself were fed up with infantry training, so we went to see Company Commander Hunke and told him we were radio specialists and wanted a transfer. We then worked in the radio station at Friedenthal and did some training there. About August 1944 about 50 members of the battalion, though not Stringer, were posted to Rumania. We were in Rumania for about three weeks during which time I helped blow up two river bridges and one railway bridge. We went near Kronstadt but did not blow up any bridges there. There was only twenty two of us left when we pulled out of Rumania. Some men were killed by Russians and others by Rumanians. I returned to Friedenthal about September 1944 where I stopped for about two weeks before my company was ordered to Hungary. We went to Budapest as it was our job to get Horthy out before Hungary packed in. We had a scrap with some Hungarians and lost a few men before we got Horthy out.[5]

In the meantime, Stringer was serving in a different company under the unfortunately named Hauptsturmführer Fucker.

The operation in Hungary to which Brady alludes was interesting in so far as it was the second mission launched by Skorzeny aimed at capturing a head of government, albeit the rationale was slightly different. During the summer and autumn of 1944 German intelligence began to receive indications that Germany's Hungarian allies, led by the regent, Admiral Horthy, were conducting secret negotiations with the Soviets with the intention of agreeing an armistice. On 30 August, Horthy dismissed the existing pro-German government and appointed a cabinet that was clearly intended to prepare for Hungary's withdrawal from the war. Just over a month later, Field Marshal Farago was sent to Moscow to arrange terms.

In the meantime, Skorzeny had been summoned to Budapest to help put together a series of operations designed to keep Hungary in the war. The aim of the German plans was to ensure that, should Hungary attempt to change sides, a pro-German government could be quickly installed in place of the Horthy regime. From late August, the senior SS leader in Budapest, Obergruppenführer Winkelmann, had been preparing Ferenc Szalasi, a local Hungarian Nazi, to take over, and a squad had been standing by to seize control of Radio Budapest. On 6 October Winkelmann decided to give the order to arrest Horthy's entourage whilst the SD were planning to catch Horthy's son Nikolaus actually negotiating with representatives of Tito's partisans.

Arrests and kidnappings of Horthy's associates began on 10 October with Skorzeny playing a leading role and on 15 October, Nikolaus Horthy agreed to a meeting with two bogus representatives of Tito. In fact this was a cue for a Skorzeny operation. The meeting was arranged to take place in the headquarters of the Danube Ports Association and Horthy took the sensible precaution of positioning a detachment of Honved national guardsmen nearby; unfortunately Skorzeny had beaten him to it. His men were concealed inside the building already. At the appropriate moment the arrival of German vehicles outside the building caused a brief skirmish but by then Nikolaus Horthy was already handcuffed and being bundled into a truck on the first step of his journey to Mauthausen concentration camp.

Later that day the Germans began to take control of the city and the 22nd SS Cavalry Division moved to seal off the government quarter and the citadel at the Burgberg, Admiral Horthy's fortress. At 6 a.m. the next morning, Skorzeny led a company of his troops in an assault on the fortress; they quickly occupied the citadel without a shot being fired, but by then Horthy had already given in to German blackmail and handed over the reins of government to Szalasi.

The last meaningful German special operation of the war was also perhaps the best-known and was again commanded by Skorzeny. Operation Greif (Griffin) was the attempt to pass a German special forces unit behind the American lines disguised in American uniforms during the Ardennes offensive of December 1944. In some respects it was a reversion to the role carried out by the Brandenburg units during earlier campaigns because Skorzeny's mission was to

> exploit the breakthrough by General Dietrich's 6th SS Panzer Army, assume the lead and take possession of the Maas bridges at Huy, Amay and Engis, between Namur and Lüttich. These bridges were to be captured intact in order to enable our panzers to advance on Antwerp. Officers and men were to wear American

uniforms as far as the Maas; after reaching the Maas they were to fight in German uniforms.

Small units, also in American uniforms, were to infiltrate behind the enemy lines and reconnoitre there, cut telephone lines, issue false orders and cause general confusion among the enemy. These units were instructed to use their weapons only in extreme emergency and to do so only in German uniform.[6]

In fact, although Skorzeny's unit, 150th SS Panzer Brigade, did enter the battle, the combat element only did so in German uniform fighting in a conventional way. Skorzeny was able to pass only eight four-man 'American' units through the lines of which two were captured, two achieved nothing of significance, two reached the Maas where they misdirected military traffic and the other two carried out minor acts of sabotage. The impact that they achieved was entirely psychological and this came about because of inflated reports on their activities put about by US security units. One strong rumour was that the SS teams were intended to assassinate Eisenhower, who was thus held as a virtual prisoner at his headquarters near Paris, but the general level of disruption caused, while irksome for individuals who didn't know who was pitcher for the Brooklyn Dodgers, or any of the other all-American questions designed to catch out disguised SS assassins, was not severe enough to inhibit operations.

In the wake of the Ardennes battles, Skorzeny and his men reverted to a conventional role in the desperate last months of the defence of Germany. The reality was that the Fatherland no longer had the resources to support complicated special operations and needed every infantry soldier it could find. Skorzeny ended up commanding the makeshift Division Schwedt an der Oder fighting the Russians as they pushed towards Berlin.

There is no doubt whatsoever that in the Western Desert in 1942, David Stirling's idea of using small raiding parties to hit Axis airfields and lines of communication had a strategic impact on the outcome of the campaign. A relatively small group of enterprising and aggressive misfits – for want of a better word – caused chaos and destruction out of all proportion to their own strength and, importantly, at very little cost to the main effort. They did not need to be closely co-ordinated with operations at army level and could, to some extent, be left to get on with matters themselves. It was a buccaneering, freebooting style of warfare whose character owed a lot to the personalities of the principal leaders involved. It is equally clear that as the war progressed out of the desert wilderness, it became much more difficult to achieve the same 'value for money'. The costs in terms of troops involved, support effort and casualties became progressively higher. SAS operations in North Africa were unequivocally successful with 250 men involved; in France, ten times that number produced a rather less clear-cut result. Nevertheless, the SAS under David Stirling, Paddy Mayne, Roddy McLeod and, in the last few months of the war, Mike Calvert (who had commanded one of Major General Orde Wingate's 'Chindit' Brigades in Burma until shortly after Wingate's death in 1944) had turned heads at the very highest level, and the end of hostilities in Europe did not spell the end for the Special Air Service.

8

Cold Warriors

The end of the Second World War left all three of the major victors, the Soviet Union, the United States and Great Britain, in possession of armed forces vastly greater than were required by political and military necessity, and in Britain's case much larger than could be afforded by its massively indebted economy, as the country had lost one quarter of its entire national wealth during the war.[1] British demobilisation began in the summer of 1945, even before the defeat of Japan, as various classes and categories of wartime conscript began their journey home. Whole battalions, brigades and divisions were eliminated from the regular ORBAT as the army shrank down to a size commensurate with the peacetime tasks it faced, and amongst the many casualties of this process were Britain's unconventional warfare specialists: the Special Operations Executive and the Special Air Service Brigade.

Discussion on the future of SOE had begun as early as November 1944 when Anthony Eden, then the Foreign Secretary, had suggested to the Prime Minister that SOE be amalgamated with its wartime rival, MI6, in any post-war reorganisation. This reflected the widely held belief in official circles that special operations and the support of resistance movements would continue after the defeat of Germany and Japan, presumably targeted against the Soviet Union. In fact, discussions had not advanced very far when Japan surrendered in August 1945, following the dropping of the atomic bombs on Hiroshima and Nagasaki, and on 31 August Clement Attlee's new Labour government accepted the advice of the Chiefs-of-Staff and ordered the amalgamation of MI6 and SOE forthwith. All that remained for SOE's organisation to do was wind down its remaining operations in the Far East, settle accounts and recommend decorations for its agents in the field, and close down its various administrative and training facilities. A number of the more professional SOE operators were recruited by MI6, including Tony Brooks, Peter Kemp and Xan Fielding, whilst the majority of the remainder returned happily to civilian life. Although now tasked with maintaining a special operations capability, MI6 maintained only a small branch capable of doing so, although it did acquire an SOE-type training facility, at Fort Monckton outside Gosport, where MI6 officers were (and are) trained in the more muscular disciplines of field intelligence work, latterly by instructors recruited from military intelligence and the Special Air Service.[2] Nevertheless, MI6 attempts to support resistance movements behind the Iron Curtain almost all failed for two reasons: firstly, the Soviet internal security apparatus, the KGB and its predecessors, maintained a ruthless policy of surveillance and suppression against groups and individuals who were, or might conceivably become, opponents of the state; secondly, one of the principal MI6 officers involved in despatching agents behind the Iron Curtain was Kim Philby, who had been working on behalf of the Soviets at least since the early 1930s.

According to Philby's memoirs, he took part in three separate operations to launch guerrillas into communist countries. The first took place in 1949 when he was sent two Georgian émigrés, who had been trained in London, with instructions to supervise them as they were passed over the border into the Soviet Union by Turkish intelligence with the aim of exploring 'the possibilities of conspiratorial existence in Georgia . . . If these preliminary sallies went well, a start could be made with setting up, by gradual stages, a resident network, its shape and style dictated by the results of early reconnaissances.'[3]

Not surprisingly, with Philby privy to the details of the plan, it did not succeed: 'The two agents had been put across the border at such and such a time . . . there had been a burst of fire, and one of the men had fallen – the other was last seen striding through a sparse wood away from the Turkish frontier. He was never heard of again.'[4]

Philby was also involved in high-level planning, with the CIA, of Operation Valuable, designed to infiltrate Albanian émigré guerrillas back into their homeland to organise resistance to the hard-line communist regime of Enver Hoxha between 1949 and 1951, with attempts to drop teams of saboteurs into the Ukraine in the summer of 1951. Both operations failed miserably and, as Philby subsequently pointed out, 'I do not know what happened to the parties concerned. But I can make an informed guess.'[5]

It is a persistent theme of post-war histories of the Special Air Service that there was a determination on the part of the War Office to get rid of the SAS at the end of the war. In 1945, as we have seen, the SAS Brigade consisted of two British regiments, two French regiments and a Belgian regiment, totalling a little over two thousand men. The French and Belgian elements were, of course, to be returned to their own national command but this left a little over one thousand British SAS members, many of them highly experienced and skilled in various forms of unconventional warfare, at the disposal of the War Office. The immediate solution was to use the SAS Brigade, under Calvert, as an occupation garrison in Norway, whilst simultaneously some thought was being given, by the now released David Stirling amongst others, to deploying SAS units to the Far East. Such speculation was ended by the Japanese capitulation, and a decision was made to disband the SAS Brigade, together with 1 and 2 SAS Regiments, pending the outcome of a study into the use of unconventional units during the war and any further requirement that the British Army might have for them. This is not to say that the SAS had not acquired enemies amongst the military establishment: they certainly had, but the established view was that the SAS had made a valuable contribution to the war effort and that similar units might do so again in the future. As SAS Brigade commander, Calvert circulated his own views on the value of the SAS to senior officers of the brigade, and it is worth examining these at length:

Future of S.A.S. Troops

The Director of Tactical Investigations, Maj-Gen ROWELL, has been ordered by the Chief of Imperial General Staff, that his directorate should investigate all the operations of the Special Air Service with a view to giving recommendations for the future of S.A.S. in the next war and its composition in the peace-time army. The actual terms of reference were:

An investigation of S.A.S. technique, tactics and organisation without prejudice to a later examination of all organisations of a similar nature which were formed and operated in various theatres of this last war.

Brigadier Churchill is Deputy Director of Tactical Investigation and lives at Flat 110, 4 Whitehall Court, London, SW1 (Whitehall 9400 Ext 1632), just behind the War Office. The Officer immediately concerned is Lt-Col C.A. Whigham. Lt-Col Wigham has in his possession all the reports on S.A.S. operations in W. EUROPE. The reports on S.A.S. operations in ITALY and in the MEDITERRANEAN Theatre are also being obtained and forwarded. I have given Lt-Col Wigham your names so that he may either have a talk with you to obtain your views and to find out about incidents which are not clear in the reports, or to ask you to write your views to him.

We all have the future of the S.A.S. at heart, not merely because we wish to see its particular survival as a unit, but because we have believed in the principles of its method of operations. Many of the above-named officers have had command of forces which have had a similar role to that of the S.A.S., as well as being in the S.A.S. at one time.

The object of this investigation is to decide whether the principles of operating in the S.A.S. manner are correct. If they are correct, what types of units should undertake operations of this nature, and who best to train and maintain such units in peace, ready for war. I will not start now by writing about the principles of S.A.S., which have been an intrinsic part of your life for the past few years, but I will mention what I think are some of the most important points which needed bringing out. The best way to do this is to consider the usual criticisms of the S.A.S. type of force.

1. 'The Private Army'

From what I have seen in different parts of the world, forces of this nature tend to be so-called 'Private Armies' because there have been no normal formations in existence to fulfil this function – a role which has been found by all commanders to be a most vital adjunct to their plans. It has only been due to the drive and initiative of certain individuals backed up by senior commanders that these forces have been formed and have carried out their role.

2. 'The taking up of Commanders' valuable time'

This has often been necessary because it has very often only been the Comds of armies who have realised the importance of operations of this nature, and to what an extent they can help their plans. The difficulty has been that more junior staff officers have not understood the object or principles of such forces. They have either given us every help as they have thought us something wonderful, or they have thought we were 'a bloody nuisance'. I feel that the best way to overcome this is, that once the principle of the importance of Special Raiding Forces operating behind the vital points of the enemy's lines is agreed to it should become an integral part of the training of the army at the Staff College, military colleges, and during manoeuvres, Etc. Students should be asked not only what orders or directives or requests they have to give to the artillery, engineers, air, etc. but also what directives they would give to their raiding forces. There should be a recognised staff officer on the staffs of senior formations whose job it is to deal with these forces, i.e. the equivalent of a C.R.E. or C.R.A. This should be included in the text books FSR, etc.

3. 'These forces, like airborne forces, are only required when we pass to the offensive, which – judging by all previous wars – is when the regular army has been nearly wiped out in rearguard actions whilst the citizen army forms, i.e. about 3 years after the beginning of the war'

The answer here, I feel, is that it is just when we are weak everywhere that forces of this nature are the most useful, and can play a most vital part in keeping the enemy all over the world occupied. Also there is little difference between the roles of S.A.S. and 'Auxiliary Forces' who duck when the enemy's offensive rolls over them and then operate against the enemy's L of C from previously constructed bases. An S.A.S. formation, by its organisation and training, is ideally suited to operate in this defensive role.

4. 'Overlapping with S.O.E. and other clandestine organisations'

My experience is that S.O.E. and S.A.S. are complementary to each other. S.A.S. cannot successfully operate without good intelligence, guides, etc. S.O.E. can only do a certain amount before requiring, when their operations became overt, highly trained, armed bodies in uniform to operate and set an example to the local resistance. S.O.E. are the 'white hunters' and produce the ground organisation of which S.A.S. operates. All senior officers of S.O.E. with whom I have discussed this point agree to this principle.

5. 'S.A.S. is not adaptable to all countries'

This has already been proved wrong. S.A.S. is probably more adaptable to changes of theatres than any regular formation. Also, as I have said in 4 above, S.A.S. work on the ground organisation of S.O.E. It is for S.O.E. to be a world-wide organisation with an organisation in every likely country. Then when necessary, S.A.S. can operate on this organisation using their guides and intelligence, knowledge, etc.

6. 'Volunteer units skim the regular units of their best officers and men'

Volunteer units such as S.A.S. attract officers and men who have initiative, resourcefulness, independence of spirit, and confidence in themselves. In a regular unit there are far less opportunities of making use of these assets and, in fact, in many formations they are a liability, as this individualistic attitude upsets the smooth working of a team. This is especially true in European warfare where the individual must subordinate his natural initiative so that he fits in to a part of the machine. Volunteer units such as the Commandos and Chindits (only a small proportion of the Chindits were volunteers although the spirit was there) have shown the rest of the army how to fight at a time when it was in low morale due to constant defeat. A few 'gladiators' raises the standard of all. Analogies are racing (car, aeroplane, horse, etc), and Test teams.

7. 'Expense per man is greater than any other formation and is not worthwhile'

Men in units of this nature probably fight 3 or 4 times more often than regular units. They are always eager for a fight and therefore usually get it. If expense per man days *actually in contact with the enemy* was taken into account, there would be no doubt which was the more expensive type of formation. I have found, as you will have done, the 'old familiar faces' on every front where we have seen trouble. I consider the expense is definitely worth it without even taking into account the extra results. One S.A.S. raid in North Africa destroyed more aeroplanes in one day that the balloon barrage did during 6 years of war.

8. 'Any normal battalion could do the same job'

My experience shows that they definitely cannot. In Norway in 1940, a platoon of marines under a Sgt ran away when left on its own, although they had orders to stay, when a few German lorries appeared. Mainly owing to the bad leadership of this parade ground Sgt, they were all jittery and useless because they were 'out of touch', and could not receive orders. By avoiding action, the unit went into a waterless area and more perished this way and later by drowning than if he had attacked.

My experience with regular battalions under my command in Burma was that there were only 3 or 4 officers in any battalion who could be relied on to take positive action if they were on their own, and had no detailed orders. This 'I'll 'ave to ask me Dad' attitude of the British Army is its worse feature in my opinion. I have found the RAF and Dominion officers far better in this respect. I have not had experience with the cavalry. They should also be better. Perhaps cavalry could take on the S.A.S. role successfully? I admit that with training both in Burma and North Africa there were definite improvements amongst the infantry, but in my opinion, no normal battalion I have seen could carry out an S.A.S. role without 80% reorganisation. I have written frankly and have laid myself open to obvious criticism, but I consider this such a vital point that I do not mind how strongly I express myself. I have repeated this for 5 years and I have nowhere seen anything to change my views, least of all in Europe.

I have mentioned some points above. You may not agree with my ideas but I write them down as these criticisms are the most normal ones I know.[6]

Calvert's view on the value of the wartime SAS is hardly surprising; he was, after all, its last commander, but it is interesting that his *aide-mémoire* ignores the most fundamental question-mark that hangs over the role of special operations forces: do they achieve their aim and is that aim worth achieving?

There is no doubt that Stirling's original conception of the SAS and the role he envisaged for it have grown somewhat with the telling. Stirling's military background was with the Commandos, although he never saw action with them, but he had spotted the essential difficulty that Commando units faced in the Middle East theatre: the scale of their operations tended to negate any prospect of achieving surprise. Surprise was what gave the highly trained, well-drilled Commandos their edge in combat against numerically superior, better-armed enemies and, in consequence, their Middle East operations repeatedly failed to achieve the desired effect in their attacks against targets on the enemy's lines of communication. Stirling quite correctly took the view that smaller groups of men would have a better chance of striking such targets and getting away again before a coherent response could be mounted by the Axis forces: that was the concept he famously presented to General Ritchie in 'one of the worst pieces of military writing ever submitted to a headquarters'.[7]

But Stirling's original idea was also misguided in many respects. In the first place, it soon became apparent that conditions in the Western Desert did not in any way suit parachuting, which was Stirling's preferred entry method; he was keen for diversionary activity on a large scale to take place, involving air-raids on major targets; and he had little conception of how he would exfiltrate his assault parties, beyond 'retiring independently ... to a rendezvous with the Long

Range Desert Group',[8] which would have actually required a march of at least fifty miles in a single night. As we have seen, by the end of the first SAS operation, the strength of L Detachment was reduced by more than half.

The crucial breakthrough was the enforced co-operation with the LRDG. With this came the serendipitous realisation (that Lawrence had reached twenty-three years before) that the desert was just as protective an environment for raiders as it was for intelligence gatherers. Only after this did the SAS achieve any measure of the success for which they became famous.

In fact the claim made on behalf of the SAS is that the regiment destroyed approximately three hundred Axis aircraft on the ground during 1942, as well as causing serious damage at Axis transport parks and logistics depots.[9] These are serious figures, not to be dismissed lightly, and clearly these SAS operations *must* have had an effect on the outcome of the campaign in the desert; evidently the SAS did achieve their general strategic aim. Even so, it was not perhaps as crucial as has sometimes been supposed: in reality, the Luftwaffe was in a position to contest Allied air superiority over Tripolitania and the Western Desert even after the battle of El Alamein in October 1942,[10] whilst the logistics problems that faced the Axis can be mainly ascribed to the effect of ULTRA decrypts which revealed the timings and positions of Axis resupply convoys, enabling them to be attacked with considerable precision.

SAS success in Sicily and Italy, and in western Europe, was, as we have seen, even less clear-cut. It is not entirely surprising, therefore, that when the Directorate of Tactical Investigation reported to the War Office in 1946, the conclusion was reached that there was no need, at that time, to retain an SAS capability as part of the regular order of battle. Instead, a territorial regiment was founded by resurrecting the traditions of the Artists' Rifles, a fashionable volunteer unit founded in central London in the 1850s but which had latterly existed only as an Officer Cadet Training Unit. This was merged with volunteers from the wartime SAS Brigade as 21st Special Air Service Regiment (Artists') (Volunteers), always referred to as 21 SAS, under the command of Lieutenant Colonel Brian Franks, who had taken command of 2 SAS from Bill Stirling in 1944. Wartime SAS personnel with a reserve commitment but who were unable to join 21 SAS were incorporated into the Z Reserve of the SAS. In theory, this would provide continuity of experience and expertise from the wartime SAS Brigade through into any future conflict in which a special operations capability might be required:

> I met Billy on the Charing Cross Road and we went for a drink in a pub on the Cambridge Circus. We were talking about old times, as you do, and he mentioned that he had joined the territorials, and that they had reformed the SAS as a territorial regiment and he was back in it, and it was a lot of the old boys from the war. My first reaction was 'good luck to him', but over the next few weeks I started thinking about it more and more, and I suppose it began to sink in just how much I missed all the old chaps.
>
> After a while I wrote off and was invited to go down to the barracks in Euston and sign up, which I did, and virtually the first chap I met there was Billy and his first words were 'I knew you'd show up eventually', but really, it was tremendous to be back in that atmosphere.[11]

The unit was initially equipped with SAS armed jeeps, but wearing the Mars and Minerva cap-badge of the Artists' Rifles (21 SAS adopted the winged dagger badge in 1949) on the airborne maroon beret. The original role conceived for 21 SAS was a simple follow-on from the Second World War: strategic reconnaissance and raiding on behalf of the commander of the 1st British Corps in Germany in the event of a Soviet invasion of the West. As time went by, however, this role became more refined. Captain Peter de la Billière was appointed adjutant of 21 SAS in 1960:

> In the early 1960's 21st SAS began to develop a new and important role. The concept of operations in Europe . . . was basically that we, the NATO forces, were on the defensive. We never expected to attack the Russians, but we did expect them to attack us. Our plan in that event was to withdraw, consolidate, hold the enemy on a given line and destroy them with nuclear weapons. To implement this plan effectively, the British Corps Commander needed an organisation which could send back accurate reports of Russian movement from far enough in front of his own troops

to enable him to identify the main enemy thrust and deploy his reserves accordingly, as well as to help target his nuclear weapons. That organisation was 21st SAS.[12]

The intention for 21 SAS was to deploy its patrols on the ground in Germany immediately before a Soviet attack and then allow them to be 'rolled over', passively allowing themselves to fall behind enemy lines in order to enable themselves to start reporting troop movements in the rear area. Clearly, however, heavily armed, mobile jeep patrols were not the best nor most subtle way of doing this and, while de la Billière was adjutant, 21 SAS began to focus on the construction and long-term occupation of underground observation posts as their principal operational technique.

As 21 SAS were converting to an essentially static role at the beginning of the 1960s, a second territorial SAS regiment was being formed (22 SAS, the regular SAS regiment, was established in 1952). The designation chosen for the new formation was 23 SAS although it had existed for a short period as the Reserve Reconnaissance Unit. Details of the original role envisaged for 23 SAS remain somewhat obscure but it does seem to have been much more akin to an SOE/MI9 task: leading, advising and training guerrillas, and organising escape lines for Allied evaders (which had been MI9's role during the war). And there have been suggestions that there were connections with the CIA's Gladio network of stay-behind resistance groups that were organised in the 1950s at the height of the Cold War. However long this role lasted, 23 SAS evolved into a parallel regiment to 21 SAS, providing stay-behind observation posts on main supply routes and 'choke points' for the commander of 1st British Corps (in which role 21 and 23 SAS were known as the Corps Patrol Unit or CPU). This remained their role until the end of the Cold War at the beginning of the 1990s.

A second element of Britain's SAS commitment to NATO is at the International Long Range Reconnaissance Patrol School at Weingarten in southern Germany, for which the SAS provided a number of instructors. Nevertheless, it is interesting to note that Britain's main NATO special forces commitment, 21 and 23 SAS, is found from part-time territorial soldiers whereas, for the majority of NATO member countries, their special forces commitment represents the best of their professional élite. Despite this, the territorial SAS have always performed well in NATO special forces competitions, most probably as a result of their rigorous selection standards, and a steady trickle of territorial SAS soldiers continue to join the regular 22 SAS Regiment. One recent example of this transition is Corporal Chris Ryan, formerly of 23 SAS, who was the only member of the famous Bravo Two Zero patrol to avoid capture by the Iraqis and escape to Syria.

Until recently, COs of 22 and 23 SAS, who are regular army officers, were former members of 22 SAS but this is no longer always the case. Each of the two territorial SAS Regiments consists of five operational 'sabre' squadrons with an administrative HQ squadron, commanded by territorials. Training support is provided to each squadron by a sergeant or staff sergeant seconded from the permanent cadre of 22 SAS, and there is a regular training major, regimental sergeant major and training wing sergeant major, as well as a number of non-regular permanent staff who are usually ex-members of 22 SAS. In practice, this generally means that members of the territorial SAS are very good at the core skills required for their operational tasks: signalling, navigation, first-aid and so on; but have only a surprisingly basic level of ability in other fields. Even though territorial SAS soldiers are allowed a much higher allocation of training days than most members of the TA, they will probably not be 'in the field' for more than three or four weeks of the year at the very most. This means that their patrol skills and fieldcraft are unlikely to be as well developed as those of a regular infantryman who might spend half of a six-month tour of Northern Ireland on rural patrolling. Still, they are evidently of sufficiently high standard to compete with Allied soldiers from armies which do not share the British level of operational preparedness. There is, nevertheless, a certain amount of friction between regular and territorial SAS members:

> The only thing that really got on my tits about the whole experience was that you couldn't really get them to practise their role. Basically their job was information reporting from stay-behind OPs in Northern Europe, but all they wanted to do was storm embassies and fight guerrillas. You'd set up a weekend

---

* A training area in East Anglia.

for them to go to Stanford,* say, to dig in and practise comms procedures and all the rest of it, and maybe ten people would turn up, but if you organised some kind of raid or target attack, they'd all be there, and they'd bring their mates as well. That did use to piss me off.[13]

The US Army's conclusions on the future role of special forces were much the same as the British, although reached via a slightly different route, the US not having created a *military* special operations unit during the war. In 1946 the US Secretary of War, Robert Patterson, proposed that the army should examine the prospects and value of creating an airborne long-range reconnaissance capability. This idea was kicked around by the US military bureaucracy for several years, and eventually came to encompass such diverse evolutionary strands as Merrill's Marauders, OSS Jedburgh teams, and Ranger-type units. One feature of the evolution of post-war US special forces was the idea that unconventional warfare would be controlled, in peacetime at least, by the Central Intelligence Agency, the post-war successor to the OSS, which had already inherited the OSS's intelligence collection role, but that manpower and training support would come from army resources. In fact what emerged, in 1951, was the United States Army Special Forces (formally activated in June 1952) consisting, at that time, of the Special Warfare Center at Fort Bragg, North Carolina, and the 10th Special Forces Group (Airborne) which deployed to Bad Tölz (the former officer training school for the Waffen-SS) in 1953 as the United States' NATO-roled special forces.

The mission of the US special forces was essentially the same as that of the Jedburghs:

The Cold War threat … in the early 1950s demanded a strategic capability which would allow the Army to gather timely intelligence utilising possible resistance movements within the Soviet Union [and its satellites] as well as US ground personnel who would carry out unilateral taskings. Though many confuse unconventional warfare to mean guerrilla warfare, the term 'unconventional warfare' was intended to apply to a series of actions which could be taken by a theatre commander in support of declared or undeclared conflicts. Special Forces teams would be expected to train and advise insurgent organisations to act as guerrillas during peace and wartime, but the trainers and advisers themselves would also be available to carry out, via special reconnaissance [the US term for long-range strategic reconnaissance and intelligence collection by special forces] activities, such missions as locating Soviet nuclear installations for future attention by US military planners.[14]

In contrast to the cautious and long-drawn-out approach of the British and American armies, France and Belgium both kept their Special Air Service units operational in the aftermath of the war: 3 and 4 SAS became 1ière and 2ième Régiments de Chasseurs Parachutistes (1 and 2 RCP) in the new French Army, whilst 5 SAS became 1ière Régiment de Parachutistes SAS of the Belgian Army. The French units moved away from the special forces role, becoming, in effect, parachute light infantry. The Belgians eventually amalgamated their Second World War special operations experience into one unit, the Regiment Para Commando, consisting of two parachute battalions (the 1st Parachute Battalion wears a metal winged dagger cap-badge), a Commando battalion and various smaller units, including a long-range reconnaissance patrol squadron (the ESR). The Regiment Para Commando now forms part of Belgium's NATO-roled forces as a component of the Multi-National Airmobile Division set up in 1991 as part of the Allied Rapid Reaction Corps.

Despite the high level of preparedness maintained by the military special operations forces of NATO (and reputedly the Warsaw Pact) during the Cold War, politicians and diplomats of both power blocs were able to maintain sufficient control over the situation that it did not spill over into direct military confrontation. Even so, most major special forces units have taken part in a wide variety of campaigns in the post-colonial wars and insurgencies that followed the break-up of the European empires after 1945, and it was in these that the special operations forces created during and immediately after the Second World War evolved the operational flexibility that has now become their hallmark.

The Wild Colonial Wars: who dares wins

One of the most important consequences of the outcome of the Second World War was the massive blow that it dealt to the European colonial powers in regions in which they had suffered military defeats, and most particularly in Asia. Britain had been summarily kicked out of Malaya, Singapore, Burma and Hong Kong, together with several smaller dependencies and colonies; France had lost control of Indo-China;* the Netherlands had lost the Dutch East Indies. The Japanese occupiers had then done their best to promote a form of bogus pan-Asian nationalism, presenting themselves as 'liberators' from European colonial oppression which, if it did not impress their new subjects overmuch, at least raised the issue of self-rule for Asian peoples who had seen their previously all-powerful European rulers firmly beaten by superior Asian troops. In consequence, when Japan surrendered in August 1945, nationalist groups throughout Asia were determined that the former colonial powers should not be allowed to simply march back in and resume control.

Nevertheless, in the vacuum created by the collapse of Japanese authority, this is more or less what happened. British troops in small numbers began to arrive in Indonesia and Indo-China towards the end of August and the beginning of September 1945, planning to re-establish order and to enable the Dutch and French to resume their civil authority. Both objectives were achieved but in both areas resistance from local groups was encountered. In Indonesia, nationalist groups based on the

* The Vichy French governor-general remained nominally in charge until March 1945 but was firmly subject to Japanese control.

island of Java fought fiercely against the British whilst in Indo-China, the British discovered that a powerful communist-nationalist group, the Viet Minh, which had fought against Japanese occupation with the support of the OSS, was in *de facto* control of large areas of the country. As French and Dutch troops began to arrive from Europe, the British were able to evacuate and concentrate on their own colonial problems.

The Malayan Communist Party had begun to organise as early as 1930 but it received its real impetus as a result of the Japanese occupation of Malaya and Singapore in 1942. Apart from the military defeat that they had suffered, the blow to British prestige and 'face' was enormous and one from which it was unlikely that they would ever recover, whatever the final outcome of the war. In Malaya and Singapore, a large but poorly equipped and inadequately led Commonwealth force was defeated by less than half their number of Japanese invaders. Singapore was, at that time, Britain's principal strategic naval base in the Far East and the island had been fortified against possible attack at enormous financial cost during the 1930s, but a lack of foresight, money and military imagination left the Malayan peninsula itself relatively undefended, and the Commonwealth forces had effectively crumbled when the Japanese attacked.

In the face of military defeat, an attempt was made in the dying days of the campaign to deploy stay-behind teams of guerrilla saboteurs into the jungle. Few survived very long but from this experience the SOE unit Force 136 was created to develop and nurture resistance to the Japanese.

The object of Force 136 was to harness the resentment created by Japanese occupation policy – for all their propaganda, the Japanese were not much less racially supremacist than the Germans – and allow it expression by supplying training, leadership and most importantly *matériel*, much as SOE had done in Europe. In Malaya, it soon became apparent that the best-organised resisters were to be found in the Malayan Communist Party and their Malayan People's Anti-Japanese Army (MPAJA); as happened elsewhere Force 136 actually provided most assistance to an avowedly communist grouping.

One particularly interesting feature of the Malayan Communist Party and the MPAJA was in its ethnic make-up: it was largely drawn from the minority Chinese population which, by and large, lived in 'Chinatown' ghettos in the towns and squatted on the fringes of agricultural areas. Despite their urban background, however, the MPAJA showed no real reluctance to operate in jungle areas and their relative ethnic exclusivity also proved an advantage in providing a ready-made support infrastructure within the Chinese population. This support structure, known as the Min Yuen, probably involved a majority of the Chinese population at one stage or another, and was just as much a result of family ties as of political affiliation. As will be readily appreciated, the conjunction of politically committed communist guerrillas, an extended ethnically homogeneous logistics and intelligence system and military support and, to some extent, leadership from the British Empire and its allies, created an effective resistance force with a very distinct political agenda.

The end of the war, however, caught the MCP unprepared, and with SOE operators already in the country, it did not take long for the colonial authorities to re-establish themselves. In fact the British had recognised that they would not be able to hang onto many of their colonies and Clement Attlee's Labour government, which had been swept to a landslide victory in July 1945, announced in October 1945 the formation of a Malayan Union designed to unify the various territorial entities that had comprised the pre-war colony with a view to guiding them towards independence. This proved to be something of a mistake.

The problem with the Malayan Union was that it ensured equal status for the various ethnic groups present in the colony, particularly the Malays, Indians and Chinese. But this caused consternation to the majority Malay group which feared domination by a coalition of minorities, thus exacerbating already existing ethnic tensions. During 1946 the colony, which had traditionally been quiescent and stable, became rapidly politicised as the Malays sought to preserve their pre-eminent position. This in turn caused tension and fear amongst the minority groups and particularly the Chinese, who saw *their* way of life now threatened by Malay intransigence. Malay nationalism was essentially conservative, but the Chinese population increasingly turned to the MCP as a vehicle to air their political frustrations and this fitted in well with the MCP leadership's ambitions.

For the first two and a half years after the end of the war, the MCP consolidated their military infrastructure (their military wing was called the Malayan Races Liberation Army or MRLA but they were almost always referred to as communist terrorists or CTs) and built up a campaign of subversion, infiltration of trades unions and other associations, disruption of industry, agriculture and commerce, and the assassination of (mainly Malayan and Indian) managerial personnel. Finally, in the summer of 1948, following the murder of three European planters, the government declared a state of emergency.

Although the regular British Army prior to the Second World War had a good deal of experience dealing with counter-insurgency and low-intensity warfare, it had not in recent years fought against such a well-organised enemy in such unforgiving surroundings. As a result the initial military response to the Malayan Emergency was marked by a distinct lack of success at both the tactical and strategic levels. The guerrilla strength amounted to about three or three and a half thousand operating permanently in the jungle in small groups, with at least five thousand committing terrorist acts on a 'part-time' basis whilst living in towns. The Min Yuen support organisation consisted of at least four hundred thousand members and probably as many as six hundred thousand. The small, relatively flexible guerrilla gangs would attack plantations, villages and other centres, and unwieldy British infantry units would respond by launching slow search and destroy operations which rarely achieved their aim. The CTs hoped that by their strategy of concentrating on rural areas they would first cripple the economy and then isolate the British and their allies in the towns; an urban uprising orchestrated by the Min Yuen should force the British out completely. Faced with the failure of their initial response to the CTs, the apparently bewildered British leadership cast around for a new method to get them out of their predicament: the man selected to study the problem in the spring of 1950, at the suggestion of General Sir William Slim (then CIGS*), was then working as a staff officer in Hong Kong: Major Mike Calvert DSO, former commander of the SAS Brigade.

Calvert was summoned to see General Sir John Harding, Commander-in-Chief Far East, at his headquarters in Singapore and given six months to study the problem of fighting the guerrillas and recommend some solutions. Calvert's fact-finding mission has since become legendary.

* Chief of the Imperial General Staff.

During his six-month, study he covered a distance of around thirty thousand miles, during which he interviewed soldiers and officers, accompanied patrols and operations, and made a recruiting trip to Rhodesia. His two most important observations were that military success against the CTs was being hampered by the confused chain of command that prevailed in Malaya, and that insufficient effort was being made to win control of the jungle and its inhabitants.

The first point was fast becoming glaringly obvious to the government back in London: it was very evident that ill-feeling and rivalry between the colonial administration, the police and Special Branch, and the army in Malaya were blocking any kind of resolution to the problem, but Calvert's second idea was more interesting. The reluctance of the British forces to operate deep in the jungle – they would not usually stay in for more than a week or so – meant that it had become a haven for the CTs (who as urban Chinese had no greater instinctive feel for the jungle environment than their opponents).

A second factor that Calvert identified in relation to this issue concerned the position of the aboriginal jungle tribesmen. About a hundred thousand of them lived deep in the jungle in longhouses, subsisting on what they were able to catch and gather in their tribal area, and showing little interest in the outside world. Although they had no particularly good reason for supporting the CTs, many of them were doing so, providing food, shelter and intelligence, partly because of intimidation but also because the CTs represented their only real contact with outsiders. In the early stages of the conflict British troops treated the locals with an entirely unwarranted degree of brutality, an attitude exemplified by the massacre of (at least) twenty-five innocent Chinese by a small patrol of Scots Guards in 1948, an incident that was covered up for many years. The occasional appearances of British patrols in the aboriginals' tribal areas were an irritation to the aborigines who would avoid them when possible and make little or no effort to help, even when they would have suffered no loss to have done so.

Calvert understood that by inserting patrols for much longer periods, and by making an effort, using medical and other forms of aid, to win the hearts and minds of the local population, it might be possible to make the jungle an extremely hostile, and possibly even untenable, environment for the CTs. Even so, he was less than sanguine about being able to achieve this aim with conventional infantry, and he recommended that a special long-range patrol unit be formed.

The majority of his report was accepted for incorporation in the Briggs Plan, the document that served as a strategic blueprint for the Malayan campaign, but Calvert himself, with his background in the jungle as a Chindit, and as a wartime SAS officer, was given the task of raising the special unit. The name selected for Calvert's unit, the Malayan Scouts, reflected the army's intention that it remain a local force raised to meet the conditions of the Malayan theatre only, but Calvert was keen to associate it with the SAS – as a military special force – and successfully lobbied to have SAS incorporated into the name, making it Malayan Scouts (SAS Regiment).

The early days of the Malayan Scouts were not dissimilar to those of L Detachment: although the idea of a long-range patrol unit was approved in principle, few resources were forthcoming to support it and Calvert, holding the acting rank of lieutenant colonel, was forced to handle most of the unit's administrative tasks as well as training and operations, whilst also attending high-level staff conferences as an acknowledged expert in jungle warfare. This led to several problems. In the first instance, discipline was intermittent and inconsistent in the unit. Calvert, like many fighting soldiers, was not particularly concerned by the trivia of, for example, military appearance; uniformity and smartness have little bearing on a unit's ability to fight but they do have an important effect on the way in which a military unit is perceived by outsiders. Traditionalists certainly made up the great majority of the officer corps in the 1950s, and probably still do today, and they have always been likely to form a poor opinion of soldiers who are scruffy in barracks, however effective they may be in the field. This prejudice can certainly lead to suspicion and misuse of units with a potentially important role to play, and Calvert's failure to enforce basic standards was a serious error:

> They had a dreadful reputation, the SAS in Malaya. Whenever one came across them they were dirty, scruffy and drunk. The problem lay in their leadership because Calvert, for all his undoubted qualities, was also dirty, scruffy and drunk a lot of the time as well! When they first started working, they were not very much use to us: it was only when they'd been

in the jungle for a few years that they started to achieve results.[1]

A second important factor was the selection of personnel. Calvert was allowed to recruit his own officers but most of the men for his first squadron were selected for him by unit commanders who, not unnaturally, took the opportunity to unload their troublemakers and wasters. At one stage Calvert was even given ten deserters from the French Foreign Legion who had jumped ship in Singapore *en route* for the war in Indo-China; not surprisingly, such recruits were worse than useless in a unit with the Malayan Scouts' projected role, but their presence, and that of similar low-grade soldiers, was to give the Malayan Scouts, and subsequently 22 SAS, an undeserved reputation that took many years to shake off.

As with L Detachment, the early operations of the Malayan Scouts were unsuccessful: on their first deployment, in August 1950, they made no contact with the enemy at all. But importantly, the more able officers and soldiers in the unit did begin to develop an understanding of what long-term jungle patrols entailed, and it was this jungle awareness that was to have an important role in the relative successes of later years.

With A Squadron formed and ready for operations, the Malayan Scouts had a continuing need for volunteers to bring the unit up to its proposed strength of four squadrons. The first source to be tapped back in Britain was, perhaps, the most obvious one, although it does not seem to have been at the forefront of the recruiters' minds: 21 SAS Regiment in London.

Following the North Korean invasion of the South in 1950, General MacArthur, the American commander of the United Nations forces, had requested two regiments of SAS troops from Britain to operate in the classic Second World War role. This was evidently not possible but nevertheless volunteers were called for from 21 SAS and the Z Reserve of the SAS* to form a squadron, known as M Independent Squadron, for service in Korea. In fact as the situation in Korea improved in early 1951 it was decided that there was no continuing need for M Squadron's services and, instead, the volunteers were offered the opportunity to go to Malaya instead. Sufficient came forward, 'between thirty or forty',[2]

---

* Wartime SAS soldiers with a peacetime training commitment.

for the squadron to go out to Malaya as a formed unit where they were to become B Squadron of the Malayan Scouts.

Arrival in Malaya was something of a shock to the well-trained, highly motivated soldiers of B Squadron:

> It was a hell of a problem. We had pretty good discipline in our Squadron and it made things difficult all round when I was making my guys shave and do all the normal things soldiers do in camp while A Squadron seemed to just do as they pleased. Roadknight, the RSM, wasn't a lot of help in things like that. We soon heard the stories of Calvert's boozing and the wild parties that went on when the lads were out of the jungle.[3]

B Squadron were joined shortly after their arrival by C (Rhodesia) Squadron, commanded by Captain (later Major) Peter Walls,* and soon after that by D Squadron, which had also been raised from UK-based volunteers and had gone through a short period of training at the Airborne Forces depot in Aldershot. All the new squadrons were put through a jungle training course organised by Major John Woodhouse, one of Calvert's original recruits, who had assumed temporary command of B Squadron when their original OC resigned in disgust at the apparent slackness of the unit under Calvert, and shortly afterwards assumed full command of D Squadron. At the time that these changes were taking place, in mid-1951, Calvert's health was beginning to collapse under the strain of a series of major tropical diseases, combined with the sheer hard work of commanding the new special force, heavy drinking and other stresses resulting from his private life. In June 1951 he was invalided back to Britain for a long period of sick leave, and command of the Malayan Scouts was passed to Lieutenant Colonel 'Tod' Sloane, a regular officer of the Argyll and Sutherland Highlanders with no experience of special operations.

Calvert has never really been given the credit he deserves for re-establishing the SAS in the regular army. As commander of the SAS Brigade he had played an instrumental role in ensuring the survival of

---

* As a three-star (Lieutenant) General he commanded the Rhodesian Armed Forces at the height of their struggle against ZIPRA (Zimbabwe People's Revolutionary Army) and ZANLA (the Zimbabwe African National Liberation Army) in the 1970s.

the SAS concept in the Territorial Army but the wartime SAS's – and 21 SAS's – behind-the-lines raiding role was entirely different to the Malayan Scouts' task of long-range reconnaissance, winning hearts and minds and denying the jungle haven to the CTs. By insisting on associating his new unit with the Special Air Service, Calvert succeeded in establishing a role for the regiment in low-intensity warfare which would not necessarily have come about otherwise. If Calvert had not made the Malayan Scouts part of the SAS (against some opposition from SAS Regimental Headquarters in London) it is entirely likely that the unit would have been disbanded at the end of the campaign.

Why has Calvert's role been ignored and downplayed by the SAS themselves? Almost certainly because of events which took place after his medical evacuation in June 1951. After several months of hospital treatment and sick leave Calvert was posted to Germany as commander of the Royal Engineers in Soltau: 'One day I got drunk and got myself into trouble.'[4] At a general court martial in Hanover he was convicted on one charge of gross indecency and two of attempting to procure gross indecency with German youths.[5] As with the most of those who have been court-martialled for homosexual offences, there was no suggestion that he had behaved improperly towards any other member of the forces, or that his behaviour had any material bearing on his ability to do his job, or to command the respect of his officers and men. On 13 July 1952 he was 'dismissed the service';[6] it was a sad and unnecessary end to a career of exceptional and largely unrecognised achievement.

The second half of 1951 saw a steady increase in the efficiency and effectiveness of the Malayan Scouts as the squadrons gained experience on longer jungle patrols and began to move into areas hitherto only visited by the CTs and aborigines, and the usefulness of the unit was fully appreciated by Headquarters Far East Land Forces, who were keen to recommend that the Malayan Scouts become part of the regular army order of battle as 22 SAS Regiment:*

> The role of the Malayan Scouts (Special Air Service Regiment) is to operate in the deep jungle areas not already covered by other Security Forces, with the object of destroying bandit forces, their camps and their sources of supply.

* Which duly happened in early 1952.

No other units in Malaya are so suitably organised or equipped for this task which is vital in bringing the bandits to battle.

The result is that the unit is becoming a 'Corps d'Élite' in deep jungle operations and is a most valuable component of our armed forces in Malaya.[7]

In the period 1952–5 as the deep jungle became a more hostile environment for the CTs, there was a shift in emphasis by the SAS towards operations on the jungle fringe, using the skills acquired during the early stages of the campaign to mount searches and ambushes against terrorist groups around their area of operations. At the same time, back in the UK, a selection process was being organised to ensure that a consistent standard of volunteer was coming out to the Far East for operational service. This came about by coincidence: in 1952 Major John Woodhouse had returned to Britain to take up an appointment as the adjutant of a territorial battalion but, having some weeks to spare before reporting to his new unit, he was asked to take control of a draft of new volunteers for 22 SAS who were assembling at the Airborne Forces depot at Aldershot. Starved of resources, he took them to Snowdonia for a period of strenuous hill walking combined with map-reading instruction and basic tactics, with the intention of giving them the best possible preparation before they left and also to weed out any unsuitable soldiers. It was from this small beginning that the now famous SAS selection course developed and it normally meant that officers and soldiers arriving in Malaya were of a high baseline standard, even if their jungle skills were not up to those of the veterans.

The success of SAS patrols in dominating the deep jungle led to a steady pressure to increase their numbers and within two years of its foundation as the Malayan Scouts, 22 SAS had reached a strength of three regular British squadrons together with the Rhodesian volunteer squadron. When the Rhodesians' tour of duty ended in December 1952, they were replaced after a two-year gap by a squadron formed in New Zealand and the regiment was augmented by a further squadron raised from the Parachute Regiment, thus increasing the strength of 22 SAS in 1955, when both contributions became ready for duty, from three to five operational squadrons. At the same time, this created a lasting affiliation between both the New Zealand Armed Forces, which have maintained an effective and efficient SAS capability ever since (with further operational experience in Borneo and Vietnam), and the Parachute Regiment, which prides itself on providing the majority of operational SAS soldiers to this day.

The tide began to turn in favour of the government forces in Malaya when political and military command were unified under Sir Gerald Templer in 1952 but the process of finding and destroying the fighting elements of the MRLA was slow and laborious and Malaysia did not become independent (within the Commonwealth) until August 1957. 22 SAS remained on operations in Malaya until the middle of 1959, although by that stage the New Zealand SAS squadron had returned home, the Parachute Squadron had been disbanded, and A and D Squadrons had deployed to the Oman in late 1958 and then relocated to Britain, leaving only B Squadron 'in at the death' under Lieutenant Colonel Tony Deane-Drummond. CT activity had declined drastically from the early days and many operations consisted largely of searches for specific small guerrilla bands. A typical example was Operation Thrust, B Squadron's successful search for the CT gang led by Ah Hoi ('the Babykiller') in the Telok Anson area in January and February 1958.

At its height the Malayan Emergency employed the services of twenty-two battalions of British and Commonwealth infantry, 180,000 police (including special constables and auxiliaries) and 250,000 Home Guards. During the period of the Emergency – 1948 to 1960 – some six thousand four hundred CTs were claimed killed with a further 3,000 captured or surrendered; 34,000 individuals were interned without trial, 10,000 deported and 226 hanged. Set against this, the contribution of 22 SAS, which was operational for nine years of the Emergency and had a peak strength of 560 men, was a total of 108 confirmed terrorist kills: a little less than two per cent of the total. Clearly there was no sense in which the role of 22 SAS was decisive: the regiment was a relatively small cog in a large, and after a somewhat shaky start, effective security apparatus which had the support of a majority of the population.

But the SAS's part was by no means insignificant. Calvert correctly saw the importance of denying the deep jungle as a safe haven for the CTs and recognised two ways in which this could be achieved: by sending effective troops to live in it, and thus dominate it, for extended periods, and by winning the allegiance of the jungle people who could sustain the CTs. In pioneering these activities, the SAS developed a major strand of the security policy that would lead to ultimate victory.

The campaign was also important from the SAS point of view in helping to refine the regiment's method of selecting and recruiting its soldiers, and in defining its role. From the end of 1952 a formal procedure existed whereby individuals could volunteer from their parent regiment or corps for service in 22 SAS, and a formal selection and training course existed to check their suitability. This was a crucial development which laid the foundations for future successes: a special forces unit can only hope to achieve its normally ambitious objectives if its members are up to the tasks set for them. Calvert's original Malayan Scouts struggled despite the sound underlying concept because many of its soldiers did not have the aptitude or the self-discipline to handle the particular demands of special forces soldiering. Jungle warfare makes great demands on its practitioners – a situation recognised implicitly by the fact that soldiers joining 22 SAS are still essentially trained as jungle soldiers – and by only selecting those who are likely to succeed, rather than relying on the lottery of blind posting or over-ambitious volunteering, the SAS ensured that it became a regiment that could achieve its aims.

Even so, the end of the Malayan campaign could well have meant an end to 22 SAS. Far from being the all-round special forces unit it is today, 22 SAS was very much a specialist long-range jungle patrol unit, albeit made up of high-quality, relatively flexible manpower, but there were no jungle campaigns on the horizon at that time and it took some imagination to realise that the general lessons of the SAS's Malayan campaign might be applied to other theatres. In fact there were no specific plans to disband the SAS but it was reorganised and streamlined, reducing from three regular squadrons to two, as a reflection of the difficulty of finding sufficient recruits of the right calibre. By the time this happened, however, the two surviving squadrons were involved in a campaign which ensured the survival of 22 SAS as part of the regular order of battle.

The crucial campaign in which 22 SAS now became embroiled took place in the Sultanate of Muscat and Oman (normally referred to simply as Oman), a country which was, at that time, obscure and backward, but which occupied a key position on the southern side of the Straits of Hormuz, at the entrance to the Persian Gulf on the eastern side of the Arabian peninsula. Over many years, rivalry and jealousy had built up between the tribes of the interior of the country – who tended to be fundamentalist and insular, and who resented the Sultan's British backing – and the inhabitants of the coastal strip and ports, who made their living by trading, and tended to be more cosmopolitan in outlook. Conflict and feuding had culminated in a treaty agreed in 1920 between the tribes' leader, the Imam, and the Sultan, recognising, in effect, the Sultan's authority to rule the country but guaranteeing certain rights and perquisites for the tribal leaders.

This arrangement had broken down in 1954 with the death of the old Imam and the election of a young radical, Ghalib ibn Ali, in his place. Ghalib, with his brother Talib, and their tribal allies of the Bani Hinya and Bani Riyam, thereupon began attacks on targets associated with the Sultan with the apparent aim of seizing control of the country. This in turn provoked a reaction from the Sultan's army, which forced the new Imam and his Bani Riyam allies to take refuge in their tribal villages, and which led Talib to leave for Saudi Arabia where he hoped to raise and arm a force of expatriate Omanis.

The rebellion began at an interesting time in Arab history. In Egypt Gamal Abdel Nasser had seized power and was attempting to reassert Egyptian control over the country which had been virtually occupied by Britain for many years; whilst the huge wealth created by oil deposits in the Gulf states was giving the Arabs a level of influence they had not enjoyed since the time of the Crusades. It was therefore a propitious time for Talib to seek help to oust a Sultan characterised by his enemies as a puppet of the British. When he returned to the Jebel Akhdar in June 1957 with a small force of Saudi-trained Omanis and the support of the two tribes, he was quickly able to seize control of the central part of Oman and declare its independence from the Sultan.

Although Talib's rebellion was not widely supported outside the Bani Riyam and Bani Hinya, he was in a strong military position because of his control of the Jebel Akhdar. This massive plateau effectively controlled the land routes inland from Muscat and was supposedly impregnable to attack by land forces. According to a long-standing defence agreement, the Sultan called on the British for assistance.

The military problem presented by the rebellion was not great. Contemporary intelligence reports record that the rebels consisted of:

60–100 operational Saudi-trained Omanis armed with SMLE.*
400–500 Bani Riyam armed with .45 Martini-Henry Rifles† (of whom 60% were operational).
Up to 10 foreigners.
A small number of semi-automatic weapons and LMGs [Light Machine Guns], 1 .50 Browning machine gun and up to 6 81mm Mortars.[8]

The real problem was political: by the time that Britain came to consider committing regular forces to resolve the situation, the ill-judged invasion of the Suez Canal zone had taken place and British prestige was at an all-time low amongst the Arab states. Committing regular British Army units or formations for long-term operations in any part of Arabia would be met with enormous hostility and suspicion, and could not be countenanced. Instead, in July 1957 an infantry brigade was deployed from Kenya to seize low-lying areas held by the rebels, and a number of British officers and NCOs were attached to the Sultan's forces to stiffen them with experienced leadership and more up-to-date tactics as they attempted to enforce a blockade of the Jebel Akhdar, to which Talib's forces withdrew after the arrival of the British brigade. At the same time RAF squadrons based in the region began a campaign of bombing suspected rebel strongholds.

The officer tasked to work out how to resolve the Oman problem was Major Frank Kitson, who was then employed as a staff officer in the Directorate of Military Operations at the Ministry of Defence, but who had already achieved some success as an intelligence officer during the Mau-Mau revolt in Kenya and as an infantry company commander in Malaya. Kitson favoured mounting a small special operation, selecting a group of thirty or forty officers and NCOs who would use 'turned' rebels and bribery to, in effect, smuggle a small infantry force onto the Jebel Akhdar. This could then take on the rebels on their own

---

* Short Magazine Lee-Enfield rifles: the British Army's standard weapon of the First World War.
† The standard British infantry weapon of the Zulu wars.

territory. This scheme was accepted and Kitson was duly despatched to the Persian Gulf to begin the process:

> Just before I left, the Director of Military Operations had an idea. Some years earlier a unit had been formed to carry out patrols in deep jungle. It was in effect a descendant of the old wartime Special Air Service and in due course it became known as 22 SAS. By the summer of 1958 the Malayan Emergency was nearly over and it was decided that 22 SAS should move to England and hold itself in readiness to carry out patrol tasks in other parts of the world if necessary. General Hamilton reckoned that 22 SAS might provide most of the soldiers needed in our teams, which would be a quicker and more efficient way of getting individuals than collecting them from the army as a whole.[9]

The signal was duly sent to the CO of 22 SAS to meet Kitson in Aden to be briefed by him. Its arrival seemed a godsend to Captain de la Billière, then serving as 22 SAS's operations officer:

> I took the message to Deane-Drummond, who seized on the opportunity as eagerly as I had, though for different reasons [de la Billière did not want to return to regimental soldiering with the Durham Light Infantry]. He saw this not merely as another operation, but as a chance for the SAS to prove to the world that it could fight effectively in environments other than the jungle. Because the Regiment had been in Malaya ever since its reformation, its soldiers had become known to outsiders as 'Jungle Bunnies', and the general assumption was that all we could do was to creep about in thick cover. Moreover, many people believed that when the Malayan campaign came to an end, the SAS would be disbanded. As Deane-Drummond at once realised, Oman would give us another chance.[10]

The reconnaissance by Kitson and Deane-Drummond showed that Kitson's scheme was workable but posting problems suggested that it would be unlikely that sufficient suitable officers would reach Oman in time to put it into effect in the short term. Consequently it was decided that an SAS squadron* would come out from Malaya and begin patrolling around Jebel Akhdar, probing the rebels' defensive positions.

At this point, it is worth recording that the blockade and aerial bombardment of the Jebel had achieved a considerable impact:

> during the week ending 12 September, Shackletons dropped 148 × 1000lb bombs; 40 rockets were fired by Venoms and a large quantity of 20mm ammunition was expended. During the latter part of this month HMS *Bulwark* [a Royal Navy aircraft carrier] arrived in the Gulf of Oman and her full complement of Sea Venoms and Seahawks joined in the air attack. In one week, forty-three offensive sorties against the plateau targets were flown from the ships as well as ten reconnaissance sorties. Within the confines of a relatively small target area, air attacks on this scale continuing for week after week against simple agricultural tribes was a terrifying experience . . . There were increasing reports that villagers were pleading with their Imam Ghalib to go down the mountain and surrender.[11]

And in the second week of November, a week before the arrival of D Squadron of 22 SAS, a patrol of the Trucial Oman Scouts, a British-officered regiment largely composed of Baluchi mercenaries, had in fact discovered an unguarded route onto the Jebel. D Squadron arrived therefore, on 18 November 1958, as the campaign was reaching its climax.

D Squadron spent approximately a week acclimatising before they began operations:

> For the SAS it was a far cry from Malaya. Conditions were totally different. In Malaya visibility was limited to 20–50 yards, and encounters were short and sharp; in Oman the air was crystal clear and a man could be picked out at 2000 yards, although with difficulty for the rebels were adept at fading into the background.

---

* The commander of the Sultan's forces, Colonel David Smiley, actually asked for 'A Parachute Regiment, Marine Commando or SAS unit', i.e. regular soldiers rather than National Servicemen.

Consequently encounters with a highly mobile adversary were liable to last for hours at long range, and to counter this, the SAS carried out extensive patrolling by night. Only thus were they able to get to grips with the rebels and outmanoeuvre them.[12]

Thereafter, their aim was set out by Colonel Deane-Drummond:

> D Squadron 22 SAS [would] carry out offensive recce on all slopes leading up the mountain and on the plateau with a view to
> a. Gaining knowledge of all possible routes up the mountain.
> b. Ambushing and killing pickets on the wadis or anywhere else.
> c. Killing Talib.

Early patrolling by D Squadron established that it was possible for the SAS to get onto and stay on the Jebel using the route pioneered by the Trucial Oman Scouts, and although they lost a man early on to a rebel sniper, they were perfectly capable of holding their own against the rebels in any confrontation. The next step was to exploit their foothold.

With D Squadron having explored various routes onto the Jebel it was now decided that the best way to bring the campaign to a swift conclusion was to bring A Squadron out from Malaya to take part in an assault on the main rebel strongholds, such as they were. This operation was launched at last light 26 January 1959 and involved a long climb up the southern slopes of the Jebel for both squadrons. There was some opposition from snipers during the next morning, during which 'occurred the only casualties, caused by a stray bullet exploding a grenade in an SAS soldier's pack; he and the two men behind were badly wounded, and although evacuated by helicopter without undue delay, two of the three died within twenty-four hours'.[13] By now the rebels were exhausted and demoralised, and they melted away from the Jebel as quickly as they could. By 31 January 1959 all resistance had ceased and within a month both squadrons were on their way back to Malaya to prepare for the regiment's move to temporary accommodation in Malvern in the West Country of England.

The Jebel Akhdar operation was undeniably physically tough on its participants and demonstrated very effectively how a small but well-trained and cohesive force could sew up a convincing victory in a very short time. It was not, however, the triumphant feat of arms that has been suggested in recent years. The majority of the rebels, including their leadership, escaped without having to fight the SAS and continued as an active source of trouble in Oman for several years afterwards (there was, for example, a campaign of mining in 1960 which necessitated further small-scale British troop deployments). It did nevertheless show that 22 SAS were flexible enough to be discreetly moved from one theatre of operations, using one set of tactics, to another in which the tactical requirements were completely and profoundly different; and still accomplish their task at a low cost in terms of men (three dead) and resources.* The two SAS squadrons deployed less than one hundred fighting soldiers combined and this was a lesson that was not lost on the ever cost-conscious War Office. As Frank Kitson subsequently wrote:

> From the point of view of the army as a whole, the most important effect of the campaign was that it ensured the continued existence of the Special Air Service. The regiment had been formed in Malaya for operations deep in the jungle and might well have been disbanded at the end of that campaign had it not been able to demonstrate that it had a use outside the jungle as well.[14]

The period which followed the Jebel Akhdar campaign was one of consolidation for 22 SAS. Discussions began in 1959 at the Ministry of Defence with the aim of regularising the position of the regiment within the army. This meant that all the various nit-picking administrative details needed to be tidied up: what badges and insignia would they wear? How long should soldiers serve with the unit? How much should they be paid?

At the same time, as the unit returned to England it was essential to broaden the training that its soldiers received and the system of specialist troops was created in order to provide a range of skills within each squadron. Thus each of the two squadrons was organised into an

---

* Although, interestingly, one criticism that was levelled at 22 SAS after the campaign was of their high level of equipment wastage: 'The practice of throwing away socks, trousers etc. as soon as a hole or tear develops cannot continue. But this is what is happening' (SAS post-operational report).

Air Troop specialising in parachute insertions, a Mountain Troop, a Boat Troop and a Mobility Troop using vehicles. The selection procedure was also formalised. When 22 SAS was in Malaya, selection had been run on a shoestring from a training camp in the foothills of the Brecon Beacons in mid-Wales, but with the arrival of the regiment in Britain, it was possible to devote much closer attention to it, and to integrate selection and continuation training into one extremely demanding package:

You start off on the course carrying a bergen [a military rucksack] with about 35lbs in it, and every day it's increasing. It's in a bog standard rucksack which is taking its toll on your back as well, ripping the skin off, knocking you about a bit. And this is still the early days of the course, and people are beginning to tweak on little injuries, the little strains here and there. You've got through the first week and there's a bit of bullshit and then we're off on the second week and you've got to start to navigate yourself about.

You get the weekends off – it's all very sensible – but you're eating like an absolute bastard, putting away quantities of scoff that even I am embarrassed about. And for the first week or so, provided you're not injured you feel all right. But as you start getting into the hills and you're really going for it there's a constant feeling of nausea. It's a combination of eating a lot of bulky food and not having long enough to digest it peacefully, together with a certain amount of tension, I guess. It means you're always a little uncomfortable even when you're not actually walking. I was up in the hills thinking to myself: 'Fuck, I'd never tell anyone this was fun; this is hard work; it fucking hurts; I feel sick!' You're close to total fucking exhaustion, basically. It's the feeling you get when you're walking like a bastard and you've got a fucking big hill in front of you and you've covered several big ones already. You don't feel a little tired, like at the end of a run, you feel FUCKED – and you want to just sit down, and have a cup of tea and let some other fucker carry the stuff over the hills 'cause you don't want to do it. This is when it becomes a mental battle.

After this you're getting a steady stream of people jacking – injuries, attitude, and then of course there are those who simply can't move fast enough over the hills, 'cos the speed is crucial to everything. People are being rifted out, people are jacking, others

aren't sure why they're there, they might have done selection simply
to get time off for training away from Germany. One or two who
were there were just not all that fussed by it. I mean, this is why
the hills are such a good test. You've really got to want to do it
because it's fucking hard work. It's not a fitness test as such –
I mean, you've got to be fit but you can't *just* be fit – because
unless you're unbelievably fit and can just take it in your stride
it's all about motivation.[15]

The physical ordeal of the selection phase – the first three weeks of
the course – could now be augmented by command and leadership
tasks for aspiring officers and the psychological ordeal of simulated
interrogation for all ranks (described here by an officer who acted as
an *interrogator* during exercises in the 1970s and 1980s):

The SAS exercise comes up twice a year at [the SAS training
area]. It's one of those things with a fearsome reputation which it
probably doesn't deserve. Although it is an unpleasant ordeal for
the people on it, it's extremely closely monitored with plenty of
doctors, psychiatrists and so on lurking about, and the pressures
which are applied to the prisoners are very restricted. Apart
from being a tester for SAS selection and the CSI [Combat
Survival Instructor] course, it's also the final exercise for the long
interrogation course, so there's training value all round.

The rest of the interrogators who do it are mostly territorials
or reservists from all three services. Generally speaking, they
get selected to do the interrogation course because of their
proficiency in languages and not because they are particularly
fearsome characters, although some of them are. It's actually
become a bit of a problem, because a lot of these old geezers
who can do the language bit are so decrepit that they wouldn't
survive the excitement of a real war; seriously, five years ago there
were still World War Two veterans doing it! What you have is
a lot of elderly civvy academics trying to put the fear of god into
potential SAS men in their late twenties: it doesn't work.

Despite what you hear, the idea isn't to 'break' the prisoners
during these exercises, it's to expose them to different interrogation
techniques. This means that the average prisoner will go through

some sort of 'trick' approach, he'll get a screaming session, a sort of 'logical' persuasion session, a 'mutt and jeff' and one or two others. Theoretically, the interrogation exercise cannot be used as a means of selecting personnel, only for training them, and the individual reports on personnel aren't supposed to be shown to the SAS DS [Directing Staff – the instructors]. But, of course, the training major and training wing sergeant major are in the control room for most of the exercise, so they usually know who has talked, and what they subsequently do is up to them. There's a whiteboard in the control room, and next to the name of any prisoner who talked they put a little red 'T', but this can mean various different things. I think it's fair to say that few SAS candidates talk during the interrogation; maybe one per course, rarely more, though you always get a handful of the CSI people to have a chat. Rather more rewarding are the courses for aircrew and such-like: aircrew seem to have a pathological aversion to keeping their mouths shut, and I would personally reckon to have about a fifty per cent hit rate with them.

The form is that you don't know who's doing selection and who isn't, though generally you can guess, particularly when they have sandal marks on their feet from sunbathing at the end of the jungle warfare course. For officers, you get to look at the Army List, and you can guess that if the guy's a second lieutenant in the Pay Corps, he's not doing selection. On Pilgrim's Progress [the final 'Escape and Evasion' exercise] all the runners are wearing old battledress uniforms and they don't carry military kit, and this masks one of the problems that faces SAS members for real. This is that, despite the fact that they don't wear badges and insignia on operations, they do wear special, high-quality uniforms and carry unusual weapons, and these are just as distinctive . . .

The SAS interrogation is certainly the biggest of these exercises, but it has the same format as the SBS equivalent, and they don't get the hardest time: that's reserved for specialist army undercover personnel who aren't, despite what everyone thinks, necessarily from the SAS. It's an experience that I've been through, and I think it's worthwhile training, but I wouldn't pretend that it is necessarily going to prepare anyone for the kind of torture that the *Bravo Two Zero* people went through: all it will do is reinforce the 'rules' for conduct after capture but in reality, the rules normally go out of the window.[16]

Operationally, the period between 1959 and 1962 was quiet for 22 SAS but towards the end of 1962, events began to stir in South-East Asia that would see 22 SAS's last large-scale jungle deployment. The origin of the Borneo confrontation lay in a revolt that broke out in Brunei in December 1962 against the rule of the hereditary Sultan. Brunei, along with Sabah and Sarawak, was one of three former British colonies which occupied the northern third of the island of Borneo (the southern two-thirds of which comprised the Indonesian province of Kalimantan) and which were, at that time, earmarked to federate with Malaya and Singapore to form Malaysia. The Brunei revolt was locally inspired and led – and was quickly put down by British troops brought in from Singapore – but it came at a time of tension between Malaysia and Indonesia to its south. As it was interpreted as an Indonesian move to destabilise Brunei, the British soldiers remained in place.

In fact the revolt was not Indonesian-inspired but it did suggest to President Soekarno, the expansionist and bombastic Indonesian leader, that it might be possible to foment trouble throughout 'British' Borneo and he began to cast around for a means by which to start the ball rolling. He found it in the Clandestine Communist Organisation, an ethnically Chinese terrorist group based mainly in the towns of Sarawak.* In addition, he decided to send his own Indonesian soldiers across the border in small groups to raid villages and intimidate the locals. The British Director of Operations, Major General Walter Walker, found himself with a 900-mile-long jungle border to guard as well as the prospect of an internal uprising, and very few troops with which to do it. Not surprisingly, he accepted the offer of an SAS squadron, and A Squadron, under Major John Edwardes, was swiftly despatched, arriving in January 1963.

Walker's original intention was to use the SAS as an airborne quick reaction force. Never having worked closely with the unit, he believed that the SAS's ability to parachute into jungle canopy might allow them to intercept Indonesians involved in cross-border raiding before

---

* Soekarno was by no means a communist, but was prepared to use the ready-made terrorist infrastructure for his own ends.

managing their getaway. Lieutenant Colonel John Woodhouse, who had now taken command of 22 SAS, managed to persuade Walker that this would not be the best use of their talents and instead they were set much the same task that they had performed in Malaya: long-range patrols aimed at winning the friendship and support of the jungle inhabitants and, at the same time, maintaining surveillance on the border. These two tasks were, of course, complementary: when the tribesmen realised that the SAS patrols were friendly, benevolent men prepared to dispense medical aid to them and their families, they were happy to pass on information that they had gleaned from their own travels in the jungle and even from relatives and friends on the other side of the largely arbitrary border. Thus a single strategically placed patrol was actually able to keep an eye on a very much larger area than might have been anticipated.

It is worth recalling that at this time – early 1963 – 22 SAS consisted of just two operational squadrons, A and D, which meant that only one could be operational in Borneo at any one time. The strain, physical and mental, of extended patrolling in the Borneo jungle was such that squadrons were restricted to four-month tours. Thus A Squadron covered January to April and then August to December, whilst D Squadron covered April to August. However, D Squadron's second tour was forcibly extended to cover another operational contingency which delayed A Squadron's return to the jungle as well as causing a serious reverse for the regiment.* This was A Squadron's brief operation in the Radfan Mountains of Aden.

The port city of Aden and its southern Arabian hinterland had been under British control since 1839; it was valuable as a refuelling and revictualling point on the route to British imperial possessions in India and the Far East. British policy in the colony, such as it was, had been to concentrate on the port, leaving the rural parts of the territory to the control of tribal leaders, whose loyalty was earned through treaties, bribery and occasional shows of force from the locally raised, but largely British-officered, Federal Regular Army (FRA). This policy had, in fact, worked up until 1962 when, under the influence of Nasser's pan-Arab nationalism and Soviet communism, the army of neighbouring Yemen

---

* To relieve the pressure of this continuous cycle of operations, 22 SAS was given permission in 1963 to reactivate B Squadron, and recruiting started immediately.

had deposed their Imam, set up a left-wing government with Egyptian and Soviet backing, and begun to infiltrate weapons and guerrillas over the Radfan Mountains into Adeni territory.

The British authorities, alerted to the threat, finally declared a state of emergency in December 1963 and sent a brigade – Radforce – into the Radfan at the beginning of 1964, but they had no strategy for dealing with the rebellion beyond occupying ground and temporarily halting the supply of arms. Thus when Radforce moved out, the rebels came straight back in.

The SAS involvement came about as the result of a coincidence. In the wake of the first attempts to deal with the Radfan problem a rethink ensued at the headquarters of Middle East Land Forces and it was agreed to launch a second operation, this time involving several British units in addition to the FRA. Whilst this was in the planning stage, Major Peter de la Billière of 22 SAS was in Aden organising a training exercise for A Squadron, which he was then commanding, and he got wind of the scheme. The plan involved using two battalions of the FRA together with 45 Commando Royal Marines (with B Company of 3 Para, then based in Bahrain, attached to them) to seize – initially – two hill objectives in rebel-held areas, one of which would be taken in an airborne assault by the Paras. De la Billière suggested that his squadron might be used to secure the Paras' DZ.

A Squadron arrived in Aden on 22 April 1964 and, without taking time to acclimatise, moved forward to a base at the village of Thumier. The first task for the squadron was to begin patrolling in order to familiarise themselves with the ground and to find a suitable drop zone for the Paras.

After less than a week of patrolling, de la Billière was given orders for his main operation: sending a patrol to secure 3 Para's DZ at the head of the Wadi Taym, inside rebel-held territory. The plan was to insert an eight-man patrol into the area of the DZ which would then lie up for a period, observing enemy activity, before emerging to clear and mark their target.

The operation started at last light on 29 April with a helicopter drop-off of the patrol, commanded by Captain Robin Edwards, 5,000 metres inside rebel-held territory. They began to move forwards towards their lying-up position (LUP) when they hit their first problem: Trooper Nick Warburton, the patrol signaller, fell ill with suspected food poisoning. Although he managed to keep going he inevitably slowed the patrol down and it became evident that they would not reach their objective before daybreak. This meant serious problems: an eight-man patrol, if spotted, would undoubtedly be outnumbered and possibly overwhelmed by rebels known to be in the area. They would be beyond artillery range and probably not strong enough to secure an helicopter landing site for helicopter extraction: all in all, a poor situation to find themselves in. Having selected an emergency lie-up, Edwards and his men settled down to wait it out.

Disaster struck during the late morning. A local goatherd appeared heading straight for the patrol's position. Fearful that he would give their position away if they allowed him to escape, he was shot and killed. The killing of the goatherd provoked an immediate reaction from armed tribesmen who were in the area. Although they did not at first realise who was responsible for the shooting, they soon started poking round to discover what had happened. Realising that their position was now well and truly compromised, the patrol opened fire on the closest tribesmen, hoping to reduce the odds against them before a major contact developed. At the same time, Warburton reported the contact back to squadron HQ from where Major de la Billière called up RAF close air support (CAS), based only eight minutes' flying time away in Khormaksar.

The remainder of the day was essentially a stalemate. Armed tribesmen attempted to work their way close in to the SAS position, whilst the British soldiers sniped at any movement and directed RAF Hunter CAS bombers onto enemy positions. According to de la Billière, the RAF expended 127 rockets and over seven thousand rounds of ammunition during the course of the day in support of the patrol, and a Royal Horse Artillery battery gave supporting harassing fire on enemy approach routes, even though the SAS themselves were out of range. It was only when twilight came that the situation changed appreciably.

Darkness meant the end of close air support but it also gave the patrol the opportunity to make a break for it. By now the enemy snipers were closing on the SAS position, possibly within fifty metres, and as the patrol prepared to move, Warburton was shot in the head and killed. This setback was followed a few minutes later by the death of Edwards himself, killed as the patrol skirmished towards a wadi that would cover their retreat to safety. During the remainder of the night, the patrol fought their way back along the wadi, occasionally 'back-ambushing' their track to deter follow-up by the rebels. By morning, the survivors were safely back in friendly territory.

The disaster of the Edwards patrol was compounded by subsequent events. The bodies of Edwards and Warburton were decapitated by the rebels and their heads taken to Taiz in the Yemen where they were exhibited. Unfortunately, this news reached the families as the result of an ill-judged press conference called by the Commander of Middle East Land Forces, Major General Cubbon, and was then incorrectly denied by the US State Department, causing further anguish.

This deployment into the Radfan was a severe blow for A Squadron, and reflected the hurried way in which they arrived in theatre and began operations. General de la Billière recounts in his autobiography that

> we finished our tour with the feeling that this had not been an ideal operation. As Mike Wingate Gray [second in command of 22 SAS at the time, and the overall commander of SAS troops in the Radfan] remarked in a letter to Woodhouse, written on 11 May, he thought that paratroops could do what we had been doing:
>
> > We are only operating in a super-infantry role of short-range penetration, and tough, well-trained troops could do it equally well. We are only using part of our skills here.[17]

But of course, as we have seen, the operation only came the SAS's way because of lobbying by de la Billière himself.

It is also worth examining why the operation went so badly wrong. It is certainly true that Warburton's illness could not be predicted before it struck but this failure is yet another example of the 'Yarmuk bridge syndrome'. No complex operation ever goes entirely according to plan and therefore, to accommodate this element of chance, or mischance, flexibility must be built in. The insertion march for Edwards' patrol was clearly at the limit of the patrol's capacity in one night and even if Warburton had not become sick, there is a strong possibility that some other setback would have emerged that would have delayed the patrol and prevented them from reaching their destination. There is also the question of shooting the goatherd – the textbook special operations dilemma: what do you do to non-combatants who inadvertently threaten to compromise your operation?

De la Billière identifies three options that Edwards could have taken: let events take their course; attempt to overpower the goatherd; kill him. Edwards went for the third, an extremely dubious moral decision bearing in mind that he had no reason to suppose that the man was anything other than a non-combatant, except that he lived in what was regarded as enemy territory. Subsequent events do not actually prove anything: neither the SAS nor the tribesmen were in a position to accurately identify their targets and it is unlikely that the tribesmen were certain about whom they were dealing with until the soldiers' air support and artillery began to arrive.

A Squadron's entanglement in the Radfan was the first of several short SAS deployments to Aden as the situation deteriorated there, and a further four members of the regiment were to be killed before the final British evacuation. By the end, political errors in London had ensured that the British left Aden in a state of relative chaos as competing factions fought it out for supremacy in the final days of the British presence. Fortunately, these errors were not repeated in the continuing campaign in Borneo.

It was during 1964 that 22 SAS's role began to evolve from what was essentially defensive information reporting within British Borneo, to offensive intelligence gathering across the border in Kalimantan. Patrols were tasked to cross the border covertly, investigating reports of Indonesian terrorist and special forces camps, in order to target them for larger, more conventional attacks. In conjunction with this, the number of SAS troops available for operations was increased, as it had been in Malaya, by introducing Commonwealth SAS (from Australia, who provided a squadron, and New Zealand, who provided a half-squadron) and by retraining British infantry in the long-range patrol role: in this case C Company of 2 Para and the Guards Independent Parachute Company.

In many respects, the SAS's experience in Borneo mirrored that of Malaya. In the early days of the campaign small tentative intelligence-gathering patrols made contact with the jungle inhabitants, befriended them and exploited *their* intelligence-gathering potential. As operational experience increased, the SAS were able to conduct more aggressive patrols, operating into enemy territory and seeking out the enemy for themselves. In the final phase, from 1965, they conducted raids in troop- and ultimately squadron-strength at targets up to 20,000 yards across the border, supported by infantry with mortars and machine guns.

In parallel with information reporting and offensive action operations came a new departure for the SAS: raising and establishing an indigenous patrol unit, the Border Scouts. This had begun in 1963 during D Squadron's first tour and was based on the fundamentally sound premise that people who lived in and off the jungle would be more adept at patrolling it than outsiders. The SAS had used native trackers during the Malayan campaign, but the Border Scouts were a more ambitious project, requiring relatively in-depth military training and careful management. Several members of D Squadron were detached to seek out recruits and begin training for the new force:

> They were not soldiers but scouts. Within a few months their uniforms were discarded and with bare feet and shotguns they became ostensibly hunters again. They were also a great deal safer should they meet the enemy. Gradually the scheme spread through Sarawak and then Sabah. Before the end of D Squadron's tour, a few Border Scouts were added to each SAS patrol, thus enlarging the area it could cover and greatly improving communications.[18]

The Border Scouts proved sufficiently successful that it was decided to create a small team of them for cross-border operations, and training began with forty selected Iban tribesmen in the summer of 1964. By July, Major Muir Walker, in charge of the scheme, was satisfied that they were ready for operations and launched a small incursion to ambush any traffic on a river just across the border. Although this and the next three attempts did not result in any success, the fifth cross-border patrol culminated in an ambush during which two Indonesians were killed: the delighted Border Scouts thereupon removed one of the heads as a trophy.

Although head-hunting was subsequently discouraged by the regiment, cross-border operations by Border Scouts in troop strength achieved increasingly more success as the confrontation between Britain and Indonesia continued. But this was not for very long. The confrontation came to an end in 1966 as political turmoil in Indonesia undermined the politicians' will to continue the costly and ineffective campaign.

Soekarno, the Indonesian President who had led the country to independence from the Netherlands, was toppled from power to be replaced by the far more pragmatic General Suharto. Negotiations began in May 1966 and concluded in August, after which incursions by Indonesian troops ceased. The part played by the SAS was, of course, relatively small but, again, not insignificant. Their involvement in border surveillance and patrolling (including the raising and training of the Border Scouts) was an important element in gathering intelligence for more conventional infantry operations, whilst their cross-border patrols (22 SAS were the first British unit authorised to cross the border) pointed the way for the later 'Claret' attacks on significant Indonesian installations. The British Commonwealth force would still have won the Borneo Campaign without the presence of the SAS, but it is likely that it would have dragged on for longer and that many of the lessons of jungle warfare would have taken much longer to learn. As it was, 22 SAS suffered only three men killed in action throughout the campaign (three others died in a helicopter crash and an Australian SAS lance-corporal was gored to death by an elephant during a cross-border patrol) out of a total of 114 British and Commonwealth deaths, which further cemented their growing reputation within the army as first-rate strategic reconnaissance troops.

The last of the colonial wars in which 22 SAS was involved was probably the most influential on their post-war development: Operation Storm, the campaign to free the province of Dhofar in southern Oman* from the presence of a communist-backed insurgency. The roots of this rebellion lay in several different areas of Omani life. The Sultan, Sai'id bin Taimur (the same man who was ruling the country during the Jebel Akhdar revolt), was a feudal and autocratic despot. Although by all accounts a charming and kindly individual, he evidently had little understanding of the modern world and was fearful of its intrusion into his fiefdom. Although oil had been discovered in Oman in the early 1960s, and the country was potentially very wealthy, Sultan Sai'id refused to borrow development funds against future oil revenue, and the infrastructure of the country was essentially medieval. This situation was compounded by Sai'id's belief that by preventing modernisation

* Oman had, of course, never been a British colony *per se* but it was very much a British client during the heyday of the empire.

he would be able to maintain control of the country. Fearful that modern education – even modern techniques of agriculture – might serve as a focus of dissent, he ruthlessly used his armed forces, which were largely composed of British officers on loan and 'contract' (i.e. mercenary) service, and Baluchi mercenaries from Pakistan, to suppress any signs of development, even going to the extent of concreting over newly dug wells and destroying crops.

Not unnaturally this caused some resentment amongst people who were perfectly capable of finding out how the world was changing outside their own borders, and who were, in fact, now being subjected to a stream of propaganda from the communist People's Democratic Republic of Yemen, as the Aden protectorate had become after British withdrawal in 1967, as well as from Cairo, Baghdad and other centres of Arab nationalism. In any case, although the Sultan was, theoretically, an absolute monarch, in practice his freedom of action had always been partly circumscribed by the tribal chiefs of the interior, who traditionally regarded him as an effete plainsman. It was not surprising then that rebellion was breaking out throughout Oman within two years of the SAS's victory on the Jebel Akhdar or that despite the best efforts of the Sultan's Armed forces (SAF), it was growing stronger all the time.

Nevertheless, the discontent of traditionally rebellious mountain tribesmen in a feudal backwater on the Arabian peninsula would have been of little interest were it not for the strategically vital position of Oman at the mouth of the Persian Gulf. Oil from Kuwait, Iraq, Iran and Saudi Arabia was transported in vast quantities through the narrow Straits of Hormuz, which divide Oman from Iran, and an unfriendly government would theoretically possess a stranglehold on a considerable proportion of the world's oil supply. Not surprisingly, there were a number of parties with a strong interest in the outcome of the Dhofari rebellion and it is believed that both Soviet and Chinese aid was making its way to the rebel factions in the mountains.

On 23 July 1970 Sultan Sai'id was deposed in a *coup d'état*, almost certainly engineered by MI6, and replaced by his son Qaboos who had been partly educated in Britain, trained at Sandhurst and had served in a British Army regiment. Since returning to Oman, he had been under virtual house-arrest. The way was now clear for a radical policy change.

One of the earliest priorities was to ensure that there were no further sudden changes of government, and shortly after the coup the first organised SAS group, a team of bodyguards under an SAS warrant officer, arrived to begin round-the-clock protection of Qaboos. This was followed in September by the arrival of fifteen more men under the command of Captain Keith Farnes, who later commanded 21 SAS, who were sent to the Dhofari coastal town of Mirbat to explore ways to defend the coastal plain, which by then was becoming increasingly hostile, and reoccupy the Jebel.

Nevertheless, despite the presence of Farnes and his team in the south of the country, the first SAS operation took place in the far north of Oman, on the Musandam peninsula, and was, as far as can be ascertained, the only operational free-fall jump ever made by 22 SAS. The background to the operation was a report, probably false, that a small group of Iraqis had landed there to subvert the primitive indigenous tribesmen. A joint helicopter and seaborne operation was mounted by the SAS and the Trucial Oman Scouts, followed by G Squadron Air Troop's jump into the Wadi Rawdah on 12 December 1970. Unfortunately this went wrong and Lance-Corporal Paul 'Rip' Reddy died when his parachute failed to open properly after free-falling from 11,000 feet. In the follow-up to the air and sea landings, no conclusive evidence of any incursion was found but there was enough suspicion to leave a troop of SAS for a month to win hearts and minds whilst the real problems of Oman were addressed.

To a very large extent the principal cause of Dhofari unrest – the Sultan – had been removed by the coup and a considerable number of the more traditionalist rebels began to drift back to areas under the new Sultan's control in the months which followed it. This actually served to highlight a division amongst the rebels between a hard-core of communists and more traditionally minded tribesmen who had simply balked at the Sultan's repressive regime; some Dhofaris were now beginning to suffer at the hands of the anti-Islamic communists who behaved in a high-handed, arrogant way in the areas under their control. Nevertheless there were many areas of policy in which rapid changes had to be made if the whole of the province was not going to fall under communist domination. Lieutenant Colonel John Watts, CO of 22 SAS, came up with a five-point plan with which he hoped the SAS might contribute to bringing the situation under control. He argued that the regiment should provide or facilitate:

1. An intelligence cell.
2. An information team.
3. A medical officer supported by SAS medics.
4. A veterinary officer.
5. When possible, the raising of Dhofari soldiers to fight for the Sultan.[19]

The provision of an intelligence cell was organised by 22 SAS's intelligence officer, Major Ray Nightingale, who arranged to staff it with several junior Intelligence Corps NCOs (this was to prove something of a precedent for 22 SAS which subsequently acquired a permanent Intelligence Corps section* at Hereford, and whose intelligence officers are now professionals supplied by the corps). In the wake of the coup they gained access to a number of former dissidents who had returned from the hills and who were in a good position to supply information on the rebels' strength and organisation.

Psychological operations – euphemistically known as 'information services' – were handled by a small team organised by an SAS corporal, John Ward, who proved to have a natural talent for the task. A field surgical team came from the Royal Army Medical Corps; a vet from the Royal Army Veterinary Corps. The role of 22 SAS, in squadron strength and using the cover name British Army Training Team (BATT), could now start in earnest.

The first task was to establish outposts from which Civil Action Teams could begin providing aid for the community. The permanent basis of the teams were medically trained SAS NCOs, living amongst the Dhofaris, providing them with healthcare and arranging other aid as appropriate, and as this fundamental project was getting underway the second major facet of 22 SAS's work was also beginning: the raising of the Dhofari militias.

The original intention was to make the *Firqats*† non-tribal in the hope that it would decrease friction within the units and make them less independent and easier to control. In practice this didn't work out: the first non-tribal unit, the *Firqat Salahadin*, suffered badly from

* Generally referred to as the 'Green Slime' because of the Intelligence Corps' usual cypress-green beret, although they actually wear the SAS beige beret when serving with the regiment.
† Band of men (Arabic).

tribal strife and thereafter *Firqats* were tribally based. For their SAS mentors, the BATT, serving with the Dhofaris could be something of a culture shock:

> 'All the news is good,' I whispered. 'We will get the automatic rifles for your Firqat but the *geysh** are short of equipment. We will have to buy it in Salalah. By the way, I have a present for you.'
>
> I felt under my shirt and produced a brand new Smith and Wesson .357 magnum, fully loaded. The pistol gleamed blue-black in my hand, accentuating the whiteness of its ivory handle.
>
> 'It is too big,' he said. 'I want one smaller, an automatic.'
>
> I was staggered. It was a beautiful and expensive pistol which I had gone to much trouble to get for him. I had thought he would be delighted with it, or if not, would have had the courtesy to pretend to be . . .
>
> It took BATT some time to understand that no such sentiment as gratitude exists in the average Dhofari's character. Since all things come from God anyway, and the giver is merely doing the will of God, he cannot help himself, so what is the point of being grateful to him?[20]

The military advantage of the *Firqats* was not in the firepower they provided but in their detailed knowledge of the ground they were fighting over and the tactics of the rebels. Their psychological impact on the *Adoo*† was enormous: having forsaken religion and traditions for communism, the rebels were shaken to see individuals that they knew and respected going back into the government fold – and being welcomed. They were not much use in set-piece battles where the superior discipline and battle drills of the SAF were very evident, but in intelligence collection and reconnaissance patrolling they came into their own, becoming an invaluable and indispensable part of the war effort, despite the suspicions of the SAF establishment towards them.

In addition to civil aid projects and raising the *Firqats*, 22 SAS were involved in wider military operations and also took part in the most significant single battle of the campaign at Mirbat on 19 July 1972.

---

* Army (Arabic).
† Enemy.

The first major operation was Operation Jaguar, launched in October 1971 and designed to regain a permanent presence on the Jebel for the SAF. This involved two complete squadrons of SAS (B and G); two companies of SAF; a pioneer platoon; some *Askars** and five separate *Firqats*; the force adding up to some seven hundred and fifty men under the command of Lieutenant Colonel Watts, CO of 22 SAS. This succeeded in seizing the strategically important airstrip at 'Lympne' as well as subsequently allowing the Sultan's forces to capture the rebel village of Jibjat, thus firmly establishing an operational toehold on what had, hitherto, been the heart of rebel territory. It also accounted for the first SAS soldier killed by enemy action in Oman – Sergeant Steve Moores – since the Jebel Akhdar campaign. For the men of B Squadron who took part, the most memorable aspect of the operation was the initial approach march to 'Lympne' with each man carrying loads well in excess of a hundred and twenty pounds across miles of broken, rocky terrain.

The battle of Mirbat in July 1972 has rightly gone down in legend as a supreme example of the courage and tactical acumen of members of 22 SAS. It resulted from the success that the Sultan's forces, including the SAS, were enjoying in their counter-insurgency campaign and the fear, on the part of the rebel leaders, that they were losing their grip on the population of Dhofar. In consequence, it appears that the rebels decided to mount a large-scale attack against the town of Mirbat to demonstrate their continued ascendancy over the SAF.

At first light on 19 July, more than two hundred and fifty guerrillas of the Dhofar Liberation Front (the combatant arm of the PFLOAG†) began to move towards Mirbat, covered by fire from both mortars and recoil-less artillery. Their opposition consisted of approximately thirty *Askars* armed with .303 Lee-Enfield rifles, twenty-five members of the Dhofar Gendarmerie (DG) armed with FNs‡ and a light machine gun, and nine members of 22 SAS under Captain Mike Kealy: eight of them from B Squadron, and one from G Squadron who was there to do a stores check before his squadron took over responsibility for the town later that day. The three groups of defenders were all occupying different

---

* Sudanese mercenaries.

† Popular Front for the Liberation of the Occupied Arabian Gulf.

‡ Fabrique Nationale, a popular abbreviation for the FN 'Fusil Automatique Leger' rifle.

locations: the *Askars* were in the town Wali's* fort; the Gendarmes were in their own fort; the SAS were in their two-storey BATT-house.

Alerted by the incoming mortar fire, the SAS team stood to, expecting that it was no more than the usual 'dawn chorus' of harassing fire from the Jebel. Instead, they soon realised that they were being subjected to a sustained attack. After sending a contact report, the SAS men began responding using their own support weapons – an 81mm mortar and a .50 Browning heavy machine gun – whilst a Fijian SAS corporal, Labalaba,† made his way across 500 metres of open ground to the DG fort to operate a 25-pounder field gun.

The rebel attack was concentrated on the DG fort, probably with the aim of capturing the field gun. After Labalaba reported that he had been 'chinned' by a bullet he was joined by Takavesi who helped him for a short period before he too was hit. By now the rebels were very close to the gun-pit and Labalaba was using the artillery piece as a direct fire weapon, aiming over open sights at the enemy only a few hundred yards away.

At this point Labalaba decided to give up on the field gun and use a 66mm mortar which was nearby. As he made his way towards it, he was shot in the neck: he died almost immediately. Takavesi was now on his own, wounded, and firing his SLR (Self-Loading Rifle) one-handed from the gun-pit at the *Adoo* less than a hundred metres away.

In the BATT-house, Captain Kealy decided to take the team medic, Trooper Tobin, to the DG fort. They covered each other across the open ground but as they arrived at the gun-pit, Tobin was mortally wounded by shots to the face. Taking cover in a nearby trench, Kealy was now able to talk to Takavesi, but they appeared to be in an impossible situation, virtually overrun by the guerrillas attacking the fort. It was now that salvation arrived in the form of Strikemaster ground attack aircraft of the Sultan's air force, which made repeated bombing and strafing runs at the guerrillas, despite heavy ground fire. As the momentum of the rebel attack faltered, members of G

---

* The Governor of Dhofar Province.

† The British Army recruited a number of Fijians during the 1950s and 1960s, several of whom gravitated towards the SAS. A second Fijian, Takavesi, was also present at Mirbat and went on to become one of the most highly decorated soldiers in the British Army.

Squadron, under Major Alistair Morrison, arrived to reinforce the position.

It was a complete coincidence that there were two SAS squadrons in Dhofar at the time of the Mirbat battle, and it was fortunate that one of them had just completed its build-up training and was literally about to take over from the first, providing an entirely fortuitous but extremely effective quick reaction force. In the face of the stiff resistance of the Mirbat garrison, close air support and unexpected reinforcements, the *Adoo* had no option but to withdraw, leaving behind thirty-eight bodies. In contrast the defenders suffered nine dead, including Labalaba and Tobin.

As well as being a stiff military defeat, the battle of Mirbat was a major symbolic blow to the rebels, demonstrating that even in strength they were unable to overwhelm a well-organised garrison of the Sultan's forces. Although it would be incorrect to ascribe the victory at Mirbat entirely to the BATT, the action of Labalaba, Takavesi and Kealy at the gun-pit, supported by the mortar and machine guns at the BATT-house, probably delayed the *Adoo* enough to ensure that they had not achieved any of their objectives by the time that air support (delayed by low cloud) arrived. Both the DG and the *Askars* in the Wali's fort fought well and deserve their share of the credit for resisting the attack.

Mirbat marked a watershed in the SAS involvement in Oman. General de la Billière later wrote: 'Now that the Sultan's Armed Forces had been built up into an effective, self-contained means of defence, properly trained and equipped, the SAS was able to step back into a supporting role ... we concentrated on rehabilitating the *Firqats* on their own territory up the mountain, helping to rebuild their villages and set agriculture in motion again.'[21]

The Dhofar campaign, Operation Storm, proved beyond all doubt that victory is only achieved in counter-insurgency campaigns when the hearts and minds of the population are won over. Again, it is important to get away from the idea that the campaign was won by the SAS on their own – approximately twelve thousand regular soldiers (10,000 members of the Sultan's Armed Forces, a battalion of Jordanians, a battalion group of Iranians as well as the British contribution) actually took part in the campaign, of whom fewer than a hundred and fifty at any one time were members of the SAS – but they did play an important role in pioneering civil aid to the population of Dhofar in a classic illustration of what can be achieved by a well-trained special forces unit without necessarily resorting to the violence of which they are undoubtedly capable. The SAS took part in a good deal of combat in the Oman – twelve members of the regiment died there – but there is little doubt that their most important role was in providing and organising civil aid for the Dhofaris, and in training and organising the *Firqats* to fight their own battles for their own territory. It is a lesson that, even now, many governments and many armed forces remain unable, or unwilling, to learn.

Britain's withdrawal from empire has taken up a great deal of effort and expenditure since the end of the Second World War, and protecting those parts of it which remain has been a major, and probably unwanted, commitment. But it has ensured that the British Armed Forces have acquired an unrivalled breadth of experience in operating under different conditions, with constantly changing levels of operational freedom and flexibility imposed from above. 22 Special Air Service had been given scope to develop from a narrow operational specialisation – jungle patrolling in low-intensity operations – into a much wider-ranging role that, by the end of the 1970s, encompassed desert and urban operations, civil aid, the raising and training of irregular militias, and counter-terrorism in the European environment. It was this extraordinary range of experience that was to establish 22 SAS as the 'senior' western special operations formation.

10

Vietnam

After Dien Bien Phu we became prisoners of the Viet Minh. We turned our backs on two thousand years of Judeo-Christian civilisation and went back into the land of the red termites.

Lieutenant Colonel Marcel Bigeard

As we have seen, the French returned to their Indo-Chinese colonies (which comprised the modern countries of Vietnam, Laos and Cambodia) in September and October 1945 to find that they had, to a large extent, fallen under the control of the local nationalist and communist movements that had been encouraged, trained and armed by the OSS, and to a lesser extent by SOE, to fight the Japanese. The largest of these, the Viet Minh led by Ho Chi Minh and his military commander Vo Nguyen Giap, had actually succeeded in driving the Japanese out of large areas of northern Vietnam (Tongkin) by the end of 1944, nine months before the final Japanese surrender. In consequence, the returning French colonial administration had no option but to take them, and their demands, seriously.

France's aim was certainly the resumption of full control of its colony, but the government hoped to be able to accomplish this subtly enough to accommodate the communists' aspirations whilst at the same time stimulating conservative and anti-communist groups that would balance out the Viet Minh's undoubtedly powerful influence. What neither side wanted in the immediate aftermath of the Second World War was a long-drawn-out guerrilla conflict.

Nevertheless, despite their efforts, that is what emerged. In November 1946 the French bombarded the Viet Minh-held town of Haiphong with the intention of forcing the Viet Minh into serious negotiation, and shortly afterwards they moved into Hanoi, the capital of Tongkin which had been under Viet Minh control since the Japanese surrender. The French tactic backfired, the Viet Minh retreated to their strongholds in the highlands and the guerrilla war began in earnest.

French strategy in their war against the Viet Minh centred on constructing military strongpoints at key locations throughout the country, attempting to locate concentrations of guerrillas and destroying them using conventional tactics. This was bound to fail: large areas of the country being in guerrilla hands meant that French logistics were stretched past breaking point, and the weakness caused by poor logistics meant that sudden concentrations of guerrilla strength could overwhelm isolated garrisons and outposts in conventional fighting. In May 1954 the beleaguered French garrison of Dien Bien Phu, close to the border with Laos, was overrun by the Viet Minh, and the French Army in Indo-China was effectively defeated. In July 1954, the country was partitioned at the Geneva conference into a communist north, ruled by the Viet Minh, and a non-communist south, in which the minority Catholic élite held sway with French backing initially, but soon as an American client state.

Insurgency in Indo-China did not end in 1954, however. For the Viet Minh of South Vietnam, concessions that they had apparently been granted at Geneva never materialised: there was no amnesty for former guerrillas; there were no free elections (there weren't any in the North either); and they were subjected to harassment by South Vietnamese security forces. In 1957 the Viet Minh began to reactivate their disused networks for propaganda and intelligence; in 1958 they began a campaign of terrorism and assassination, killing approximately seven hundred South Vietnamese officials that year; and in 1959 the government of North Vietnam began supplying arms and advisors to the rebels.

It is worth pointing out at this stage that the rebellion in South Vietnam was not, in its early days, purely communist in character. Although it was dominated by communists, much of its support came from individuals, particularly in rural areas, who were disaffected by the authoritarian policies of Ngo Dinh Diem, the South Vietnamese President. The National Liberation Front, or Viet Cong, was genuinely supported by a wide cross-section of the population: in 1961, it was estimated that of approximately thirty-five thousand operational Viet Cong in South Vietnam, only 400 were from the North.

The rapid escalation of Viet Cong activity in South Vietnam excited a considerable amount of interest in the US government. As we have seen, the CIA was the primary agency with responsibility for conducting special operations in peacetime and in 1961 and 1962 they began the process that would lead to full-scale US military involvement in Vietnam by introducing ten twelve-man special forces A-teams, of the 1st and 7th Special Forces Groups, into Darlac Province. The mission of the Green Berets was a civil aid programme: the US soldiers protected the Rhade tribe, who inhabited the area, in a network of fortified villages, and also trained and armed locally recruited militia as Civilian Irregular Defence Groups (CIDG). While this was taking place schools and dispensaries were established and a mobile reaction force of locals was organised to help any villages in the area that came under attack. Two years later, several hundred villages, 300,000 civilians and several hundred square miles of territory had been effectively secured from the Viet Cong.[1]

Unfortunately, this was not the way the US Army wanted to fight its war. As the number of American military personnel in Vietnam increased, it was inevitable that the army would assume responsibility for counter-insurgency operations from the CIA. This led to a change of emphasis: conventional forces need a yardstick to measure their performance and the most convenient one, in counter-insurgency operations, is usually body count. There was no particular dispute that special forces' tactics worked: they clearly did; but such subtle, long-term operations could not satisfy the pressure to resolve the situation *now*. Almost inevitably, special forces teams came under pressure to mobilise their Montagnard* tribal protégés into structured, full-time counter-guerrilla units, whilst conventional units, with their South Vietnamese counterparts, conducted search and destroy operations, supported by US Air Force bombing of Viet Cong-held areas of the South and strategic targets in the North. As we have seen, the majority of Viet Cong recruits came from South Vietnam and the consequence of the US Army's search and destroy tactics was that even when the casualties were VC members (and as many as forty per cent of those killed were innocent bystanders as early as 1963),

---

* Mountain-dwelling Vietnamese tribes.

they were still the fathers and mothers, sons and daughters, brothers and sisters of the population the US was claiming to be saving from communism.

The 5th Special Forces Group (5th SFG) deployed to Vietnam in October 1964 as the nucleus of the special forces counter-insurgency programme. When they left in 1970, they had been responsible for 'setting up 49,902 economic aid projects, 34,334 educational projects, 35,468 welfare projects; supplying 14,934 transportation facilities; supporting nearly half a million refugees; digging 6,436 wells and repairing 1,949 kilometres of road; building 129 churches, 272 markets, 110 hospitals and 398 dispensaries; and building 1,003 classrooms and 670 bridges'.[2] But this enormous effort was a drop in the ocean in comparison to the vast effort expended by the South Vietnamese and United States armies on killing members of the same population that the special forces were trying to aid: in reality, the special forces civil aid programmes had no prospect of working as an effective part of a counter-insurgency programme after the commitment of US air and ground forces in a conventional role.

The civil aid programmes were not, however, the only arena of activity for US special forces in Vietnam. In addition to the 5th SFG, the Military Assistance Command Vietnam (MACV) also created, in April 1964, a strategic reconnaissance and special operations force under the cover-name Studies and Observation Group (MACV-SOG), using high-quality personnel channelled into it through 5th SFG (which also administered the unit). Highly classified during the war and working direct to the US Joint Chiefs-of-Staff rather than to the American commander in theatre, SOG was, in command terms, a truly strategic unit, although its actual impact on the course of the war was negligible.

SOG's first operation in the spring of 1964 was Project Leaping Lena, a joint American-Vietnamese effort to conduct strategic long-range reconnaissance and target acquisition patrols against Viet Cong targets in South Vietnam and across the border in Laos. Small teams of South Vietnamese were parachuted into Laos targeted against the Viet Cong logistics infrastructure, but inadequate training meant that the majority of them were compromised, captured and killed by the Viet Cong and their allies in the Pathet Lao (the Laotian communist insurgency). This was followed, in the autumn of 1964, by Project

Delta, which was to become the principal special operations unit of the Vietnam war.

Project Delta's main role was

> to conduct . . . long-range reconnaissances inside South Vietnam. We were asked to go ahead of large operations – division or two-brigade sized operations – and test the water. We were to go in a week or ten days before and look the country over. If we got discovered and got into a heavy firefight, we'd know we were in a hot area. Then, it was up to MACV in Saigon to decide what the big operation did. DELTA also did bomb damage assessment, hunter-killer missions, and special purpose raids. Our job was hairy. A guy could get killed.[3]

The first year of Delta's existence was undistinguished but in June 1965 it was taken over by Major Charlie Beckwith, a special forces officer who had spent 1962 and 1963 on exchange as a troop commander in 22 SAS. Beckwith's SAS service was a revelation to him: he was impressed by the British regiment's relentless pursuit of excellence and sought, on his return to the US special forces, to persuade his superiors that an SAS capability was something the US Army should have. This was not a message that the US military hierarchy wanted to hear from a junior officer but, despite this, Beckwith was given control of Delta in Vietnam as the next best thing. The majority of the operations they conducted were remarkably similar to those of the SAS in Borneo:

> The job was to look at two large trail complexes coming out of the TRI-Border area and hitting route 19. When we were about four kilometres away from one of the junctions, we decided to stop. There were mountains to the west, but where we stood it was hilly. We spent the night in a thicket. I thought the Vietnamese made a good choice. We sat there all night. I didn't sleep a damn wink. You couldn't have drilled a flax seed up my ass with a sledgehammer. I was scared . . .
>
> Around noon we hit the first trail. There was nothing moving, but looking at the ground we could tell there had been a lot of activity in the area.
>
> The Vietnamese lieutenant in charge said we should break up

in a circle and observe the trail from hidden positions. This was a good little drill I'd learned in Malaya [with the SAS]. I climbed into a large bamboo brake adjacent to the trail. I figured, shit, ain't nobody going to see me in here. I felt I could even smoke. I had just settled down for a long quiet wait, pulled out some rations, added a little curry powder to my little plastic bag of rice, when all of a sudden, directly over my head, I heard an ear shattering scream. I nearly pissed all over myself. An enormous black gibbon ape swung down and looked me straight in the face.[4]

Delta was not the only special forces unit operating in the long-range reconnaissance role. SOG developed several 'projects' designed to conduct cross-border operations including Shining Brass which operated in Laos, and three field commands – Command and Control South, Central and North (CCS, CCC and CCN respectively) – which used mercenaries and Montagnard tribesmen as proxies for cross-border incursions. Many of the operations of these later projects remain classified but it is believed that CCN mounted a number of incursions into North Vietnam and even China. Three of the CCN reconnaissance teams (RT* Idaho, RT Michigan and RT Ohio) were trained in HALO (high-altitude low-opening) parachute techniques but it is not altogether clear whether any were used in this role.

One aspect of special operations that the US developed in Vietnam and which remains high on their special operations agenda is the rescue of POWs. Between 1966 and 1973, 119 operations were launched to rescue prisoners of which ninety-eight were specifically intended to rescue Americans. None of these ninety-eight was successful: only one American serviceman was retrieved and he died of wounds received during the operation. The most interesting, and most spectacular, of these operations was Operation Ivory Coast: the Son Tay raid.

Operation Ivory Coast, which took place on 20–21 November 1970, was mounted amidst intense secrecy. It came about because of painstaking work by Norval Clinebell, an air force intelligence analyst based at Fort Belvoir, Virginia, whose task was to collate information regarding the whereabouts of US POWs in North Vietnam. In early 1970, Clinebell became convinced that he had located the site of a

---

* Reconnaissance Team.

POW compound in the town of Son Tay, twenty-three miles from Hanoi. Clinebell briefed his superiors, who agreed with his analysis, and planning immediately began to launch a rescue mission.

Operational security for such a highly sensitive raid into North Vietnam forced the decision that US commanders within Vietnam should be kept in the dark about the mission, and the raiding force was recruited entirely from special forces based at Fort Bragg. Command of the ground element was given to Colonel Arthur 'Bull' Simons, recently returned from serving with SOG, and his unit was allocated a section of Eglin air force base in Florida to prepare, train and rehearse for the operation.

From the middle of June, the fifty-six-man assault team prepared for their task, provisionally scheduled for October, but one disquieting factor began to enter into the planning of the raid: from July 1970, air reconnaissance of Son Tay began to indicate that the compound was empty. It is not entirely clear why the operation was not abandoned at this stage. This can partly be explained by the fact that senior special forces officers were desperately keen to gain formal authority to mount further raids into the North and felt that even a raid on an empty camp would help their cause. In addition, the evidence of the abandonment of Son Tay was equivocal and inconclusive; there was also probably an element of wishful thinking.

Shortly before midnight on 20 November the assault force lifted off from their forward mounting base in Thailand. In the month before the raid new evidence had suggested that the Son Tay compound was reoccupied but there was no confirmation of any prisoners there. Three hours after lift-off, the assault force, in five HH-53 Jolly Green Giant helicopters and one Sea King, with C-130 gunships and fighter bombers in support, reached their objective. Having flown in as low as fifty feet along carefully planned routes, they were undetected and achieved complete surprise. Part of the force was accidentally landed in a compound containing hundreds of Chinese military advisors, but the overwhelming firepower available to the Americans enabled them to effectively eliminate any threat that they posed. At the prison itself the assault team, led by Captain Dick Meadows, did encounter guards but no prisoners: the intelligence had been correct.

From a technical point of view, Operation Ivory Coast was a success: intelligence analysis and reporting were virtually perfect; Simons' assault force reached its objective, dealt with any threats, searched the prison compound and exfiltrated without any serious casualties; and had any POWs been there, it is certain that they would have been rescued. But there weren't any, and this fact was at least half-known to the officers who organised and led the operation. The Son Tay raid was a bold undertaking that could easily have turned into a suicide mission for those taking part in the assault; the decision to send the assaulters in when it was known they were unlikely to achieve their aim was profoundly flawed.

Along with US special forces and their South Vietnamese allies, other contributors to the Vietnam War also sent special forces units, the most important of which were the Australian and New Zealand SAS. The New Zealand SAS, as we have seen, was directly formed to bolster 22 SAS for their campaign in Malaya but the Australian SAS Regiment, as it became in August 1964, had slightly different roots.

During the Second World War the Australian Army had formed independent companies to operate in the Pacific theatre, successfully harrying the Japanese rear areas on islands like Borneo and New Guinea but, along with most special forces units of the Allies, these had not survived the general demobilisation at the war's end. During the reorganisation of Australia's Armed Forces in the late 1940s, there were no plans to incorporate any special forces capability and it wasn't until the early 1950s that pressure began to mount to create an SAS-type unit.

In the immediate post-war era Australian defence policy was based on the concept of operating as part of a British Commonwealth command structure. With Japan defeated, there was no obvious threat to Australian security that could not be countered by using volunteer reserve-type formations, and Australian regular forces were to a large extent integrated into British-led operations like the Commonwealth Division that fought in Korea. Nevertheless, thinking changed in the 1950s with the use of nationalist and communist resistance to the colonial powers of South-East Asia, following the defeat of France in Indo-China, for example, as well as the Malayan Emergency. Strategically, it became evident that Australia needed to be able to field formations independent of British or Commonwealth support, alongside existing defence commitments. Consequently, in October

1956, plans were announced to form a regular brigade group for service safeguarding Australia's immediate strategic interests in the Pacific/South-East Asian region, and that the brigade would include an SAS squadron.

The SAS unit was formed, initially as an independent company (1st Special Air Service Company, Royal Australian Infantry), towards the end of 1957, and based in the Perth suburb of Swanbourne, Western Australia. Training was orientated towards raiding, harassment operations and surveillance patrols – the classic capabilities developed by the SAS of the Second World War but adapted to Australian/South-East Asian conditions.

Selection for the new SAS unit was initially made on paper by the infantry postings branch but experience on exercises made it clear that some form of aptitude course was essential in order to find the right soldiers to man the unit and, in November 1960, the Recondo (reconnaissance-commando) course was introduced. This combined arduous physical selection with training in patrol and raiding techniques, operating in small teams, and it had to be passed by all members of the unit.

The characteristics required by the Australian Army for their SAS soldiers were much the same as for their British counterparts:

> SAS training is tough and exacting. The role of the unit demands a particular type of soldier of outstanding personal qualities. These qualities and make up count more than technical efficiency in his own arm or service. Technical efficiency can be taught, the personal qualities required for long range, long-term operations in enemy territory however are part of a man's character and, although they may be developed over a period, they must be learnt in childhood. These qualities are: initiative, self-discipline, independence of mind, ability to work without supervision, stamina, patience and a sense of humour. The aim is to find the individualist with a sense of self-discipline rather than the man who is a good member of a team. The self-disciplined individualist will always fit well into a team when team work is required but a man selected for team work is by no means always suitable for work outside the team.

The first operational deployment for the Australian SAS was in Borneo, where they operated under the command of 22 SAS conducting hearts and minds operations with jungle tribes, undertaking long-term border surveillance patrols and attacking cross-border targets. Although this was a gruelling initiation for the Australians, in extremely arduous conditions, the unit suffered only three fatal casualties, none of which was the result of enemy action – one man was gored to death by an elephant, two others were drowned during a river crossing; even so, Borneo was to give the SAS an enormous advantage when they were finally deployed to Vietnam.

The first Australian SAS soldiers to reach Vietnam arrived as members of the Australian Army Training Team (AATTV) sent to assist the government of South Vietnam in 1962, but it wasn't until the middle of 1965 that a battalion-sized combat unit, the 1st Battalion Royal Australian Regiment (1 RAR), reached the war zone. 1 RAR operated initially under US command, but in 1966 the Australian Prime Minister, Harold Holt, announced that he was increasing the Australian commitment to the war from the 1,400 men of the 1 RAR battalion group and the AATTV, to a task force of 4,500, comprising two infantry battalions, support arms and services, an RAAF helicopter squadron and an SAS squadron, commanded by an Australian brigadier.

When the Australian SAS had been raised to regimental status in 1964, work had started to increase its strength from one squadron to three. By the beginning of 1966 this was complete and it was decided that 3 Squadron would be the first to go to Vietnam. Before the deployment, there had been some misgivings about how the task force commander would employ his SAS troops, and it was particularly feared that he might allocate them to the infantry battalions as reinforcements to their reconnaissance capability, but in the event this was not the case.

The Australian task force began to arrive in Vietnam in June 1966. They had been allocated a TAOR* in Phuoc Tuy province to the south-east of Saigon, a rural area believed to contain at least seven Viet Cong battalions which mainly operated in mountainous rainforest in the north of the province. It was the Australians' job to find them and to eliminate them.

The general principle governing the employment of the Australian

---

* Tactical Area of Responsibility.

SAS in Vietnam was very simple, and not radically different from SAS tasks in Malaya and Borneo. They were inserted from their base at Nui Dat – usually by helicopter – into areas that were believed to contain enemy and patrolled until they found them, after which the Australian task force commander had the option to continue surveillance, to attack them using the SAS patrol on the ground (provided it was a small enemy force!), to bring in infantry or to request an air strike from his American allies. The differences between the Australians' experience in Vietnam and that of the mainly British SAS operations in Malaya and Borneo were in the numbers of enemy that were being confronted and the sheer intensity of much of the fighting.

There were differences also in the conditions in which the Australians operated. In Borneo the shape of the terrain and the nature of the primary jungle effectively ruled out any prospect of night movement but in Vietnam, which was much more densely populated and in which large swathes of the jungle had been cultivated at one time or another, this was not necessarily the case. This had several different effects on operations. In the first instance it ruled out the building of shelters, cooking or smoking at night, all of which had been possible, at least to some extent, during patrols in Borneo. This in turn led to more rapid physical deterioration during operations because it became impossible for patrol members to remain at all dry and thus meant that they would spend a good proportion of each night cold, wet and shivering. The threat of VC movement at night also meant that there was no question of removing boots, which meant that most SAS members suffered from severe fungal infections in their crotches and feet which could become both painful and extremely distracting during operations. Other hazards remained much the same: the jungles of Vietnam contained the usual profusion of stinging and biting insects, together with potentially poisonous snakes, scorpions and spiders; the occasional tiger was also to be encountered.

Although the great majority of SAS patrols in Vietnam were reconnaissance and information reporting, some SAS patrols were specifically tasked to take offensive action, including assaulting potentially large Viet Cong bases:

> The assault was great fun . . . We killed about six plus VC in the first round and grenaded all bunkers on the western perimeter.

From the noises in the bunkers they were definitely occupied. Dennis Cullen pushed forward about ten metres in front and was held by about four VC firing on the assault party with M1 carbines and M3 SMGs. This confused us initially as I thought the support might have mistaken us for VC. We grenaded this trench then neutralised the area behind with M79 rounds. The results were unknown so I decided we had better find the radio before a counter attack was organised. Lobb and Kerkez kept fire up to our line of advance. From the sounds further down the spur line it seemed that a flanking party was setting out.

I stumbled across the radio roughly in the centre of the camp. It was sitting on a rough table under a camouflage of hessian and undergrowth. Fortunately Lobb and Kerkez had missed seeing it otherwise there would have been little to pick up. I grabbed the radio under one arm and stuffed all the documents I could find down my tunic. Fire was now coming from across the valley. Yellow tracer usually signified an RPD in the vicinity so I ordered withdrawal. Several of the more agitated VC were now moving towards us but they were dealt with by Cullen ... The only bodies we claimed were the ones we had shot again to ensure they did not come to life behind us during the assault.[6]

But despite the evident success of the Australian SAS in Vietnam (together with the NZSAS – the New Zealanders provided an SAS troop from December 1968 to February 1971), their operations were the subject of criticism from both inside and outside the regiment. Brigadier 'Sandy' Pearson commanded the Australian task force from October 1968 until September 1969 and later wrote:

In Vietnam, some of their operations appeared to be successful. That is, they provided information and greatly contributed to harassment and attrition. But we were never successful in contacting enemy – based on that information – by normal infantry. What happened too, was that the time spent on the ground between insertion and extraction of SAS patrols got progressively shorter. In fact, they were requesting almost

immediate extraction – in some cases minutes only – which made
the whole operation farcical and expensive in helicopter hours.

SAS officers accept the validity of some of Pearson's criticisms but the
reality is that the SAS were being used in a medium reconnaissance
role which, although easily within their capabilities, was not entirely
appropriate for the level of operational support and effort that an SAS
patrol requires. Pearson evidently did not want to tie up resources by
inserting small patrols which could not effectively defend themselves
against the type of forces he was expecting – and hoping – that they
would meet, but as that was inevitable in the role in which he was
using them, it was clearly a vicious circle. The only solution would
be to insert larger, more aggressively armed patrols, thus losing the
advantage of stealth that the SAS clearly possessed.

Strategic special forces operations undoubtedly took place during
the Vietnam War but the Australian troop commitment – in effect a
brigade – essentially ruled out any but the most peripheral SAS role.
The fact that the US government was prepared to conceal 'illegal' strategic
cross-border operations from the US Congress made it highly unlikely
that they would involve an ally in them. As a result, Australian SAS
operations outside Phuoc Tuy province were limited to training South
Vietnamese soldiers in SAS skills, and giving advice and assistance to
their American special forces colleagues.

The Australian SAS left Vietnam in October 1971 after five years of
hard jungle operations and with many lessons learned. Of the many
special forces/Commando/Long Range Reconnaisance Patrol units that
took part in the Vietnam War, the Australian SAS Regiment probably
earned the highest reputation amongst both their friends and their
enemies: to the Viet Cong they had become the 'Phantoms of
the Jungle'.

It is worth mentioning, at this point, the recurrent rumours that
members of 22 SAS became involved in the Vietnam War. There is
very little hard evidence that this happened to any great extent, but it is
undoubtedly true that members of 22 SAS who had left the British Army
and joined the Australian Army served there, and in at least one case an
officer who had served in the Australian SAS in Vietnam subsequently
joined 22 SAS. Nevertheless, a senior former SAS officer did suggest
to the author during the course of a private conversation that he had

visited Vietnam during the war and an account has emerged recently suggesting how members of 22 SAS might have become involved in some aspects of the war. This account is supposedly by a participant and claims that in 1966–7 an SAS team was involved in training the Royal Thai Special Forces, and that the SAS subsequently took part in operations with the Thais inside Laos aimed at the Ho Chi Minh Trail, the North's principal supply route into South Vietnam. In the absence of corroboration it is impossible to assess the truth of this story.

11

Special Forces and Counter-Terrorism: fighting fire with fire

International and domestic terrorism has been a plague in society since the nineteenth century but it is only in recent years that democratic governments have sought to directly counter it by resorting to specialist military – rather than police or paramilitary – force. The impetus that led to the development of special counter-terrorism capabilities by military special forces was provided by one major incident – the Black September attack on the Israeli team at the Munich Olympics in 1972 – and also, to a very large extent, by the Republican violence in Northern Ireland which re-erupted in 1969 after a seven-year lull.

The terrorist attack at the Munich Olympics began on 5 September 1972 when a group of eight armed terrorists of the Black September group, cover-name for a faction of the Palestine Liberation Organisation, infiltrated the athletes' 'village' and burst into an apartment holding eleven members of the Israeli team. Two of the Israelis resisted the terrorists and were shot and killed; the rest were taken hostage.

The terrorists' demands were that 234 Palestinian prisoners held in Israel be released along with members of the Red Army Faction (the Baader-Meinhof gang) held in West German prisons. The West German government was prepared to accept the terrorists' blackmail but the government of Israel steadfastly refused. After seventeen hours of negotiations the terrorists agreed to move, by military helicopter, to Fürstenfeld military airfield from where they expected to be flown to Cairo but where, in fact, the police and army planned to ambush them.

As the terrorists and hostages left the helicopters, several police snipers opened fire killing two of the terrorists and wounding several others, and a military assault team with armoured car support began to move forwards. But two of the police snipers, with terrorists in their sights, lost their nerve and failed to fire, allowing the surviving terrorists to get the hostages back on board the helicopters and, as a firefight developed, to blow them up. All of the hostages, a German policeman and five terrorists died; three terrorists were wounded and captured.[1] This appalling outcome was compounded by the fact that it had been broadcast live on television, and the shockwaves ran round the Western world: the Munich massacre was a disaster for the West German government.

Probably the first military force to react was 22 SAS. Lieutenant Colonel Peter de la Billière had taken over as commanding officer in January 1972 at the height of Operation Storm, having served in and around 22 SAS since 1956.* In the spring of 1972 he had asked a young troop commander, Captain Andrew Massey (formerly of the Royal Corps of Transport), to write a paper outlining a role for the SAS in countering terrorism. Massey came up with the idea of a special team, on short notice standby, trained in techniques of close-quarter battle and hostage rescue, which could be deployed in support of the police to help end any terrorist incidents on British soil. De la Billière was so impressed by Massey's concept that he 'staffed' it through to SAS Group HQ and from there to the Ministry of Defence where it came to rest. Not surprisingly, the government was most unwilling to be seen to be developing a role for the military in policing mainland Britain and it was no doubt hoped, with the naïve optimism that tends to characterise politicians, senior civil servants and high-ranking military officers who are faced with difficult decisions, that the problem of major terrorist incidents would not affect Britain.

In fact within three days of the Munich massacre the Prime Minister, Edward Heath, had asked the Director of Military Operations what measures the army could take to respond to a similar incident. The DMO turned to de la Billière at Hereford and Massey's concept was

---

* De la Billière was probably the first 'professional' SAS officer: after leaving the 1st Battalion of the Durham Light Infantry for 22 SAS in 1956, he never again served with his regiment.

revived and brought to life in the form of Operation Pagoda, the SAS counter-terrorist team: a permanent squad on twenty-four-hour standby to deal with any major terrorist situation in Britain. Similar processes in France and Germany caused the establishment of, respectively, the Groupe d'Intervention de la Gendarmerie Nationale (GIGN) and Grenzschutzgruppe 9 (GSG9) which formed part of the Bundesgrenzschutz or Federal Border Protection Service,* and, somewhat later, Special Forces Operational Detachment – Delta in the United States.

The counter-terrorist squadron provides manpower for three distinct units in the fight against terrorism: the red and blue special projects teams, identically manned and equipped units which would, *in extremis*, be able to deal with at least two major incidents at the same time; and the nucleus of the Northern Ireland troop, based in Ulster, where they are the focus of the regiment's part in the ongoing campaign to contain Republican terrorism. The Special Projects Teams are the subject of much scrutiny and imitation by Britain's allies: both the Australian and New Zealand SAS have added a very similar capability to their armoury of operational techniques, whilst the United States created Delta Force in direct and conscious imitation of 22 SAS under Colonel Charlie Beckwith, a hugely experienced Vietnam veteran who had served in 22 SAS in the 1960s. It is an acknowledged fact that counter-terrorist techniques are willingly shared between the democracies in order to maximise their chances of defeating this menace, and the Western world has become an enormously more hostile environment for terrorists since 1972.

Two successful hostage rescues in the 1970s set the tone for the practical response to terrorism that characterised the 1980s and they resulted in a dramatic reduction in the number of major international terrorist incidents aimed at the Western powers.

On 27 June 1976, an Air France flight from Tel Aviv to Paris was hijacked after a stopover in Athens by two Germans and two Palestinians. They ordered the pilot to fly the aircraft to Benghazi in Libya where it was refuelled and then on to Entebbe Airport in Uganda where it landed in the early hours of the morning the next

---

* The German government was, at that time, sensitive about the creation of a military élite force which might come to be regarded as, for example, a new Waffen-SS.

day. The 258 hostages were then taken from the aircraft to the terminal buildings where they were corralled under guard by the four terrorists from the aircraft and another five who had flown in from elsewhere, additional security being supplied by members of Idi Amin's Ugandan Armed Forces. The terrorists' demand was the release of a number of their colleagues from prisons in France, Germany, Kenya, Switzerland and Israel, and whilst the French, Germans and Swiss were prepared to make a deal, the Israelis were not.

Nevertheless, despite the Israelis' traditional willingness to use force to resolve hostage situations, they held back on this occasion for fear of causing heavy loss of life amongst the many foreign nationals involved in the hijack. This obstacle, however, was removed by the hijackers themselves: during the four days following the hijacking, they released all of the non-Jewish hostages, clearing the way for Israel to take the military option.

Three plans were considered for releasing the hostages: the first involved an airborne descent on Lake Victoria followed by an amphibious assault on the airport; the second involved a ground assault from Kenya; the third, which was ultimately adopted, was for a tactical air landing at the airport itself, using deception to get as close as possible to the airport buildings and massive firepower to suppress opposition from within.

The raiders set off from Lod Airport during the early hours of 3 July on the first leg of their 2,250-mile flight to Entebbe. After a refuelling stop in Sinai they set course south flying over the Red Sea at low level to avoid radar detection and after a final approach over Ethiopia and Kenya closed on the Ugandan airport.

The raiders were being carried aboard four C-130 transports: the first to land carried the mission commander, American-born Lieutenant Colonel Yoni Netanyahu with thirty-five members of the Sayaret Matkal anti-terrorist commando unit dressed as Ugandan soldiers, fifty-two paratroopers, two Land-Rovers and a black Mercedes disguised to look like Idi Amin's personal limousine; the second held seventeen more paratroopers, two armoured personnel carriers and a command jeep; the third held thirty infantrymen from the élite Golani Brigade with another two APCs and a jeep; the fourth carried twenty more Golani infantry, a refuelling crew and a medical team ready to deal with casualties amongst the hostages.

In fact, as the first C-130 touched down and members of the assault team deployed landing lights alongside the runway, the Ugandans were still completely in the dark about what was going on. The bogus limousine with its two escorting Land-Rovers got within forty yards of the airport buildings before a challenge was issued by one of a pair of sentries; the Israelis immediately killed one of them but the other was able to run a little way before he was shot down. This meant that the terrorists in the building were alerted but without any clear idea of what was going on and it was only when the first Israelis appeared in the building that the terrorists began shooting at the hostages.

Netanyahu's men shouted to the hostages to lie down, making the standing terrorists easy targets: two Germans and five Palestinians were swiftly killed (the rest of the terrorists had left the airport) together with an unknown number of Ugandan soldiers and two of the hostages, one of whom was killed by the hijackers and one accidentally by the Israelis. In the meantime, the paratroopers and Golani infantry were securing the perimeter of the airport, engaging the Ugandan security forces and destroying a squadron of eight Ugandan MIG 17 fighters that could have been used to intercept the assault force on its way out. During the fifty minutes that the Israelis were on the ground one Israeli soldiers was seriously wounded and Netanyahu himself was shot and killed whilst directing operations outside the building. One other hostage, Mrs Dora Bloch, a British citizen, had been taken from the airport for medical treatment. She was subsequently murdered by the Ugandan Army in revenge for the assault. With little time for rehearsal and preparation, the Israeli team had expected 20 per cent casualties amongst the hostages.

With their mission complete, the Israeli force took off and flew to Nairobi for an agreed refuelling stop and to rendezvous with a Boeing 707 fitted out as a flying hospital and a second Boeing that acted as an aerial command post.

The lessons of Entebbe were reinforced fifteen months later by the German anti-terrorist group GSG9. On 13 October 1977 four Palestinian terrorists hijacked a Lufthansa Boeing 737 bound from Majorca to Frankfurt. During the next four days they flew to Rome, Cyprus, Bahrain, Dubai, Aden and finally to Mogadishu in Somalia, demanding the release of ten members of the Baader-Meinhof gang from West Germany and two Palestinians held in Turkey, together with $15,000,000. The Germans were prepared to negotiate a peaceful settlement but, at the same time, GSG9 was placed on alert and a twenty-six-man team began to follow the hijacked aircraft around in their own chartered Lufthansa Boeing. At Dubai Airport two members of 22 SAS, Major Alastair Morrison and Sergeant Barry Davies, met up with the GSG9 men, bringing with them a supply of newly developed British stun grenades designed to emit a deafening bang and a blinding flash to disorientate terrorists in the vital first few seconds of an assault.

GSG9 had hoped to be able to launch their assault in Dubai but the plane left on the next leg of its journey, finally arriving in Somalia where the frustrated terrorists vented their spleen at the government's refusal to give in to their blackmail by murdering the airliner's pilot. This first killing represented a crucial watershed in the hijack. Most psychologists agree that once a hostage is deliberately killed by the hijackers, their inhibitions against further killings rapidly fall away and a massacre may result. GSG9 was authorised to move in.

Shortly before midnight on 17 October, Somali soldiers lit a fire on the runway near to the cockpit of the aircraft and, when two terrorists appeared in the cockpit to see what was happening, the attack began. GSG9 operators carrying rubber-coated ladders approached the aircraft and placed the ladders next to the front and rear entrances and the overwing emergency exists. In the next few moments the doors were opened and Morrison and Davies threw in their stun grenades. In the confusion after the explosion, GSG9 men inundated the aircraft, killing three of the terrorists and wounding and capturing the third. Although two of the terrorists had managed to throw grenades, these exploded relatively harmlessly beneath the passenger seats and only four hostages and one GSG9 operator were slightly injured.

Entebbe and Mogadishu were superb examples of simple aggressive hostage rescue operations by highly trained specialist units, which achieved a notable deterrent effect, but their impact was undermined two years after Mogadishu by a US operation which went catastrophically wrong. In November 1979 a large mob of Islamic Revolutionary Guards attacked the United States Embassy in Teheran and took the majority of its staff hostage. Although the Iranian government showed some inclination to negotiate, it was clear that there was no one person or group within the government with the power to deliver a solution and within a few days of the attack, President Jimmy Carter's administration had directed the military to prepare a rescue plan. By coincidence, the attack on the embassy had taken place almost simultaneously with the final proving exercise of the United States' new counter-terrorist unit, Delta Force. As observers were preparing for the post-exercise debrief, Delta's operators were quietly deploying to a secure holding area to begin planning for a rescue mission.

The problem that faced the rescuers was unlikely to be in the assault phase of the rescue mission – storming buildings and freeing hostages is, after all, the bread and butter of units like Delta – but in getting the assault force into position to carry out the rescue undetected and then getting them out again with the rescued hostages.

The solution eventually reached by the American planners was a poor one. It was decided that the operation would be extended over a number of days. The plan was for the assault team to be flown in six C-130s to a staging post in Iran – Desert One – on the first night of the mission, where they would marry up with a fleet of eight helicopters flown off an aircraft carrier. The helicopters would then refuel from aviation gasoline carried aboard three of the C-130s and fly the assault team to Desert Two, a hilly area to the south-east of Teheran where the force would be concealed for the remainder of the day: the helicopters themselves would be located some distance away in a third site. On the second night of the mission, a pre-positioned team commanded by Dick Meadows, a civilian employee of Delta (who as a soldier had led one of the assault groups on the Son Tay raid), would drive out to Delta's location and collect them in six 2½-ton trucks and drive them from there to the compound to begin the assault. The Delta assault force was to be divided into three elements: red, white and blue, each with different highly specific tasks relating to the embassy compound; a second assault force comprising thirteen members of the 10th Special Forces Group formed and trained in Germany would, in the meantime, assault the Iranian Foreign Ministry. The assault force was authorised to kill any Iranians who impeded the progress of the mission.

As the attacks began, the assault force air controller would be bringing the helicopters in from their location outside Teheran and, simultaneously, a company of Rangers would be securing a disused, paved airstrip at Manzireyah. Once the compound had been seized and the surviving hostages centralised, the force would attempt to clear a helicopter landing site within the compound and, if this proved impossible, would then move the hostages to a nearby sports stadium which would act as a defended helicopter landing site. When the hostages and rescuers were clear of the embassy, the entire compound was to be levelled by C-130 gunships. The hostages and assault teams would then be flown to Manzireyah where all personnel would board C-141 Starlifter aircraft and the helicopters would be destroyed and abandoned. The C-141s would then airlift everybody out under cover of fighter escort. Unfortunately, when the mission was launched on 24 April 1980, it did not go according to plan.

Many reasons have been advanced why Operation Rice Bowl failed. These range from political interference in military decision-making by the hated liberal President Carter, through over-complication in the plan, to the strange insistence by the Joint Chiefs-of-Staff that each of the US's four services have a role in the operation. In reality what finished it was poor maintenance by US Navy mechanics on the eight Sea Stallion helicopters. The aircraft were being flown by US Marine Corps pilots and had, for several weeks, been in the care of mechanics who knew that they would have to be flown in desert conditions, but when the time came for the actual operation, the helicopters were prepared by navy mechanics with no experience of preparing helicopters in such a way. Although this might not have been important in the normal course of events, an unforeseen sandstorm on the helicopters' route to Desert One caused one severe malfunction in a helicopter which had to ditch; one other had to turn back whilst a third became unsafe to fly because of hydraulic malfunctions at Desert One. With only five flyable helicopters, the assault group commander, Colonel Beckwith, was obliged to abort the mission.

Unfortunately this tough decision was then compounded by an accident as the helicopters were refuelling prior to evacuation. One of the helicopters collided with a C-130, killing eight men and wounding several others, and Operation Rice Bowl turned from a disappointing but not irretrievable failure into a disaster.

This is not to say that the operation would have worked without the helicopter problem: many of the criticisms levelled at it are perfectly valid. It is impossible to imagine that every other element of such a complex plan would have gone like clockwork but it is equally impossible to predict what else would have gone wrong, and looking for deep structural reasons why Operation Rice Bowl failed is illogical and pointless.

Perhaps the most famous successful hostage rescue took place, with cruel irony, only two weeks after the Desert One fiasco: the SAS assault on the Iranian Embassy in Princes Gate, London, on 5 May 1980. Six days before, on 30 April, a group of six Iraqi-sponsored terrorists had entered the embassy and seized twenty-six hostages, including an armed Metropolitan Policeman, Trevor Lock. The terrorists were ethnic Arabs from the oil-rich Iranian province of Khuzestan (also called Arabistan). Khuzestan had been annexed by Persia in 1926 and the mainly Arabic population were undoubtedly the victims of persecution by the ethnically Persian authorities who had been put in place above them; nevertheless, it is most likely that the terrorists were agents of Iraqi intelligence, intent on causing trouble for the unstable Islamic government of Iran.

The SAS were initially alerted to the incident by PC 'Dusty' Gray, an ex-corporal from the regiment who was now working as a police dog-handler, and the Special Projects Team actually began its move to London before a formal request had been made for SAS assistance. After a brief stopover at the army's language school in Beaconsfield, Red Team were deployed into a building close by the embassy in the early hours of 1 May and set to work on an immediate action option (IA), a rough and ready plan for use in the event that the terrorists started killing their hostages before a deliberate assault plan could be developed.

As the siege dragged on Red Team were relieved by Blue at the embassy and headed for Regent's Park Barracks, where a mock-up of the embassy had been constructed by the Irish Guards Pioneer Section and they were able to work out their plans for a deliberate assault.

The crisis came to a head shortly after midday on 5 May. The terrorists had been assured by their controllers that they would be flying out of Britain with their hostages within twenty-four to forty-eight hours and were not psychologically prepared for a long siege. By day six they were extremely edgy and anxious: at 12.40 p.m. their leader warned the police negotiators that he would start killing hostages in two hours' time but in fact the first shots were heard from inside just fifteen minutes later.

It seemed evident to the police and the SAS assault team that a hostage had been shot, but a decision had been made at ministerial level that the SAS assault could only begin when *two* hostages had been killed. This was based on the principle that a single killing might have been an accident but that a second was much less likely to be so (in reality, it smacks of the futile condition-setting beloved of politicians and civil servants at all levels in order to establish their authority and place in the pecking order). In any event it meant a further delay whilst the Home Secretary was briefed on the current military assessment by de la Billière, who needed permission to bring the assault team to immediate 'notice to move' (i.e. ready to go as soon as the order was given). This order was given (by the police commander at Princes Gate) at about 3.50 p.m. and the assault team were declared ready at 5 p.m., nearly an hour ahead of schedule; thereafter, it was a question of waiting for developments. These were swift in coming.

At 6.20 p.m., the police deployed a priest from the Regent's Park Mosque to talk to the terrorist leader, but whilst the conversation was in progress further shots were heard and shortly afterwards a body was dumped on the steps of the embassy. After permission had been given to remove it, a quick autopsy was carried out which swiftly established that the body (of Abbas Lavasani, the embassy's press officer) had been dead for some hours. The logic of this discovery was that it was now possible, if not probable, that the required two hostages were dead. The police sought a decision from the Home Secretary, who in turn consulted Prime Minister Margaret Thatcher, and permission was given to send the SAS in on the orders of Assistant Commissioner John Dellow who was in command of the incident.

Once the decision had been made to use the military option, the aim of the negotiators shifted somewhat. At least part of their task now became to lull the terrorists into a false sense of security, and they sought to do this by agreeing to the terrorists' demand that they bring a bus to transport the terrorists and hostages to Heathrow Airport. In reality, as this was happening, the assault team was moving into position for the attack. The surviving recording of the negotiator talking to the terrorist leader culminates in the following sequence:

Salim (terrorist leader): We are listening to some suspicion . . . er . . . movements.
Negotiator: There are no suspicious movements.
Salim: There is suspicion, OK. Just a minute . . . I'll come back again . . . I'm going to check.

The sounds that Salim had heard were members of Red Team on the roof, preparing to abseil down the rear of the building, and a pair from Blue Team placing a frame charge on the front window prior to scurrying back into cover. As Salim left the phone, the assault commander, Major Hector Gullan, gave the order 'Go! Go! Go!' and a large stun charge in the embassy's light well was detonated. The explosion was audible halfway across London; even so, the tape clearly shows the negotiator repeating *after the detonation*: 'Salim, there are no suspicious movements'!

It is not technically difficult to storm a single building like the Iranian Embassy, but it is difficult to storm such a building *and* rescue all or most of the hostages within, and it was here that the enormous skill and long months of training paid off for the SAS assault force. In the first few seconds of the assault, one of the terrorists did open fire on the hostages, killing one of them, but very shortly afterwards the assault force had killed four of the terrorists and a fifth was shot by a sniper stationed in Hyde Park. The sixth survived because the soldiers were unable to positively identify him within the building; only two of the hostages died.

The successful conclusion to the Iranian Embassy siege caused a worldwide ripple of admiration for the capabilities of the SAS as a hostage rescue force and caused a shudder of fear amongst terrorists, and since May 1980, Great Britain has seen very little international (as opposed to Irish Republican) terrorism. Despite this, the hostage rescue training has not been in vain and the Special Projects Teams have been sent into action several times to less public events including, for example, the rescue of a prison officer held hostage by inmates at Peterhead prison in Scotland in the late 1980s.

In parallel with the threat from overseas terrorist groups attempting to further their aims by attacking 'third party' countries, Britain was also faced with its own home-grown terrorist problem resulting from sectarian strife in the province of Northern Ireland. Irish Republican terrorism has never been far from the surface of politics in Ireland since home rule was granted and the island partitioned; organised campaigns of IRA intimidation, robbery, shooting and bombing in Ireland and on the mainland took place on several occasions leading up to the outbreak of the present troubles in 1969. During the Second World War, the IRA had actively sought to assist Nazi Germany, albeit in a small and ineffectual way (in reality, the roots of violent Irish Republicanism are founded in a misty-eyed, sentimental 'blood and soil' fascism very similar to that espoused by the more ideologically inclined German Nazis of the 1930s).

The Republican outbreak in 1969, however, came in response to Protestant Loyalist intimidation of the Roman Catholic Nationalist minority community and their claim for equal civil rights. By mid-August of that year the province of Northern Ireland was close to civil war as Protestant die-hard groups sought to undermine concessions won by the Nationalist community through violence and rioting, and on 14 August members of the 1st Battalion, the Prince of Wales's Own Regiment of Yorkshire (1 PWO), were the first British soldiers deployed onto the streets of Londonderry to separate Protestant from Catholic and attempt to keep the peace.

In the early days of the troubles, the presence of British soldiers was welcomed by most Catholics. They were correctly viewed as having saved several communities from the wrath of drink-fuelled mobs of Loyalist hooligans, but as time passed and the Unionist government of Northern Ireland reasserted itself and its traditionally bigoted stance, the army, which was, of course, operating on behalf of the Northern Ireland government, became increasingly resented and disliked by the Nationalists. After the army was welcomed in 1969, an uneasy truce obtained between the army and Republican paramilitaries through 1970, which broke out into violence and murder on 5 February 1971 when Gunner Robert Curtis of the Royal Artillery was killed by an IRA volunteer named Billy Reid. After that, violence escalated remarkably quickly. The next month three IRA men met three off-duty soldiers in a bar in Belfast city centre and lured them into their cars with a story about going to a party to find some women. All three soldiers, two of whom (John and Joseph McKaig) were brothers aged only seventeen and eighteen, were shot dead by the side of the road where they had stopped to urinate. All three were still clutching beer glasses when they were found.

But by the time that the IRA began to kill soldiers in Northern Ireland, the army had already set up its first special operations unit in the province. In September 1970, Brigadier Frank Kitson was appointed commander of the army's 39 Brigade, a formation which covered Belfast and the east of the province, and he had sought and received permission to create a small special unit for reconnaissance and intelligence collection duties. At this time, Kitson was one of the British Army's foremost experts in counter-insurgency, having served in the Kenya, Malaya and Jebel Akhdar campaigns, and had studied the subject in depth as a defence fellow at University College, Oxford. Kitson recognised that good intelligence was the key to success in counter-insurgency and set about obtaining it. The unit he created at the beginning of 1971 was given the name Mobile Reconnaissance Force (MRF).

The MRF operated in several ways. One strand of their operations involved the use of a handful of 'turned' IRA members (known as 'Freds') who were housed in the married quarters of Palace Barracks in Belfast. They had, typically, been arrested and threatened with long jail sentences (and subsequently internment) if they refused to co-operate with the army. After a thorough debriefing, they were then used to accompany plain-clothes patrols through Belfast, pointing out 'players'* and places of possible interest. Another side of the MRF's work was the attempted interception of IRA bombing teams. Plain-clothes patrols would stake out places where it was believed that a bombing might take place, either on the basis of a tip-off or a hunch, and attempt to ambush the terrorists. Other imaginative ideas included the setting up and running of a bogus laundry service in hard Republican areas and a bugged massage parlour where it was hoped that tired and stressed Republicans might unburden themselves in the course of the range of sexual services on offer.

The idea behind the 'Four Square Laundry' was that it would provide undercover soldiers with a reason for driving around Catholic estates in a van that contained, more often than not, two hidden observers in its roof compartment and which, theoretically, gave the army access to the dirty laundry of terrorist suspects that might contain some physical evidence of their involvement in terrorist activities. There is no good evidence that any analysis of dirty sheets took place although surveillance and covert photography certainly did, but both the laundry and the massage parlour operations were fatally compromised by two of the Freds who had been 'arrested' by the IRA. On 2 October 1972 IRA hit squads visited the Twinbrook estate, killing the laundry van's driver, Sapper

* Security forces' jargon for terrorists.

Ted Stuart, and the massage parlour at 397 Antrim Road, from where the terrorists fled in panic after accidentally discharging one of their weapons. The two Freds who had become, in effect, double agents, Seamus Wright and Kevin McKee, were interrogated at length by the IRA, and subsequently murdered and given secret burials.

The collapse of the Four Square Laundry and massage parlour operations in effect sounded the death knell for the MRF which was now fatally compromised as an intelligence-gathering unit, and this was compounded by the trial of one of its members who was charged with attempted murder for an incident which had taken place that June. In a very short period, the IRA and the general public had gained access to a great deal of information about the unit and there was no way that it could continue to operate. Even so, for a period the MRF gave 39 Brigade intelligence staff a very worthwhile insight into the activities of the Belfast IRA and caused the arrest and internment of a number of key IRA players, and this pointed the way forwards towards a far more professional organisation with similar aims.

This came into being in 1974 and, indeed, still exists as the third branch of British special forces: the Army Surveillance Unit in Northern Ireland, better known by its former cover-name 14 Intelligence Company (or 14 Int). 14 Int was founded to provide a capability to conduct extended, in-depth surveillance of terrorist targets beyond the normal level available to the police and army, recognising that its members would be operating in an extremely hostile environment. Up until 14 Int was established, the only specialised surveillance capability within the British Army was a unit of the Intelligence Corps whose task was to covertly track members of the Soviet military mission in Germany and it was, therefore, to the Intelligence Corps that the army turned to provide surveillance teams for Ulster. This proved impossible: the Intelligence Corps was a small and therefore relatively inflexible organisation which was already, at that stage of the 1970s, stretched to its limits by its operational commitments in Germany, Cyprus, Hong Kong, Oman and, of course, Ulster – not to mention myriad other small-scale commitments. The most the corps was able to provide was specialist training and a handful of volunteers. Instead the job went to 22 SAS: a number of members of B Squadron were 'debadged', posted out of the regiment back to their parent units, then enrolled in the surveillance unit and sent to Ulster.

Initially, 14 Int consisted of three detachments, or 'Dets', roughly equivalent in size to an SAS Troop, and commanded by a junior officer. Geographically, they followed the approximate boundaries of the three operational Brigades in the east and west of the Province, and in the border region of the south, although the correlation is not precise. However, in addition to these regionally-based teams, task-based sub-units were set up to augment the surveillance effort. The most important of these was tasked with monitoring terrorist arms caches and, on occasion, planting surveillance devices within weapons and explosives.*

It is worth briefly examining the selection and training procedures for 14 Int which are probably unique amongst military units worldwide. Volunteers are sought from men *and women* throughout the British Armed Forces for a selection process that is held twice a year. After an initial pre-screening, during which applicants are tested on their physical fitness and mental agility, candidates assemble at a Territorial Army training camp for Camp One, a three-week period of assessment and basic training during which they are subjected to sleep deprivation, strenuous physical activity and dislocation of expectation, designed to indicate whether they have the potential to conduct stressful long-term surveillance operations. Camp One ends with a day-long hike over the Black Mountains, following which the candidates are taken to a special forces training area and subjected to a short resistance to interrogation exercise. After a weekend off, Camp Two begins.

Camp Two comprises the core training package for 14 Int. The first week requires 14 Int recruits to go to Ulster and undergo NIRTT training, a short course designed to indoctrinate all military personnel in the basic operational procedures which apply in the province.† At this point the raw recruits to 14 Int are joined by other special forces units, volunteers from 22 SAS and the Special Boat Service who are exempted from Camp One and NIRTT, and together they go through an intensive course in close-quarter

---

* This unit has occasionally been mis-identified as the Weapons Intelligence Section (WIS). WIS is actually a unit comprising military policemen who co-operate with the RUC in making forensic identifications of weapons used in terrorist crimes.
† Northern Ireland Reinforcement Training Team. Every soldier, whether a padre or a paratrooper, who goes to Ulster as an individual reinforcement must go through the NIRTT course.

battle, driving, covert signals procedures, photography, close target reconnaissance and static and mobile surveillance, together with a realistic and psychologically traumatic simulated terrorist interrogation. With this training concluded, and after a final exercise which takes place, partially at least, in the suburbs of a large city, the recruits are finally ready to join 14 Int itself. It is only at this point that recruits are formally briefed on the full scope of their duties (although it is fair to say that if they have not worked them out after five months of training they are idiotically stupid).

Throughout the period 1974–5 14 Int was the only British special forces unit operating in Northern Ireland, despite propagandist claims by Republican sources, and it was only at the beginning of 1976 that 22 SAS was finally committed to Ulster in a counter-terrorist role.* This was the result of a campaign of sectarian murders by both the IRA and Loyalist gangs in South Armagh which had caused the deaths of a large number of civilians in the previous six months. The population of South Armagh, by an anomaly of the partition in 1922, was of largely Catholic/Nationalist orientation and this, together with the difficult terrain and ease of escape into the relative safety of the Republic, had created a uniquely difficult area of operations for the security forces. The various IRA units in the area were, for a time in the mid-1970s, able to achieve a measure of equilibrium with the security forces: neither side was in a position to dominate the situation. In the six months leading up to January 1976, sectarian death squads had murdered a total of twenty-four civilians from the Nationalist and Loyalist sections of the population, culminating in the appalling massacre of eleven Protestant workmen in a revenge attack for five Catholics previously murdered by Loyalists. The press had by now given South Armagh the nickname 'Bandit Country' and there was a widely held perception that the area was getting out of control; the response from the government of Harold Wilson was to publicly announce that he was sending in the SAS.

* D Squadron 22 SAS deployed to Ulster briefly in 1969, but in an overt patrolling role.

The very public arrival of the SAS in South Armagh had a massive psychological impact on terrorists and the Nationalist community in the area. Although the IRA/Sinn Fein propaganda machine had been claiming the presence of SAS soldiers in the province for several years, the news that they were actually there caused a dramatic reduction in terrorism in South Armagh. D Squadron was based in Bessbrook Mill, a disused linen mill in a small, largely Protestant village surrounded by Catholic communities, which served as the headquarters of the Armagh Roulement Battalion (ARB) and various minor army units, and also contained what was, then, the busiest heliport in the world. The SAS squadron was, unusually for 'strategic troops', placed under the direct command of the commanding officer of the ARB, although in practice he would be guided in their use by higher authority. Their role, according to one army officer quoted at the time, was to 'kill terrorists'. This they began to do with considerable success.

In March 1976, Sean McKenna, a local IRA commander, was snatched from his home in the Irish Republic by armed men who took him north and delivered him to a waiting regular army patrol which promptly arrested him. Two months later, Peter Cleary, another Provo wanted by the security forces in the north, was arrested by a four-man SAS team that had staked out his fiancée's house for some time. They moved him to a nearby field and called in a helicopter to take him back to Bessbrook but, as three of the exhausted soldiers marked out the helicopter landing site, Cleary attacked the fourth man who had been left to guard him and, in the struggle, was shot and killed.

Nevertheless, SAS successes were tempered by reverses. On the night of 5 May 1976, an unmarked car containing three heavily armed plain-clothes SAS men was detained by a member of the Garda a little way south of border crossing-point 'Hotel One' south of Newry. Shortly afterwards two more carloads of SAS appeared and were arrested by the same officer. In total, eight SAS men were under arrest in the Irish Republic having crossed the border illegally.

The soldiers' explanation was that they were on a reconnaissance operation and had made a map-reading error but it was easy enough for Republicans to make propaganda about SAS 'hit squads' operating in the south. In fact, the 'cock-up' explanation is the most likely: the road that crosses the border at that point is narrow and twisting, and is painted in one place with misleading markings several hundred metres north of the actual border.[2] Even so, the wide publicity that the error received can only have undermined the reputation of the regiment whilst hinting at nefarious cross-border activities.

Worse, however, was the loss of Robert Nairac. When the first SAS squadron arrived in South Armagh, it was decided that they would need their own liaison officer to ensure that SAS operations were cleared with local police and army commanders, and to liaise with the Police Special Branch and army intelligence to ensure that the SAS received the best possible briefing for their operations. Accordingly, an officer with good local knowledge was appointed to the staff of 3 Brigade, based in Armagh, with the specific title SAS LO: this was Captain Robert Nairac of the Grenadier Guards.

Nairac knew the area well, having served as second in command of a detachment of 14 Int (then using the cover-name 4 Field Survey Troop) operating from Castledillon, and he was thus well known to a number of SAS officers, although he was not, in fact, a member of the SAS Regiment. Early in his tour, Nairac was a source of useful advice for members of the squadron, circulating a paper to them explaining the best way to approach the Nationalist population for information:

South Armagh is traditionally a lawless and independent-minded area. It is resentful of authority of any kind. Furthermore certain things are taboo. It is said that if you raped your next door neighbour it would soon be forgotten; if your grandfather had been an 'INFORMER' you would soon be an outcast. It follows that there are certain deep-rooted traditions that will shut people up like a clam. Never ever use the words INFORM, INFORMATION, WITNESS or INTIMIDATE. Never write anything down; it smacks of police work. Never offer money for 'INFORMATION'. (It may come to that after months of cultivation but to offer it is fatal.) There are ways round these taboos. 'May I call for a chat?', 'can you help?'. Avoid the direct question: hint, suggest and work round the subject. If you wish to say 'It is high time the bad men were locked up' try to get them to say it for you. Ask their advice, opinion in very general terms.[3]

But soon he became more ambitious. Nairac took his responsibility for collecting intelligence seriously; he grew his hair long in order to blend in when dressed in civilian clothes and would visit bars and pubs hoping to be able to pick up tit-bits of raw intelligence useful to the squadron. In Crossmaglen he was well known as a member of the armed forces, and treated with great suspicion and circumspection by the locals (who nicknamed him 'Danny Boy'), but in the smaller villages he felt able to try out his pose as a Belfast Republican called Danny MacErlean.

On 14 May 1977, Nairac called in at the Three Steps Inn in the small village of Drumintee to have a few drinks and to listen to an Irish folk group. There is no reason to believe that he was visiting for any specific intelligence collection purpose: more that he was simply there to 'sniff the air' and see if he could pick up any gossip. He stayed for several hours, drinking and chatting with the locals, relying on his fake Belfast accent, singing along to the band. Although he was confident in his disguise, he was actually creating intense suspicion amongst local Republicans who were present, and who were making efforts to find out who he was. As the evening came to an end and Nairac left the bar, he was confronted by a group of local Republicans, beaten up in the pub car park and driven off to a field to meet an IRA executioner who had been summoned, drunk, from a pub in Dundalk, across the border. After a violent and vicious torture/interrogation, during which Nairac clung to his cover story and twice managed to snatch his executioner's revolver, which failed to operate, the drunken gunman, an English civil servant's son named Liam Townson, eventually managed to shoot him. Nairac was buried in an unmarked grave and his body has never been found.

Nairac's horrific murder was a salutary lesson to the SAS and other covert forces operating in Northern Ireland. Despite the fictional image pushed by thriller writers and in television dramas, it is virtually impossible for an outsider to mimic the accents and attitudes of a group to the extent that he will become accepted by them, even during the space of a couple of hours of casual conversation in a pub. It is also believed that Nairac had become careless in his operational drills. Although he had told the SAS squadron's duty officer at Bessbrook Mill, Captain David Collett, that he would return to base at 11.30 that night, the officer didn't actually raise the alarm for a further thirty-five minutes, essentially because Nairac had slipped into a habit of checking in late. Finally, it is believed that Nairac had not taken his personal weapon, a Browning Hi-Power 9mm pistol, into the pub but had left it in his car. During the fight in the pub car park, when Nairac was first confronted, he made great efforts to retrieve the weapon, but by then it was too late. The lesson that the SAS have learned over many years is that it is only by getting the basics right that successful operations can be built.

Despite this setback, the SAS and 14 Int were involved during the next fifteen years in a series of more or less successful operations as techniques for combating terrorism in Ulster became more refined; of the forty-one terrorists killed by the security forces between 1976 and 1987, for example, thirty-two fell victim to the SAS and 14 Int.[4] This period also saw a reorganisation of counter-terrorist responsibilities, starting with the policy of 'police primacy' which was declared in 1976. Operationally, this meant that ultimate authority for deploying the SAS fell to the Chief Constable of the Royal Ulster Constabulary, delegated in practice to three Tasking and Co-ordination Groups (TCGs). These are, in essence, combined operations and intelligence centres, manned by CID, Special Branch and military intelligence personnel, whose role is to assess intelligence reports from all sources available to the security forces and then to assign priorities and task units of the police and army to follow them up. This took place at much the same time as the special forces commitment to Ulster was reorganised. From the end of 1978 the SAS squadron and 14 Int were grouped together as Intelligence and Security Group (NI),* a cover-name designed to suggest that its components were relatively innocuous Intelligence Corps personnel. This integration

---

* Always referred to as 'the Group'.

led to closer co-operation, particularly on operations in rural areas, and ultimately the realisation that an entire squadron of SAS in Ulster was unnecessary, leading to a reduction to troop strength in 1980.

Also in 1980 came the formation of the last special unit designed for service in Northern Ireland. Although the unit is not strictly part of special forces in the sense that it is not under the administrative umbrella of the Directorate of Special Forces in London, its members do receive special forces pay and receive training to much the same level as 14 Int and SAS personnel in close-quarter battle, driving, signals and resistance to terrorist interrogation. In fact, their purpose is somewhat more refined than that of 'the Group': their task is to recruit and handle agents with access to information about Republican and Loyalist terrorism. Throughout the 1980s, the unit was known as the Force Research Unit (NI) or FRU.

Prior to the formation of the FRU, agent handling by the army in Northern Ireland was run on a fairly *ad hoc* basis. The only field intelligence collection unit, apart from 14 Int, was the Special Military Intelligence Unit (SMIU), a small group of officers and NCOs tasked to maintain liaison between the Special Branch and the army. During the years of their deployment in Ulster they had acquired a small roster of agents of their own but, by and large, they were more involved in making sure that army and police operations did not come into conflict. Other agents, 'touts' in the Irish vernacular, were often recruited and run by the intelligence sections of infantry battalions during the course of their tours in the province, but the relatively casual way in which these people were recruited and handled by personnel with superficial training, at best, meant that they were rarely useful for much more than low-level gossip. In 1977, each brigade organised a 'research office'* to take over the running of almost all of the army's agents and this was followed by the creation of the FRU, on the orders of Major General James Glover as Commander Land Forces in Northern Ireland (and thus the operational-level military commander).

* 'Research' is the military jargon for agent-handling operations.

The FRU is commanded and officered by members of the Intelligence Corps, and about fifty per cent of its strength is also drawn from the Intelligence Corps, the remainder being volunteers, normally relatively senior NCOs in their late twenties and early thirties, from other arms of the British Army, and particularly the infantry. Like 14 Int, recruits join after an initial assessment, but there is no corresponding 'selection' phase: 'either you make it through the training or you don't',[5] according to a former member of the unit. The training, which takes place at a special facility within a well-protected barracks in mainland Britain, is conducted by the Intelligence Corps with weapons instruction from 22 SAS NCOs seconded to the unit: 'at least fifty per cent of the course is weapons training; in the unit you are not just working in a "hostile environment", you're actually making approaches to, and arranging to meet terrorists, and if you can't protect yourself, you're no use to the unit'.[6]

Organisationally, FRU is not dissimilar to 14 Int. Divided into a number of regional 'Dets' and sub-dets throughout the province, its operators are generally NCOs with considerable experience in Northern Ireland. Although the FRU is commanded by an Intelligence Corps Lieutenant Colonel – and is thus, in theory, a battalion-level command – the unit is actually relatively small and closely knit, reflecting the great expertise of its members. Naturally, for a unit with this specialisation, close liaison with the Royal Ulster Constabulary and other intelligence collecting agencies is close, although, anecdotally, the relationship between the FRU and the RUC Special Branch can be rocky.

The purpose of special forces in Northern Ireland is to provide and act on the kind of hard intelligence needed to take on a dedicated, hard-core terrorist organisation like the IRA, and the statistics indicate that the one hundred and fifty or so special forces personnel deployed to Northern Ireland are an unalloyed success. But that has not been achieved without controversy and it is worth examining a few of their operations to understand why.

In July 1978, a sixteen-year-old Catholic farmer's son, John Boyle, was playing in a disused graveyard outside the village of Dunloy, a small Catholic enclave in a largely Protestant area of rural Antrim. After a while he noticed something beneath a fallen gravestone and, on investigating, found it to be an arms cache containing an Armalite rifle and a pistol. John Boyle ran home to tell his father, Con, who immediately telephoned the RUC to report the find.

After some discussion, a decision was made by the RUC and army, presumably at TCG East, to send an SAS patrol to stake out the graveyard in case the terrorists came back to collect their weapons, and on 10 July a four-man team deployed into two observation posts covering the cache.

The next morning at about 10 a.m. a series of shots were heard from the graveyard and Con Boyle and his elder son Harry went to investigate. As they approached the graveyard they were detained by two SAS soldiers who told them that 'The other bastard's lying dead'.[7] In fact what had happened was that John Boyle had returned to take another look at the cache and had apparently taken the Armalite from it, whereupon the SAS had opened fire and killed him. It is quite probable that the SAS men genuinely had no idea who Boyle was, and did believe him to be a terrorist, but several aspects of the incident did raise serious doubts about this operation and others of a similar nature.

In the first instance, it is entirely legitimate to ask whether the soldiers had in fact *allowed* Boyle to arm himself on the basis that they would then be able to justify killing him under the army's 'yellow card' guidelines. It is reasonable to suggest that it would have been possible for the soldiers to have challenged or arrested Boyle as he entered the graveyard, as he poked around in the cache prior to removing the weapon or at least before they opened fire on him. Instead, they subsequently claimed that it had been impractical to do so. In fact, forensic examination of the weapon showed it to be unloaded, a fact which could have been ascertained by a covert examination of the arms find by the soldiers but apparently was not.

Despite an early realisation by the soldiers at the scene that they had killed the wrong person, the army press office in Lisburn put out a series of misleading and downright untrue statements suggesting, amongst other things, that the Boyle family were terrorists, that the soldiers had shouted warnings to Boyle and that the weapon was loaded. None of this impressed either journalists or the RUC who promptly charged two of the SAS men, Corporal Alan Bohan and Trooper Ron Temperley, with murder.

When the case eventually came to trial, the prosecution case depended on forensic evidence which suggested that Boyle had been shot in the back, and on the soldiers' own accounts of what had happened. Bohan testified that he had been briefed that the weapons had been discovered by a ten-year-old boy, but the judge – Lord Justice Lowry – was extremely dubious about the soldiers' other main claim that the weapon had been brought to bear against himself and Temperley, eventually concluding that Bohan was 'an untrustworthy witness'.[8] Despite this, both soldiers were acquitted of murder because the forensic evidence proved ambiguous – a pathologist hired at the army's expense, at the insistence of Brigadier de la Billière, actually showed that it was more likely that the bullets had entered Boyle from the front, thus supporting, to some extent, Bohan's claims.

The degree of anxiety felt by the SAS over the shootings can be gauged by a passage in de la Billière's 1994 autobiography *Looking for Trouble* describing the circumstances of the shooting, which took place while de la Billière was Director of the SAS, and which is a grotesque misrepresentation of what actually took place:

> Our soldiers had found a weapons cache in a grave, and had staked the site out, lying up for several days and nights hidden in a wet ditch at the edge of the churchyard. One night a man appeared, lifted the top of the grave and took out a semi-automatic weapon, which he had pointed in the direction of the watchers. They, thinking that he was about to shoot, opened fire and killed him.
>
> Clearly the dead man had been a member of the IRA; but he was only sixteen, and probably a low-grade operator. The IRA opened up a vociferous propaganda barrage, producing pictures taken seven or eight years earlier, when the youth was singing in a choir, and presenting us as having killed a choirboy.[9]

Almost every detail of this version of events is false: the weapons were not originally discovered by soldiers but by Boyle himself; the stake-out had lasted less than twenty-four hours; the shooting happened in broad daylight at 10 a.m.; and the victim was not and never had been a member of the IRA. Indeed, 'it would be difficult to imagine how any Catholics finding an arms cache could have behaved more responsibly'.[10] This attitude on the part of the professional head of British special forces almost certainly explains why Bohan and Temperley continued to serve in 22 SAS after the incident (Bohan was a member of 22 SAS's training wing as recently as 1991).

Despite the fall-out from the Dunloy incident, special forces have continued, on occasion, to ambush and kill terrorists and civilians in circumstances that can be interpreted as being of doubtful legality. However, there was a five-year lull between December 1978 and December 1983 when, for a variety of reasons, one of which may well have been a change in security forces policy, the SAS killed no terrorists at all.* During this period, several special forces operations took place which indicated that it was possible to use them in a relatively effective manner that fell short of lethal force.

On 14 March 1981, for example, members of 'the Troop', as the SAS is referred to in Ulster, surrounded a farm building near Rosslea, County Fermanagh, and called upon its four occupants to surrender: they duly did so. Out of the building came Seamus McElwaine, the twenty-year-old commander of the IRA in Fermanagh, and three comrades. Inside the house police found four rifles and 180 rounds of ammunition, and all four terrorists, together with another man linked by forensic evidence to the weapons, were convicted of a range of crimes and received sentences varying from ten years to life imprisonment. McElwaine was an extremely effective terrorist who had been active in the IRA since the age of sixteen, and it is a measure of the fear that the SAS inspires in the IRA that he gave himself up on this occasion.†

Special forces ambushes resumed in Ulster in December 1983 and continued until December 1992, during which period a further thirty-two terrorists were killed (excluding the three shot in Gibraltar in 1988). The most significant operation during this phase took place in May 1987 in the small Armagh village of Loughgall.

---

* A 14 Int officer killed two IRA terrorists in Londonderry in May 1981 whilst shooting his way out of an ambush.
† He subsequently took part in the Maze prison mass escape in September 1983 and was ultimately shot and killed by the SAS in April 1986 when he was involved in setting up a command-wire bomb in rural Fermanagh.

After a tip-off from an informer, 14 Int and E4A (a police surveillance team) units had watched an eight-man Active Service Unit of the Provisional IRA's so-called 'Tyrone Brigade' developing and preparing an attack against the part-time RUC station at Loughgall. With a reasonably accurate idea of when the attack was going to take place, 'the Troop', with reinforcements brought in from G Squadron in Hereford and some members of 14 Int, set up an ambush in and around the target and waited for developments.

The IRA gang, led by a hard-core terrorist, Jim Lynagh, planned to crash a stolen JCB excavator through the perimeter of the police station, and then detonate a large bomb held in the scoop, designed to demolish the building. The security forces, backed up by massive firepower (at least two 7.62mm General Purpose Machine Guns were deployed), had set up the main 'killer group' within the police station together with 'cut-offs' on all likely escape routes.

Just after 7.20 p.m. on 8 May 1987, a blue Toyota Hiace van containing five members of Lynagh's gang pulled up outside Loughgall police station. The IRA men got out, lined up and opened fire with a selection of automatic rifles, possibly with the intention of giving covering fire to the JCB which now headed towards the fence carrying another three members of the gang. The JCB crashed through and stopped close to the building and the three terrorists leapt off and ran back for cover, but as they did so, the waiting soldiers opened fire. Almost simultaneously, the bomb in the JCB detonated, flattening the end of the police station and wounding several members of the security forces.

Three terrorists, Seamus Donnelly, Patrick McKearney and Jim Lynagh, were killed in the Toyota as they tried to shelter from the hail of SAS bullets; one, Patrick Kelly, was killed as he stood by the driver's door, whilst Eugene Kelly and Declan Arthurs died as they pathetically tried to find shelter behind the van. Meanwhile, two of the others were running for their lives. They both reached the cut-offs and died there. One of the terrorists, as it happened, was a long-serving and highly paid police informer, but he carefully selected the jobs that he 'touted' on to avoid incriminating himself with the IRA's internal security teams and had said nothing about Loughgall.

But along with the terrorists, an entirely innocent local man, Anthony Hughes, who was driving past with his brother Oliver, was also targeted by the soldiers. Both were hit several times, and while Oliver survived, Anthony did not.

This was followed, the next year, by Operation Flavius, the attempted arrest of three IRA terrorists in Gibraltar in March 1988. The IRA's plan to detonate a car bomb during the changing of the guard outside the Governor's residence in Gibraltar was supposedly an attempt by the IRA to retaliate against the British Army for the Loughgall incident. Had it succeeded it would undoubtedly have caused a great deal of injury and loss of life, although whether it would have been much of a 'propaganda coup', as some writers have claimed, is open to question. Attacks on 'soft targets' – military or civilian – have never aroused much sympathy from anyone and a similar bombing, launched against a Remembrance Day parade in Enniskillen in 1987, had drawn widespread condemnation even within the Republican movement.

The first indication that British intelligence received that a bombing was planned in Gibraltar came from an informer who tipped off his handlers that two prominent, active IRA terrorists were due to fly to Malaga where an IRA reconnaissance team had previously cached a supply of weapons and explosives. From this tip it wasn't difficult to infer that their target was likely to be Gibraltar. Subsequent surveillance by the Spanish police identified Danny McCann and Sean Savage as they were returning to Ireland, travelling on false passports. Thus whilst the Spanish police kept watch for their return, an MI5 and Special Branch team moved to Gibraltar to work with the local police and await events.

Surveillance operations during February 1988 had shown that an Irishwoman, travelling on a stolen passport, was appearing in Gibraltar on Tuesdays, the day on which the resident infantry battalion normally mounted a full-dress changing of the guard ceremony. In fact the ceremony had been temporarily suspended, but when it resumed, on 23 February, and a week later, on 1 March, the woman was seen to take a close interest in the route that the soldiers followed. On this evidence, the duty Special Projects Team drawn from A Squadron of 22 SAS, and commanded by 'Soldier F', moved to Gibraltar on 3 March to make preparations for an arrest operation.

As it happens, the IRA team left Belfast the next day and rendezvoused at Malaga Airport where, by chance, they managed to 'lose' the Spanish surveillance. During the next twenty-four hours it is evident that the IRA gang were involved in some quite detailed preparation. A bomb consisting of 141lb of Semtex plastic explosive had been manufactured and smuggled into Spain for them, and they had to obtain vehicles to conceal it and bring it into Gibraltar. Whilst the IRA team were making their preparations, so were the security forces, with a senior MI5 officer briefing the soldiers about their opposition:

> The briefing I gave was as follows – that there was reason to believe that the Provisional IRA was going to carry out an attack in Gibraltar, the target being the changing of the guard ceremony on March 8.
>
> It was believed that a three-man active service unit, as the IRA calls it, was despatched to carry out this operation, and that they were intending to kill as many soldiers as possible using a bomb detonated by remote control. We believed that it would be brought across the border in a vehicle and that the bomb itself would remain hidden inside that vehicle.
>
> The ASU would comprise three members – two of whom were known to be Danny McCann and Sean Savage, and the third was later identified as Mairead Farrell. It was known that Savage and McCann were active, extremely dangerous terrorists. More was known about McCann than Savage. They were believed to be dangerous terrorists who would almost certainly be armed, and if confronted by security forces personnel, would be likely to use their weapons and it was further believed that if the method of detonation of the device was indeed a radio control device, they might seek, if confronted, to detonate that device.
>
> Radio control would be much the safest way to explode a device from the terrorists' point of view: they would be away from the bomb when it went off. We also considered the possibility of them using a timing device – a bomb with some form of clock in it, but we considered that highly unlikely. Very

recently there had been the explosion in Enniskillen where a
large number of innocent civilian bystanders had been killed
and we assessed that they would not be likely to use a
timing device. It seemed to us far more likely it would be a
remote-control device. We believed they would probably drive it
in some time before the parade, either Monday night or Tuesday
morning.

With the intelligence aspects of their briefing covered, the soldiers
were given detailed orders by their overall commander, the squadron OC. Broadly speaking, it would seem that the team were
split up into two-man groups with the intention of providing
armed back-up to an MI5 surveillance team who were there to
keep tabs on the terrorists; and with the capability to make 'hard
arrests' at the appropriate moment, on the instructions of the
police commissioner. 'Soldier F', the squadron commander, takes
up the story:

I was the senior military advisor to the Police Commissioner of Gibraltar during the operation which took place
in early March. In that capacity I was a permanent member of the advisory group which had been established to
run the operation against an IRA active service unit. The
purpose of the military force in Gibraltar at that time was
to assist the police in arresting the IRA unit. It was clear
to us that we were subject to the instructions of the Police
Commissioner.

We were mindful of the priorities which he had laid down
himself, and that the execution of that plan was to follow the
sequence that he had requested. We were to arrest the offenders,
detain them and defuse the bomb.

We had been told that the Provisional IRA were under
pressure to produce what they, in their terms, describe as
a 'spectacular'. In other words, some obscene act against the
security forces. We were told that it was going to be a
button job – that it would be detonated at the press of
a button.

At 2.30pm on 6 March, in the joint operations room, we

received a message on the radio of a possible sighting of Farrell and McCann entering Gibraltar on foot. At the same time there was a possible sighting of Savage in the town.

At about 2.50pm McCann and Farrell, with a second man, were identified in the assembly area: looking at it, walking through it and paying particular attention to one of the cars parked there. The second man was then identified as Savage, and almost simultaneously information was passed that it was Savage who had been seen parking the car at 12.15pm and fiddling with something in the front for several minutes before leaving it. The presence of these three in the band's assembly area was a clear indication that they were about to launch their attack. Our preferred option was to arrest them whilst they were on foot in the area, but we knew from the briefing that they were dedicated and ruthless terrorists and, if compromised, would be likely to resort to the force of arms to carry out their operation.

On the day of the operation, the terrorists were kept under surveillance and at 3.25pm were seen to return to the assembly area and examine it and the car once again before heading towards the border. At 3.40pm the Police Commissioner finally handed control over in a signed form to me. By this stage, the ATO* had examined the car and was convinced that it contained an IED.†

From this point, I could hear the tactical commander on the ground moving his soldiers into position and checking with the Gibraltar police officers assisting them. At about 4.00pm we received reports over the radio that the terrorists had been apprehended and that shooting had taken place. Once we received reports that the scene on the ground had returned to Gibraltar police control and that the soldiers had been removed from the scene, I formally returned control to the Police Commissioner.

Events had, in fact, moved much faster than anticipated by the police and army team. The soldiers and surveillance team believed that the car brought in by the terrorists and parked in the assembly area for

* Ammunition Technical Officer: a bomb disposal expert.
† Improvised Explosive Device.

the ceremony contained the bomb and that it might well be primed and ready for detonation. The decision was made to go for the arrests and effective control passed to the soldiers on the ground. 'Soldier A' continues:

I saw that all three terrorists were together, talking and smiling. They were looking back up the road in the general direction of us. I decided I would then move down the right-hand side of the road to effect the arrests as all three were together, and I knew that C and D were nearby.

As I was moving up, Savage moved away and started walking south towards us. I wasn't expecting the split. As he moved past, Soldier B was about to turn round to arrest Savage, but I stopped him and said we should keep moving and arrest Farrell and McCann: I was told over the radio that C and D would effect the arrest of Savage.

Farrell and McCann then started moving off again towards the border and I was about ten metres behind them when McCann turned round. He had a smile on his face and he looked over his shoulder, and he looked right at me. We had eye to eye contact. We looked directly at each other. The smile went off his face. It is hard to describe how he looked. He had a look that he knew who I was, a look of alertness that I was a threat.

At that stage I was going to shout a warning to stop. At the same time I was getting out my pistol. I went to shout 'stop': I don't know if it came out . . . I honestly don't know. He looked at me, his right elbow moved across the front of his body . . . At that stage, I thought he was going for a button: for me the whole thing was the bomb in the band area.

I fired at him, one round into his back from about three metres. I caught out of the corner of my eye some form of movement by Farrell. She had a bag under her arm and she was going for it. I thought she was also going for a button so I also shot Farrell in the back once. I fired a further three rounds at McCann: one to the body, two to the head.

McCann was down on the ground and so was Farrell, and their arms were away from their bodies. I then turned round to see if Savage was behind them, but I couldn't see him.

As two SAS men fired at Farrell and McCann, another two were approaching Sean Savage:

Before I could get any closer I heard the sound of gunfire. [Soldier C] shouted 'Stop'. Savage spun round, he didn't stop, and his hand went towards the pocket in his hip area.

Uppermost in my mind at that point was that a bomb had been left in the Ince's Hall car park. I believed Savage had a detonator and was going to detonate that device. I had to make a decision. There were gunshots to my left rear: a threat to people around me; and to C and me. I had milliseconds to make a decision.

I had to move a woman away with my left hand, draw my pistol with my other hand and engage Savage. I fired nine rounds. The last two rounds were aimed at his head. He was possibly just inches away from the ground. I kept firing until he was on the ground and his hands were away from his body because at any time he could press a button and detonate the bomb which I had been told was in Ince's Hall car park.[11]

In the course of approximately four seconds, Farrell was hit three times, twice by 'Soldier B' and once by 'Soldier A'; McCann was hit nine times, four shots from 'Soldier A', five from 'Soldier B'; Savage was hit fifteen times, six rounds from 'Soldier C', nine from 'Soldier D'. It is a tribute to the enormous skill of the soldiers that in this cataclysmic explosion of violence, no bullets missed their targets and no civilians were hit. As the noise died away and the soldiers were sure that the terrorists posed no further threat, control was handed back to the police on the scene. It was then that it was discovered that the terrorists were unarmed and none of them was in possession of a remote-control device. Investigations later that afternoon were to show that the car left by the terrorists in Ince's Hall car park did not contain a bomb and that it was actually a 'blocking car', left to keep the parking space for the actual bomb (which was later found in a car park across the border in Marbella). What had, at first, appeared to be a triumphant success for the SAS was now clouded with doubt as to whether they should have opened fire at all.

The debate over the Gibraltar operation encapsulates the problem of using a military force like the SAS in what is, fundamentally, a policing role. SAS men are trained, first and foremost, to react as soldiers, using firepower, aggression and their tactical skill to resolve combat situations: to 'win the firefight', as military jargon puts it. But in counter-terrorist operations the law constrains the security forces to use minimal levels of firepower and aggression, and most people would accept that gunfights and killing are best avoided when enforcing the law in a democratic society. There is a good argument for saying that the ruthless, split-second decision-making skills developed by SAS soldiers are not necessarily appropriate for individuals ostensibly being sent to make arrests in the interests of justice. After all, whatever the significance of the movements made by Farrell, Savage and McCann, they were neither 'going for a button' nor a weapon: they were unarmed.

The final incident to be examined, and also one of the last to result in killings by the SAS, took place in the village of Coagh, County Tyrone, in June 1991.

The operation was mounted because intelligence had been received of an attempt by a Cookstown-based IRA gang to attack a Protestant UDR reservist as he went about his morning routine. Before the operation members of the SAS and 14 Int carried out a reconnaissance of the village and formulated a plan to mount what Mark Urban has described as a 'Reactive OP' involving both the SAS and 14 Int, together with a mobile back-up force from the RUC's HMSU. The security forces plant involved substituting an SAS soldier for the IRA's intended victim and positioning a team of SAS nearby to act as the main ambush party. In addition, several mixed teams of 14 Int and SAS personnel were to be close at hand to prevent any escape from the immediate area of the ambush.

On this occasion, the intelligence information proved to be correct and just before 7.00am on the nominated day a vehicle containing three terrorists pulled up alongside their intended victim's car in Coagh High Street. Watching members of the security forces saw the terrorists about to open fire and immediately returned fire. The terrorists clearly had a brief period in which they realised they were being ambushed because they attempted to drive away but as the car began to move, it exploded, leaving all three terrorists dead.

The dead men were Peter Ryan, Tony Dorris and Lawrence McNally; all hardened, experienced terrorists; and few tears were shed outside Republican circles at their passing. Under the circumstances in which the security forces opened fire on them there was clearly no sensible alternative to lethal forces' knowledge of the terrorists' intentions might have allowed them to intervene earlier. A security forces source, who was not present during the ambush, has suggested to the author that the terrorists might have been subject to Police or Army surveillance as they approached Coagh. This raises the prospect that the terrorists could have been intercepted and arrested before they reached the ambush site. Other sources deny this, suggesting that the security forces' knowledge of the proposed IRA attack was limited to little more than the target.

It is difficult to feel any sympathy for terrorists killed in these circumstances. The law abiding citizens of Northern Ireland have never been subjected by the authorities to the violence and horror with which the Republican terrorists routinely oppress the community, nevertheless, it is entirely appropriate to question whether it is right, in a democracy, to use *military* special forces at the cutting edge of law enforcement.

The British experience of finding military solutions to problems of counter-insurgency has been mixed. Victory in Malaya was achieved through a major campaign, which included the use of special forces, but which largely concentrated on separating the terrorists from their supporting communities by a wide variety of psychological, political and economic means. Once that separation had come about, attrition of the terrorist groups became almost inevitable. In Northern Ireland however, efforts to create a wider counter terrorist campaign, over and above routine policing with military support, have been spasmodic and unfocused. This has allowed a policy of attrition to become the orthodoxy, despite good evidence to suggest that the killing of terrorists by the security forces is one of the Republican movement's best recruiting sergeants.

It would be ridiculous to question the use of surveillance and agent-handling units like 14 Int and the FRU: they clearly have an important role to play in the campaign against terrorism in Northern Ireland. But we must ask whether it is appropriate, in a Province which is as much a part of the United Kingdom as Cornwall or Northumberland, that the Special Air Service should be called upon to enforce the rule of law on a regular basis.

12

The Empires Strike Back:
the Falklands, Grenada and the Gulf

The origins of the Falkland Islands war of 1982 rest in the decision by an Argentine scrap-metal dealer of Russian extraction, Constantino Davidoff, to purchase, in 1979, the remnants of a commercial whaling station on the South Atlantic island of South Georgia from the Edinburgh-based company of Christian Salveson. He first visited his purchase briefly in December 1981 before returning to Buenos Aires to make arrangements to dismantle the station the following March. On 17 March 1982, an Argentine freighter, the *Bahia Buen Suceso*, arrived off the deserted port of Leith to begin the task and Davidoff's forty-one civilian workers started work two days later, unloading equipment and setting up living accommodation to keep them sheltered during the harsh South Atlantic winter that was, even then, drawing on.

Davidoff's operation would have caused no excitement whatsoever had his men not failed to observe one formality required by their visit to South Georgia: they did not get a landing permit from the British Antarctic Survey research station at Grytviken, twenty miles down the coast. There is some debate still over whether or not this was a calculated move by the Argentines: certainly they were aware of the requirement, but their excuse, which is of some validity, was that they had neither the time nor the means to make the journey. Their ship, chartered from the Argentine Navy but crewed by civilians, had left them as soon as their kit was unloaded, although it would not have been too difficult for them to make the journey cross-country. Even so, two days after their arrival, a British scientist surreptitiously observed that the scrap-men had hoisted a flag above their living quarters, and he also heard the sound of rifle shooting in the area. He immediately reported this back to his base.

At Grytviken, the British Antarctic Survey team leader, who doubled as the magistrate on the practically uninhabited island, sought the advice of his superior, Rex Hunt, the Governor of the Falkland Islands, 800 miles away. His decision was to report the matter to London and also to order the BAS team to tell the Argentines by radio to lower their flag and send a representative to Grytviken. The flag was grudgingly lowered but no Argentine appeared at the BAS base. The matter then began to take on an international dimension.

Governor Hunt of the Falkland Islands was fully aware that the Argentine government disputed British sovereignty over South Georgia as well as the Falklands themselves and was alive to the possibility that the Argentines were launching a 'provocation' against the British. Misinterpreting the information that the BAS had heard shooting from Leith, he reported to London that Argentine *military* personnel had come ashore and he gave his opinion that the Argentine Navy were attempting to establish a presence on the island.[1] From that moment, Britain and Argentina began to move inexorably towards conflict.

The British reaction to Hunt's note was a formal diplomatic protest to Argentina which demanded that the *Bahia Buen Suceso* return to South Georgia and remove the entire Argentine party or else 'the British Government would take whatever action seemed necessary'.[2] London backed up this stiff protest by despatching the patrol ship HMS *Endurance* from Port Stanley, capital of the Falklands, with a party of twenty-two Royal Marines under the command of Lieutenant Keith Mills.[3] As far as the Argentine government was concerned, this escalated the situation to an entirely new level: the pride of the military regime was affronted and a naval ship exercising nearby was ordered to proceed to Leith to land a group of Argentine Marines.

Unbeknown to the Foreign Office in London, their overreaction to a mild territorial infringement gave the Argentine government an excuse to launch an operation that they had been planning since the previous December: the invasion of the Falkland Islands.

The Falklands invasion was an initiative of Admiral Jorge Anaya, the naval member of the three-man junta that had ruled Argentina since 1976 and, in 1981, its longest-serving member. He had spent time in

London as Naval Attaché during the early 1970s and, perhaps because of this, perceived Britain to be ruled by weak, vacillating governments; his judgement was that if Argentina seized the Falkland Islands by force, the British government would not risk military action in an attempt to win them back and that they would become Argentinian by *fait accompli* whatever subsequent discussions took place in the United Nations and other diplomatic forums. Anaya was a fervent believer that the Falklands should be 'returned' to Argentine sovereignty and was equally clear that the navy should play a leading role in this objective. When General Roberto Viola resigned the Argentine presidency in December 1981 in favour of General Leopoldo Galtieri, Anaya apparently briefed him that recovery of the Falklands was a significant national priority.[4]

The Argentine claim to the Falklands rested on two basic points: the Falklands Islands are on the supposedly 'Argentine' section of the South American continental shelf, and Argentina had ruled the islands between 1826 and 1831, both of which facts were undoubtedly true but more or less meaningless in terms of modern international law. Since 1833, despite the proximity of the islands to mainland South America, they have been ruled and settled by Britain, the population is almost exclusively of British origin, and is overwhelmingly in favour of remaining a British colony. The Argentine claim simply does not recognise the principle that territorial disputes are nowadays usually resolved on the basis of self-determination by the population of the area in question. Whatever the historical rights and wrongs of the situation, any Argentine claim to the islands stumbled and fell against the wishes of the Falklanders to remain British; inevitably it would have continued to do so in any tribunal to which the Argentine government had appealed.

Anaya's planning team devised an operation centred around naval assets but using elements from all three Argentine armed services. It wasn't a particularly difficult task; the Falklands were garrisoned by a 'naval party' of British Royal Marines not normally stronger than fifty all-ranks, supported by the survey ship HMS *Endurance*, and the British had neither heavy weapons nor any hope of rapid reinforcement. The order was given to go ahead with the operation in the last week of March and D-Day was set for 1 April.

The Argentine plan was straightforward enough. Specialist Commandos would seize the Royal Marines' barracks at Moody Brook outside

Stanley, whilst a smaller team were tasked to capture the Governor and his official residence, Government House. Following this *coup de main* a Marine battalion would land outside Stanley and take control of the town and the nearby airport, allowing army reinforcements to be flown in from the mainland to establish an Argentine garrison. The intention of the Argentines was to avoid British casualties if possible in the expectation that Britain would accept a bloodless loss of face far more easily than it would a pitched battle.

The Argentine fleet set sail on Operation Blue on Sunday 28 March, leaving Puerto Belgrano on a course designed to take them along the Argentine coast to a position south of the Falklands. A fierce storm blew up on the 29th which lasted for two days and set back the timetabled landings by twenty-four hours; the first Argentine troops would now set foot on the islands during the night of 1–2 April.

The British government was alerted to the possibility of serious Argentine military action the day before the ships sailed. British diplomats in Argentina reported unusual troop movements and intense activity at Puerto Belgrano as the fleet prepared to depart, and reporting from GCHQ, the government's signals intelligence (SIGINT) agency, suggested a wider mobilisation of Argentine naval assets. By chance, the crisis had erupted as the Royal Marines garrison in the Falklands was changing over and consequently there were double the normal number of soldiers present (sixty-nine Royal Marines and eleven sailors from HMS *Endurance*. Even so, it was a pitifully small force with which to mount a credible defence of the islands, and in London it was realised that if Argentina went ahead and launched a full-scale invasion, the Falklands would be lost.

The commander of the Falklands garrison, Major Mike Norman of the Royal Marines, was told during the afternoon of Thursday 1 April that an Argentine landing appeared to be imminent. He called his men together for an initial briefing:

> I gave them the good news that tomorrow we would start earning our pay. They took it remarkably well but the sailors from *Endurance* became very wide-eyed. Most of them were keen to get on with it and, although we were all military men, they took it as a personal affront. There was a 'Who the hell do they think they are!' attitude, although we all knew that we couldn't really stop them.[5]

Norman had only a very limited stock of defence stores – a few coils of barbed wire – but he sent a team of Marines to lay this out on a potential landing beach near the airfield. The airstrip itself was temporarily blocked by the simple expedient of parking earth-moving vehicles out on the runway. At 11 p.m., Norman gave his final orders for the defence of Port Stanley and shortly afterwards his men were dropped off at their positions by truck.

Even as Norman was briefing his Marines, the first Argentine troops – also Marines but of the Amphibious Commando Company – were landing at an unnamed and unguarded beach close to Lake Point, about four kilometres south of Port Stanley. For the next six hours, the Argentine Commandos carefully infiltrated north towards their two targets, Moody Brook barracks (which had been abandoned by the British) and Government House, now being used as a headquarters and the focal point of Major Norman's defensive plan. Just after 6 a.m., the defenders heard the sound of firing and grenade explosions coming from Moody Brook as the Argentines 'cleared' the empty buildings, and ten minutes later the first probes were made at Government House.

Earlier in 1982, an Argentine tourist claiming to be an architect had managed to obtain a copy of the plans of Government House from Governor Hunt, who said that 'like a fool, I gave them to him'.[6] It is likely that these had formed the basis of the original attack plan. But when the Argentine assault began on Government House, it was not the originally tasked army unit that took part but a detachment of sixteen members of the Amphibious Commando Company under Lieutenant Commander Giachino. Giachino had not seen the architect's drawings and led a small five-man party into what he thought was the main building in order to demand Hunt's surrender. In fact, Giachino and his squad were attacking the empty servants' quarters which were in an outbuilding and, following this error, he had to take his squad out into the courtyard at the rear of the main building. Here, as they prepared to try to break into the house, they were met by well-directed machine-gun and rifle fire from the forty-five defenders located inside. Giachino was hit and knocked down, still holding onto a grenade from which he had pulled the safety pin, and several of the other Argentines, one of whom was also wounded, fled back into the servants' block. Seriously wounded, Giachino shouted for help but a medic who came forward was wounded by a British grenade and had to withdraw. Shouting and brandishing his hand-grenade, Giachino slowly bled to death from his wounds in the courtyard of Government House whilst his men waited for reinforcements.

Even as the Commandos launched their farcical attack on Government House, amtracks of the 2nd Marine Infantry Battalion were leaving the hold of the *Cabo San Antonio* heading towards the landing beach of Yorke Bay. After a short skirmish on the outskirts of Stanley when a group of British Marines fired their 84mm Carl Gustav (anti-tank rocket launcher) at the lead vehicle (they missed, despite subsequent over-optimistic claims). By 8 a.m. the Argentines occupied the town and Government House was surrounded. It was then only a matter of time until the Governor was forced to order the Marines to surrender. By 9.30 a.m., the islands were under Argentine control. The occupation of the Falkland Islands cost Argentina one dead and a handful of wounded (two seriously); there were no British casualties.

News of the Argentine invasion was largely greeted with incredulity by the British intelligence and military establishment, and in the confusion that followed, as the task force was hastily assembled, there was no clear thinking on how special forces might be employed and how many would be required. It was at the initiative of the CO of 22 SAS, Lieutenant Colonel Michael Rose, that D Squadron, under Major Cedric Delves, were despatched to the forward mounting base at Ascension Island, close to the Equator, on 4 April.

Rose joined D Squadron the next day, bringing with him an SAS headquarters element, and soon linked up with Brigadier Julian Thompson, commander of 3 Commando Brigade (which was then the task force's principal land element). As a member of Thompson's planning staff, Rose was able to develop a special forces strategy which envisaged using D Squadron in a raiding or OA (offensive action) role, together with G Squadron in the IR (information-reporting) role. In addition to the two SAS squadrons, the special forces effort was bolstered by the presence of the Royal Marines' Special Boat Squadron, commanded by Major Jonathan Thomson, as well as the Arctic and Mountain Warfare Cadre, a Royal Marines training unit whose specialised fieldcraft skills suited them for use as an additional source of IR patrols. Both of these Royal Marine units brought with them the advantage of wide experience of operating with 3 Commando Brigade.

Although it is a principle of special forces operations that they should be commanded at the strategic level – that is, by the overall commander in any particular 'theatre' – Operation Corporate, as the campaign to regain the Falklands was codenamed, was a naval-led operation being controlled by the Headquarters of the Commander-in-Chief of the Fleet (HQ Cincfleet) at Northwood in Middlesex, in a bombproof bunker deep below ground. However, as we have seen, Lieutenant Colonel Rose had decided to take himself and his regimental tactical headquarters to Ascension Island where, for better or for worse, together with D and, shortly afterwards, G Squadrons, they became *de facto* components of 3 Commando Brigade under Brigadier Thompson. This posed certain problems.

The first difficulty to be overcome stemmed from the unfamiliarity of the naval hierarchy with the potential scope and the degree of support required for SAS operations. This was solved comparatively easily by establishing an SAS liaison cell within HQ Cincfleet, and by the personal intervention of Brigadier de la Billière, still the Director of the SAS in 1982, who ensured that the C-in-C, Admiral Fieldhouse, was fully briefed on SAS capabilities. The second difficulty was less tangible but, anecdotally at least, considerably more problematic: the chain of command and reporting. The full extent of the confusion over who was responsible for tasking special forces patrols at each stage in the campaign, and how the intelligence they acquired should be disseminated within the force, never seems to have been completely resolved. The whole picture has also been crowded by inter-unit rivalries and jealousy which have tended to obscure facts in relation to some aspects of SAS operations.

The first special forces operation of the campaign, which involved both the SAS and SBS, were the moves to recapture the island of South Georgia, 800 miles to the south-east of the Falklands group, which were still held by a small force of Argentine Commandos. South Georgia is a little over a hundred and five miles long and approximately eighteen miles wide at its widest point, but its mountainous terrain and relative proximity to the Antarctic make it geographically and climatically a very different proposition to the Falklands, being icy and bleak, and buffeted by severe katabatic winds carrying ice and snow particles at up to 100 m.p.h. For practical purposes, the island is uninhabited, apart from a small scientific team from the British Antarctic Survey, whose leader doubles as the island's magistrate and immigration chief. It had been occupied by the Argentines on 3 April after a brief skirmish with a small party of Royal Marines detached from the Falklands garrison at short notice and landed from HMS *Endurance*, the Royal Naval Antarctic survey ship which eluded the Argentines and continued to lurk in the area.

The plan, developed in London, was to send a Royal Marines company (M Company of 42 Commando) together with an SBS section and a troop of SAS in a small task group consisting of the destroyer *Antrim*, the frigate *Plymouth*, and two auxiliaries, *Fort Austin* and *Tidespring*. The idea was that the special forces would mount OPs providing information for the Marines who would then capture the enemy garrison with the assistance of naval gunfire support. The Argentine garrison was believed to be no more than about sixty strong, to be based solely in the two tiny settlements of Grytviken and Leith (both former whaling stations) and to be well out of range of land-based air cover, although a serious threat to the task group was present in the form of a submarine that was thought to be cruising the area.

The South Georgia task group left Ascension Island on 9 April for the voyage south with most of D Squadron embarked on the *Fort Austin* – the squadron commander, Major Delves, felt that none of them would want to 'miss a scrap' – and making intense preparations for their forthcoming operation.

The commander of the land element of the South Georgia task group was Major Guy Sheridan, the second in command of 42 Commando, but the SAS were placed under the command of the captain of the *Antrim* who was the overall task group commander. In reality, this meant that the SAS commander could act as his own boss – few naval officers would have sufficient experience or knowledge of special operations to question his decisions – but it led to the SAS attempting an operation that came close to disaster: a helicopter insert onto the Fortuna Glacier.

The SAS scheme to land on the glacier and then move along the coast to positions overlooking Leith was strongly opposed by several members of the crew of *Endurance*, onto which the SAS had moved as the last step before landing on the islands, and by Major Sheridan, who was a highly experienced arctic and mountain warfare specialist, because they argued that the weather would be too severe. Despite this, the SAS team, from 19 (Mountain) Troop under Captain John Hamilton, decided to go ahead. During the afternoon of 21 April, and after two abortive attempts, the troop bundled out of their helicopter and onto the glacier, the first British forces to return to the islands.

They soon realised that they had been wrong. The glacier was being buffeted by 50 m.p.h. winds that blew ice particles into their equipment and weapons, and it was criss-crossed by dangerous crevasses. Having covered about five hundred metres in the first five hours' march, they were obliged to seek shelter in a crevasse for the night, having decided to request evacuation the next morning. This came in the form of three Wessex helicopters:

The helicopters lifted off, the Mark 3 Wessex with navigational equipment leading and the two Mark 5's following. I was in the first Mark 5. The flight plan was to follow the glaciers down to a land fall and then out to the ships. The Mark 3 put in a shallow right-hand turn, height probably about 200–300 feet, the first Mark 5 started the turn but was hit by a sudden whiteout in which the pilot lost all his horizons and we crashed into the ice. The pilot managed to pull the nose up before impact so that the tail rotor hit first and the helicopter rolled over on its left-hand side. The main door being uppermost everyone got out quickly, the only injury being Corporal Bunker who hurt his back.

The remaining Mark 5 and Mark 3 then landed and we transferred to them ... the two helicopters lifted off again and exactly the same thing happened, whiteout followed by crash. This time the Mark 5 rested on its right-hand side. The Mark 3, unable to return because of extra payload, then flew back to *Antrim*. I and the other passengers were taken to the wardroom where an emergency medical room had been set up. After refuelling, the Mark 3, with the same crew still aboard, returned to the area of the second crash, but was unable to land because of the weather. It returned to the ship, having contacted the troops on the glacier who had no serious injuries. They had in fact managed to erect a survival tent carried by the helicopter and had also retrieved equipment from the first crash.

The Mark 3 then returned to the second crash, and this time picked everyone up and returned to *Antrim*. It had seventeen passengers, very much overloaded, and the pilot had to fly the helicopter straight onto the flight deck as he was unable to hover and approach normally.

For this and other examples of superb flying during the campaign, the pilot, Lieutenant Commander Ian Stanley, was awarded a DSO.

A second attempt to land SAS soldiers was then made using the Boat Troop's Gemini inflatable motor-boats into Stromness Bay. This was similarly unsuccessful: three of the inflatables failed to start and had to be towed behind the two which would. Caught in a sudden squall, two of the unpowered boats broke free from their tows and were carried away; the crews of both were fortunate to be retrieved some time later: 'I don't mind admitting that I was shitting myself. We were lucky to get away with it. I had visions of us bobbing around in the South Atlantic for days. Who would we eat first: Ha! Ha! . . . Seriously, I did think we were fucked and I was very, very happy to get back on board that nice warm ship'![7]

As it turned out, the special forces OPs (the SBS managed to get some men ashore as well) were virtually irrelevant to the final outcome of Operation Paraquat. This was precipitated by the sighting, on 25 April, of the Argentinian submarine *Santa Fe* on the surface approximately five miles from Grytviken. Attacked by anti-submarine helicopters from the task group, it was severely damaged and forced to put into the harbour. With the main threat to the operation now neutralised, Major Sheridan requested and received permission to attack Grytviken without delay:

All SAS troops were helicoptered ashore, landing on an area of flat ground known as the Hesterleten, two kilometres south-east of the BAS. The troop formed up in all-round defence to await the arrival of some thirty men from M Company, 42 Commando, and the commander of the operation, Major Sheridan, Royal Marines. Prior to our insertion a Forward Observation Officer and party had inserted to control the naval gun support. Having shaken out for an advance to contact, we engaged likely enemy positions, and by this time naval gunfire was supporting our advance.

In the area where the Brown Mountain ridge line joined the coast we saw what appeared to be men in brown balaclavas among the tussock grass. They were engaged by GPMG fire from approximately 800 metres and by naval gunfire. Captain Hamilton and I also engaged a possible enemy position on the top of Brown Mountain with Milan. Advancing across open ground towards the ridge line we discovered that the balaclava'd enemy were in fact seven or eight elephant seals, which were now somewhat the worse for wear! The enemy position on Brown Mountain had been a piece of angle iron on which we had scored a direct hit.[8]

Unnerved by the naval gunfire, the Argentinians were now busy stringing up white sheets to hang out of the windows of the BAS station, and the SAS troop, led by Major Delves and Captain Hamilton, and covered by the Marines on the ridge line, moved through the whaling station to take the Argentine surrender. On the next day, 26 April, the small Argentine garrison at Leith surrendered without a shot being fired.

The next phase of SAS operations was the insertion of the G Squadron IR patrols which started on 1 May. In all, ten teams were inserted by naval Sea-King helicopter into strategically important areas around the islands, together with six SBS patrols tasked to examine possible beach landing sites. Locations covered by the SAS at this stage included Port Stanley, Darwin/Goose Green, Fitzroy, Bluff Cove, Fox Bay and Port Howard, whilst the SBS appear to have concentrated on the San Carlos area and the inlets and natural harbours along the north coast of East Falkland. In the meantime, an offensive action target had been located for D Squadron: the Argentine airstrip at Pebble Island off the north coast of West Falkland.

Pebble Island, known to the Argentines as Isla de Borbon, was home to an Argentine Navy Turbo-Mentor attack squadron of four aircraft. It had been located by a patrolling British Harrier which had picked up emissions from the base's air-traffic control and early warning radars. D Squadron's Boat Troop, under Captain B, were tasked to recce the area and were inserted during the night of 10 May. They evidently reported favourably because the rest of D Squadron followed on 14 May:

45-minute flight by three Sea Kings onto LS secured by 17 Troop. Captain B then briefed the Squadron and Troop officers on the ground. Distance from LS to base – six kilometres. The moon was bright and very little cover was afforded by the ground. Each man carried two 81mm mortar bombs, which were dropped at the base-plate. 16 and 19 Troops were led to their respective targets by scouts from 17 Troop.

Base-plate to forward RV* four kilometres. Captain B led 19 Troop onto airstrip via the forward RV manned by Captain W and Sergeant Major Gallagher. Once on the edge of the airstrip we began to engage visible aircraft with small arms and 66mm rockets. By this time naval gunfire and illumination was being produced by HMS *Glamorgan* and our mortars were also firing some illuminating rounds. We were aware of some incoming enemy small arms fire, but it was totally ineffective.

I was a member of Staff Sergeant Currass's patrol and was the extreme right-hand man. I was hit in the lower left leg by shrapnel at about 0700 hours. Staff Sergeant Currass helped me put a shell dressing on the wound. The Troop moved onto the airstrip and started systematically to destroy the aircraft with standard charges and 66mm. Captain Hamilton covered Trooper A who went forward to destroy the last aircraft. The Troop then shook out and started to fall back off the airstrip. A land mine was then detonated in the middle of the Troop, Corporal Bunker being blown some ten feet backwards.

I was beginning to feel faint from loss of blood and consequently was told to head back towards the forward RV with two others. Just off the airstrip we heard Spanish voices, at least four or five, shouting some fifty metres towards the settlement. I opened fire with M-203 and put down some sixty rounds in the direction of the voices. Two very pained screams were the only reply. The Troop came down behind us and we moved back through the forward RV at about 0745 hours. During the move back I was helped over various obstacles and so was Corporal Bunker. The helicopter pick-up was on time at 0930, and the flight back to *Hermes* lasted about one hour twenty minutes. Corporal Bunker and I went directly to the sick-bay where we were looked after admirably.

With great good fortune, D Squadron's attack came on a night when six Pucara ground attack aircraft had been dispersed to Pebble Island from the Goose Green airstrip to avoid Harrier attacks, and they, the four Turbo-Mentors and an Argentine Coastguard Skyvan were all rendered inoperable by the attack. The airstrip had been guarded by a platoon of Marine conscripts but it appears that the majority of them were ill and only a skeleton guard had been mounted. Although a relatively easy and uncomplicated operation which wouldn't have been beyond the capacity of a well-trained infantry or Marine company, the Pebble Island raid was of genuinely strategic impact. For the loss of two men lightly wounded (there were no fatal casualties on either side), D Squadron knocked out ten of the thirty-four Falklands-based ground attack aircraft being operated by the Argentine Air Force and Navy, in what was a virtual re-enactment of the desert airfield raids of 1941 and 1942. If properly employed by the Argentines (although Argentinian military incompetence was almost mind-boggling), these aircraft could have had a significant impact on the ability of the British to move troops about the island and might even have threatened the main landings which took place a week later. As it was, the aircraft crews were deployed on hilltops with radios to act as early warning observers.

Unfortunately for the SAS, the great success of Pebble Island was followed by the tragedy of the Sea King crash of 19 May in which eighteen members of the regiment, mostly from 19 Troop but including D and G Squadron sergeant majors, a forward air controller and his signaller, members of 264 SAS Signals Squadron, and some non-Sabre personnel (such as cooks, storemen, clerks etc.) were killed during a routine cross-decking flight. Although this was clearly a serious blow it did not, in the short term, critically affect the regiment's ability to conduct operations in the Falklands.

The main landing of 3 Commando Brigade was scheduled to take place at San Carlos during the morning of 21 May. By this stage SBS recce had established that there was a small detachment (of slightly less than company strength) of Argentinians in the area, occupying Fanning Head and Port San Carlos, and a rather confused attempt was made to neutralise them using naval gunfire and persuasion by a Spanish-speaking Royal Marines captain. Simultaneously, D Squadron were sent to Darwin/Goose Green to mount a diversionary raid.

Goose Green contained a small Argentine air force base equipped with a number of Pucara ground attack aircraft together with a battalion of conscript infantry, forming the largest concentration of Argentine forces outside the Port Stanley area (there were approximately eleven hundred Argentinians there). The D Squadron group, numbering about forty and led by Major Delves, were carrying an average of 80lb in weight per man, mostly consisting of ammunition and other ordnance, and were presumably guided by the IR patrol, under Corporal B, that had been in the Goose Green area for sixteen days. Their intention was to persuade the Argentine garrison that they were under attack by about a battalion in the hope that this would prevent any move from Goose Green in the direction of the landings; to reinforce this impression they were to be supported by the guns of HMS *Ardent*.

In the event, the raid did not work out quite as planned. A Naval Gunfire Forward Observer who was tasked to direct the *Ardent*'s gunfire found that his codes were now out of date and the ship was unable to open fire during the night; and the considerable amount of firepower of the SAS did not actually hit the main Argentine positions. The SAS's shooting was reported to Port Stanley by Lieutenant Colonel Piaggi, the Argentine commander, but more out of puzzlement than fear; still unaware of the landings to the north, he placed his garrison on alert. Far more effective, psychologically at least, was *Ardent*'s bombardment which finally arrived after daylight and which was concentrated around the north side of the grass airstrip. Although it caused no casualties, a 20mm anti-aircraft gun was damaged and widespread fear was engendered.

Far more crucial to the success of the landings was an opportunistic air strike called in by the G Squadron IR patrol, commanded by Captain Aldwin Wight, in the hills above Port Stanley. Wight and his team had noted the existence of a helicopter hide area east of Mount Kent and, after several abortive attempts, succeeded in directing in a Sea Harrier attack on 21 May which destroyed four enemy troop-carrying helicopters. In fact these aircraft were earmarked to provide lift for the Argentine strategic reserve (Agrupación de Ejercito Malvinas Reserva Z) which was therefore stranded well away from the landings and was not committed against the British beach-head (which was probably just as well for its members: the Argentine reserve consisted of a single conscript infantry company).

In the period immediately after the landings, the contribution of the SAS – and other special forces – was less obviously useful than before the arrival of main force troops of 3 Commando Brigade. The three Commandos (in effect battalions) and two airborne battalions brought with them their own highly trained reconnaissance sub-units (the Patrols Companies of 2 and 3 Para, it is worth remembering, are the direct descendants of the Parachute Squadrons of 22 SAS from Malaya and Borneo) and the brigade also had the Mountain and Arctic Warfare Cadre as a brigade recce asset. As a result the no man's land between the main Argentinian position around Stanley and the British beach-head became somewhat crowded. A distinguished SAS officer, serving at that time with a Parachute battalion, recalls:

> One of the problems with the Falklands was that there were too many guys out front wandering around recce-ing in an area that is normally reserved for battalion patrol units. You had our own patrol company, you had the SAS, you had the Arctic Warfare Cadre, you had SBS patrolling a bit, you had neighbouring units also doing their bit. The companies had great difficulty doing their own recces. Everyone was trying to get in on the act: they should have said, 'Right, one lot will do it.' You had strategic troops operating alongside tactical troops, which is not the best way of doing it.

General de la Billière has noted that 'After the war criticisms were made that the intelligence which they [the G Squadron IR patrols] produced was never passed on far enough down the chain to be of practical use; I think this was true, but the fault lay with the system, not with the men on the ground.'

But although these two critiques of the SAS are valid for the special forces role in the campaign as a whole, they do not apply to the battle which has prompted most criticism of the regiment: Goose Green.

The Goose Green action was prompted, above all, by increasing disquiet amongst Margaret Thatcher's war cabinet at the lack of action and mounting *matériel* losses. It seems that there was concern that Britain might be perceived to be losing the war and it was decided that action was needed to quell this impression. On 25 May the container ship *Atlantic Conveyor* was sunk by an Exocet missile, destroying a number of support helicopters that were earmarked to provide the land force's heavy lift capability. As Brigadier Thompson and his staff tried to think their way through the problems that this posed, Thompson was ordered, from London, to provide a major success. His only realistic option was to launch 2 Para at Goose Green.

The criticism that is levelled at 22 SAS regarding Goose Green is that they gave Lieutenant Colonel 'H' Jones, 2 Para's CO, a misleading impression of what he should expect to face when he arrived there with his battalion. Brigadier Julian Thompson, in his account of the campaign, remarks that 'Jones went on board the *Intrepid* to see the SAS Squadron that had attacked Darwin on D-Day and they told him that, in their opinion, the whole isthmus was held by about one company.' But this statement is contradicted by the 2 Para O Group for the attack, which took place the next day (27 May), during which Jones's intelligence officer informed the assembled company commanders and attachments that there were 'a minimum of three companies' in the area. The intelligence officer, Captain Allan Coulson, was right: there was a battalion of Argentine infantry at Goose Green, and after their epic observation of the area, it is difficult to believe that the SAS can have had a false impression of what was there. The reality of Goose Green is bound up in a combination of understandable euphoria at 2 Para's eventual victory and unsurprising military ignorance on the part of media representatives who were present.

When Goose Green was eventually captured, 2 Para took approximately a thousand prisoners and there were about fifty dead Argentines scattered around. The battle had proved to be much harder fought than expected for the simple reason that the British had an unrealistically low expectation of the quality of the Argentine soldiers and had relied on a battle-plan that was over-complicated and over-optimistic. Six-figure grid references given out for Argentine company positions turned out to have been wrongly transcribed at some stage, and, amongst other things, Jones had told his officers that 'All previous evidence suggests that if the enemy is hit hard he will crumble'. This comment had no basis in reality for the simple reason that the only ground combat, at that point, had been the retaking of South Georgia and the scrap between an SAS squadron and the sick, frightened, conscript guards at Pebble Island airstrip. The battle for Goose Green lasted as long as it did because the Argentine garrison did not roll over and put its hands up as soon as the British appeared. Whatever briefing Jones received from 22 SAS, it is evident that he based his plan on facing approximately a battalion of fighting troops – which is precisely what 2 Para were up against. In the euphoria of victory, the numbers of prisoners taken became exaggerated and the inexperienced journalists with the task force did not fully understand the difference between the five hundred or so Argentine infantry who were captured and the similar number of air force personnel who took no part in the fighting. The rumour that 2 Para defeated a vastly superior enemy has now passed into military myth, so much so that a recent book confidently states that 2 Para were outnumbered ten to one! The debate on this subject does tend to ignore the reality that it was a considerable feat for 2 Para to defeat an equally strong enemy in prepared positions.

For the remainder of the conflict both squadrons continued to operate but the increasingly restricted real estate available for special forces tended to marginalise their efforts. Even so, their contribution included seizing the important high ground at Mount Kent after a D Squadron patrol had discovered it to be unoccupied (a large part of D Squadron, together with elements of 42 Commando, were flown forward to take possession) and maintaining observation on the Argentine garrison on West Falkland. It was there, on 10 June, that a D Squadron IR patrol was finally discovered by a four-man Argentine special forces patrol (from Compañía de Commando 601) outside Port Howard.

In a sharp firefight, the patrol commander, Captain John Hamilton, was wounded in the back but ordered his signaller to attempt to make a break whilst he gave covering fire. Shortly afterwards he was killed and, although the signaller was captured, two members of the patrol did get clean away. The signaller then used a novel form of resistance to interrogation: 'Yeah, poor old Roy "the Fonz" got nabbed, but he got away with it. He's a bit swarthy is Roy, and he persuaded the Argies that he was John's servant. They had no problem believing that, and so they didn't bother with much of an interrogation, they thought he was the cook or something.'[9]

It was also during this period (in fact on 2 June) that a clash took place between a G Squadron patrol and an SBS patrol, led by Sergeant 'Kiwi' Hunt, near Teal Inlet. Hunt's patrol had been dropped off by helicopter in the wrong position and they were making their way to their correct target area when they were spotted by an SAS patrol commanded by an officer. The SAS set up a hasty ambush, and when Hunt and his men were about ten metres from it, the SAS officer challenged them in

English. Hunt and two others stopped and behaved correctly but the rear man in the patrol attempted to creep away and an SAS machine gunner opened fire, killing Hunt.

This tragic 'blue on blue' incident, of a sort inevitable in war, was perhaps made worse because it occurred between two small units whose tasks mean that they must often work closely together. Although blame *per se* cannot be directed squarely at anyone involved, the death of 'Kiwi' Hunt did serve to poison the atmosphere between the SAS and the SBS for some time, and the reaction of several SAS men, that 'Hunt had strayed into "their" area and got what he deserved',[10] did not help to calm matters.

The final offensive operation of the war by the SAS was a diversionary attack launched during the night of 13–14 June by a combined force from D and G Squadrons (together with six SBS members and a handful of Marine coxswains from 3 Commando Brigade's Raiding Squadron) against Cortley Hill Ridge, a feature that formed the northern arm of Port Stanley harbour and which housed several fuel storage tanks. The force travelled in four Royal Marines Rigid Raider craft from a lie-up in Berkeley Sound but, as they approached land, they were spotted by a crew member aboard the Argentine hospital ship anchored in the harbour who alerted the nearest ground unit, an anti-aircraft battery (this was technically a breach of the hospital ship's neutrality but it is virtually unimaginable that the crewman would have acted differently, Argentine or British) which was positioned, unsuspected, nearby. The anti-aircraft battery brought fire to bear on the raiding party who soon realised that they were in real trouble as large splinters and cannon rounds began to tear into their craft. Whilst this was happening, the major battalion assaults against Wireless Ridge and Mount Tumbledown were taking place and were naturally receiving priority for artillery and naval gunfire support, but this made it difficult to bring down fire to support the raiders' now essential withdrawal. Nevertheless, after a somewhat fraught period, a short barrage from the guns of 29 Commando Regiment RA allowed the SAS to make their excuses and leave, having suffered three minor casualties and with their Rigid Raiders looking somewhat the worse for wear.

The Port Stanley harbour raid was an operation that was widely criticised after the war for having been more of a diversion to the British than the Argentines. Confusion about where the SAS were going to be and what they were going to be doing led 2 Para on Wireless Ridge to impose a restrictive boundary to their west which was to prove a constraint to the easy manoeuvring of at least one rifle company, whilst the use of limited artillery resources to get them out of trouble in the middle of a planned shoot on other targets was also a disruption to the main effort. As far as can be judged, the anti-aircraft battery was the only Argentine unit to be involved in the action (with the exception of the hospital ship) and so it cannot easily be said that the raid diverted Argentine resources. With hindsight it can be argued that launching a diversionary raid within an operation taking place in such a comparatively small area was never likely to achieve all that much impact. The Argentine leadership in the Falklands was of such a low standard that they had little concept of using reserves at all, let alone diverting them from the more important battles taking place to the south and east, and they were only ever likely to attempt to deal with the raid in a piecemeal, positionalist way: the Argentines were fortunate that the nearest unit happened to have sufficient firepower to utterly overwhelm the relatively lightly armed SAS force.

Argentine resistance in the Falklands collapsed the day after the Stanley Harbour raid: with 3rd Commando and 5th Infantry Brigades dominating the high ground around Port Stanley, poised to sweep into the capital for the last battle, the Argentine commanders had no realistic option, although Lieutenant Colonel Rose, the SAS commander, helped them along to this decision in a nicely judged negotiation. Thus it was that the most interesting special forces operation planned for the Falklands campaign never actually took place.

On 4 May the British type-42 destroyer HMS *Sheffield* was struck amidships by a French-built Exocet missile fired from a Super Etendard bomber of the Argentine naval air arm. In the ensuing explosion and fire twenty members of the crew died and many more were injured. The ship was abandoned and sank whilst under tow six days later.

The loss of the *Sheffield* had a galvanic effect on both the task force and the war cabinet. The Chiefs-of-Staff had informed the cabinet that an amphibious landing, if it was to take place, needed to happen before 30 May, when the onset of the southern winter was likely to have made the weather too unpredictable, but the Super Etendard/Exocet threat appeared to be a potential war-loser even though the Argentines were known to have only a limited number of them. If an Exocet was to destroy one of the aircraft carriers or a troopship it might prevent the landings taking place at all. Some means, therefore, needed to be found to neutralise the Exocets.

Various ideas were considered, and then rejected, at government level. It would appear that the Director of the SAS and his staff developed a plan for a target attack against the Rio Grande naval airbase on Tierra del Fuego, the rugged island off southern Argentina, from where the Super Etendards with their deadly payload were believed to be operating. In essence, the concept was simple: two C-130 aircraft carrying B Squadron would take off from Ascension Island and fly, courtesy of air-to-air refuelling, across the South Atlantic ocean to Rio Grande where they would land and be abandoned. Once on the ground, B Squadron would fan out across the base, destroying as many Super Etendards and Exocet missiles as they could find and killing any Argentine aircrew that happened to be there. With the attack completed, B Squadron and their RAF aircrew would tactically evade across country, making for RVs on the other side of the border with Chile.

Amazingly, this audacious option was accepted by the military and political leadership, and B Squadron began specific training and rehearsals in the second week of May. However, it soon began to emerge that there were considerable reservations in the squadron about the operation, not least from the squadron commander and some of his most senior NCOs, who apparently believed that it would lead to the destruction of the entire squadron. One NCO has been quoted as saying that B Squadron were 'all going to die to fulfil an old man's fantasies',[11] the old man in question being Brigadier de la Billière.

With hindsight it is hard to believe that it was seriously intended to launch such an attack on Rio Grande. The problems facing the assault force were enormous and the plan, in so far as details are known, seems to ignore many of the earliest lessons learned by the SAS in 1941 and 1942.

The first of these is that the entry phase of any special forces operation needs to be as secure – and flexible – as possible. The first operation against the airfields at Gazala and Tmimi in November 1941 failed because the parachute entry chosen was a one-shot, succeed or fail method which offered no real prospect of a rethink: on the day that

Covered by police and SAS snipers, two members of 22 SAS 'Special Projects' team prepare to lay a 'frame charge' against the armoured front window of the Iranian Embassy. *(Press Association)*

With the front window blown out, the lead assault pair enter the Embassy. *(Press Association)*

As the building starts to burn, hostage Sim Harris, a BBC journalist, escapes through the front window and is ushered to safety by an SAS trooper. *(Press Association)*

The next day, firemen remove the body of a terrorist from the charred remains of the Embassy. *(Press Association)*

British special forces personnel training in two-man Klepper canoes. *(Defence Picture Library)*

Captain Robert Nairac GC, SAS liaison officer on the staff of HQ 3 Brigade in Northern Ireland, who was murdered by the IRA in 1977. *(Press Association)*

Members of the SAS Special Projects team training in the Garrabach Range ('The Killing House') at their training area near Hereford. The black clothing protects the soldiers from the effects of smoke, irritant chemicals and flames, as well as frightening their opponents. *(Defence Picture Library)*

The remains of an Argentine Pucara aircraft at Pebble Island airbase in the Falklands, attacked by members of D Squadron 22 SAS in May 1982. *(Defence Picture Library)*

Commandos of the Royal Marines Mountain and Arctic Warfare Cadre, who acted as 3 Commando Brigade's reconnaissance force during the Falklands war, practise river crossing. *(Defence Picture Library)*

Chinook helicopter of the RAF's Special Forces Flight during the Gulf War. These helicopters were used to insert B Squadron's roadwatch patrols deep inside Iraq. *(Defence Picture Library)*

SBS men abseil from a Royal Navy Sea King helicopter to secure the British Embassy in Kuwait City at the end of the Gulf War. *(Defence Picture Library)*

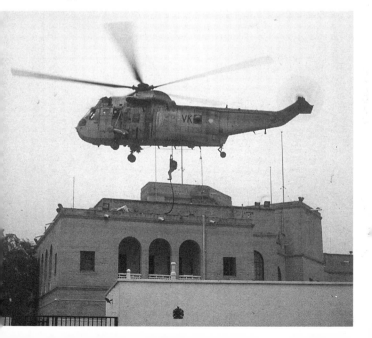

British Special Forces members in HALO parachuting kit, including emergency oxygen supplies. *(Defence Picture Library)*

Training at the Killing House: an SAS Trooper prepares to throw a stun grenade during a hostage rescue exercise. *(Defence Picture Library)*

Firepower: US Special Forces personnel carrying M16 Armalite rifles fitted with the M203 40mm grenade launcher. *(Defence Picture Library)*

SAS HALO parachutist dropping in full kit. *(Defence Picture Library)*

SAS HALO parachutist comes into land beneath a highly manoeuvrable square canopy parachute. *(Defence Picture Library)*

Members of 22 SAS Boat Troop prepare to dive from a Klepper canoe. *(Defence Picture Library)*

US Navy SEALs spearheaded the invasion of Grenada. *(Defence Picture Library)*

the operation was launched, conditions were known to be wrong but there was a great deal of pressure on Stirling and his men to succeed; they went ahead and the parachutists ended up scattered, captured and killed; they didn't achieve their aim. Flying two C-130s over a great distance would invite any number of things to go wrong, all of which might cause the mission to abort or, if it continued, to fail. These include: mechanical failure in either or both of the aircraft; failure to reach a refuelling RV; illness amongst the flight crew; detection by the enemy; navigational errors, etcetera, etcetera. Although these things may seem obvious, they do happen – the SAS had the example of the failed US attempt to rescue hostages in Iran two years before to go by – and there is no easy way to avoid them. Stirling's airfield attacks in the desert began to succeed because he switched to a method of entry – jeep convoys across the desert – that could within reason be relied on and which was flexible enough to accommodate the unexpected. The final approach and landing at Rio Grande would also have been problematic: even if the Argentines had not detected the British approach sufficiently early to respond aggressively, it is possible that the aircraft would have had to land on an unfamiliar airfield without the normal aids to navigation and landing, and with the prospect of finding other aircraft blocking their approach.

But even if B Squadron had reached their target successfully, there was still no outright guarantee of success. One problem that Stirling and his men never resolved was what to do if their quarry was not there. On a number of occasions, the early SAS successfully penetrated airfield defences only to find that the aircraft were absent; apart from shooting up empty hangars and blowing up storage facilities, there was nothing they could do about it except wait for the next opportunity to present itself. This would not have been the case at Rio Grande where there could be no second bite at the cherry. Even with top-class intelligence resources there would be no certainty of all the aircraft, all the missiles or all the pilots being present on one airfield nor even, given that the squadron would have limited 'time on target', that they would be able to find them all even if they were there. In any case, although it is fair to argue that the SAS would have had a big edge over any defenders present at the airfield, there is a big difference between carefully penetrating an airfield from the outside before launching an attack and landing two huge Hercules aircraft in the middle of it before

starting: one alert GPMG gunner in the wrong place might have wiped
out half of the squadron before the assault could begin.

The final worry for the squadron was the exfiltration. However
incompetent and inexperienced the Argentines were in conventional
war, their forces certainly had good knowledge of counter-insurgency
and internal security procedures, developed during the ruthless 'Dirty
War' against left-wing guerrillas in the 1970s. The follow-up after a
raid on Argentinian soil would probably have been enormous and it
is likely that a proportion of those who had survived the assault would
have been caught as they made their way to Chile; it is difficult to
predict what would have happened to them. Despite these objections
and others, the operation was to go ahead.

The first phase was to land a small party near the airbase to conduct
reconnaissance prior to the arrival of the main force and, on 17
May, a Sea King helicopter left HMS *Hermes* carrying three aircrew,
nine members of 22 SAS commanded by B Squadron's Boat Troop
commander, and a huge extra fuel load. They reached their landing
site apparently undetected but, as they prepared to unload, they saw
a flare being fired over the sea and came to the conclusion that they
were compromised. The commander then made the decision to abort
and the helicopter took off again, now heading for Chile where the
SAS men were to be dropped off before the crew took the helicopter
further and simulated a crash landing, after which they burned the
aircraft. A few of the SAS men in the Sea King had briefly set foot on
Argentine soil but it seems that they were the only ones to do so.

Despite aborting the reconnaissance, the main operation remained
'on' for some time, but during this period the squadron apparently
became polarised between those who felt the operation should be
cancelled and those who wanted to continue. This came to a head
on the night before the squadron flew out to Ascension when the Boat
Troop staff sergeant – one of the most senior members of B Squadron –
voluntarily resigned from the SAS, believing it to be a 'suicide mission',
and the B Squadron commander was sacked by Brigadier de la Billière,
who replaced him with the regiment's second in command.

The operation was finally halted with B Squadron sitting in aircraft
with the engines running, ready to go. By now it had been discovered
that the Argentines had established a radar guardship off Tierra del
Fuego and were likely to have considerable advance warning of the

SAS's arrival; instead, B Squadron flew down to the islands, parachuting into the sea, to replace the exhausted IR patrols of G Squadron. They did not see any action before the surrender.

The Falklands campaign was not an unqualified success for the SAS although, on balance, they did make a significant and worthwhile contribution. Part of the problem was that less than two years after the Iranian Embassy assault, members of the regiment were saddled with a reputation as military supermen that they mostly neither liked nor wanted. This reputation was current amongst the media covering the campaign, amongst politicians and civil servants, and to some extent amongst the military as well. As a result, expectations were high and, in combination with a command hierarchy that was largely naval-led – and thus unfamiliar with special operations, there was a degree of over-emphasis on offensive action tasks coupled with an unrealistic expectation of what might be achieved by them.

At the same time, the SAS hierarchy was anxious that the regiment should benefit from the experience of taking part in the campaign and this may have led to the acceptance of roles that were not necessarily entirely appropriate for strategic troops. The reality was that the Royal Marines and Parachute Regiment battalions which made up the bulk of the infantry strength on Operation Corporate were units trained to work with a higher degree of autonomy and flexibility than their 'line' counterparts, and it would not be too outrageous to suggest that a well-led Marines or Para company would have been just as capable of conducting the Pebble Island raid as D Squadron were.

In stark contrast to the tough and arduous conditions faced by British and Argentine troops in the South Atlantic, the next major military operation in which special forces were involved was in the idyllic setting of the Caribbean. Grenada is a small island some twenty-one miles long and twelve miles across at its widest point, with a population of a little under ninety thousand people and an economy based on the growing of bananas, spices and cocoa. Until 1974 it had been a self-governed British colony but had then gained independence and had settled down to life as a typical Caribbean elective democracy under Prime Minister Eric Gairy.

In 1979, however, Gairy was overthrown in a bloodless coup by a local Marxist politician, Maurice Bishop, whose New Jewel Movement began to stifle opposition groups, consolidating power entirely in its own hands. Bishop established ties with Castro's Cuba and accepted aid proffered by the Soviet Union, North Korea and Vietnam, including small quantities of weapons (rifles, machine guns and anti-aircraft cannon). He also, to the alarm of the United States' intelligence community, began a project to improve the runway at the island's 'international airport', in order that modern jets would be able to land there. Finance for this project came from Britain, but the construction force consisted largely of Cubans. This move took place at much the same time as Ronald Reagan was elected President of the United States and it fitted well with his administration's anti-communist stance to characterise Grenada's new runway as a potential base for Soviet attacks against the US. In July 1981, therefore, the CIA put up a plan to begin a programme of destabilisation against the Grenadan government through 'a propaganda campaign, a reduction in aid and other measures designed to cause . . . economic problems',[12] despite Bishop's frequently reiterated claims that he only wanted to improve the airport to bolster the island's tourist industry.

This situation was complicated on 13 October 1983 by a second coup, organised by Bernard Coard, a left-winger within Bishop's party who thought the Prime Minister 'too moderate'.[13] Bishop was arrested and detained by the People's Revolutionary Army, a newly formed group based on the Grenadan Defence Forces and controlled by General Austin, Grenada's military chief. This immediately caused concern within the US State Department and on 18 October the US government sought assurances from Grenada that the one thousand or so US citizens on the island would be safe. The Grenadans replied in the affirmative but failed to reassure the US, even though there had been no suggestion that anything would be done to harm American citizens or interests on the island.

The next day, as opposition to the latest coup grew in Grenada, a large crowd converged on Bishop's residence, where he was under house-arrest, and freed him. Thereupon the crowd made its way to Fort Rupert in the hope of rescuing another member of the Bishop government. At this point the situation deteriorated. At Fort Rupert, the People's Revolutionary Army rearrested Bishop, three of his ministers and two union leaders, took them into the fort and murdered them; at the same time, they opened fire on the crowd, killing more than fifty and wounding many others. Although there was still no obvious threat to US citizens, this event provoked America's diplomatic representative in the region, the US Ambassador to Barbados, to recommend to the US government that a protected evacuation of US citizens take place.

This alarmist assessment of events automatically brought the US military into the planning cycle. On 20 October, a meeting of the Joint Chiefs-of-Staff (JCS) took place at which two outline plans were discussed. One, put forward by the Joint Special Operations Command at Fort Bragg, envisaged using special forces for the entire operation, a second from the Headquarters of the Commander-in-Chief Atlantic (Cinclant) proposed that a task force of Marines should handle the situation. Ultimately, it was decided to use elements of both plans: the Marines would take the northern half of the island, the army would take the south.

Detailed planning for the operation swiftly assumed farcical proportions. Each of the four services (in the US, the Marine Corps is separately represented on the JCS) was evidently keen that its forces have a 'piece of the action' and within a very short time a large number of units had been lined up with particular tasks, but at the same time, basic information regarding the situation on the island was virtually non-existent: the strength, organisation and armament of the People's Revolutionary Army were entirely unknown; it was not known whether there were any Cuban troops on the island (there were none); it was not known whether the Cuban construction workers had any military training or role; and the Marine planners, aboard the assault ship *Guam*, had only an 8-inch by 5-inch 1:500,000 tourist map which had last been updated in 1895.

The main elements of the plan to seize Grenada, codenamed Operation Urgent Fury, were that:

1. A thirty-five-man Delta team would land by parachute at Point Salines airfield before dawn on 25 October and clear the runway of construction machinery. This would allow a battalion of Rangers to tactically air-land and seize control of the airport and its immediate surroundings, which would in turn allow a brigade of the 82nd Airborne Division to be landed conventionally to conduct the protected evacuation.

2. A second Delta unit would attack the prison at Richmond Hill and release political prisoners.
3. A SEAL team* would assault the governor-general's residence and 'rescue' him from the new government.
4. A second SEAL unit would seize control of Radio Free Granada to prevent it from broadcasting propaganda and rallying islanders against the US forces.
5. Two further SEAL detachments would reconnoitre the intended Marine landing beach and the airstrip at Pearl's (Grenada's second airfield). After which a Marine battalion, in three company groups, would seize and hold objectives in the north of the island.

By the time that the invasion was launched US planners put the enemy forces' total at about eleven thousand (more than ten per cent of the island's entire population), including up to seven thousand Cubans.

In the early hours of 25 October, Operation Urgent Fury moved into its operational phase with the Delta Force assault on Point Salines Airport. Landing in darkness, the Delta operators were quickly spotted by Grenadan guards at the airport who opened fire on them. Apparently summoned by the noise of shooting, Grenadan and Cuban construction workers were quickly armed and joined in the firefight, and the Delta team started taking casualties, finding themselves pinned in a small ravine at the edge of the airfield; during the next four hours they suffered six dead and sixteen wounded. The Ranger follow-up force, a composite unit inexplicably formed from the 1st and 2nd Ranger Battalions, and consisting of men who had never trained or worked together before, was by then already airborne, but rather than turn back – the runway had not been cleared and their aircraft could not land – they decided to parachute onto the airfield instead.

The Delta operation at Point Salines had put the Grenadan forces on general alert and as fighting continued at the airfield, key points were being reinforced and militiamen were reporting for action. The SEAL detachment from the élite counter-terrorist SEAL Team 6(ST6)† thus met with opposition as they attempted to infiltrate through the town of

---

* US Navy Sea, Air, Land Commando unit.
† In effect, the US equivalent of the SBS.

St George's, the island's capital, coming under heavy fire which killed two and wounded two of the eight-strong group sent to silence Radio Free Grenada. They withdrew without getting within range of the radio station. A second ST6 detachment, targeted at beaches around Grenville Port, had decided to parachute into the sea with boats and equipment, but in a heavy swell the first four members of the group are believed to have been dragged to the bottom by their loads and drowned, whilst the four remaining members of the team, having spotted a fishing boat emerging from the harbour, cut the engines of their dinghy and were unable to restart them. They were swept away out to sea and eventually rescued some eleven hours later by a navy helicopter.

The second Delta operation, taking control of Richmond Hill prison, also ran into difficulty. The first problem came from the Black Hawk helicopters being used by the US Army's special operations squadron, Task Force 160. These had been broken up and flown to Barbados in the holds of huge Starlifter aircraft but had taken much longer to reassemble than expected so that, when the operation was finally launched, it took place in broad daylight. The plan was that the Delta operators would 'fast rope' or abseil from the helicopters into the prison, kill or capture the guards and release the prisoners. In reality, their daylight approach meant that one Black Hawk was shot down as the unit crossed the coast, causing a second to divert to protect the crew of the first, whilst between two and five helicopters* were brought down by heavy ground fire in the vicinity of the prison. In an effort to relieve the Delta men now pinned down near their target, an air strike only succeeded in flattening the island's mental hospital, killing twenty-one civilians.[14]

In the meantime the SEALs who were supposedly rescuing the governor-general were also in bad trouble. Having infiltrated close to the governor-general's residence and then assaulted it, the SEALs, also from ST6, were apparently quickly surrounded and pinned down. The SEAL team commander immediately called for assistance, informing the Marines' command element on the *Guam* that eight of his thirteen men were wounded. In response they despatched two Cobra gunships, both of which were shot down, killing three Marines aircrew.

At the airport, where the original Delta assault element were pinned down awaiting the arrival of their Ranger reinforcements, it was after

---

* Figures are disputed.

dawn before the first two C-130s came in, now intending to drop the Rangers. The aircraft began to drop the paratroopers but almost immediately aborted their run as they began to receive small arms fire from Grenadan troops around the airport, leaving twelve Rangers, who had already jumped, isolated without support for several terrifying minutes before the third aircraft, carrying the Rangers' headquarters team, appeared and successfully dropped its troops.

In all, the first wave of Rangers took more than two hours to land and even then, with 600 men on the ground, they failed to act decisively against a handful of poorly trained and equipped Grenadans. Instead of securing the airfield and moving off to their next objective – the campus of a medical school for American students unable to obtain places to study medicine in the US – they dug in to await reinforcements. Alarmed by the messages he was receiving from the ground where, it appeared, the Rangers and Delta were receiving stiff opposition, the task force commander, Admiral Metcalf, decided to call forward the 82nd Airborne. As a result, the second wave of Rangers was not actually used during the battle.

In the meantime, the Marines' assault on the northern part of the island was going much better. The Marines actually formed the 22nd Marine Amphibious Unit (22 MAU) and had been *en route* for a deployment in the Lebanon when they were diverted to Grenada and, although they were unprepared for this particular operation and were very poorly briefed, they were nonetheless accustomed to working together and had their own integrated SEAL team commanded by a long-term veteran, Lieutenant Michael Walsh. Walsh and his men were Fleet SEALs, accustomed to co-operation with navy and Marine units for whom they provided a highly specialised reconnaissance and sabotage capability, whereas ST6, who undertook the majority of the SEAL missions on the island and took all of the SEAL casualties, had been organised specifically as a counter-terrorist force. Walsh's team had successfully reconnoitred the beach close to the airstrip at Pearl's and the Marines had managed to get ashore unopposed and begin their move inland.

By mid-morning, the leading elements of the 82nd Airborne began to arrive only to find that the airfield still wasn't secured – Grenadan troops and Cuban construction workers still held one end of it and were firing at every aircraft that came in to land – and that the airfield was, in any case, only big enough to handle one C-130 at a time. Even so, the Rangers and 82nd Airborne were finally able to link up and, with the support of helicopter gunships and airstrikes, begin their move towards the capital.

The final part of the special forces phase of the operation was resolved the next morning at 03.00 hours when a Marine unit relieved the SEAL team at the governor-general's residence. There they found that the SEALs had not been under as much pressure as they had claimed and had not taken any casualties: 'In fact, they had not been surrounded but had simply panicked and lied to get help',[15] according to one officer involved.

Organised resistance to the American invasion ceased during the early hours of the morning of 26 October when members of the People's Revolutionary Army were ordered to get rid of their guns and their uniforms and try to blend in with the civilian population. Nevertheless, US offensive operations continued throughout the day having assumed a brutal and stupid momentum of their own. During an effectively unopposed attempt to evacuate US students from the college campus at Grand Anse, US forces shot down one of their own helicopters and severely damaged another whilst a Ranger assault on the People's Revolutionary Army headquarters at Calvigny Barracks cost four lives and a number of serious casualties when two helicopters collided: the barracks turned out to have been abandoned and the only opposition was a negligible amount of intermittent, ineffective, long-range sniping.

When all resistance had ceased and the US was completely in control of the island – largely, it should be said, because of the efforts of 22 MAU – it was finally possible to make a reasonably accurate assessment of enemy strength. It turned out that there had been 784 Cubans on the island, but the majority of these *were* only construction workers and only about fifty had military training. There were also about two thousand Grenadan troops who had actually borne the brunt of the fighting, but who were mostly armed with small arms and whose heaviest weapons were Soviet-made 23mm anti-aircraft cannon. In any case 600 of the Cubans had been captured within the first few hours of the invasion.

In contrast the United States had deployed: Delta Force; elements of SEAL Teams 4 (the 22 MAU detachment) and 6; the 1st and 2nd Ranger Battalions; 22 MAU (in effect, a battalion group); the 82nd Airborne

Division; and a carrier battle group centred on the USS *Independence*. Out of this enormous force – more or less equivalent to the British task force sent to the Falklands – some seven thousand men were involved in the combat phase of the operation. Twenty-nine Americans were killed and 152 wounded; 110 Grenadan and 71 Cuban combatants died, together with 45 civilians; 358 Grenadan civilians were wounded.

There is no doubt that in Grenada the United States was using a sledgehammer to crack a nut. The experience of 22 MAU was that competently executed drills by a well-integrated force were sufficient to achieve their aims and more (22 MAU ended up in possession of much more of the island than had originally been bargained for) and it is reasonable to speculate that the Marines could have taken the entire island without too much difficulty. The special forces operations, despite their air of farce, failed for two very specific reasons: in the first place they were launched without any realistic intelligence whatsoever because in the short timescale available to the planners none could be obtained; and in the second place they were fundamentally misconceived: small-scale special forces operations were launched against what were likely to be the most strongly defended targets on the island! The rationale behind the invasion was the safeguarding of US citizens, but despite the presence of units specifically formed in order to rescue Americans held hostage – Delta Force and SEAL Team 6 – an inexplicable reversal took place and the students (who had never been threatened by the revolutionaries or the Cubans anyway) were ultimately 'saved' by main force units.

The next seven years brought about something of a lull in 'conventional' special operations. The United States Green Berets continued to train anti-communist forces in Latin America and Asia, and, following the American lead, the SAS's training activities also spread to a wider clientele, with British teams operating as far afield as Cambodia, where they trained members of anti-communist groups (though not the Khmer Rouge as has been occasionally alleged); Colombia, where a joint team of SAS, SBS and Intelligence Corps personnel helped train the Anti-Narcotics Police in 1988 and 1989; Botswana, where in 1986 B Squadron trained members of the Botswana Defence Force in techniques for resisting South African incursions; and Kenya, where an SAS squadron took part in operations aimed at eliminating ivory poaching from the national parks.

This was a key period for the SAS. After their success at the Iranian Embassy, their apparent success in the Falklands and with the ongoing campaign in Ulster, the regiment had found great favour with the right-wing government of Mrs Thatcher. In the United States as well, and despite the débâcle of Grenada, special forces were very much in favour with Ronald Reagan's administration as a symbol of American resolution and toughness. For the first time since they were founded, the West's special operations forces were gaining access to funding and facilities on a greatly more lavish scale than conventional forces of the same size on the premise that for the limited, relatively low-intensity conflicts that had dominated warfare since the end of the Second World War, special forces appeared to deliver cheaper, more cost-effective solutions. It came as something of a surprise when this trend was completely reversed and a war was fought dominated by aircraft, tanks, artillery and infantry and where special forces, despite entirely bogus claims made on their behalf, turned out to be irrelevant.

The Iraqi invasion of Kuwait on 2 August 1990 did not come as a complete surprise to Western governments but the timescale left virtually no opportunity for an effective response. In some measure this was the result of dithering by politicians who would not believe the warnings that were coming from the intelligence community, but whatever the fundamental cause, the military response did not begin for some days.

The only member of the SAS to be involved in any way with the invasion and its immediate aftermath was a major with the Kuwait Liaison Team, the British Army loan service training and technical unit attached to the Kuwaiti Army. He, together with the rest of the team, was arrested during the morning of 2 August and removed the next day to Baghdad as part of Saddam Hussein's 'human shield' which consisted of Western expatriate workers and their families from both Iraq and Kuwait. Reports that members of the SAS flew into Kuwait on a British Airways 747 which landed a few minutes before Iraqi aircraft attacked the airport are untrue.*

As the military build-up continued through the autumn of 1990, two squadrons – D and G – moved to the Gulf to conduct reconnaissance and

---

* The author conducted intelligence debriefs of several passengers and members of the crew of this flight, who made no mention of the presence of any 'mysterious soldiers' as subsequent press reports have claimed.

carry out training exercises in the United Arab Emirates (G Squadron later returned to the UK and were replaced by A Squadron shortly after Christmas 1990; additionally half of B Squadron joined the task force in early January 1991, as 'battle casualty replacements').

On 29 September Lieutenant General Sir Peter de la Billière was appointed commander of all British forces deployed in the area, serving under the US General, Norman Schwarzkopf. After his arrival in theatre in early October, he gave orders that the SAS should examine the possibility of rescuing Saddam Hussein's hostages. In fact this would have been an almost impossible mission to fulfil: the hostages were being held in small groups scattered widely around installations deemed to be likely bombing targets by the Iraqis, ranging from military bases to oil refineries. In fact Saddam Hussein spontaneously released the hostages on 6 December and the rescue mission plans could be abandoned.

This left the problem of how the SAS were to be employed. The traditional SAS tasks in conventional desert warfare, harking back to the Second World War, encompass raiding, harassment and information reporting, but many senior officers in theatre, including de la Billière, felt that these could be achieved through air power (it was abundantly clear that the Allies would have overwhelming air supremacy): 'Paddy [Air Chief Marshal Sir Patrick Hine] then asked if I could think of any better use for Special Forces [than hostage rescue] and I said that at the moment I could not. Our technological capability on the battlefield and in the air seemed to be so overwhelming as to leave no gap which Special Forces could reasonably fill.'[16]

In any case, the Commander-in-Chief of Allied Forces was notoriously sceptical of the utility of special forces, having witnessed at first hand the comparatively poor performance of the Green Berets in Vietnam and in Grenada where, as a major general, Schwarzkopf had been sent in on the second day of the invasion to attempt to restore order to the chaotic situation that prevailed.

The role that was ultimately given to the SAS was one that they had developed for themselves. General de la Billière wrote that 'Their task would be to cut roads and create diversions which would draw Iraqi forces away from the main front and sow fears in the mind of the enemy that some major operation was brewing on his right flank. At the back of my own mind was the idea that the SAS might also be able to take out mobile SCUD missile launchers.'[17]

The first phase of the liberation of Kuwait began in the early hours of 17 January 1991 with a massive wave of aircraft and missile attacks aimed at destroying Iraqi air capability and suppressing air defences. Five days later, after a two-day delay, the first SAS patrols crossed the border: Bravo 10, 20 and 30 were tasked to maintain watch on an Iraqi main supply route to the west of Baghdad, reporting significant sightings – and particularly Scuds – back to the special forces headquarters at Al Jouf in Saudi Arabia.

The three patrols were drawn, as their Bravo call-signs imply, from B Squadron which, as we have seen, had been the last SAS squadron deployed to the Gulf. One consequence of this was that they were last in the queue for specialised operational stores, including silenced weapons and purpose-built claymore mines, as well as more fundamental equipment like vehicles. There was also a question mark over their training: B Squadron were moving into a period of 'team tasks' when the squadron would normally be broken up into small groups and sent around the world on various training and advisory missions. This meant that patrols would not have been working closely together in a 'green' (SAS members divide their tasks into 'green' or uniformed tasks and 'black' counter-terrorist tasks) role prior to the deployment and would therefore need time to become accustomed to each other and to develop standard operating procedures (which although supposedly standard to the entire regiment are, in reality, normally fixed at troop level). All three were eight-man patrols but Bravo 30 was mounted in hastily converted Land-Rovers whilst Bravo 20 and 10 had opted to operate on foot.

Immediately after the three roadwatch patrols were landed, during the night of 22 January, it became apparent that a serious miscalculation had been made: instead of finding themselves in a relatively warm sand desert, in which they would have been able to construct secure and relatively comfortable OPs, they were on a windswept rocky plateau with a night-time temperature around freezing point. The commander of Bravo 10, after consulting with their helicopter pilot, opted to turn around and fly straight back: he considered, almost certainly correctly, that there was little possibility of remaining in the area for long without compromise. Bravo 30 stayed in their location a little longer but ultimately reached the same conclusion and opted to drive back into Saudi Arabia, a journey which took them two nights.

Bravo 20's commander decided, after ascertaining that the patrol was close to an Iraqi military position and that cover was limited, that he would relocate.

In fact Bravo 20 were unable to make any immediate move because they discovered that their radio didn't appear to be working. Although the PRC 319 EMU appeared to be sending messages, they were not being acknowledged and there was no way to tell if they had got through. After lying up through the first day, and conducting recces of their immediate area during the next night, the patrol decided to rely on their 'lost comms' procedure – whereby a helicopter would fly to a pre-arranged location with a new radio – to solve the problem. This was not to be: during the second day a local civilian goatherd stumbled across the patrol's lie-up. Unlike Captain Robin Edwards and his patrol twenty-one years before, Sergeant Andy McNab decided that his men should not shoot a non-combatant. The Iraqi ran away and raised the alarm.

Compromised, the patrol now attempted to evade across country towards Syria which was 130 kilometres to the west. As is now very well known, one member of the patrol, Trooper Robert Consiglio, was killed by the Iraqis, Sergeant Vince Phillips and Trooper 'Legs' Lane died of exposure, four were captured (and subjected to ferocious treatment by the Iraqis) and one, Corporal Chris Ryan, escaped, evaded and returned to Al Jouf via Damascus, Cyprus and Riyadh.

More successful, technically at least, were reconnaissance teams of the US 5th Special Forces Group, deployed along the Saudi-Iraqi border and inside Iraq, including roadwatch patrols deployed in the Euphrates valley on 23 February, surveilling the road that the SAS patrols had earlier failed to cover. But the date is significant: by the time these later patrols were deployed, almost every significant target in Iraq had been on the receiving end of air attacks, and Iraqi troop movements at any level were cut to the minimum. Even so back-up for these deployments worked and those that were compromised were successfully extracted.

In the meantime, after a long period of build-up training, A and D Squadrons deployed in force on 23 January in half-squadron-sized fighting patrols into the 'Scud box', an area of several thousand square kilometres in the western Iraqi desert. At much the same time, the SBS conducted Operation Maude, a successful attempt to cut the fibre-optic communications cable connecting Baghdad with the port city of Basra which they did by the simple expedient of landing a Chinook loaded with a digging team and a cover party, digging down to the cable with pneumatic drills, cutting and removing a length of it, and placing demolitions charges and booby traps.

These SAS 'Scud-hunting' patrols have been described as bearing a close similarity to SAS operations in the Western Desert in the Second World War and in some respects that is the case, but there were important differences, not least in the circumstances in which they were conducted. Alpha Three Zero, a patrol from A Squadron, was described by one of its members as consisting of

> eight Land Rovers type 110, most of which were armed with a Browning .5 heavy machine gun. Additional weapons included GPMGs, American Mark 19s, 40mm Grenade Launchers and Milan anti-tank missiles . . . In each column a Mercedes Unimog was used as the mother vehicle and carried the bulk of the stores. The Unimog's great advantage is that it can be loaded to the gunwhales and still go anywhere. And it most certainly was loaded, with extras of every variety: rations, fuel, ammunition for a wide range of weapons, NBC equipment and spares.[18]

There is little doubt that the patrols of A and D Squadrons, and of the American Delta Force, who joined the Scud hunt shortly after the SAS deployment, were involved in hard fighting in extremely challenging and difficult terrain in the western Iraqi desert, but there is a question mark over whether they actually achieved their aim, which by then was to disrupt launches of Scud missiles aimed at targets in Israel and Saudi Arabia. Between 17 and 26 January twenty-one Scuds were fired at Israel and twenty-two at Saudi whereas from 27 January to the end of the war, nearly a month later, nineteen Scuds were fired at Israel and twenty-three at Saudi; in other words, there was a reduction in the number of firings but not a huge one, and it would be difficult to claim that it was the result of specifically SAS action rather than, for example, air attacks.

A second question mark has been raised over the number of Scuds that were actually destroyed. A United States Congressional Investigation, as well as the United Nations team investigating and destroying Iraqi weapons of mass-destruction, both concluded independently that there was no solid evidence that any Scuds had been destroyed, either by air power or special forces. Intelligence information collected after the war indicated that the Iraqis had possessed nineteen mobile Scud launchers and the UN were able to account for all of them.* Special forces attacks on communications centres and infrastructure targets probably had little ultimate effect on an enemy who were shown, after the launch of the main ground offensive on 24 February, to have neither the will nor the means to resist.

---

* This is not to say that no *missiles* were destroyed – but without the launchers the missiles are useless anyway.

13

Conclusion

It is evident from an examination of some of the major campaigns and operations involving special forces in the last century that the case in favour of them is perhaps not as watertight as might be imagined when one observes the resources and interest that are currently devoted to them. What special forces have almost always done is capture the popular imagination by the courage, daring and technical skill of the operations that they undertake, but what they seem to do less often is conclusively achieve their aim, particularly in conventional warfare.

It is quite clear, for example, that LRDG, L Detachment and 1st SAS Regiment did have a significant effect on the outcome of the campaign in the Western Desert up to the battle of El Alamein in October 1942, but after that their impact waned for two particular reasons. In the first place the terrain changed: as Montgomery pursued the Axis forces into Tunisia, the special forces lost the great open flank of the desert and were forced into closer and closer contact with the enemy; and in the second place, the character of the fighting changed. After El Alamein, the Allies held the initiative as well as material superiority and there was little danger that Montgomery would squander it. Victory, Montgomery knew, was going to be achieved by bringing his enemy to battle and destroying his capacity to continue the fight, not by raids on line-of-communication targets.

Much the same can be said about the Gulf War. For all the hype that has surrounded the activities of special forces, the reality is that their impact was marginal at best and the claim that, by undertaking the Scud hunt in western Iraq, special forces kept Israel out of the war is based on a ludicrously pessimistic view of Israeli pragmatism. The attempt to repeat the role of the Second World War SAS was elbowed into irrelevancy by the massive Allied material and technological superiority.

The deduction to be made from this is that 'successful' offensive special forces operations are characteristic of armies on the defensive, and one might well speculate that the benefits they bring are, to a great extent, psychological: they comfort commanders that they retain the ability to take the initiative, at least in a small way. This is equally the case in counter-insurgency as it is in conventional operations: killing members of the IRA does not appear to have brought about a solution to the problems of Northern Ireland; it simply raises the morale of the security forces and the Loyalist population.

But it is wrong to dismiss offensive special operations entirely. There is no doubt that widespread acts of sabotage by resistance movements organised and armed by SOE caused a great deal of disruption to the German war effort but the question here is one of scale. By the time of the Normandy invasion in 1944, SOE had armed half a million Frenchmen, who were committing hundreds, if not thousands, of acts of sabotage every month: a level of operations that a typical small-scale special forces unit could not hope to emulate. However, small-scale raids with a specific technical or intelligence task like the first Lofoten attack by the Commandos and the Bruneval raid by the Parachute Regiment were completely successful and provided specific, demonstrable benefits to the war effort.

This brings us to intelligence-gathering operations. The LRDG in the Western Desert, and 22 SAS in Borneo and the Falklands were able to provide strategic commanders with vital timely intelligence of enemy activity which could not be easily gathered by other means. There is always a need for intelligence in military operations, and special forces are an ideal adjunct to SIGINT, photographic reconnaissance and other traditional means of collecting information. The technical skills of special forces enable them to get to places that other intelligence means cannot reach and to get their reports out. This is the crucial role for special forces in conventional operations over and above offensive action tasks.

In counter-insurgency, as we have seen, there are two main areas in which special forces work: military action, collecting intelligence and acting upon it; and civil aid. History shows us that the most effective of these options is the latter, although it is a long slow process that does not produce the quick results that military commanders and politicians like. The campaigns in Malaya and the Oman were won because those in command took a long view which allowed them to co-ordinate effective civil aid with sufficient military activity to maintain security, and special forces played an important role in this. The campaign in Northern Ireland has stagnated because these lessons were ignored. Hostage rescue, which has become a special forces task in the past twenty-five years, is a special case: someone has to do it and the SAS, GSG9, GIGN and their counterparts have proved themselves admirably suitable for the role.

Whatever one's view of the importance of special forces and special operations in warfare, however, one cannot but admire the men (and women, to some extent) who take part in them. Even if they do not entirely fit in with the stereotypes – and as we have seen, several important special operations commanders were homosexual, for example – they are almost invariably highly motivated, determined, intelligent and clear thinking, and their presence in modern armed forces adds an essential element of flexibility to military planning. A British War Office civil servant discussing proposals to pay members of the SAS extra money during the 1960s admirably summed them up. He opposed the idea as unnecessary: they were all 'true believers' anyway.

Notes

Introduction

1 Personal experience.
2 Combined sales of the two 'Andy McNab' books, *Bravo Two Zero* and *Immediate Action*, in hardback and paperback, were in the region of two and a half million by the end of 1996.
3 In 6th impression, November 1949; Jonathan Cape.
4 Briefing to the author by Army staff officer, November 1996.
5 Good examples of this are: the US which created Delta Force in 1979 as a specialist counter-terrorist unit; the UK which set up 14 Intelligence Company in 1974 for operations in Northern Ireland; and the Federal Republic of Germany which created GSG9 in the wake of the Munich tragedy in 1972.
6 Urban, *Big Boys' Rules*, p. 250.
7 There is usually one troop of about twenty members of 22 SAS in Northern Ireland, together with the sixty or so members of 14 Intelligence Company based around the province.

Chapter 1: Historical Origins

1 Young, p. 98.
2 United States Special Operations Command, *A Special Operations Primer*, 1996.
3 Personal experience of the author during training at Sandhurst in 1985.
4 USSOC.
5 Hopkirk, p. 4.

6 Ibid., p. 55.

Chapter 2: Lawrence and the Arab Revolt

1 James, p. 24.
2 Ibid.
3 Ibid., p. 36.
4 Lawrence, p. 193.
5 And certainly not now. Military history and the classics of military theory are virtually excluded from the professional training of modern British army officers.
6 Lawrence, p. 42.
7 James, p. 82.
8 Liddell Hart, *First World War*, p. 134.
9 Ibid., p. 96.
10 Ibid., p. 155.
11 James, p. 148.
12 Ibid., p. 159.
13 Ibid., p. 161.
14 Clayton papers, quoted in James, p. 164.
15 Lawrence, p. 92.
16 James, p. 173.
17 Lawrence, p. 298.
18 James, p. 204 ff.
19 Gardner, p. 137.
20 Lawrence, p. 169.
21 Quoted in James, p. 212.
22 Lawrence, p. 396.
23 Gardner, p. 144.
24 Churchill, *The Aftermath*, p. 70.
25 Sir Samuel Hoare, quoted in Andrew, p. 207.
26 Teague-Jones, p. 101.

Chapter 3: On the Road to War

1 John Weeks, 'Paratrooper', *War Monthly*, no. 26 (May 1976).
2 Lucas, p. 24.
3 Ibid., p. 25.

4 Ibid., p. 40.
5 Höhne, p. 156.
6 Adolf Hitler, quoted in Höhne, p. 238.
7 Höhne, p. 241.
8 Ibid., quoting Naujocks, p. 243.
9 Adolf Hitler, quoted in Höhne, p. 238.
10 Hoe, *David Stirling*, p. 38.
11 Skorzeny, p. 34.
12 Calvert, p. 30.

Chapter 4: Leopards

1 Lucas, p. 44.
2 Calvert, p. 33.
3 Young, p. 8.
4 Churchill, *The Second World War*, vol. 2, p. 217.
5 Ibid., p. 147.
6 Ibid., p. 572.
7 Young, p. 5.
8 Niven, p. 219.
9 Cooper, p. 9.
10 Hastings, *Evelyn Waugh*, p. 415.
11 Waugh, diaries, quoted in ibid., p. 416.
12 Niven, p. 220.
13 Sergeant Ernie Chinnery, quoted in Arthur, p. 11.
14 Churchill, *The Second World War*, vol. 2, p. 218.
15 Major Tony Hibbert, quoted in Arthur, p. 2.
16 Calvert, p. 48.
17 Deane-Drummond, quoted in Arthur, p. 24.
18 Ibid.
19 Young, p. 23.
20 Cox, quoted in *RAF Flying Review*.
21 Clark, p. 179.

Chapter 5: The Baker Street Irregulars

1 Andrew, p. 471.
2 Philby, p. 32.

3 Ibid.

4 West, *The Story of SOE*, p. 11.

5 Philby, p. 32.

6 West, *The Story of SOE*, p. 20.

7 M.R.D. Foot, 'SOE', in *The Oxford Companion to the Second World War*, p. 1018.

8 Foot, p. 46.

9 George Langelaan, quoted in Foot, *SOE*, p. 64.

10 Ibid., p. 69.

11 *The Oxford Companion to the Second World War*, p. 1021.

Chapter 6: The Laboratory

1 W.L. Kennedy-Shaw, quoted in Barrie Pitt, 'Desert Raiders', *War Monthly*, no. 67.

2 Churchill, *The Second World War*, vol. 2, p. 542.

3 Pitt, 'Desert Raiders'.

4 Young, p. 40.

5 Waugh, quoted in Hastings, *Evelyn Waugh*, p. 422.

6 WO 218/97.

7 Fitzroy Maclean, interview with the author.

8 Cooper, p. 24.

9 Sergeant Bob Bennett, quoted in Hoe, *Re-enter the SAS*.

10 Fitzroy Maclean, interview with the author.

11 Churchill, *The Second World War*, vol. 3, p. 498.

12 Campbell, quoted in Young, p. 54.

13 WO 218/97.

14 Ibid.

15 Lieutenant R. Seekings, quoted in Bradford and Dillon.

16 Skorzeny, p. 267.

Chapter 7: D-Day to the End of the War

1 WO 218/114.

2 Cooper, p. 89.

3 WO 218/116.

4 Ibid.

5 WO 71/1149.

6 Skorzeny, p. 331.

Chapter 8: Cold Warriors

1 Morgan, p. 52.
2 Private information.
3 Philby, p. 167.
4 Ibid., p. 171.
5 Ibid., p. 188.
6 Quoted in Strawson, p. 278.
7 Hoe, *David Stirling*, p. 64.
8 Ibid.
9 Strawson, p. 149.
10 Hamilton, p. 24.
11 Interview with the author.
12 De la Billière, *Looking for Trouble*, p. 161.
13 Interview, PSI 21 SAS.
14 Walker, p. 33.

Chapter 9: The Wild Colonial Wars

1 C.M. Porter, interview with the author.
2 Hoe, *Re-enter the SAS*, quoting RSM Bob Bennett, p. 64.
3 Ibid.
4 Calvert, p. 208.
5 WO 71/1206.
6 *The Times*, 14 July 1952.
7 Letter, HQ FARELF, dated 22/12/51.
8 RHQ/SAS/9214.
9 Kitson, *Bunch of Five*, p. 170.
10 De la Billière, *Looking for Trouble*, p. 129.
11 Lees, p. 133.
12 WO 337/9.
13 Ibid.
14 Kitson, *Bunch of Five*, p. 201.
15 Interview with the author.
16 Interview with the author.
17 De la Billière, *Looking for Trouble*, p. 224.

18 Dickens, p. 58.
19 Jeapes, p. 31.
20 Ibid., p. 51.
21 De la Billière, *Looking for Trouble*, p. 278.

Chapter 10: Vietnam

1 Figures from Adams, p. 50.
2 Ibid., p. 54.
3 Beckwith, p. 57.
4 Ibid., p. 59.
5 Australian Army requirements for volunteers for the SAS Company, 1960.
6 Lieutenant Sam Simpson, quoted in Horner, p. 259.

Chapter 11: Special Forces and Counter-Terrorism

1 Account of Munich Airport operation from Adams.
2 Personal experience.
3 R.L. Nairac, *Talking to People in South Armagh*.
4 Urban, *Big Boys' Rules*.
5 FRU officer, interview with the author.
6 Ibid.
7 Con Boyle, quoted in Urban, *Big Boys' Rules*, p. 63.
8 Ibid., p. 65.
9 De la Billière, *Looking for Trouble*, p. 315.
10 Urban, *Big Boys' Rules*, p. 64.
11 Inquest transcript.
12 Interview with the author.
13 Ibid.

Chapter 12: The Empires Strike Back

1 Middlebrook, *Fight for the Malvinas*, p. 10.
2 Ibid.
3 Now known within the Royal Marines by the nickname 'Fairly Famous'.
4 Middlebrook, *Fight for the Malvinas*, p. 44.

5 Middlebrook, *Task Force*, p. 31.
6 Middlebrook, *Fight for the Malvinas*, p. 31.
7 Interview with the author.
8 Quoted without attribution in Strawson.
9 Corporal 22 SAS, interview with the author.
10 McManners, *Scars of War*, p. 231.
11 McCallion, p. 176.
12 Adams, p. 223.
13 Ibid.
14 Ibid., p. 243. Much of the detail regarding SF operations in Grenada is drawn from Adams, and Walker.
15 Ibid., p. 244.
16 De la Billière, *Storm Command*, p. 102.
17 Ibid., p. 192.
18 Crossland, p. 60.

Select Bibliography

Adams, James, *Secret Armies*, Hutchinson, 1987

Aldington, Richard, *Lawrence of Arabia*, Collins, 1955

Andrew, Christopher, *Secret Service: The Making of the British Intelligence Community*, Heinemann, 1985

Arthur, Max, *Men of the Red Beret*, Hutchinson, 1990

Asher, Michael, *Shoot to Kill*, Viking, 1990

Beckwith, Colonel Charlie, and Kno, *Delta Force*, Arms & Armour Press, 1984

Bishop, Patrick, and Mallie, Eamonn, *The Provisional IRA*, Heinemann, 1987

Bond, Brian, *The Pursuit of Victory*, Oxford University Press, 1996

Boyle, Andrew, *The Climate of Treason*, Hutchinson, 1979

Bradford, Roy, and Dillon, Martin, *Rogue Warrior of the SAS*, John Murray, 1987

Calvert, J.M., *Fighting Mad*, Airlife Publishing, 1996

Churchill, The Rt. Hon. Winston S., *The Aftermath* (sequel to *The World Crisis*), Macmillan, 1941

Churchill, The Rt. Hon. Winston S., *The Second World War*, 5 vols, Cassell, 1949

Clark, Ronald W., *The Rise of the Boffins*, Phoenix House, 1962

Cooper, Johnny, *One of the Originals*, Pan, 1991

Crossland, Peter 'Yorky' (pseud.), *Victor Two*, Bloomsbury, 1996

De la Billière, General Sir Peter, *Looking for Trouble*, HarperCollins, 1994

De la Billière, General Sir Peter, *Storm Command*, HarperCollins, 1992

Dear, I.C.B., and Foot, M.R.D. (eds), *The Oxford Companion to the Second World War*, Oxford University Press, 1995

Dickens, Peter, *SAS: The Jungle Frontier*, Arms & Armour Press, 1983

Dillon, Martin, *The Dirty War*, Hutchinson, 1991

Foot, M.R.D., *SOE: The Special Operations Executive 1940–46*, BBC, 1984

Gardner, Brian, *Allenby*, Cassell, 1965

Geraghty, Tony, *Who Dares Wins*, Little, Brown, 1992 (revised and expanded edn)

Hamilton, Nigel, *Monty: Master of the Battlefied 1942–44*, Sceptre, 1987

Harris, Robert, and Paxman, Jeremy, *A Higher Form of Killing*, Chatto & Windus, 1982

Hastings, Max, *Das Reich*, Michael Joseph, 1981

Hastings, Selina, *Evelyn Waugh: A Biography*, Sinclair-Stevenson, 1994

Hibbert, Christopher, *Mussolini*, Pan/Ballantine, 1972

Hinsley, F.I.I., and Simkins, C.A.G., *British Intelligence in the Second World War*, 5 vols, HMSO, 1979

Hoe, Alan, *David Stirling*, Little, Brown, 1992

Hoe, Alan, *Re-enter the SAS*, Leo Cooper, 1994

Höhne, Heinz, *The Order of the Death's Head*, Secker and Warburg, 1969

Holland, Jack, and Phoenix, Susan, *Policing the Shadows*, Hodder & Stoughton, 1996

Holland, R.F., *European Decolonization 1918–1981*, Macmillan, 1985

Holroyd, Fred, *War Without Honour*, Medium Publishing, 1989

Hopkirk, Peter, *The Great Game*, John Murray, 1990

Horner, D.M., *SAS: Phantoms of the Jungle*, Battery Press (US), 1989

James, Lawrence, *The Golden Warrior: The Life and Legend of Lawrence of Arabia*, Abacus, 1995

Jeapes, Tony, *SAS: Operation Oman*, William Kimber, 1980

Jennings, Christian, and Weale, Adrian, *Green-Eyed Boys: 3 Para and the Battle for Mount Longdon*, HarperCollins, 1996

Kennedy, Michael Paul, *Soldier I*, Bloomsbury, 1989

Kipling, Rudyard, *Kim*, Macmillan, 1901

Kitson, Frank, *Bunch of Five*, Faber & Faber, 1977

Kitson Frank, *Low Intensity Operations*, Faber & Faber, 1970

Large, Donald 'Lofty', *One Man's SAS*, William Kimber, 1987

Lawrence, T.E., *Seven Pillars of Wisdom: A Triumph*, Jonathan Cape, 1935

Lees, Sir David, *Flight from the Middle East*, HMSO, 1980

Liddell Hart, Sir Basil H., *History of the First World War*, Cassell, 1970

Liddell Hart, Sir Basil H., *T.E. Lawrence: In Arabia and After*, Jonathan Cape, 1935

Lucas, James, *Kommando: German Special Forces of World War Two*, Arms & Armour Press, 1985

McCallion, Harry (pseud.), *Killing Zone*, Bloomsbury, 1995

McManners, Hugh, *Falklands Commando*, William Kimber, 1984

McManners, Hugh, *Scars of War*, HarperCollins, 1994

McNab, Andy (pseud.), *Bravo Two Zero*, Transworld, 1993

McNab, Andy (pseud.), *Immediate Action*, Transworld, 1995

Middlebrook, Martin, *Fight for the Malvinas*, Viking, 1989

Middlebrook, Martin, *Task Force: The Falklands War 1982*, Penguin, 1987

Morgan, Kenneth O., *The People's Peace: British History 1945–1989*, Oxford University Press, 1990

Niven, David, *The Moon's a Balloon*, Hamish Hamilton, 1971

Parritt, Brigadier B.A.H., *The Intelligencers: The History of British Military Intelligence up to 1914*, Intelligence Corps Association, 1983

Philby, Kim, *My Silent War*, Pan, 1967

Ramsey, Jack, *SAS: The Soldiers' Story*, Macmillan, 1996

Roberts, Andrew, *The Holy Fox*, Weidenfeld & Nicolson, 1992

Ryan, Chris (pseud.), *The One that Got Away*, Century, 1994

Sheehan, Neil, *A Bright and Shining Lie*, Jonathan Cape, 1989

Skorzeny, Otto, *My Commando Operations*, Editions Albin Michel, 1975

Strawson, John, *A History of the SAS Regiment*, Secker and Warburg, 1984

Teague-Jones, Reginald, *The Spy Who Disappeared: Diary of a Secret Mission to Central Asia in 1918*, Victor Gollancz, 1990

Urban, Mark, *Big Boys' Rules*, Faber & Faber, 1992

Urban, Mark, *UK Eyes Alpha*, Faber & Faber, 1996

Walker, Greg, *At the Hurricane's Eye*, Ivy Books, 1996

Warner, Phillip, *The Special Air Service*, William Kimber, 1969

West, Nigel, *The Secret War for the Falklands*, Little, Brown, 1997

West, Nigel, *Secret War: The Story of SOE*, Hodder & Stoughton, 1992

Young, Peter, *Commando*, Pan/Ballantine, 1974

Index